前言

从考研英语试卷结构来分析，阅读理解包含三种题型，共计60分，占总成绩的60%。考生能否在这60分的试题中取得较好的成绩，直接关系到考研英语成绩是否合格。

根据我们平时的考研教学经验，考生要取得好成绩，必须有针对性地进行大量而快速的练习，通过严格、系统、科学和有针对性的训练，考生便能培养出超强的应试能力，在考试中做到心中有数、稳操胜券。

本书是根据2010年版《全国硕士研究生入学统一考试英语(一)考试大纲》(非英语专业)编写的。其主要特点是给阅读理解文章配备了精准译文，考生可以通过中英文对照，准确把握句子意义，熟练掌握词汇和语法。同时配备了"生词及短语"、"答案与解析"等，使考生能够对文章精确理解。

在精选的90篇阅读理解文章中，A篇(多项选择题)60篇，B篇(选择搭配题)15篇，C篇(英译汉)15篇，内容涵盖英语国家政治、经济、文化、历史、科技、人文、语言和社会等背景知识，能帮助强化对英语词汇、短语、句型等习惯表达方式的使用，使考生快速具备综合解题能力。

本书的第一章详细介绍了多种解题方法和技巧，考生应在练习中结合自己的特点不断地总结和提高。

由于作者水平有限，书中定有不尽如人意之处。敬请广大读者不吝指正。

最后预祝考生取得好成绩！

编者

2010年1月

考研英语(一)分项复习指导与训练·阅读

主　编　张　沛

北京航空航天大学出版社

图书在版编目(CIP)数据

考研英语(一)分项复习指导与训练. 阅读 / 张沛主编. -- 北京:北京航空航天大学出版社, 2010.2
ISBN 978-7-5124-0016-0

Ⅰ. ①考…　Ⅱ. ①张…　Ⅲ. ①英语-阅读教学-研究生-入学考试-自学参考资料　Ⅳ. ①H31

中国版本图书馆 CIP 数据核字(2010)第 015887 号

考研英语(一)分项复习指导与训练·阅读

主　　编　张　沛
责任编辑　江小珍

北京航空航天大学出版社出版发行
北京市海淀区学院路 37 号(100191)　发行部电话: 010-82317024　传真: 010-82328026
http: //www.buaapress.com.cn　Email: bhpress@263.net
涿州市新华印刷有限公司印装　各地书店经销
*
开本: 787×1092　1/16　印张: 17.75　字数: 421 千字
2010 年 2 月第 1 版　2010 年 2 月第 1 次印刷
ISBN 978-7-5124-0016-0　定价: 29.80 元

本书编委会

主　编　张　沛

编　者　张利萍　许海初　李子正

陈伟生　谭正飞　陈达坤

侯德凤　谷柏松　王　寰

李彦波　王维庚

目 录

阅读理解解题技巧

阅读理解解题技巧

第一节 阅读理解A篇要点

一、A篇解题要领

1. 出题方式和标准

新大纲规定：考生应能读懂不同类型的文字材料（生词量不超过所读材料总词汇量的3%），包括信函、书刊和杂志上的文章，还应能读懂与本人学习或工作有关的文献、技术说明和产品介绍等。根据所读材料，考生应该掌握的有：

(1) 理解主旨要义；

(2) 理解文中的具体信息；

(3) 理解文中的概念性含义；

(4) 进行有关的判断、推理和引申；

(5) 根据下文推测生词的含义；

(6) 理解文章的总体结构以及单句之间、段落之间的关系；

(7) 理解作者的意图、观点或态度；

(8) 区分论点和论据。

A篇阅读文章共4篇，阅读量约为1,600词，共20题，计40分，答题准确率要求在70%以上。毫无疑问，阅读理解部分成了试题内容的重中之重。

2. 试题题型和测试要求

对历届试题的题型加以分析后，可以将其归为以下六种类型：

(1) 中心主题题型；

(2) 辨认事实题型；

(3) 猜测词义题型；

(4) 难句理解题型；

(5) 推理题型；

(6) 判断题型。

从考试大纲和历年试题来分析,阅读理解 A 篇主要是对考生三方面的能力进行测试:

(1) 理解能力;

(2) 阅读技巧;

(3) 阅读速度。

阅读速度要求达到每分钟 60 词以上,同时要求全面理解文章主旨大意,准确做出判断和概括。这不但要求考生具有扎实的语言基础,同时还要求考生掌握一定的阅读技巧,包括精读、泛读、略读、扫读等多种技能。

就目前的情况来看,大部分考生仍然不能在阅读理解试题上取得良好的成绩。这主要是因为他们缺乏系统和专项训练,平时未养成良好的阅读习惯,没有掌握正确的阅读方法和技巧,阅读速度和理解准确率影响了成绩。

养成正确的阅读习惯,掌握一定的阅读技巧,同时通过专门和系统的练习,就一定能大大提高考生的阅读速度和理解能力,以下分别加以叙述。

3. 纠正不正确的阅读习惯

对于考生来说,要提高阅读能力,除了具备扎实的语言基础,包括词汇和语法基础,以及一定的文化背景知识,更重要的还得掌握正确的阅读方法。

不科学的阅读习惯有:出声阅读、默读、指读、阅读时头部摆动、复视、停下来查字典和翻译式阅读等。不良的阅读习惯不仅影响了考生的阅读速度和理解效果,而且最终影响到考试成绩。

4. 掌握正确的阅读方法

一般来说,根据不同的阅读目的,可以采用不同的阅读方法,心理语言学家总结出了四种不同的阅读方法:略读、寻读、细读和评论式阅读。

要了解一篇文章的主旨大意,可采用略读的方法;要取得某些特定的答案,获取要求的信息,适于采用寻读的方法;要非常精确地掌握文章内容,体会词句的确切含义,应该考虑采用细读的方法;如果要求对文章的观点、作者的看法作出评论,从而提出自己的看法观点,就得采用评论性阅读的方法。

阅读过程中常常是综合使用几种阅读方法。"略读"快速浏览全文,抓住文章中心大意;"寻读"找出与答题相关的词语、句子和段落;"细读"进一步弄清上下文含义,精确地找出答案所在。评论性题目在考研英语中偶尔也会碰到,这时就得找出论点、论据并作出推理,最后得出结论。实际上,写作试题就多为评论性文章。

5. 掌握正确的解题要领

在阅读方法上,可采用短语速读法(Phrase Reading),即在阅读时把句子分成许多小节或意群,找出每个小节的中心词,扫读每个句节的非重点词,以获取最佳阅读效果。

答题时有以下几个具体步骤:

(1) 浏览问题,明确要求;

(2) 快速阅读,读懂大意。由于要在10—12分钟内完成一篇文章后的问题,阅读时就要抓紧时间,同时根据文章难度采取不同方法,力求抓住主要信息,掌握短文的主旨和大意。要注意抓住关键词句,不可忽视每段开头和结尾句子的含义;碰到生词,可以猜测或直接跳过;利用上下文或构词法推断某些关键词的含义;

(3) 抓住要点,逐一解答。根据文章体裁、题材和内容,针对题型和解题方法的不同特点,认真思考,准确作出判断;

(4) 复读全文,加深理解。做完题之后,若还有时间,应该把短文再快读一遍,这时你对短文思想、内容、结构已经有了一定的了解,可以进一步核实答案,同时进一步确认原来没有把握的答案。

考生必须记住,解题方法和技巧固然重要,但是对于一篇文章的理解是否深入,关键仍是对词汇、语法和背景知识的掌握和运用。

二、阅读理解A篇常见题型

根据大纲要求,阅读理解A篇的试题中常出现以下题型:

1. 中心主题题型

中心主题题型通常以下列形式提出问题:

疑问句形式:

1. What is the subject of this passage?
2. Which of the following best reflects the main idea of the passage?
3. What is the best title for this passage?
4. What is the main topic for this passage?
5. Which of the following statements best summarizes this passage?
6. What is the main point the author makes in the passage?
7. With what topic is the passage primarily concerned?

肯定句形式:

1. The best title of this passage is ________.
2. The central idea of this passage is ________.
3. This article is mainly about ________.
4. This passage discusses ________.
5. This passage mainly deals with ________.
6. The passage was written to explain ________.
7. The title that best expresses the ideas of the passage is ________.
8. The author's purpose in writing this passage is ________.
9. The best summary of the passage is ________.

10. Choose the title that best expresses the ideas of the passage ________.

11. The proper subject of this article is ________.

中心主题题型在历届试题中出现的频率极高，几乎成了必考题型。这是因为中心主题题型是针对文章的主题和中心思想而设计的。是否能迅速地抓住文章的主题中心，体现了考生在阅读过程中对阅读材料综合、概括、归纳和分析的能力。

在阅读材料中，文章有文章的中心思想，段落有段落的中心思想，所以有的主题题型是针对整篇文章提出来的，也有的是针对某一段落提出来的。回答主题题型问题的关键是能否准确找出文章的主题句或段落的主题句(Topic Sentence)，它一般是文章或段落的首句或尾句，代表文章的中心思想或作者的主要观点，是作者对自己要表达的中心思想的最全面的概括。要想找出文章的中心思想，最有效的途径便是首先找出段落的主题句。

2. 辨认事实题型

在一篇文章中，作者总是要列举一系列例证和论据来支持自己的论点和阐述主题。考生对这些具体的内容，包括例证、主要事实和有关细节了解得越清楚，便越能深刻地理解文章的中心思想。这类题目通常由 who, what, where, when, why, how 等疑问词来引导，如：

1. Which of the following statements is (not) true?
2. Which of the following best supports the idea of the passage?
3. Which of the following is (not) included in the article?
4. Which of the following is (not) mentioned in the article?
5. It is suggested in the passage that ________.
6. The author states all of the items listed below except that ________.
7. What is the purpose of ________?
8. What is the meaning of ________?

对于这类问题，如文章中确已列出事实和细节，通过“细读”便可以直接从中找到答案。但是如果问题中不是直接陈述文章中的事实，而是间接地使用同义词或不同的表达方式来陈述，考生就得弄清楚问题，同时带着问题用“寻读”的方法寻找答案所在，查找与解题相关的关键词，细读该句话和上下文，在完全弄清具体内容的情况下作出选择。

3. 猜测词义题型

在阅读题中，每年总有猜测词义的题型，一般在两题以上。这些词往往是考生不熟悉的，在不允许翻查词典的情况下考生只能运用一些猜词技巧来猜出词义，主要从上下文内容的提示、构词知识去着手。这种题型常用的提问方式有：

1. By the author means ________.
2. Which of the following is closest in meaning to ________?
3. According to the author, the word means ________.
4. The word most probably means ________.
5. The word/phrase refers to ________.

6. By the word the author intends to render the idea that ________.

7. The word can best be replaced by ________.

8. From the passage, we can infer that the word is ________.

9. Which is the probable definition of the word ________?

10. The phrase ________ in the passage suggests ________.

在阅读过程中,我们总是会遇到生词或意义不明确的词。一般来说,如果个别词不影响对文章内容的理解,可以忽略。如果涉及解题或对文章的理解,就应借助猜题技巧,特别是从上下文或利用构词法来猜出词义。(参阅:本节的"三、八种猜词技巧")

4. 难句理解题型

试题中对句子意义的测试一般均针对较难的句子, 对于难句的理解也和词汇的理解一样,须结合上下文或上下句的逻辑关系加以确定。这类试题一般可以分为两种:

(1) 上下句之间或段落逻辑关系的理解测试;

(2) 对各句之间指代关系的测试。

这类试题常用的提问方式如下:

1. Which of the following best describes the author's method?

2. The author develops the thesis primarily by ________.

3. It can be assumed that the paragraph preceding (following) the passage most probably discusses ________.

4. The paragraph preceding (following) this one probably talks ________.

5. In line ________, the word "it" can be substituted by ________.

6. In paragraph ________, "they" stands for (refers to) ________.

7. The word "one" in line ________ could best be replaced by which of the following words?

8. In paragraph ________ line ________, the pronoun " ________ " refers to ________.

对于这类逻辑推理题,自然要应用一些逻辑推理方法。一是要弄清楚指代关系,代词究竟指代的是什么,在逻辑上能否说得通,根据上下文逻辑关系作出判断;二是要注意句子和段落之间的逻辑连接词,弄清前后句或上下段之间的转承关系,最后才能确定单句的意义。

5. 推理题型

推理题型要求考生从一个或几个已知信息推断出结论性的未知。信息推理有直接推理和间接推理两种形式。直接推理往往从一个已知信息得出结论,间接推理要从两个或两个以上的已知信息中才能得出结论。常用的推理方法有演绎法、归纳法和类比法。在阅读过程中,我们根据文章所提供的信息,根据试题提出的要求,判断出作者的观点、意图和态度。常见的提问方式有:

1. The passage implies that ________.

2. What's suggested by the author?

3. We can infer from the passage that ________.

4. The passage is intended to tell us that ________.
5. It can be concluded from the passage that ________.
6. The paragraph would most likely state ________.
7. The author would most probably suggest that ________.
8. The passage gives us the impression that ________.

这类题常采用 infer, imply, suggest, conclude, intend, refer to, state, discuss, deal with 等表示判断的词。解题时,考生第一步应细读试题的要求,审题首先要准确,搞清楚出题者的意图,然后要在文章中找到可以推断的信息。它们可能是一个或几个具体的事实或细节,也可能是全文或段落的中心思想,或是作者在字里行间表示出来的意图、态度、看法、风格、思想、思路等等。无论是哪一类试题,考生都要在文章所提供的信息之上加以归纳、演绎、分析、比较,不能凭自己的经验和主观看法来推断。

6. 推论题型

在不同的文体中,诸如议论文、记叙文和说明文等,作者均会在字里行间流露自己的观点和态度。有的很明显,一目了然,而有的则很隐蔽,不易察觉。作者的观点态度和感情色彩均可以从一些关键的词中反映出来,其态度表现为幽默、讽刺、批判、赞美、中立、自信、恐惧、悔恨、悲观、乐观、认真、正式、非正式、反对、赞成、同情、冷漠、憎恶等。其观点有鲜明的、隐含的、阐明的、辩论的、分析的、归纳的、推理的、总结的或考证的等等。

推论题型常见的提问形式有:

1. The tone of this passage is ________.
2. The author's view is ________.
3. Most probably the author intends to ________.
4. The author gives the impression that ________.
5. Most likely the author feels that ________.
6. Which of the following can best describe the author's attitude towards ________?
7. The author suggests in the passage that ________.
8. What's the mood of the passage ________?

答题时考生要注意不同含义或具有不同感情色彩的词的使用,它往往表明作者对某些事物或问题的不同观点及态度。特别是一些关键词,诸如动词、副词和形容词的选用,它们能代表作者论述的基调。

三、八种猜词技巧

1. 根据文中的定义或解释猜测词义

在一些情况下,作者经常会对那些难词和关键词加以定义或进一步解释,或以同义词或近义词的方式向读者暗示。这时考生便可通过阅读给出的定义、解释或同义词和近义词推测和判断该词词义，这种提示或暗示常用 that is, i.e., which means, which refers to, that can be defined as, it implies that, is known as, is called, is considered to be 等连接。

♨ Example 1

The earliest authentic works on European alchemy are those of the English monk Goger Bacon and the German philosopher St. Albertus Magnus. In their treatises they maintained that gold was the perfect metal and that inferior metals such as lead and mercury were removed various degrees of imperfection from gold. They further asserted that these base metals could be transmuted to gold by blending them with a substance even more perfect than gold. This elusive substance was referred to as the "philosopher's stone".

The "philosopher's stone" was ________.

(A) lead which was mixed with gold

(B) an element which was never found

(C) another name for alchemy

(D) a base metal

[答案为(B)] "philosopher's stone"实际上意为"点金石",它在文中已得到解释:这种捕捉不到的物质被称为"点金石",与"一种永远找不到的元素"相符,故答案应为(B)。

♨ Example 2

Imagine a world in which children would be the rules and could decide not only the outcome of each and every occurrence, but also dictate the very structure and form of the environment. In this world, a child's wildest thoughts would become reality limited only by the extent of his or her imagination. While such a world might sound both fantastic and frightening, at least from a logical, adult perspective, it does exist. What's more, it has been in existence for some time and is populated by hundreds of thousands of children who spend hours within its boundaries experimenting and learning. This world is not real, at least not in the traditional sense, but exists within a computer and is generated by an educational programming language called LOGO.

LOGO is ________.

(A) an education testing program

(B) a computer language

(C) an information dispenser

(D) an unreal world

[答案为(B)] LOGO 对于大多数考生来说是一个陌生的技术术语,但由于文中已给出了定义，考生可以根据定义加以判断:"____ and is generated by an educational programming language called LOGO."(……由名为 LOGO 的教育程序语言所产生。)，所以它是一种计算机语言，故应选择(B)。

2. 根据上下文内容猜测词义

从语义学的角度来看,单词本身的意义是确定的。只有把单词放到句子中,“适当的词放在适当的位置,这个词才有确切的含义”。考生可通过上下文提供的有关信息运用自己的知识和经验找出该词在文中形成的“特定含义”。

Example 1

Dorothea Dix left home at an early age — of her own free will — to live with her grandmother. At fourteen, Dorothea was teaching school at Worcester, Massachusetts. A short time after she had begun teaching, she established a school for young girls in her grandparent's home. Stress was placed on moral character at Dorothea's school, which she conducted until she was thirty-three.

The word “Stress” could best be replaced by ________.

(A) Emphasis (B) Strain

(C) Relative loudness (D) Physical pressure

[答案为(A)] 就“stress”一词本身的含义来说,与(A),(B),(C),(D)四个选项均有关联,但从内容来看:“多萝西亚·迪克斯自幼离开家和祖母一起生活。多萝西亚 14 岁执教于麻省伍塞斯特的一所学校。在她从事教学不久,就在祖父母家里办起了一所女子学校。该校着重培养学生的道德品行,多萝西亚亲自在该校执教直到 33 岁。” Strain 意为“紧张”;Relative loudness 意为“较大声”;Physical pressure 意为“身体上的压力”,均与学校培养学生的道德品行无关。而 Emphasis 意为“强调”,与上下文相符,故选(A)。

Example 2

George Washington Carver showed that plant life was more than just food for animals and humans. Carver's first step was to analyze plant parts to find out what they were made of. He then combined these simpler isolated substances with other substances to create new products.

In Line 2, the word “step” could best be replaced by ________.

(A) footprint (B) action

(C) scale (D) stair

[答案为(B)] step 为一个多义词,要确定它在本文中的意思必须将它放到上下文中来判断:“乔治·华盛顿·卡弗证明植物不只是动物和人类的食物。他的第一个步骤是分析植物的成分以弄清它们是由什么组成的。然后,他把这些更简单的分离物质与其他物质合成新的产品。”从四个选项来看,footprint 意为“脚印”;action 意为“行动”;scale 意为“尺度”;stair 意为“阶梯”。经过比较,action“行动”与“步骤”同义,故选择(B)为宜。

3. 根据背景常识猜测词义

一些词的词义,可以根据背景常识猜测出来。考生可以用自己平时积累的知识和经验,再结合试题中所理解的部分内容作出推测,以确定词义。

♨ **Example**

Most systems use synchronous satellites that stay in one position over the Earth. Synchronous satellites are launched to an altitude of 22,300 miles. At this altitude, the satellite's revolution is synchronized with the Earth's rotation. This means that the satellite completes one orbit during the same length of time that the earth makes one rotation on its axis. Three of these satellites, properly placed, can link stations in any two parts of the world.

It can be inferred from the passage that synchronous satellites are called "synchronous" because ________.

(A) they can synchronize three-way transmissions to all parts of the world

(B) each one rotates on its axis simultaneously with the Earth's rotation

(C) their orbits are perfectly timed to coincide with the Earth's rotation

(D) each one's movements are synchronized to one-third of the speed of the earth

[答案为(C)] 试题提问"同步卫星之所以称为同步是因为……"。这类问题明显是测试考生的常识性问题。从文章的内容来看,我们也可以找到答案:"在这一高度上卫星与地球的旋转同步。这意味着,卫星在轨道上完成一次运行所花的时间与地球绕轴自转一次的时间相同。"对照四个选项,只有 their orbits are perfectly timed to coincide with the Earth's rotation "它们的轨道与地球的旋转在时间上完全相符"与上下文一致。实际上,考生如果稍了解一点儿卫星方面的知识,便可以立即选出答案。

4. 根据文章中的举例猜测词义

作者有时常在某些词后面用"诸如、好像、例如、如此……等等"来列举数例以归纳该词的范畴,考生可以运用从一般到具体的方法归纳出该词的意思。这种列举常用 like, as, for example, for instance, such as, in such case 等词语或破折号等连接。

♨ **Example**

As many as one thousand years ago in the Southwest, the Hopi and Zuni tribes of North America were building with adobe-sun-baked brick plastered with mud. Their homes looked remarkably like modern apartment houses. Some were four stories high and contained quarters for perhaps a thousand people, along with storerooms for grain and other goods. These buildings were usually put up against cliffs, both to make construction easier and for defense against enemies. They were really villages in themselves, as later Spanish explorers must have realized since they called them "pueblos"(西班牙语:村镇), which is Spanish for town.

The people of the pueblos raised what are called "the three sisters" — corn, beans and squash. They made excellent pottery and wove marvellous baskets, some so fine that they could hold water. The author uses the phrase "the three sisters" in the passage to refer to ________.

(A) Hopi women (B) Family members

(C) Important crops (D) Main ceremonies

[答案为(C)] 文中提到的"the three sisters"是一种比喻,由于作者用破折号进行了连接,并在后面接着列举了三种作物的名字:玉米、豆子和南瓜。所以"three sisters"应是指"重要的农作物",故答案应选为 (C)。

5. 根据对比、比较的词语猜测词义

对比与比较是两种写作手法,用于进一步说明和解释一件事物或一种语义。对比可使读者了解事物和意义之间的区别;比较可使读者了解事物和意义之间的相同或相似之处。常用 like, as, but, yet, while, however, despite, in spite of, unlike 等词连接,有时还用 and 连接两个对比的部分。

♨ Example 1

Herons nest and roost in flocks, but hunt for food alone.

The word "flocks" in the sentence most probably means ________.

(A) cycles (B) groups

(C) threes (D) dens

[答案为(B)] 本句意为"苍鹭成群地筑巢和栖息,但是单独地觅食"。But 在句中为考生提示了两种意义的对比关系,in flocks 为介词短语作状语修饰 "nest and roost",alone 为副词作状语修饰"hunt"。alone 意为"单独地",与 flocks 形成对比,故该词应该意为"成群地"。在四个选项中,cycles 意为"周期;循环";groups 意为"群,组";threes 意为"三个人或物(一组)";dens 意为"穴,窝"。显然,groups 与 alone 构成鲜明的对比关系,因此(B)为正确答案。

♨ Example 2

The long-eared owl is found only in North America; the short-eared owl is ubiquitous. In the sentence the word *ubiquitous* is most probably means ________.

(A) nocturnal (B) endangered

(C) widespread (D) omnivorous

[答案为(C)] 本句意"长耳猫头鹰在北美才能找到,而短耳猫头鹰却无处不在"。将两个并列句前后分开的分号以及 long-eared owl 和 short-eared owl 表达了鲜明的对比关系。而前句的状语 only in North America 为我们提示了地理范围的局限性,所以我们应该找出具有与地理范围局限性相对立的词。在四个选项中,nocturnal 意为"夜里的";endangered 意为"受到危害的";widespread 意为"普遍的";omnivorous 意为"杂食的"。(C)项与上述分析相符,为正确答案。

6. 根据语法知识猜测词义

对于阅读中遇到的生词,往往可以运用自己平时学到的语法知识猜出词义,例如运用时

态、语态、名词的单复数形式、抽象与具体、固定搭配和习惯用法等等。

Example 1

When carbon is added to iron in the proper proportions, the result is steel. The word "proportions" in the sentence most probably means ______.

(A) container (B) sequence

(C) laboratories (D) amounts

[答案为(D)] 这里 proportions 为名词复数形式,而在四个选项中,container 和 sequence 为单数形式,laboratories 和 amounts 为复数形式。考生可以运用名词单复数这一语法知识首先将(A)和(B)排除。在(C)和(D)中,laboratories 意为"实验室",amounts 意为"数量,总额",而 proportions 意为"份额,大小,比例",故(D)最符合题意。

Example 2

Tranquilizers are often used in the treatment of tension.

The word "tension" in the sentence is most closely related in meaning with ______.

(A) stress (B) headaches

(C) broken bones (D) muscle spasms

[答案为(A)] 名词 tension 在表示"紧张"之意时应为不可数名词,故不能加"s"。选项中 broken bones 和 muscle spasms 均为可数名词的复数形式,故可排除。stress 意为"紧张",同时也为单数形式,与 tension 在单复数形上和意义上均相符,故应选(A)。

Example 3

Current hiring policies in the United States seek to provide equal employment opportunities for women and minority groups. The word "provide" in the sentence most probably means ______.

(A) furnish (B) demand

(C) confirm (D) continue

[答案为(A)] provide 在英语中的固定搭配形式一般为 provide sb. with sth.或 provide sth. for sb., 在本题中为 provide sth. for sb.。四个选项中,只有 furnish 可以构成与 provide 同样的搭配形式:furnish sb. with sth.。同时从意义来看,furnish 意为"提供、供应"与 provide 同义,而 demand 意为"需要、要求";confirm 意为"批准、证实";continue 意为"使继续",均与 provide 意义不符,故选(A)。

7. 根据定语或同位语猜测词义

定语常用来说明词义,而同位语则表示意义相同的词义,所以考生可借助定语或同位语猜出词义。引出同位语可用括号或破折号,也可以用 or, that is, in other words 等来连接。

Example

Alaska boasts of several climates due to its lofty mountains, warm ocean currents, and frozen seas.

The word "lofty" in Line 1 is most closely in meaning with ________.

(A) towering (B) countless

(C) rugged (D) ageless

[答案为(A)] 形容词lofty在这里用作定语修饰mountains,意为"山,山脉"。在一般情况下,修饰"山"的形容词常为"巍峨的"、"低矮的"、"绵延的"。在四个选项中,towering意为"屹立的、高耸的"; countless意为"无数的";rugged意为"不平的、崎岖的";ageless意为"永恒的、不老的";只有towering在含义上能与mountains搭配,而lofty意为"极高的、高耸的",故(A)为正确答案。

8. 根据构词法猜测词义

掌握单词构词法,能帮助考生具备分析单字的能力,渡过"生字多"的"难关",增加词汇量,同时在解题时,利用构词法,如:前缀、后缀、词根及其含义,往往能给我们以提示来猜测词义。

《考研大纲》词汇表明确规定:学生还应理解本词汇表中所出现的单词加词缀构成的派生词。

因此除了掌握运用大纲中的词汇外,掌握加词缀构成的派生词也成为复习的一个重要组成部分。

◇ 主要构词法:

(1) 转化(Conversion):由一种词类转化为另一种词类,例如:

watch(*v.*) 观看 → watch(*n.*) 手表 chair(*v.*) 主持 → chair(*n.*) 椅子

(2) 派生(Derivation):加前缀或后缀构成另一个词,例如:

un-(不,非,未) → unfair 不公平的;un-(不,非,示) unlimited 无限的

(3) 合成(Compounding):由两个或更多的词合成一个词,例如:

名 词 + 名 词	silkworm	蚕
形容词 + 形容词	double-dealer	两面派
动名词 + 名 词	sleepingpill	安眠药
动 词 + 名 词	pickpocket	扒手

◇ 根据前后缀识别单词:

单词是由词素(词根、词缀)构成的,词义是由词素产生的。单词的核心是词根,认识一个词根,再加上前缀或后缀,就等于认识了一群单词。常用的词根大约有100多个,常用的前缀大约有130个,后缀大约有160个。常用的词缀形式构成如下:

(1) 前缀 + 词根

pro-	+	pel	→	propel
(向前)		(推)		(推进)

(2) 词根 + 后缀

port + -able → portable
(拿,带) (可……的) (可携带的)

(3) 前缀 + 词根 + 后缀

im- + mort + -al → immortal
(不) (死) (……的) (不死的,不朽的)

(4) 前缀 + 前缀 + 词根

re- + ex- + port → reexport
(再) (出) (运) (再输出)

(5) 词根 + 后缀 + 后缀

cord + -ial + -ly → cordially
(心) (……的) (……地) (衷心地)

(6) 前缀 + 词根 + 词根

tri- + gon(o) + metry → trigonometry
(三) (角) (测量) (三角学)

(7) 前缀 + 前缀 + 词根 + 后缀 + 后缀

un- + pre- + ced + -ent + -ed → unprecedented
(无) (先,前) (行) (表事物) (……的) (无先例的)

在阅读过程中,我们如果了解了一个单词的构词元素(前缀、词根、后缀),不但记词变得容易,而且猜出词义也不会很难。

♨ Example 1

In the United States senatorial race of 1858 Abraham Lincoln was the Illinois Candidate of the new Republican party, a coalition of antislavery groups. The word coalition in Line 2 could best be replaced by ________.

(A) a benefactor (B) an opponent
(C) a forerunner (D) an alliance

[答案为(D)] 从名词 coalition 的后缀 -tion 来分析,该词为表示抽象概念的名词。在四个选项中,benefactor 意为"捐助人"和 forerunner 意为"先驱者"的后缀 -or 和 -er 均表示具体概念的名词,主要是指人;opponent 意为"对手"也是表示人的具体名词,因此均可排除。alliance(意为"联盟")的后缀-ance 是用来表示抽象概念的名词,故可以肯定(D)为正确答案。

♨ Example 2

Maria Callas became one of the world's most widely known opera singers because of her musical talent, acting ability, and fiery disposition.

The word "disposition" in the sentence can most probably be replaced by ________.

(A) voice (B) producer

(C) reputation　　　　(D) temperament

[答案为(D)] 如上题所述,后缀-tion 表示抽象概念的名词,但在四个选项中,-ment 也是表示抽象名词的后缀,voice 意为“话音”,producer 意为“制造者”,两者均为具体名词,可排除。答案应在 eputation(意为“名声”)和 emperament(意为“性情”)之间选择,由于 disposition 前面的形容词fiery 意为 “火爆的、激烈的”, 不能形容 reputation, 故应排除。答案应为 temperament,它与disposition 同义。

♨ Example 3

Native New Yorker Catherine Malfitano was chosen by the Paris Opera for the title role in its 1984 production of Manon, which marked the opera's centennial.

The word “centennial” means most probably ________.

(A) hundredth anniversary　　　　(B) final performance

(C) revival　　　　(D) premiere

[答案为(A)] 考生如不了解 centennial 的含义,但其前缀 cent-在英语中含义为“百”。四个选项中,hundredth anniversary 意为 “一百周年纪念日”;final performance 意为 “最后的演出”;revival 意为“复活”;premiere 意为“初次”。只有(A)与前缀 cent- 在含义上相符,故应为正确答案。

第二节 阅读理解 B 篇要点

一、B 篇解题要领

B 篇属于选择搭配题,一般为一篇长度为 500~600 词的文章,是试卷新增加的部分,主要考查考生对诸如连贯性、一致性、逻辑性等语篇、语段整体性特征以及文章结构的理解,即要求考生在理解全文的基础上弄清楚文章的整体结构和微观结构。

该题型分为两个部分:主干部分和选项部分。主干部分的原文约 500~600 词,其中有 5 段空白处。空白处的位置可能在段首、段落中间、段末,但不会在文章的第一句,一般情况下也不会是最后一句。选项部分为 6~7 段文字,每段可能是一个句子,可能是两三个短句,也有可能是完整的段落。其中 5 段属于主干部分的空白处。要求考生根据自己对文章的理解从选项中选择 5 段文字放回到文章中相应的 5 段空白处。

这种题型的难度在于要从 7 段文字中找出正确的一段,如果选择错误,就会影响到其他题的选择。此外,对考生的要求不仅仅是能读懂文章内容,而且要求从文章的整体和细节两方面在文章内容的连贯性、一致性和逻辑性方面对考生进行考查,这就要求考生具有较高水平的阅读能力。

为了解答好B篇,考生需要认真阅读文章主干部分内容,搞清楚主干内容和结构上的关系、布局,从而分辨出选项部分从结构和内容上看是属于文章的哪一个部分,并可以与空白处的上下文有机地衔接起来。

一般情况下不可能有特别明显的词汇、句子等语言方面的提示,也并不要求考生过分关注某一具体的细节。而是要着眼于全文,在理解全文大意、文章结构、逻辑关系(诸如时间、地点、因果、从属等关系)的基础之上才能做出正确的选择。

二、B篇例题详解

♨ **Example**

If you smoke and you still don't believe that there's a definite link between smoking and bronchial troubles, heart disease and lung cancer, then you are certainly deceiving yourself. No one will accuse you of hypocrisy. Let us just say that you are suffering from a bad case of wishful thinking. This needn't make you too uncomfortable because you are in good company. Whenever the subject of smoking and health is raised, the governments of most countries hear no evil, see no evil and smell no evil. Admittedly, a few governments have taken timid measures. 1. ________________.

2. ________________. The answer is simply money. Tobacco is a wonderful commodity to tax. It's almost like a tax on our daily bread. In tax revenue alone, the government of Britain collects enough from smokers to pay for its entire educational facilities. So while the authorities point out ever so discreetly that smoking may, conceivably, be harmful, it doesn't do to shout too loudly about it.

This is surely the most short-sighted policy you could imagine. 3. ________________. Enormous amounts are spent on cancer research and on efforts to cure people suffering from the disease. Countless valuable lives are lost. In the long run, there is no doubt that everybody would be much better-off if smoking were banned altogether.

Of course, we are not ready for such a drastic action. But if the governments of the world were honestly concerned about the welfare of their peoples, you'd think they'd conduct aggressive anti-smoking campaigns. Far from it! The tobacco industry is allowed to spend staggering sums on advertising. Its advertising is as insidious as it is dishonest. We are never shown pictures of real smokers coughing up their lungs early in the morning. That would never do. 4. ________________.

5. ________________. Smoking should be banned in all public places like theatres, cinemas and restaurants. Great efforts should be made to inform young people especially of the dire consequences of taking up the habit. A horrific warning—say, a picture of a death's head—should be included in every packet of cigarettes that is sold. As individuals, we are certainly

weak, but if governments acted honestly and courageously, they could protect us from ourselves.

(A) For a start, governments could begin by banning all cigarette and tobacco advertising and should then conduct anti-smoking advertising campaigns of their own.

(B) You don't have to look very far to find out why the official reactions to medical findings have been so luke-warm.

(C) If smoking is banned in our life, some economists would worry about a great loss in cigarettes economy.

(D) While money is eagerly collected in vast sums with one hand, it is paid out in increasingly vaster sums with the other.

(E) The advertisement always depict virile, clean-shaven young men. They suggest it is manly to smoke, even positively healthy! Smoking is associated with the great open-air life, with beautiful girls, true love and togetherness. What utter nonsense!

(F) Smoking is discouraged among the students at all of our colleges, the subject of smoking and health is widely discussed there.

(G) In Britain, for instance, cigarette advertising has been banned on television. The conscience of the nation is appeased, while the population continues to puff its way to smoky, cancerous death.

答案与解析

本文谈论各个国家对于吸烟的态度,以及对广告宣传的政策等。

1. [答案](G)

[解析]空白前提到一些国家采取了一些谨慎的措施,(G)以英国为例,指出该国已经禁止电视打广告。

2. [答案](B)

[解析]空白后面的句子明显是对空白内容的回答,回答很简单,是钱的问题。(B)提出了问题:你不用费劲就可以得出为什么官方对医学的发现会一直很冷淡。

3. [答案](D)

[解析]空白前面的句子指出,这肯定是最目光短浅的政策(指不敢大胆禁烟),(D)指出为什么是目光短浅:一方面是大肆搜刮钱财,另一方面是更大的付出。后面提到大量的资金投入到癌症研究和治疗。

4. [答案](E)

[解析]空白前提到广告都在对吸烟做虚假宣传,从来没有暴露它的危害。(E)进一步作出阐述,广告总是宣传健康男性抽烟有益健康,并与户外生活、漂亮女孩、爱情和

团结联系起来,真是一派胡言。

5. [答案](A)

[解析] 空白后面提到禁烟措施,(A) 提出应该由政府开头,首先禁止广告,掀起反对吸烟的广告宣传。

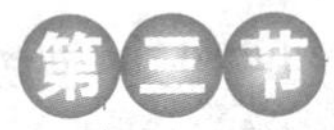

阅读理解 C 篇英语长句的翻译方法

从近几年的试题来看,要求翻译的画线部分基本上为长句,所以长句翻译技巧也应是复习的重点。长句翻译实际上是多种翻译方法的综合应用。在翻译时,考生首先要弄清楚原文的句法结构,找出中心思想及各层意思,分析各层意思之间的逻辑关系再翻译,不拘泥于原文的形式。常用的翻译方法有顺序法、逆序法、分译法、综合法,下面分别加以介绍。

一、顺序法

如时间或逻辑顺序与中文表达相一致,可按照原文顺序译出:

The Committee prepared this paper because its members recognized that the government has failed to establish an energy policy capable of providing a comprehensive energy source that can meet our requirements for the last portion of this century and the greater portion of the next.

该委员会制订这份文件,是因为该委员会的成员看到政府已不能制订一个能提供全面能源的能源政策,以满足我们在本世纪和下大半个世纪的需要。

(这句话由四个句子组成,有从属关系,是一种纵向关系,故顺序译出。第三句由于形容词capable 引导的词组较长,中间还有动名词 providing 作为定语,置于所修饰的名词 policy 之后,译时为紧凑可置于 policy 之前。)

On August 1, the gunboat began her mission, which was, in the eyes of the defenders, a provocative act and seemed to be part of the overall assault which had begun on July 31.

8 月 1 日炮舰开始执行任务。在防御者看来,这是一次挑衅行动,而且似乎是 7 月 31 日开始的全面攻击的一个组成部分。

本句由一个主句和两个定语从句组成,其逻辑顺序与中文习惯相符,故顺序译出。

二、逆序法

英语原文长句的表达次序与汉语表达习惯不同,或完全相反,汉译时必须从原文后面逆着顺序译:

Primary colors are colors in terms of which all other colors may be described, or from which all other colors may be evolved by mixture.

原色就是所有其他颜色可以用它们来表示或者可用它们来调制的颜色。

在英语中,名词、代词、形容词或动名词作定语时一般都放在所修饰的名词前面;从句和各种短语作定语时则放在所修饰的名词之后。汉语却不同,它的定语都会放在所修饰的词之前,因此翻译时,需要对原文结构的排列顺序作部分调整。本句有两个限制性定语从句,均要用到逆序法。

The method normally employed for free electrons to be produced in electron tubes is thermionic emission, in which advantage is taken of the fact, if a solid body is heated sufficiently, some of the electrons that it contains will escape from its surface into the surrounding space.

将固体加热到足够温度时,它所含电子就有一部分离开表面,飞逸到周围的空间中,这种现象叫做热离子放射。电子管就是利用这种方法来产生自由电子的。

本句主句比较简单,有一个较长的过去分词短语作后置定语。由于"in which"引出的长非限制性定语从句十分复杂,它有一个"fact"的同位语从句,在同位语从句中又含有一个"if"引出的条件状语从句和一个"that"引导的定语从句。翻译时,须把次序颠倒过来,以符合汉语表达习惯。

And I take heart from the fact that the enemy (1), which boasts that it can occupy the strategic point in a couple of hours (2), has not yet been able to take even the outlying regions (3), because of stiff resistance that gets in the way (4).

由于受到顽强的抵抗(4),吹嘘能在几小时内占领战略要地的敌人(2)却还没有能占领外围地带(3),这一事实增强了我的信心(1)。

本句由一个主句、一个同位语从句、两个定语从句和一个宾语从句组成。翻译时将顺序做了适当调整,按(4) (2) (3) (1) 的次序译出,以符合汉语表达习惯。

三、分译法

分译也称拆译,就是把一些曲折层叠的长复合句拆成短句,再分别进行翻译。在英语原文的主句与从句或修饰语之间的关系并不是十分密切时,可按照汉语多用短语的习惯,把长句中的从句或短语化为句子,分开来叙述;为使语意连贯,有时可适当增加词语。

The site at Poverty Point, Louisiana, has been known to archeologists since the early 1900s, but it wasn't until 1953, when aerial photographs were taken, that the ridge pattern was first spotted.

考古学家早在本世纪初就已经知道路易斯安那州波佛迪波安特的这处遗址了。然而,直到1953年进行了空中摄影之后,才第一次发现了土岗排列的图形。

本句可以把 but 连接的并列句拆开分译, 其他由 and, although 等连词连接的并列句也可采用这种译法。注意各并列句的译法要因句而异,有的顺译,有的逆译,有的分译。

The great difficulty of introducing radically new computer architectures which requires

customers to rewrite most of their software excluded the possibility for these techniques to find their way to the commercial marketplace.

采用全新的计算机体系结构,势必要求用户改写其大部分软件,因此难以付诸实现。这就排除了这种技术进入商品市场的可能性。

本句的主语是带介词短语,其中又有定语从句的复杂结构,很难直译。译文拆散了原文句子结构,重新组合,先把定语从句拆出分译,再把"great difficulty"抽出来译为"难以付诸实现",独立构成一词,这样就解决了翻译困难,可以使译文通顺流畅。

Computer languages may range from detailed low level close to that immediately understood by the particular computer, to the sophisticated high level which can be rendered automatically acceptable to a wide range of computers.

计算机语言有低级的也有高级的。前者比较繁琐,很接近于特定计算机直接能懂的语言;后者比较复杂,适用范围广,能自动为多种计算机所接受。

句中"range from... to..."之类的结构,在汉语中没有相应的表达结构,故将原文结构顺序打乱,加以重新组合,采用增字、减字、变序等技巧,将形容词短语和定语从句拆出分译,并把作短语的过去分词和形容词短语组合在一句中,读起来更为地道。

四、综合法

当顺译、逆译都感觉不适,而分译也有困难时,便可以进行综合法处理,或按时间先后,或按逻辑顺序,有顺有逆,有主有次地进行分译。事实上,长句翻译本身就是一个综合运用语法分析和各种翻译技巧的复杂过程,往往也会采用其中两种甚至三种译法。

With the advent of the space shuttle, it will be possible to put an orbiting solar power plant in stationary orbit 24,000 miles from the earth that would collect solar energy almost continuously and convert this energy either directly to electricity via photovoltaic cells or indirectly with flat plate or focused collectors that would boil a carrying medium to produce steam that would drive a turbine that then in turn would generate electricity.

随着航天飞机的出现,有可能把一个沿轨道运行的太阳能发电站送到离地球24,000英里的轨道上去。这个太阳能发电站几乎从不间断地采集太阳能。它还能够用光电池将太阳能直接转换成电能,或者用平板集热器或聚焦集热器将太阳能间接转换成电能,即集热器使热传导体气化,驱动涡轮机发电。

本句由it作形式主语,用动词不定式短语作逻辑主语的结构。主语中的名词"solar power plant"带有一个相距较远的定语从句,该从句中又包含另外三个定语从句。这四个定语从句均由that引导,环环相扣。另外还有介词短语、省略成分和并列成分组合在一起,为一个很复杂的长复合句。译文把四个定语从句拆开,独立成句,采用分译法;从整个句子的结构顺序看,译文与原文相近,也可采用顺译法;而在个别地方把原文顺序做了局部颠倒,采用了逆译法。

To head the development division they chose a forty-year-old engineer, Kenichi Yamamoto, who in the succeeding few years emerged as one of the handful of Men — Froede, Bentele, Bensinger of Daimler-Benz — who have made major contributions to rotary technology.

为了领导这个开发部,他们选择了一个40岁的工程师山本健。他在以后的几年中,成了少数几个名人 —— 福来迪、本特尔、戴姆勒-奔驰公司的本辛格之一,这些人对转子技术都作出了重大贡献。

本句用关联词 who 承上启下,使首尾相接。汉语则必须独立成句,因此必然重复出现上句中有关的词。

By the middle of the year, he warned, the Soviet Union would overtake the United States in the number of landbased strategic missiles, the result of a massive Soviet effort beginning in the mid-1960s, after the Cuban fiasco, to achieve at least parity and possibly superiority in nuclear weapons.

他告诫说,到本年年中,前苏联在陆上发射的战略导弹将在数量上超过美国,因为前苏联在古巴事件中遭到失败后,从60年代中期就大力发展导弹,目的是为了在核武器方面至少同美国均等,并力争超过美国。

本句为一个简单句。有一个插入语 he warned 可以提前译出。另外有一个表示结果的名词短语,但这个短语中有两个表示时间的短语和一个表示目的的短语,需要按逻辑关系来安排。表示结果的名词短语可译为表示原因的句子。

阅读强化练习一

阅读 A 篇

Directions:

Read the following four texts. Answer the questions below each text by choosing A, B, C or D. Mark your answers on ANSWER SHEET 1. (*40 points*)

Passage 1

The theory of plate tectonics describes the motions of the lithosphere, the comparatively rigid outer layer of the Earth that includes all the crust and part of the underlying mantle. The lithosphere is divided into a few dozen plates of various sizes and shapes; in general the plates are in motion with respect to one another. A mid-ocean ridge is a boundary between plates where new lithospheric material is injected from below. As the plates diverge from a mid-ocean ridge they slide on a more yielding layer at the base of the lithosphere.

Since the size of the Earth is essentially constant, new lithosphere can be created at the mid-ocean ridges only if an equal amount of lithospheric material is consumed elsewhere. The site of this destruction is another kind of plate boundary: a subduction zone. There one plate dives under the edge of another and is reincorporated into the mantle. Both kinds of plate boundary are associated with fault systems, earthquakes and volcanism, but the kinds of geologic activity observed at the two boundaries are quite different.

The idea of sea-floor spreading actually preceded the theory of plate tectonics. In its original version, in the early 1960's, it described the creation and destruction of the ocean floor, but it did not specify rigid lithospheric plates. The hypothesis was substantiated soon afterward by the discovery that periodic reversals of the Earth's magnetic field are recorded in the oceanic crust. As magma rises under the mid-ocean ridge, ferromagnetic minerals in the magma become magnetized in the direction of the geomagnetic field. When the magma cools and solidifies, the direction and the polarity of the field are preserved, in the magnetized volcanic rock. Reversals of the field give rise to a series of magnetic stripes running parallel to the axis of the rift. The oceanic crust thus serves as a magnetic tape recording of the history of the geomagnetic field that can be dated independently, the width of the stripes indicates the rate of the sea-floor spreading.

21. What is the main topic of the passage?
    (A) Magnetic field reversal.
    (B) The formation of magma.
    (C) The location of mid-ocean ridges.
    (D) Plate tectonic theory.

22. According to the passage, there are approximately how many lithospheric plates?
    (A) Six.
    (B) Twelve.
    (C) Twenty-four or more.
    (D) One thousand nine hundred.

23. Which of the following is true about tectonic plates?
    (A) They are moving in relationship to one other.
    (B) They have unchanging borders.
    (C) They are located far beneath the lithosphere.
    (D) They have the same shape.

24. According to the passage, which of the following statements about the lithosphere is LEAST likely to be true?
    (A) It is a reactively inflexible layer of the Earth.
    (B) It is made up entirely of volcanic ash.
    (C) It includes the crust and some of the mantle of the Earth.
    (D) It is divided into plates of various shapes and sizes.

25. What does the author imply about the periodic reversal of the Earth's magnetic field?
    (A) It is inexplicable.
    (B) It supports the hypothesis of sea-floor spreading.
    (C) It was discovered before the 1960's.
    (D) It indicates the amount of magma present.

生词及短语

tectonics [tek'tɔniks]	*n.*	筑造学，构造
lithosphere ['liθəusfiə]	*n.*	岩石圈，陆界
crust [krʌst]	*n.*	外壳，硬壳
underlying [ˌʌndə'laiiŋ]	*a.*	在下面的，潜在的
mantle ['mæntl]	*n.*	地幔，覆盖物，斗篷
with respect to		关于，至于
ridge [ridʒ]	*n.*	背脊，山脉
diverge [dai'vəːdʒ]	*vi.*	分叉，分歧
yielding ['jiːldiŋ]	*a.*	易弯曲的，易受影响的，出产的
constant ['kɔnstənt]	*a.*	不变的，持续的
reincorporate [ˌriːin'kɔːpəreit]	*v.*	(使)再合并，再并入
geologic [dʒiə'lɔdʒik]	*a.*	地质(学)的，地质(学)上的
precede [ˌpri'siːd]	*v.*	领先(于)，在…之前，先于
destruction [dis'trʌkʃən]	*n.*	破坏，毁灭
subduction [sʌb'dʌkʃən]	*n.*	潜没，消亡作用
zone [zəun]	*n.*	地带，地域，地区，圈，环带
hypothesis [hai'pɔθisis]	*n.*	假设
reversal [ri'vəːsəl]	*n.*	颠倒，反转，反向，逆转
magma ['mægmə]	*n.*	岩浆
ferromagnetic [ˌferəumæg'netik]	*a.*	铁磁的，铁磁体的
geomagnetic [ˌdʒiːəumæg'netik]	*a.*	地磁的
solidify [sə'lidəˌfai]	*v.*	(使)凝固，巩固
polarity [pəu'læritiː, pə-]	*n.*	极性
stripe [straip]	*n.*	条纹，斑纹
axis ['æksis]	*n.*	轴
rift [rift]	*n.*	裂缝，裂口，断裂，长峡谷

答案与解析

21. [答案] (**D**)

[解析] 本题为主旨题。文章第一句就写道："The theory of plate tectonics describes the motions of the lithosphere,…"，后文全是由此展开的论述，故(D)为正确答案。

22. [答案] (C)

[解析] 从第一段第二句“The lithosphere is divided into a few dozen plates of various sizes and shapes;”可知板块的数目为几十块,故(C)为正确答案。

23. [答案] (A)

[解析] 第一段第二句后半句 “in general the plates are in motion with respect to one another.” 表明本题答案为(A)。

24. [答案] (B)

[解析] 此题采用排除法。根据第二段第一句 “Since the size of the Earth ... material is consumed elsewhere”, 第三段第二句 “... but it did not specify rigid lithospheric plates.”可排除(A);由第一段第一句中的“...that includes all the crust and part of the underlying mantle.” 可排除 (C); 由第一段第二句中的 “The lithosphere is divided into a few dozen plates of various sizes and shapes;”可排除(D),故答案只能为(B)。

25. [答案] (B)

[解析] 文章第三段第三句写道 “The hypothesis was substantiated soon afterward by the discovery that periodic reversals of the Earth's magnetic field...”, 其中 substantiate 的意思与(B)项中的 support 一致,而(B)项正好与此句的意思一致,故(B)应为正确答案。

译文

板块结构理论描述了陆界的运动。陆界是地球相当坚硬的外层结构,包括所有的地壳以及部分下层地幔。陆界被分成几十块大小和形状相异的板块。一般来说,这些板块间是相对运动的。一个中海屋脊就是一个板块间的边界,新的陆界物质从下面注入。当板块从中海屋脊分离时,它们在陆界基底更易弯曲的地层上滑动。

由于地球的大小基本上是不变的,因此只有当其他地方的陆界材料消耗掉时,才能在中海屋脊形成等量的新的陆界。被毁掉的地方成为另一种板块的边界:潜没地带。在这里一个板块沿着另一个板块的边缘下潜再并入地幔。两种类型的板块边界都与断层结构、地震和火山爆发有关,但在这两类边界所观察到的地质活动的类型是极不相同的。

海床扩展观念实际上先于板块结构理论。20 世纪 60 年代早期的原始著作中,描述了海床的形成和毁灭,但它未提及坚硬的陆界板块。这一假设在发现海洋地壳地磁场的周期性反转后不久便得到了证实。当岩浆从中海屋脊渗出时,在岩浆中的铁磁性矿物沿着地球磁场的方向磁化。当岩浆冷却并固化时,磁场方向和极性在磁化的火山岩中保存下来。磁场的反转导致了与裂谷轴线平行的一系列磁性条纹的形成。因此海底地壳作为一种磁带,记录了可以独立标注年代的地磁的历史。条纹的宽度说明了海床扩展的速度。

Passage 2

The United States court system, as part of the federal system of government, is characterized by dual hierarchies: there are both state and federal courts. Each state has its own system of courts, composed of civil and criminal trial courts, sometimes intermediate courts of appeal, and a state supreme court. The federal court system consists of a series of trial courts (called district courts) serving relatively small geographic regions (there is at least one for every state, a tier of circuit courts of appeal that hear appeals from man), district courts in a particular geographic region, and the Supreme Court of the United States. The two court systems are to some extent overlapping, in that certain kinds of disputes (such as a claim that a state law is in violation of the Constitution) may be initiated in either system. They are also to some extent hierarchical, for the federal system stands above the state system in that litigants (persons engaged in lawsuits) who lose their cases in the state supreme court may appeal their cases to the Supreme Court of the United States.

Thus, the typical court case begins in a trial court—a court of general jurisdiction—in the state or federal system. Most cases go no further than the trial court: for example, the criminal defendant is convicted (by a trial or a guilty plea) and sentenced by the court and the case ends; the personal injury suit results in a judgment by a trial court (or an out-of-court settlement by the parties while the courts suit is pending) and the parties leave the court system. But sometimes the losing party at the trial court cares enough about the cause that the matter does not end there. In these cases, the "loser" at the trial court may appeal to the next higher court.

26. What does the passage mainly discuss?
    (A) Civil and criminal trial courts.
    (B) Typical court cases.
    (C) The court system in the United States.
    (D) The appeal court process.

27. According to the passage district courts are also known as ______.
    (A) circuit courts
    (B) supreme courts
    (C) intermediate courts
    (D) trial courts

28. In the last sentence of the first paragraph, the phrase "engaged in" could best be replaced by which of the following?
(A) Committed to.
(B) Involved in.
(C) Attentive to.
(D) Engrossed in.

29. It can be inferred from the passage that typical court ______.
(A) always appealed
(B) usually resolved in the district courts
(C) always overlapping
(D) usually settled by the Supreme Court

30. Which of the following is most likely to be the subject of the paragraph following the passage?
(A) The process of an appeal.
(B) Out-of-court settlements.
(C) The state court structure.
(D) Sentencing procedures.

生词及短语

dual [ˈdjuːəl]	*a.*	双的,双重的
hierarchy [ˈhaiərɑːki]	*n.*	层次,层级
intermediate [ˌintəˈmiːdiət]	*a.*	中间的
tier [tiə(r)]	*n.*	层,等级
circuit courts	*n.*	巡回法庭
overlap [ˈəuvəˈlæp]	*v.*	交叠,重叠
initiate [iˈniʃiət]	*v.*	开始,发起
litigant [ˈlitigənt]	*n.*	诉讼人
lawsuit [ˈlɔːsjuːt]	*n.*	诉讼
jurisdiction [ˌdʒuərisˈdikʃən]	*n.*	权限,司法
defendant [diˈfendənt]	*n.*	被告
convict [kənˈvikt]	*vt.*	证明……有罪,宣布……有罪
plea [pliː]	*n.*	恳求,请求,辩解

pending [ˈpendiŋ]	*a.*	未决的
appeal [əˈpiːl]	*n.*	上诉,请求

答案与解析

26. [答案](C)

[解析]本题为主旨题。文章在开头第一句即开门见山地提出了本文将讨论的主要内容:The United States court system, 故答案明显应为(C)。

27. [答案](D)

[解析]从第一段第三句"The federal court system consists of a series of trial courts (called district courts)..."可知答案为(D)。

28. [答案](B)

[解析]engaged in 出现在第一段最后一句括号中 "that litigants (persons engaged in lawsuits) who..."很明显,它是对单词 litigants"诉讼人"的说明,所以括号中的意思应为"涉及诉讼的人",engaged in 在此处与(B)involved in 同义,故答案应为(B)。

29. [答案](B)

[解析]从第二段第一句 "Thus, the typical court case begins in a trial court—a court of general jurisdiction—in the state or federal system."可推断出答案应为(B)。注意:(B)项中 resolved 的词义为"解决"。

30. [答案](A)

[解析]当问及后面段落可能讨论的问题或内容时,一般要注意该段最后一句话。本文最后一句讲的是官司打输了的人可向高一级法院上诉,故下一段最可能讲述的是(A)"上诉程序"。

译文

作为联邦政府制度一部分的美国法院系统,以双层结构为特征:既有州法院,又有联邦法院。每个州都有自己的法院系统,包括民事和刑事审判法院,有时还有中级上诉法院以及州最高法院。联邦法院系统包括一系列审判法院(称为地区法院),负责审判较小地区之内发生的案件(每个州至少有一个地区法院);更高一层的巡回上诉法院,其任务是受理一个特定地理范围内来自许多地区法院的上诉;还有美国最高法院。这两种法院系统在某种程度上是重叠的,在这种情况下某些争议(例如:声称州的某条法律与宪法相抵触)可能会在两个系统中的任一个中产生。它们在某种程度上也是等级分明的,因为联邦法院系统凌驾于州法院系统之上,诉讼人(涉及诉讼的人)在州最高法院败诉之后,可以向美国最高法院上诉。

因此,典型的案件审理是从州或联邦系统中的审判法院——具有一般司法权的法院——开始。大多数案件在审判法院判决后就到此为止,例如:一个刑事被告(通过审讯或承认有罪)被法庭宣布有罪并判刑后,案件也就结束;个人伤害诉讼在审判法庭做出判决(或在诉讼审理未决时,双方在法庭外私了)之后,诉讼双方即脱离法院。但有时,在审判法院中败诉的一方,对案件非常关心,事情就不会到此结束。在这样的情况下,审判法庭上的"败诉人",就可能向高一级的法院提起诉讼。

Passage 3

To produce the upheaval in the United States that changed and modernized the domain of higher education from the mid-1860s to the mid-1880s, three primary causes interacted. The emergence of a half-dozen leaders in education provided the personal force that was needed. Moreover, an outcry for a fresher, more practical, and more advanced kind of instruction arose among the alumni and friends of nearly all of the old colleges and grew into a movement that overrode all conservative opposition. The aggressive "Young Yale" movement appeared, demanding partial alumni control, a more liberal spirit, and a broader course of study. The graduates of Harvard College simultaneously rallied to relieve the college's poverty and demand new enterprise. Education was pushing toward higher standards in the East by throwing off church leadership everywhere, and in the West by finding a wider range of studies and a new sense of public duty.

The old-style classical education received its most crushing blow in the citadel of Harvard College, where Dr. Charles Eliot, a young captain of thirty-five, son of a former treasurer of Harvard, led the progressive forces. Five revolutionary advances were made during the first years of Dr. Eliot's administration. They were the elevation and amplification of entrance requirements, the enlargement of the curriculum and the development of the elective system, the recognition of graduate study in the liberal arts, the raising of professional training in law, medicine, and engineering to a postgraduate level, and the fostering of greater maturity in student life. Standards of admission were sharply advanced in 1872—1873 and 1876—1877. By the appointment of a dean to take charge of student affairs, and a wise handling of discipline, the undergraduates were led to regard themselves more as young gentlemen and less as young animals. One new course of study after another was opened up—science, music, the history of the fine arts, advanced Spanish political economy, physics, classical philology, and international law.

31. Which of the following is the author's main purpose in the passage?
   (A) To explain the history of Harvard college.
   (B) To criticize the conditions of United States universities in the nineteenth century.

(C) To describe innovations in United States higher education in the latter 1800s.

(D) To compare Harvard with Yale before the turn of the century.

32. According to the passage, the changes in higher education during the latter 1800s were the result of ______.

(A) plans developed by conservatives and church leaders

(B) efforts of interested individuals to redefine the educational system

(C) the demands of social organizations seeking financial relief

(D) rallies held by westerners wanting to compete with eastern schools

33. According to the passage, Harvard College was in need of more ______.

(A) students

(B) money

(C) land

(D) clergy

34. According to the passage, which of the following can be inferred about Harvard College before Progressive changes occurred?

(A) Admission standards were lower.

(B) Students were younger.

(C) Classes ended earlier.

(D) Courses were more practical.

35. From the passage it can be concluded that which of the following was a characteristic of the classical course of study?

(A) Most students majored in education.

(B) Students were limited in their choice of courses.

(C) Students had to pass five levels of study.

(D) Courses were so difficult that most students failed.

生词及短语

upheaval [ʌp'hiːvəl] *n.* 巨变

domain [dəu'mein] *n.* 领域，范围，领地

interact [intər'ækt] *vi.* 互相作用，互相影响

emergence [i'məːdʒəns]	*n.*	露出,出现
outcry ['autkrai]	*n.*	大声疾呼
alumni [ə'luːmni]	*n.*	毕业生,男校友
override [əuvə'raid]	*vt.*	跨越过,不考虑
rally ['ræli]	*v.*	召集,集合
citadel ['sitədəl]	*n.*	根据地,大本营
treasurer ['treʒərə]	*n.*	财政总监,司库,出纳员
elevation [eli'veiʃən]	*n.*	上升,提高
amplification [æmplifi'keiʃən]	*n.*	扩大
entrance ['entrəns]	*n.*	入门,门口(entrance examination 入学考试)
curriculum [kə'rikjuləm]	*n.*	课程
elective [i'lektiv]	*n.*	选修课程　*a.* 有选举权的
foster ['fɔstə]	*vt.*	养育,抚育,培养

答案与解析

31. [答案] (C)

[解析] 本题为主旨题。本文第一段论述了 19 世纪下半叶整个美国高校教育的改革,第二段以哈佛大学的教育改革为例进一步加以说明。故(C) 应为正确答案。

32. [答案] (B)

[解析] 在第一段中谈到美国 19 世纪 80 年代高等教育改革的主要因素时,提到教育界的一些领导人、老牌大学的校友和朋友、耶鲁大学的年轻人、哈佛大学的毕业生,他们要求教育制度的变革,最后形成了一种运动。在第二段中举例说明哈佛大学在查尔斯·埃利奥特的领导下所进行的高等教育制度改革所取得的成绩。这些均说明 19 世纪下半叶美国高等教育的变化是由于一些对高等教育感兴趣的个人所努力的结果。故答案应为(B)。

33. [答案] (B)

[解析] 第一段的倒数第二句提到,哈佛大学的毕业生联合起来帮助大学解决财政困难。这说明当时学校很需要钱,故(B) 应为正确答案。

34. [答案] (A)

[解析] 第二段谈到哈佛大学所取得的五项改革成果中的第一项就是入学条件的提高,而且提到 1872—1873 年度和 1876—1877 年度入学标准急剧提高。这说明在教育改革之前入学标准偏低,故(A) 应为正确答案。

35. [答案](B)

[解析] 第二段在提到五项改革成果时指出改革后课程增多,同时还实行了选修课制度,这说明传统学习课程的特点是学生在课程选择上受到一定范围的限制。故答案应为(B)。

译文

从19世纪60年代中期到19世纪80年代中期，使美国高等教育领域产生巨变和现代化的是三种互相影响的因素。首先，教育界的部分领导人的出面为改革提供了所需要的人力。此外,几乎所有老校友和朋友都疾呼实现一个更新式、更实际和更先进的教育制度,这形成了一个压倒所有保守反对派的运动。敢作敢为的"青年耶鲁"运动出现了,它要求校友参与管理,争取更自由的精神和更多的课程设置。哈佛大学的毕业生不约而同地集合起来解决学校的资金短缺,同时要求开拓新的事业。在东部各地,教堂的领导地位被抛弃;在西部,学习范围扩大,新的责任感被培养起来,教育被推进到一个更高的水平。

老式的传统教育在哈佛大学的大本营遭到最沉重的打击。35岁的年轻上校查尔斯·埃利奥特博士——哈佛大学前财政总监的儿子,成了改革队伍的领导人。在查尔斯·埃利奥特博士行政管理的前几年里取得了五项革命性进展:提高了入学标准,课程增多并实行选修课制度,承认人文学科研究生的学习,在法律、医学和工程学学科中将专业学习提高到研究生水平,培养了一种更成熟的学生生活作风。在1872—1873年度和1876—1877年度,入学标准迅速提高,通过指派系主任直接负责学生事务,更明智地管理学校纪律,使大学生们认识到自己应更像年轻的绅士,而不再是年幼的"动物"。新的课程一个接一个地开设:理科、音乐、美术史、高等西班牙语、政治经济学、物理、古典文学和国际法。

Passage 4

As the English language has changed at a fast speed in this century, so has the use of the English language.

After the British Broadcasting Corporation (BBC) was founded in 1927, the particular style of speech of the BBC announcers was recognized as Standard English or Received Pronunciation (RP) English. Now, most people still consider that the pronunciation and delivery of BBC announcers is the clearest and most understandable spoken English.

English has had a strong association with class and social status. However, since the Second World War there has been a considerable change of attitude towards speech snobbery, and hallmarks of class distinction such as styles of speech have been gradually discarded, especially by the younger generation.

As the need has arisen, new words have been invented or found from other languages and incorporated into English. Similarly, old words and expressions have been discarded as their usefulness has diminished or the fashions have passed. This also happens to styles and modes of speech which became fashionable at a particular time and in specific circumstances.

By the end of the 1960s it became apparent that it was not necessary to speak Standard English or even correct grammar to become popular, successful and rich. The fashionable speech of the day was no longer the prerogative of a privileged class but rather a defiant expression of classlessness.

The greatest single influence of the shaping of the English language in modern times is the American English. Over the last 25 years the English used by many people, particularly by those in the media, advertising and show business, has become more and more mid-Atlantic in style, delivery and accent.

In the 1970s, fashion favored careless pronunciation and a language full of jargon, slang and "in" words, much of it quite incomprehensible to the outside world. What is considered modern and fashionable in Britain today is often not the kind of English taught in schools and colleges.

36. Which one of the following is NOT true?

(A) The use of the English language has not changed much in this century.

(B) The BBC announcers speak Standard English.

(C) English has no association with class and social status now.

(D) Young people all speak English in the same way.

37. What does the author imply by saying "there has been a considerable change of attitude towards speech snobbery" (Para. 3)?

(A) People all speak English like BBC announcers.

(B) There is a great change of attitude about how English should be spoken.

(C) Some people still think their way of speaking is superior.

(D) Most people don't believe their way of speaking is superior.

38. According to the author, there was a trend in the U. S. for the young people ______.

(A) to speak Standard English

(B) to speak English without class distinction

(C) to speak English with class distinction

(D) to speak English with grammar mistakes

39. The word "mid-Atlantic" in the passage (Para. 6) probably means ______.

(A) American and European

(B) American and British

(C) the Atlantic Ocean

(D) in the middle of the Atlantic Ocean

40. It can be concluded from the passage that ______.

(A) Standard English is taught in school and colleges

(B) the young people are defiant because they refuse to speak standard English

(C) English language is influenced by American English in the last 25 years

(D) there has been a great change in the English language in this century

生词及短语

association [əsəusi'eiʃən]	n.	结合,联系
social status		社会地位
snobbery ['snɔbəri]	n.	势利
hallmark ['hɔːlmaːk]	n.	标记,特点
distinction [dis'tiŋkʃən]	n.	区别,差别
discard [dis'kaːd]	vt.	丢弃,抛弃
incorporate [in'kɔːpəreit]	v.	合并,组成
diminish [di'miniʃ]	v.	(使)减少,(使)变小
prerogative [pri'rɔgətiv]	n.	特权
privilege ['privilidʒ]	n.	特权,特别待遇
defiant [di'faiənt]	a.	挑战的,挑衅的
show business		娱乐性行业
accent ['æksənt]	n.	口音,重音
jargon ['dʒaːgən]	n.	行话
slang [slæŋ]	n.	俚语

答案与解析

36. [答案] (A)

[解析] 本题用排除法可得出答案。从第一句可知,英语的使用在本世纪发生了巨大的变化,(A) 项与此意明显不相符;(B) 项在第二段被提到;(C) 项内容在第三段第二句中被提到:“现在英语与阶级和社会地位已经没有什么必然联系”;(D) 项内容可从第三段第二句看出,年轻人所讲的英语基本相同。故只能选(A)。

37. [答案] (D)

[解析] snobbery 意为“势利言行”,指一些绅士认为讲英语要比其他人高一等,但现在讲英语已经是大众的行为,故答案应为(D)。

38. [答案] (B)

[解析] 从第三段和第五段可知,讲英语的阶级差异已经被消除,变为“classlessness”,特别是在年轻人中间。故答案应为(B)。

39. [答案] (B)

[解析] 从第六段可知,近 25 年来,美国英语对现代英语的影响巨大,由于说英语的人越来越多,而且媒体有各种宣传,使得英语在文体、口音等方面变得更“mid-Atlantic”,意指美国英语与英国英语的融合。故答案应为(B)。

40. [答案] (D)

[解析] 本篇主要叙述本世纪以来英语所发生的巨大变化,(A)、(B)、(C) 均不能概括全文内容,因此(D) 应为正确答案。

译文

由于英语在本世纪以一个非常快的速度发生着变化,英语语言的使用也发生了同样的变化。

1927 年英国 BBC 广播公司成立以来,BBC 播音员独特的说话方式被公认为标准英语或标准发音英语。现在,大多数人仍然认为 BBC 播音员的发音和讲话方式是最清楚和最易懂的英语口语。

英语一直与阶级和社会地位有着密切的联系。然而,自从第二次世界大战以来,对于语言的势利态度发生了根本的变化,诸如说话方式等的阶级差别逐渐被抛弃,特别是对于年青一代。

随着日常需求的出现,新词不断被发明或从其他语言中找来,合并到英语当中。同样,旧词和旧的表达方式由于用得少或已经过时而被丢弃。这种情况也同样发生在特定时期和特别环境中曾经很时髦的说话风格和方式方面。

到 20 世纪 60 年代末,很明显,人们再没有必要说标准英语,甚至讲求语法了,语言表达更通俗、易懂和丰富。时下使用时髦语言不再是特权阶级的权利,而成为一种无阶级的反叛传统的表达方式。

现代英语语言形成的最大一种影响力来自美国英语。过去 25 年来,英语被许多人使用,特别是被媒体、广告和娱乐性行业的人们采用,它在风格、说话方式和口音方面已经变得更加“中部大西洋化”。

在 70 年代,时髦导致了发音不准确和俚语盛行,多数词不能为外界所完全理解。在今天的英国,人们认为现代和时髦的语言往往不是在学校或学院中所传授的语言。

阅读 B 篇

Directions:

In the following article, some sentences have been removed. For Questions 41—45, choose the most suitable one from the list A—F to fit into each of the numbered blanks. There are two extra choices, which do not fit in any of the blanks. Mark your answers on ANSWER SHEET 1. (10 points)

Japanese students seem to be losing patience with work, unlike their counterparts in the United States and Korea. In a 1993 survey of college students in the three countries, only 10% of the Japanese regarded work as a primary value, compared with 47% of their Korean counterparts and 27% of American students. 41. ________.

42. ________. Data collected by the Japanese government in 1993 shows that only 23% of Japanese youth are thinking about supporting their aged parents, in contrast to 63% of young Americans. It appears that many younger-generation Japanese are losing both respect for their parents and a sense of responsibility to the family. 43. ________.

The shift toward individualism among Japanese is most pronounced among the very young. According to 1991 data from the Seimei Hoken Bunka Center of Japan, 50% of Japanese youth aged 16 to 19 can be labeled "self-centered", compared with 33% among those aged 25 to 29. 44. ________.

Diminishing social responsibility, according to Yoshizaki, is tied to the growing interest in pleasure and personal satisfaction. A study comparing society-conscious youth from 1977 to 1990 found that the Japanese had slipped far behind American and Australian students. 45. ________.

Yoshizaki concludes that the entire value system of Japanese youth is undergoing major transformation, but the younger generation has not yet found a new organized value system to replace the old.

(A) To earn the self-centered label, the young people responded positively to such ideas as "I would like to make decisions without considering traditional values" and "I don't want to do anything I can't enjoy doing."

(B) Compare with the old generation, the young Japanese seems more to enjoy life rather than work hard.

(C) Japanese youth is vigorous and fresh, but lacks experience in work and life.

(D) Author Yoshizaki attributes the change to Japanese parents' overindulgence of their children, material affluence, and growing concern for private matters.

(E) Concern for family values is waning(减弱) among younger Japanese as they pursue an inner world of private satisfaction.

(F) Only 11% of Japanese aged 18 to 24 said they get personal satisfaction in doing something on behalf of society, according to 1993 data from the Japanese government, while four times as many Americans said so.

(G) A greater proportion of Japanese aged 18 to 24 also preferred easy jobs without heavy responsibility.

内容提要

本文讨论日本青年在社会责任和个人享乐之间价值观的变化，指出这是个严重的社会问题。

文章第一段指出，日本学生看起来对工作失去耐心，这和美国和韩国学生不同。根据1993年对三个国家大学生的调查，只有10%的日本学生认为工作是第一位的，而韩国有47%的大学生认为工作是第一位的,有27%的美国学生认为工作是第一位的。大部分18岁至24岁的日本学生宁愿选择容易的工作,没有强烈的责任感。

最后一段指出,调查者得出结论,日本青年的所有价值观正在发生重大转变,年青一代还没有找到一个可以取代传统价值观的新的有序的价值体系。

答案与解析

41. [答案] (G)

[解析] 空白前一句提到对三个国家的大学生的调查表明，只有10%的日本学生认为工作是第一位的。(G)继续提到18岁至24岁的大部分日本学生情愿选择容易的工作,没有强烈的责任感。

42. [答案] (E)

[解析] 空白后面提到日本政府收集的数据表明只有23%的日本青年人考虑赡养年老的父母,(E)提到日本年轻人关心家庭的意识淡薄,只追逐个人内心的满足。前后表达一致。

43. [答案] (D)

[解析] 空白前句提到许多日本年轻人既不尊重父母,也没有家庭责任感。(D)列举出一位作家认为这种变化归结于日本父母过度放纵孩子，且孩子们的物质生活过于丰富和以“自我为中心”的品性。

44. [答案](A)

[解析]空白前的内容提到调查表明50%的16岁到19岁的日本年轻人属于以"自我为中心"型的,(A)对这种结论做了解释,年轻人肯定这样回答:"我决定事情不想考虑传统价值","我不想做任何我不喜欢做的事"。

45. [答案](F)

[解析]该段提到社会责任问题,空白前提到由于关注个人的快乐和满足,日本青年的社会责任感越来越小。(F)提到在18岁至24岁的日本青年中,只有11%的表示为社会作贡献时会有满足感。

阅读 C 篇

Directions:

Read the following text carefully and then translate the underlined segments into Chinese. Your translation should be written neatly on ANSWER SHEET 2.(10 points)

Both common sense and research say memory declines over time. The accuracy of recall and recognition are at their best immediately after encoding the information, declining at first rapidly, then gradually. (46) The longer the delay, the more likely it is that information obtained after the event will interfere with the original memory, which reduces accuracy. Admittedly, subsequent interviews or media reports can create such distortions. (47) "People are particularly susceptible to having their memories modified when the passage of time allows the original memory to fade, and will be most susceptible if they repeat the misinformation as fact."

Leading questions can lead to mistakes. If witnesses are asked whether the offender had a beard, they may incorporate an imaginary beard into their memories. Subsequent questioning can reinforce the error through repetition.

It is generally agreed that the memories of adults and children are fallible. Nevertheless, even preschoolers can form reliable memories. Young children depend on context to promote memory, and naturally report less. Children may recall more information with adequate support, but the type of support and questioning is critical. Methods of drawing out information have to be carefully monitored.

Although research shows the accuracy of both adults and children can be affected by leading or suggestive questions, the ability to resist the influence of external suggestion increases with age. (48) Children may change their account of an event, not because their memory has altered but because they wish to comply with the suggestion of an adult in authority, or because they interpret repeated questioning as an indication that their first response is judged wrong.

An area of research still relatively unexplored is whether young children have difficulties distinguishing between real and imagined events. We conclude that while children are often seen as unreliable witnesses, research does not bear that out. (49) The code provides alternative ways for children to give evidence to increase accuracy, and gives judges guidance on what to tell a jury to help assess the evidence of very young children.

It is generally agreed some adults who experience sexual abuse may recall memories of the abuse after forgetting it. There is no research to indicate the recalled memories are more or less accurate than memories available all along. We believe it is impossible to distinguish a true from a false memory and it is dangerous to use confidence, vividness and detail as indicating truth. (50) False memories can be induced under hypnosis, and experiments have indicated it is possible, although difficult, to implant false memories of entire events by suggestion.

Hopefully, further research is required into interview techniques and conditions under which false memories and reports of abuse are most likely to arise. It seems that deciding whether any memory is to be finally assessed as reliable or the treacherous ally of invention will largely remain a challenge for judges and juries.

生词及短语

common sense		常识
recall [ri'kɔːl]	*n.*	回忆,回想
recognition [rekəg'niʃən]	*n.*	识别,认可
encoding [in'kəudiŋ]	*n.*	编码,译码
distortion [dis'tɔːʃən]	*n.*	扭曲,失真
susceptible [sə'septəbl]	*a.*	易受影响的,易感动的
fade [feid]	*v.*	褪色,消失
witness ['witnis]	*n.*	证人,目击者 *vt.* 目击,为……作证
offender [ə'fendə]	*n.*	罪犯,冒犯者
beard [biəd]	*n.*	胡须,络腮胡
incorporate [in'kɔːpəreit]	*v.*	合并,混合
reinforce [riːin'fɔːs]	*v.*	加强,增援,修补
fallible ['fæləbl]	*a.*	易错的,可能犯错的
preschooler	*n.*	学龄前儿童
context ['kɔntekst]	*n.*	上下文,环境
adequate ['ædikwit]	*a.*	适当的,足够的,鉴定的,评论的
critical ['kritikəl]	*a.*	关键的,危急的
draw out		使……吐露实情
external [eks'təːnl]	*a.*	外部的,客观的

account of		说明,认为
alter [ˈɔːltə]	*v.*	改变
comply with		照做
indication [indiˈkeiʃən]	*n.*	指出,暗示,迹象
unexplored [ʌniksˈplɔːd]	*a.*	未调查过的
conclude [kənˈkluːd]	*v.*	推断,认定,作出结论
bear out		证实
jury [ˈdʒuəri]	*n.*	陪审团
sexual abuse		性虐待
all along		自始至终,一直
distinguish from		区别,辨别
induce [inˈdjuːs]	*v.*	导致,引起
hypnosis [hipˈnəusis]	*n.*	催眠
implant [imˈplɑːnt]	*v.*	灌输
assess [əˈses]	*v.*	评估,估定
treacherous [ˈtretʃərəs]	*a.*	背叛的,奸诈的,叛逆的

全文译文与答案

实践和研究证明记忆力会随时间而下降。回忆和识别的最佳时间是在信息编码之后,记忆衰退最初很快,然后逐步减弱。(46)间隔的时间越长,事后获得的信息就越有可能干扰原来的记忆并因而降低准确性。不可否认的是,后来不断的面谈或者媒体报道能产生记忆失真。(47)"当时间的流逝使原来的记忆淡去时,人们很容易更改自己的记忆。如果他们反复将错误信息当成正确的,这时最容易改变原来的记忆。"

诱导性的问题会导致错误。如果证人被问到罪犯是否留着胡须,证人会将一个想象中的胡须植入记忆中。随后的询问会由于重复而强化这种错误。

一般认为成年人和儿童的记忆都会出错。然而,学龄前儿童也都可能形成可靠的记忆。年幼的儿童依靠环境来提高记忆,自然报告很少。在有充分事实支持的情况下,儿童可以回忆更多的信息,但事实支持和提出问题的方式非常关键。获取信息的方法必须认真加以检查。

尽管研究表明成年人和儿童记忆的准确度都会被诱导性或暗示性问题所影响,但抵制外部暗示性问题影响的能力会随年龄增长而增加。(48)儿童可能会更改对事件的叙述,不是因为他们的记忆发生变化,而是他们想按照有权威的成年人的暗示去回忆,或是因为他们认为重复性的提问表明他们最初的回答是错误的。

年幼儿童是否在识别事实和想象事件之间存在着困难是一个尚待研究的领域。我们推断是由于儿童总是被视为不可靠的证人，故研究没有进行证实。(49) 该法规为儿童提供了作证时提高精确度的几种办法，并指导法官如何让陪审团协助评判年幼儿童的证词。

通常认为某些有被性虐待经历的成年人在事情发生之后仍然能够回忆。没有研究表明这种重新唤起的记忆会比始终没有忘记的记忆更精确。我们坚信要区别正确和错误记忆是不可能的，而将信心、生动和详细作为事实的根据是很危险的。(50) 催眠状态下可以产生错误回忆，实验表明，暗示可能灌输对整个事件的错误回忆，但这并非是很容易办到的事。

但愿最有可能产生错误记忆和滥用报告的面谈技巧和环境会得到进一步研究。看起来，决定任何记忆最后是可靠的，还是由不可信的事情捏造而成的，这对于法官和陪审团来说仍然是一个挑战。

阅读强化练习二

阅读A篇

Directions:

Read the following four texts. Answer the questions below each text by choosing A, B, C or D. Mark your answers on ANSWER SHEET 1. (40 points)

Passage 1

On October 24, 1929—Black Thursday—a wave of panic selling of stocks swept the New York Stock Exchange. The Great Depression began. By 1932, thousands of banks and businesses had failed. Industrial production was cut in half, farm income had fallen by more than half, wages had decreased 60 percent, new investment was down 90 percent and one out of every four workers was unemployed.

The Republican president, Herbert Hoover was unable to take measures to deal with the economic collapse. So in the 1932 election, he was defeated by Democrat Franklin D. Roosevelt who promised "a New Deal for the American people."

Within the "Hundred Days", Roosevelt rushed through Congress a number of laws to aid the recovery of the economy. The Civilian Conservation Cops put young men to work in reforestation and flood control projects.

The Federal Emergency Relief Administration aided state and local relief funds. The Agricultural Adjustment Administration paid farmers to reduce production, thus raising crop prices. The Tennessee Valley Authority built a network of dams in the Tennessee River area to generate electricity, control floods and manufacture fertilizer. The National Recovery Administration regulated fair competition among businesses and ensured bargaining rights and minimum wages for workers.

The Social Security Act of 1935 established *contributory* old age and survivors' pensions, as well as a joint federal-state program of unemployment insurance.

The Wagner Labor Relations Act banned unfair employer practices and protected the workers right to collective bargaining.

The Work Progress Administration was one of the most effective of the New Deal measures. Financed by taxes collected by the federal government, the WPA created millions of jobs by undertaking the construction of roads, bridges, airports, and other public buildings. It kept workers on the job, thus preserving their skills and their self-respect.

The New Deal programs did not end the Depression. But the economy improved as a result of this program of government intervention.

21. According to the passage, "Black Thursday" is the day ______.
   (A) of selling stocks
   (B) of reducing industrial production
   (C) the Great Depression began
   (D) the New Deal was implemented

22. The New Deal is a number of laws ______.
   (A) to make young people plant trees and build dams
   (B) to aid state and local relief funds
   (C) to deal with workers
   (D) to deal with economic problems

23. The word "contributory" (Para. 5) probably means ______.
   (A) paying
   (B) providing
   (C) giving
   (D) receiving

24. The WPA was an effective measure because ______.
   (A) it provided workers jobs of building roads and airports
   (B) it preserved workers' skill and self-respect
   (C) it provided financial aids to workers
   (D) it ensured workers' minimum wages

25. Roosevelt made his New Deal programs effective through ______.
   (A) his presidential power
   (B) government taxation

(C) congress reputation

(D) government intervention

生词及短语

panic ['pænik]	*n.*	恐慌,惊慌
Stock Exchange		证券交易所
Great Depression		大萧条
collapse [kəː'læps]	*n.*	崩溃
New Deal		新政(指罗斯福在20世纪30年代实施的内政纲领)
The Hundred Days		百日王朝(拿破仑一世第二次统治法国时期的称谓,从1815年3月20日至6月28日,约百日)
rush through		快速通过,赶紧做
civilian [si'viljən]	*a.*	民间的,民用的
conservation [kɔnsə(ː) 'veiʃən]	*n.*	保存,保持
cops [kɔps]	*n.*	堆,顶
reforestation [riːfɔris'treiʃən]	*n.*	重新造林
emergency [i'məːdʒnsi]	*n.*	紧急情况,突然事件
relief funds		救济金
fertilizer ['fəːtilaizə]	*n.*	肥料
bargain ['bɑːgin]	*v.*	议价,讲条件
contributory [kən'tribjutəri]	*a.*	费用分担的,贡献的,捐助的
pension ['penʃən]	*n.*	养老金,退休金
preserve [pri'zəːv]	*vi.*	保护,保持,保存
government intervention		政府干预

答案与解析

21. [答案] (C)

[解析] 从第一段第一、二句中"Black Thursday—a wave of panic ... The Great Depression began."可知"黑色星期四"意味着大萧条的开始,(A)、(B) 两项是萧条时期的现象,(D) 指开始实施新政,与题意不相符。故答案应为(C)。

22. [答案] (D)

[解析] 从第二段最后一句和第三段第一句,我们可知罗斯福实施新政的目的是制定"... a number of laws to aid the recovery of the economy."是为帮助经济复苏。(A)、(B) 两项为新政的具体内容,(C) 与题意不符。故答案应为(D)。

23. [答案] (A)

[解析] 第五段第一句中的"contributory"意为"费用分担",与 paying"支付"在意义上最接近,故答案为(A)。

24. [答案] (B)

[解析] 从第七段最后一句"It kept workers on the job, ... their self-respect."可知 WPA 的作用在于使工人能保持自己的技能并维护自己的尊严。答案应为(B)。

25. [答案] (D)

[解析] 从最后一段的两句 "The New Deal programs ... government intervention." 我们可知,尽管新政没有结束萧条,但政府干预的措施使经济得以好转。所以答案应为(D)。

译文

1929 年 10 月 24 日,"黑色星期四"——一场抛售股票的恐慌浪潮席卷了纽约证券交易所。大萧条开始了。到 1932 年,数千家银行和商行倒闭。工业品削减了一半,农业收入下降超过一半以上,工资减少 60%,新投资减少 90%,每四个工人中便有一个失业。

共和国总统胡佛没有能采取措施对付经济崩溃,于是在 1932 年的大选中,他被民主党领袖罗斯福击败。罗斯福承诺"为美国人民实施新政"。

在"百日"中,罗斯福在国会迅速通过了一系列法律以帮助经济恢复。《平民保护法令》使年轻人能在重新造林和防洪项目中工作。

联邦紧急救助管理部为政府和地方提供了救助基金。农业调节部为农民支付费用以减少产品,这样可以提高农作物价格。田纳西流域当局在田纳西河流域建造了一个大坝用来发电,同时控制洪水和生产肥料。国家复苏管理部在商业领域制订出平等的竞争政策,保证工人讨价的权利并维持最低工资。

1935 年颁布的《社会安全法令》建立起了老年和生存者退休金分担制度,同时推出一个失业保险联邦政府联合计划。

《瓦格纳劳动者关系法令》禁止不平等雇工行为,保护工人的合法权利。工作发展管理部的建立是新政中最有效的措施之一。

在联邦政府的税收资助下,WPA 通过实施道路、桥梁、机场和其他公共设施建设,提供了数百万个工作机会。可以使工人继续工作,这样保存了他们的技能同时也维护了他们的尊严。

新政计划并没有结束大萧条,但政府干预的措施使经济得到了改善。

Passage 2

In November 1965, New York was blacked out by an electricity failure. The authorities promised that it would not happen again. Pessimists were certain that it would occur again within five years at the latest. In July 1977, there was a repeat performance which produce varying degrees of chaos throughout the city of eight million people. In 1965, the failure occurred in the cool autumn and at a time of comparative prosperity. In 1977, the disaster was much more serious because it came when unemployment was high and the city was suffering from one of its worst heat waves.

In 1965, there was little crime or looting during the darkness, and fewer than a hundred people were arrested. In 1977, hundreds of stores were broken into and looted. Looters smashed shop windows and helped themselves to jewelry, clothes or television sets. Nearly 4,000 people were arrested, but far more disappeared into the darkness of the night. The number of policemen available was quite inadequate and they wisely refrained from using their guns against mobs which far outnumbered them and included armed men.

Hospitals had to treat hundreds of people cut by glass from shop windows. Banks and most businesses remained closed the next day. The blackout started at 9:30 p.m., when lightning hit and knocked out vital cables. Many stores were caught by surprise.

The vast majority of New Yorkers, however, were not involved in looting. They helped strangers, distributed candles and batteries, and tried to survive in a nightmare world without traffic lights, refrigerators, elevators, water and electrical power. For twenty-four hours, New York realized how helpless it was without electricity.

26. What caused the blackout in 1977?
   (A) The passage does not mention the cause.
   (B) The vital cables were knocked out.
   (C) There was an earthquake.
   (D) There was a gun fight between policemen and some armed men.

27. The disaster in 1977 was more serious than in 1965 because ______.
   (A) it was at a time of prosperity
   (B) it was a repeat performance
   (C) a lot of people were unemployed and it was hot
   (D) a lot of people were prepared to rob and it was in the cool autumn

28. Although the authorities promised that the blackout would never happen again, some people thought it would occur again within ______.

(A) four years at the latest

(B) five years at the latest

(C) nine years at the latest

(D) twelve years at the latest

29. Why did many looters manage to escape?

(A) There were not enough policemen to catch them.

(B) The policemen did not have guns.

(C) They ran away before the policemen came.

(D) They hid in the dark shops until the policemen left.

30. From the passage, we can conclude ______.

(A) the vast majority of New Yorkers are kind enough to help others

(B) heat waves can cause people to commit crimes

(C) a larger number of policemen are needed

(D) electricity is important in our life

生词及短语

black out		熄灯,中断,停止
electricity failure		电路故障
pessimist ['pesimist]	*n.*	悲观主义者
chaos ['keiɔs]	*n.*	混乱
loot [luːt]	*v.*	抢劫
looter ['luːtə]	*n.*	抢劫者
smash [smæʃ]	*v.*	打碎,粉碎
jewelry ['dʒuːəlri]	*n.*	珠宝
inadequate [in'ædikwit]	*a.*	不足的,不充分的
refrain [ri'frein]	*vi.*	(from)节制,避免
mob [mɔb]	*n.*	暴徒
outnumber [aut'nʌmbə]	*vt.*	比……多,数目超过
blackout ['blækaut]	*n.*	灯火管制
vital ['vaitl]	*a.*	至关重要的,关键的
candle ['kændl]	*n.*	蜡烛

nightmare [ˈnaitmɛə(r)] *n.* 噩梦,梦魇

答案与解析

26. [答案](B)

[解析] 从第三段第三句"The blackout started at 9:30 p.m., when lightning hit and knocked out vital cables." 可知灯火管制是因为主要电缆被雷电击中而断裂所致,故答案应为(B)。

27. [答案](C)

[解析] 从第一段最后两句可知,1977年的灾难比1965年严重是因为当时失业率高同时城市正遭受着热浪的袭击,故答案应为(C)。

28. [答案](B)

[解析] 从第一段第三句"Pessimists were certain that it would occur again within five years at the latest."可知一些悲观的人们认为至少在5年之内灾难还会发生,故答案应为(B)。

29. [答案](A)

[解析] 从第二段最后一句"The number of policemen ... included armed men."可知,许多抢劫犯逃跑是由于警察人数太少。故答案应为(A)。

30. [答案](D)

[解析] 本题为主旨题,最后一句点明了主题"For twenty-four hours, New York realized how helpless it was without electricity."指出电在人们生活中的重要性。

译文

1965年,纽约市因为一次电路故障而停电。官方承诺此类事件不会再发生。悲观者却认为至少在五年内还会再发生。1977年7月,电路故障再次出现,它使城市八百万人口发生了不同程度的混乱。1965年,电路故障发生在凉爽的秋季和相对繁荣的时期。1977年,灾难显得更加严重,因为当时失业率很高,同时城市正遭受一次最严重的热浪袭击。

1965年,在黑暗中发生了一些犯罪或抢劫,有接近100人被逮捕。1977年,数百家商店被破门而入并遭到抢劫。抢劫者砸碎窗户玻璃,窃取珠宝、衣服或电视机。大约有4,000人被捕,但更多的抢劫者都消失在夜晚的黑暗中。可以动用的警察数量不足,他们只好使用枪支来对付暴徒,因为暴徒们在数量上大大超过警察,而且还有人带着武器。

医院不得不对数百名被商店玻璃窗玻璃划伤的人进行治疗。银行和大多数商业部门第二天依旧没有开门。当闪电击中并将主要电缆破坏时,灯火管制于晚上9点半开始。这使许多商店感到意外。

然而,大多数纽约人并没有卷入到抢劫中。他们帮助陌生人,分发蜡烛和电池,尽力在一个没有交通指示灯、电冰箱、电梯、水源和动力的梦魇世界中生存下来。在24小时中,纽约意识到没有电时自己是多么的无助。

Passage 3

Although America is such a huge country, traveling is usually very quick and easy. The visitor who wants to see as much of the country as possible should travel by bus—that is, if he hasn't got a friend who owns a car. It's fun. There is fast bus service between cities: for example, the Greyhound Bus Service, which has a picture of a greyhound (a dog which can run very fast) on the side of the bus. Some buses have an upper and lower level. The roof is often made of glass, and in the summer the heat of the sun through the glass may make you feel too hot. Although the buses are cooled by air-conditioning, it does not always seem to work with such good effect on the top level. The seats are soft with a reading lamp over each one and they lean back for sleeping at night. On these long-distance buses there's a toilet and other comforts on board. Stops are made for meals at roadside restaurants and there is time to stretch your legs. It takes about three and a half days to cross America by bus with short stops for meals.

Flying is as simple as going by bus. There are two kinds of service—a "regular service" on which free meals are provided, and a "stop-over" service where the plane "stops over" at various cities. Most cities have an airport. You can often buy your ticket and arrange your aeroplane trip all within about twenty minutes. Businessmen who are in a hurry do all their traveling by plane.

The roads, or "highways" as they are called, are splendid, running straight for hundreds of miles. Some are "freeways" which means that there is no charge for using them. On others, called "turnpikes", the driver has to pay. There are no crossroads or traffic lights; other roads run either above or underneath the highways, with roads leading up or down to them either side.

31. This passage tells us ______.
    (A) how to travel by bus in America
    (B) how to travel by plane in America
    (C) how to travel in America
    (D) how to travel by train in America

32. According to the passage, which one of the following statements is NOT true?
    (A) The buses are cool enough because they are air-conditioned.
    (B) There are toilets in the buses.
    (C) Meals are not served in the buses.
    (D) Travelers can sleep in the buses.

33. It takes aboutto cross America by bus ______.

(A) two days and a half

(B) three and a half days

(C) one day and a half

(D) four and a half days

34. It often takes you about ______ to buy your ticket and arrange your trip by plane.

(A) two days

(B) twenty hours

(C) twenty minutes

(D) ten minutes

35. "Highways" in America means that ______.

(A) there is no charge for using them

(B) they run straight for hundreds of miles

(C) there is charge for using them

(D) there are no crossroads or traffic lights

生词及短语

greyhound ['greihaund]	*n.*	灰狗
roof [ruːf]	*n.*	顶
lean [liːn]	*vi.*	依靠,倾斜
splendid ['splendid]	*a.*	极好的,辉煌的
freeway ['friːwei]	*n.*	免费高速公路
turnpike ['təːnpaik]	*n.*	收费公路
crossroad ['krɔsrəud]	*n.*	十字路口

答案与解析

31. [答案] (**C**)

[解析] 本题为主旨题。第一段第一句即点明了主题 "Although America is such a huge country, traveling is usually very quick and easy."指出在美国旅游一般又便捷又简单,以下分别介绍如何在美国旅行。故答案应为(C)。

32. [答案](A)

[解析] 第一段第五句指出 "Although the buses are cooled by air-conditioning, it does not always seem to work with such good effect on the top level."(A) 的答案明显与此不符,故选(A)。

33. [答案](B)

[解析] 从第一段最后一句 "It takes about three and a half days to cross America by bus with short stops for meals."可知(B) 应为正确答案。

34. [答案](C)

[解析] 从第二段第三句"You can often buy your ticket and arrange your aeroplane trip all within about twenty minutes."可知(C) 应为正确答案。

35. [答案](B)

[解析] 从第三段第一句 "The roads, or 'highways' as they are called, are splendid, running straight for hundreds of miles."可知(B) 应为正确答案。

译文

尽管美国很大,但旅行却即便捷又简单。旅行者如想尽量多地了解这个国家就应该乘汽车旅行,就是说,如果他没有拥有汽车的朋友的话。这种旅行很有趣。在城市之间都有快速公交车,例如,"灰狗公共汽车业务",在汽车的边上有一张灰狗的照片(灰狗是一种跑得很快的狗)。一些公共汽车有上层和下层。车顶通常用玻璃制成,在夏天太阳光透过玻璃会让人感觉很热。虽然汽车有空调,但在顶层效果并不很好。座位都很柔软,上方还有一盏供你阅读的灯,人们在晚上可以靠在座位上睡觉。在这些长途汽车上,有一个盥洗室和其他舒适的设备。在路边有饭店可以停靠吃饭,同时你可以伸展一下自己的双腿。乘车横穿美国只需 3 天半的时间,中途有几次短暂的停靠用来吃饭。

乘飞机旅行与乘汽车旅行一样简单。它有两种业务:"正规业务",在机上可提供免费就餐,另一种"中途停靠"业务,飞机在不同的城市中途停留。大多数城市都有飞机场。通常在 20 分钟之内你就可以买好机票并安排好你的空中旅行。忙碌的商人们都乘飞机出行。

公路,或称"高速公路",路况极好,可直接跑到数百英里。一些公路属于"免费高速公路",无需付费。而另外一些称为"收费公路",司机必须交费。公路没有交叉路口或红绿灯;其他公路沿着高速公路的上方或下方延伸,两边有道路从上下方向与它们连通。

Passage 4

Just as the telegraph in the late nineteenth century and the radio in the early twentieth century produced revolutions in communications, so it now seems apparent that another revolution is emerging: the laser revolution. This time, however, communications is not the sole beneficiary, for the laser is also being put to use in fields as diverse as chemistry, medicine, weaponry, and manufacturing.

The laser is a comparatively recent invention, the first model having been constructed in 1960. We are still in a transitional period where we are only beginning to see how the laser can be used, but it is clear that it will have an increasingly great effect on our lives in the years ahead.

A laser is a device that generates and emits an extraordinarily intense beam of light. The name is an abbreviation based on the initial letters of the words light amplification by stimulated emission of radiation. In a laser atoms of a particular substance are excited to increase their energy, and then stimulated in such a way that this energy is released in the form of light rays.

Lasers are highly attractive in communions because a laser beam is theoretically capable of carrying a much greater number of messages simultaneously than any other means of transmission so far developed. Some problems still remain to be solved, however, before laser-based systems become ready to replace conventional communications systems completely. One serious problem is that the laser beam is after all simply light, and therefore may be blocked by clouds or atmospheric dust. Another problem that must still be solved is that the items of equipment needed for converting a message into a form suitable for laser transmission are still rather primitive and extremely complex. We can be assured, and that many more applications of the laser, completely unexpected at present, will make it an even more important part of life in the future.

36. According to the author, three of the following produced revolutions in communications, which one is not mentioned?
   (A) Telegraph.
   (B) Radio.
   (C) Computer.
   (D) Laser.

37. "A transitional period" (Para. 2, Line 2) in the passage probably means ______.
   (A) a period of changes
   (B) a period of importance
   (C) a transitory period
   (D) a period of communication development

38. According to the passage, the laser ______.
   (A) produced revolutions in the early twentieth century
   (B) can be applied to other fields apart from communication

(C) is a device that releases energy in the form of light rays

(D) is more expensive than any other means of carrying me sages

39. Which one of the following is TRUE?

(A) The laser has already taken the place of other means of communications.

(B) We know how to prevent clouds and atmospheric dust from affecting the laser beam.

(C) It is difficult to change the form of a message to suit the laser transmission.

(D) It is still doubtful whether a laser beam can carry more messages than other means of transmission.

40. It can be inferred from the fourth paragraph that ______.

(A) the laser will play a very important part in communications

(B) the laser will play a very important part in many fields

(C) something unexpected will be discovered to take the place of the laser in the future

(D) scientists will try to solve the problems to make the laser more effective in communications

生词及短语

emerging [iˈməːdʒiŋ]	*vi.*	显现,出现
beneficiary [beniˈfiʃəri]	*n.*	受惠者,受益者
diverse [daiˈvəːs]	*a.*	不同的,变化多的
weaponry [ˈwepənri]	*n.*	武器,军备
manufacturing [mænjuˈfæktʃəriŋ]	*a.*	制造业的
transitional [trænˈziʃənl]	*a.*	转变的,过渡的
emit [iˈmit]	*vt.*	发出,发射
abbreviation [əbriːviˈeiʃən]	*n.*	缩写,缩写词
amplification [æmplifiˈkeiʃən]	*n.*	扩大,放大
emission [iˈmiʃən]	*n.*	散发,发射
radiation [reidiˈeiʃən]	*n.*	辐射,放射

答案与解析

36. [答案] (C)

[解析] 从第一段可知,(C) 未被提及,其他三项均提及,故答案应为(C)。

37. [答案] (A)

[解析] 在第二段第二句中,“transitional”意为“变化的,过渡的”,与(A) 同义。

38. [答案] (B)

[解析] 从第一段最后一句中“... for the laser is also being put to use in fields as diverse as chemistry, medicine, weaponry, and manufacturing.” 可知激光除了应用于通信外,还可广泛应用于其他领域。故答案应为(B)。

39. [答案] (C)

[解析] 从最后一段倒数第二句“Another problem that ... and extremely complex.”可知与(C) 项意义相符,故答案应为(C)。

40. [答案] (B)

[解析] 从第四段最后一句“We can be assured, ... in the future.”可知激光将在今后我们的生活中有更多的应用,故答案应为(B)。

译文

正如19世纪末的电报和20世纪早期的无线电在通信中发生的革命一样,现在看来,很明显的,另一项革命正在出现:激光革命。然而这一次通信并不是惟一的受益者,因为激光同样可以应用到诸如化工、医药、军事和制造业等其他不同领域。

激光相对来说是一种新发明,第一个模型已经在1960年制造出来。我们仍然处于一个过渡阶段,在这个阶段我们仅仅开始看到激光该如何加以应用,但很清楚的是它在未来的日子中将对我们的生活产生巨大影响。

激光器是一种产生和发射一种高强度光束的设备。它是建立在光放大器一词基础上的缩写词。光放大器激励光的发射。在一个激光器中,特定物质的原子被激发以提高它们的能量,然后这种能量被以光束释放的方式发射出来。

激光器在通信中具有很高的吸引力, 因为从理论上讲一个激光光束可以同时传输比迄今为止所开发出来的任何传输手段都多得多的信息。然而,在激光系统能够完全取代传统通信系统之前,一些问题仍然需要解决。一个严重的问题是激光光束还是一种简单的光束,所以会被云层或大气灰尘所阻挡。另一个必须解决的问题是用于将信息转换为适合于激光传输的设备种类非常原始而且特别复杂。我们可以相信,完全超出我们目前的预测,更多激光的应用在我们未来的生活中将起到更重要的作用。

阅读 B 篇

Directions:

In the following article, some sentences have been removed. For Questions 41—45, choose the most suitable one from the list A—F to fit into each of the numbered blanks. There are two extra choices, which do not fit in any of the blanks. Mark your answers on ANSWER SHEET 1. (10 points)

Training is intended primarily for the service of society; education is primarily for the individual. Society needs doctors, lawyers, engineers, teachers to perform specific tasks necessary to its operation, just as it needs carpenters and plumbers and *stenographers*(速记员). 41. ________. And these needs, our training centers—the professional and trade schools—fill. But although education is for the improvement of the individual, it also serves society by providing a leavening of men of understanding, of perception, and wisdom. 42.________. They serve society by examining its function, appraising its needs, and criticizing its direction. They may be earning their livings by practicing one of the professions, or in pursuing a trade, or by engaging in business enterprise. They may be rich or poor. They may occupy positions of power and prestige, or they may be engaged in some humble employment. Without them, however, society either disintegrates or else becomes an anthill.

43. ________. In the one, the recruit is training to become a professional baseball player who will make a living and serve society by playing baseball; in the other, he is training only to improve his own body and musculature. The training at the baseball camp is all relevant. The recruit may spend hours practicing how to slide into second base, not because it is a particularly useful form of *calisthenics* (柔软体操) but because it is relevant to the game. The exercise would stop if the rules were changed so that sliding to a base was made illegal. Similarly, the candidate for the pitching staff spends a lot of time throwing a baseball, not because it will improve his physique—it may have quite the opposite effect—but because pitching is to be his principal function on the team. At the gym, exercises have no such relevance. 44. ________.

45. ________. What is taught at law school is the present law of the land, not the Napoleonic Code or even the archaic laws that have been scratched from the statute books. And at medical school, too, it is modern medical practice that is taught, that which is relevant to conditions today. And the *plumber* (水管工人) and the carpenter and the electrician and the *mason* (泥瓦匠) learn only what is relevant to the practice of their respective trades in this day with the tools and materials that are presently available and that conform to the building code.

(A) Education refers to the knowledge or skill obtained or developed by a learning process.

(B) They are our intellectual leaders, the critics of our culture, the defenders of our free traditions, the instigators of our progress.

(C) The intention is to strengthen the body in general, and when the members sit down on the floor with their legs outstretched and practice touching their fingers to their toes, it is not because they hope to become galley slaves, perhaps the only occupation where that particular exercise would be relevant.

(D) The difference between the two types of study is like the difference between the discipline and exercise in a professional baseball training camp and that of a gym.

(E) Training supplies the immediate and specific needs of society so that the work of the world may continue.

(F) In general, relevancy is a facet of training rather than of education.

(G) Training is to make proficient with specialized instruction and practice.

内容提要

本文讨论教育与培训的差别和意义。第一段指出，培训主要是为社会服务；而教育主要是为个人服务。社会需要医生、律师、工程师、教师来执行特殊使命以使社会正常运转，这和社会需要木工、水管工和速记员一样。培训为社会提供及时和特殊的需要，这样世界才能继续发展进步。尽管教育是为了提高个人水平，但它同样是为社会服务，它培养人们理解、观察能力和思维方式。受教育者是我们的知识领导者、文化的批评者、自由传统的保卫者和进步的推动者。

答案与解析

41. [答案] (**E**)

[解析] 空白前提到培训与教育的区别。(E) 提到培训向社会提供及时和特殊的需要，这样全世界的工作才得以发展进步。

42. [答案] (**B**)

[解析] 空白前提到尽管教育是为了对个人的提高，但它同样为社会提供能理解、观察和充满智慧的有影响的人物。(B) 继续提到这些人是智慧的领袖、文化的批评家、自由传统的保卫者，进步的推动者。

43. [答案] (**D**)

[解析] 空白后面提到培训的特点，比如培训一个职业棒球运动员，而(D) 提及两种形式学习的差异，提到对于职业棒球训练营和体操馆训练原则和练习的不同。前后有关联性。

44. [答案] (**C**)

[解析] 空白前提到体操馆的练习没有这种棒球的相关性，(C) 对此说法加以说明：练体操的目的是强身健体。

45. [答案] (F)

[解析] (F) 为尾段的总结:总的来说,相关性是训练而不是教育的方面。后面的内容对此进行了说明:在法律学校学习的是当前的法律,不会是拿破仑时代的法规,或者古代的法律。

阅读 C 篇

Directions:

Read the following text carefully and then translate the underlined segments into Chinese. Your translation should be written neatly on ANSWER SHEET 2. (10 points)

Hewlett-Packard has regarded its proposed acquisition of Compaq Computer as a bold move to build a portfolio of computing systems and services to take on IBM. and Dell Computer. It has argued that the $24 billion deal would strengthen the company's sales of personal computers, data-serving computers and technology consulting.

(46) But behind the deal is another Hewlett-Packard ambition: to extend the reach of its dominant printing and imaging division, which registered $20 billion in sales this year, 43 percent of the company's revenue.

In the last two decades, Hewlett-Packard built itself into the world's largest vendor of desktop printers. It had done so under the command of Richard A. Hackborn, now a Hewlett-Packard board member and a leading advocate of the merger. (47) Today, the company tests so many printers, inks and papers that, if one could stack up all the test sheets printed during an average month, the pile would reach 6,000 feet.

(48) The printer division is widely regarded as the company's crown jewel, but how Hewlett can best exploit it is a matter of dispute. Walter Hewlett, the oldest son of the company's co-founder, and other critics of the Compaq acquisition argue that the deal will dilute the printing business by burying it in an even larger, slower-moving computer company. The division's $2 billion in operating profits this year propped up Hewlett-Packard's sagging computer business, which lost $450 million.

(49) Some analysts have advocated that instead of merging to become a larger company, Hewlett-Packard should sell off its other businesses and focus on selling more printers and imaging devices like digital cameras and scanners, which increase sales of ink cartridges and paper.

The company, however, says it has no intention of narrowing its scope. Instead, proponents of the merger say the acquisition will fix Hewlett's computing business, freeing up more research and development money for the printing division to tackle new markets, like the $400-billion-a-year commercial printing business.

Hewlett-Packard wants to drive this transition to digital publishing, much as IBM, through a combination of products and services, helped businesses push into online sales in the late-1990s. (50) If the strategy is successful, it would result in a surge in digital files that would stimulate sales of the powerful computing systems needed to create, store and move the files. To do that, Hewlett-Packard argues, it must become larger and stronger. The bigger it is the more influence it will have on corporate technology managers.

生词及短语

acquisition [ækui'ziʃən]	*n.*	获得,收购
portfolio [pɔːt'fəuljəu]	*n.*	文件夹,一组投资
take on		与……较量;接受……的挑战
strengthen ['streŋθən]	*v.*	加强,巩固
consult [kən'sʌlt]	*v.*	商量,请教
ambition [æm'biʃən]	*n.*	抱负,野心
extend [iks'tend]	*v.*	扩展,延展
division [di'viʒən]	*n.*	部门,部分,划分
register ['redʒistə]	*v.*	登记,记录
revenue ['revənjuː]	*n.*	收入,收益
vendor ['vendɔː]	*n.*	卖主,小贩
advocate ['ædvəkit]	*v.*	提倡,鼓吹
merger ['məːdʒə]	*v.*	兼并,合并
stack up		堆积,堆起
crown jewel		王冠珠宝
exploit [iks'plɔit]	*v.*	开拓,开发
dispute [dis'pjuːt]	*n.*	争论,辩论
co-founder		合伙创始人
dilute [dai'ljuːt]	*v.*	冲淡,稀释
operating profits		经营利润
prop up		维持,撑住
sag [sæg]	*v.*	下垂,下跌
advocate ['ædvəkit]	*v.*	提倡,鼓吹
ink cartridges		墨盒
proponent [prə'pəunənt]	*n.*	建议者,支持者
tackle ['tækl]	*v.*	应付,处理

surge [səːdʒ] *n.* 汹涌,澎湃
stimulate [ˈstimjuleit] *v.* 刺激,激励

全文译文与答案

惠普公司将提议中的对康柏公司的收购视为迈向计算系统和业务组合投资的一次大胆行动,目的是要与IBM和戴尔公司较量。它认为240亿美元的交易将增强公司的个人电脑、服务器和技术咨询的销售。

(46) 但是在这场交易的背后隐藏着惠普公司的另一个目的:拓展其占统治地位的打印和成像部门。该部门今年的销售额是200亿美元,占公司总收入的43%。

在过去的20年中,惠普发展成为世界上最大的桌面打印机制造商。这是在理查德·哈克伯恩的领导下实现的,他现在是惠普董事会成员,也是兼并的主要鼓吹者。(47) 现在,公司测试大量的打印机、油墨和纸张,如果把平均每个月份打印的所有测试纸张堆起来,可高达6,000英尺。

(48) 打印机部门被广泛认为是公司的一颗明珠,但是在公司应如何最好地对它加以利用方面颇有争议。沃尔特·休利特,公司合伙创始人的大儿子,和其他兼并康柏公司的批评者认为,由于购买的是一家更大、发展更慢的计算机公司,这笔交易会冲淡打印机生意。打印机部门今年20亿美元的营业利润支撑着惠普下滑的计算机生意,它的损失达4.5亿美元。

(49) 一些分析家主张,惠普公司不应该合并成一个更大的公司,而应当卖掉其他的生意,致力于销售更多的打印机、数码相机和扫描仪等成像设备,这些产品可带动墨盒和纸张的销售。

然而,公司认为它不打算缩小范围。相反,兼并的支持者认为这次兼并将巩固惠普的计算机生意,释放出更多的研究和开发经费以为打印机部门开辟新的市场,就像每年4亿美元的商业打印机生意一样。

惠普希望通过产品和业务的结合,将这种转换推动到数字出版,就像IBM一样,在90年代后期实现网上销售。

(50) 如果这一策略奏效,会引发数码文件的激增,从而刺激创建、存储和移动这些文件所必需的强大的计算机系统的销售。为了达到这个目的,惠普认为,它必须变得更大和更强。公司越强大对公司技术管理者的影响就越大。

阅读强化练习三

阅读 A 篇

Directions:

Read the following four texts. Answer the questions below each text by choosing A, B, C or D. Mark your answers on ANSWER SHEET 1. (40 points)

Passage 1

There are various ways in which individual economic units can interact with one another. Three basic ways may be described as the market system, the administered system, and the traditional system.

In a market system individual economic units are free to interact among each other in the marketplace. It is possible to buy commodities from other economic units or sell commodities to them. In a market, transactions may take place via barter or money exchange. In a barter economy, real goods such as automobiles, shorts, and pizzas are traded against each other. Obviously, finding somebody who wants to trade my old car in exchange for a sailboat may not always be an easy task. Hence the introduction of money as a medium of exchange eases transactions considerably. In the modern market economy, goods and services are bought or sold for money.

An alternative to the market system is administrative control by some agency over all transactions. This agency will issue edicts or commands as to how much of each good and service should be produced, exchanged, and consumed by each economic unit. Central planning may be one way of administering such an economy. The central plan, drawn up by the government, shows the amounts of each commodity produced by the various firms and allocated to different households for consumption. This is an example of complete planning of production consumption, and exchange for the whole economy.

In a traditional society, production and consumption patterns are governed by tradition:

every person's place within the economic system is fixed by parentage, religion, and custom. Transactions take place on the basis of tradition, too. People belonging to a certain group or caste may have an obligation to care for other persons, provide them with food and shelter, care for their health, and provide for their education. Clearly, in a system where every decision is made on the basis of tradition alone, progress may be difficult to achieve. A stagnant society may result.

21. What is the main purpose of the passage?
   (A) To outline contrasting types of economic systems.
   (B) To explain the science of economics.
   (C) To argue for the superiority of one economic system.
   (D) To compare barter and money-exchange markets.

22. In the second paragraph, the word "real" in "real goods" could best be replaced by which of the following?
   (A) High quality.
   (B) Concrete.
   (C) Utter.
   (D) Authentic.

23. According to the passage, a barter economy can lead to ______.
   (A) rapid speed of transactions
   (B) misunderstandings
   (C) inflation
   (D) difficulties for the traders

24. According to the passage, who has the greatest degree of control in an administered system?
   (A) Individual households.
   (B) Small businesses.
   (C) Major corporations.
   (D) The government.

25. Which of the following is NOT mentioned by the author as a criterion for determining a person's place in a traditional society?
   (A) Family background.
   (B) Age.

(C) Religious beliefs.

(D) Custom.

生词及短语

interact (with)	*vi.*	相互作用,相互影响
administer [əd'ministə]	*v.*	管理,执行
transaction [træn'zækʃən]	*n.*	交易,事务,处理
barter ['bɑːtə]	*n.*	物品交换,以物易物
short [fɔːt]	*n.*	短裤
in exchange for		交换,以此易彼
medium ['miːdjəm]	*n.*	方法,媒介
an alternative to		替代物
issue ['isjuː]	*vt.*	发布,发行
edict ['iːdikt]	*n.*	布告,法令
parentage ['pɛərəntidʒ]	*n.*	出身
caste [kɑːst]	*n.*	社会地位,社会等级
stagnant ['stægnənt]	*a.*	停滞的,迟钝的

答案与解析

21. [答案] (A)

[解析] 本题为主旨题。文章第一、二句点明了主题,“个别经济单位相互作用的方式有好几种。这些基本的方式可描述为市场系统、管理系统和传统系统。”因此答案为(A)。

22. [答案] (B)

[解析] real goods 意为“实物”,指后面所列举的汽车、短裤和比萨饼之类的具体物品,在意义上与 concrete“具体的”近义。high quality 意为“高质量”;utter 意为“完全的”;authentic 意为“可信的”,均与“real”在这里的意思相距甚远,故答案为(A)。

23. [答案] (D)

[解析] barter 意为“实物交换,以物易物”,它对考生可能是个生词,但它出现在第二段第三句中,通过 or 与 money 并列,修饰 exchange,而上下文讲的都是交易和买卖,因此不难猜出其词义“以物易物”,并根据常识判断出正确答案为(D)。同时也可以从紧接着下一句中的“... not always be an easy task”得出同样的结论。

24. [答案] (D)

[解析] 本文第三段集中讨论"administered system",从本段第三、四句中"Central planning may be one way of administering such an economy. The central plan, drawn up by the government, ...",即可选出正确答案为(D)。同时也可根据常识得出同样答案。

25. [答案]·(B)

[解析] 从最后一段第一句中的后半句"every person's place within the economic system is fixed by parentage, religion, and custom",可知 age 没有提到,故(B) 为正确答案。

译文

个别经济单位相互作用的方式有好几种。这些基本的方式可描述为市场系统、管理系统和传统系统。

在市场系统中,个别经济单位可以在市场上自由地相互作用。可以从其他经济单位购买商品,或将货物出售给它们。在市场上,交易可以通过以货易货或钱物交易来进行。在以货易货的经济中,汽车、短裤和比萨饼这样的实物是以相互抵付来交易的。显然,要找到某个想用我的旧汽车来替换一只帆船的人并不总是件容易的事。因此,使用金钱作为交易手段使交易大为方便。在现代市场经济中,货物和服务都可以金钱来购买或出售。

市场系统的一种替代办法是由某个机构对所有的交易进行行政控制。该机构发布命令规定每个经济单位必须生产、交换和消耗多少物品和服务。中央计划可能是管理这种经济的一种方式。由政府制定的中央计划显示了由各个企业生产和分配到不同家庭消费的每种商品的数量。这是对整个经济的生产消费和交换进行全面计划的一个例子。

在传统社会中,生产和消费的模式由传统支配:每个人在经济系统中的地位由血源、宗教和习惯所确定。交易也在传统的基础上进行。属于某一团体或等级的人有义务关心别人,为他们提供食宿,关心他们的健康,为他们提供教育。显然,一个所有决定都建立在传统基础上的社会是很难取得进步的。结果将导致一个停滞不前的社会。

Passage 2

Whereas George Gershwin worked in the glare of critical and commercial success, Charles Ives worked in obscurity. Though Ives created the bulk of his output before Gershwin appeared on the scene, his music was almost completely neglected until he was "rediscovered" in the 1940s and 1950s. He earned his livelihood, for most of his adult life, in the insurance business and created some of the most striking examples of American music in his spare time. Ives' composing was restricted to weekends, holidays, vacations, and long evenings, Ives himself was quite philosophic about this and never considered his business career a handicap to artistic production. On the contrary, he regarded his music and the business in which he earned his livelihood as complementary activities.

His raw material for all of his work was the ordinary musical life of a small New England town. In evolving his highly individualistic musical language, Ives used popular dance hall tunes, fragments of hymns and patriotic anthems, brass band marches, country dances, and songs which he integrated into works of enormous complexity.

But Ives' music was hardly popular with the broad public at the time it was written. The composer found it all but impossible to get his music performed. For example, Ives' Second Symphony, which he worked on between 1897 and 1902, received its first performance in 1951 when it was played by the Philharmonic-Symphony Orchestra of New York, under Leonard Bernstein. His Third Symphony, completed in 1911, was first performed in 1945. The Fourth Symphony, written between 1910 and 1916, received its premiere in 1965 under the direction of Leopold Stokowski. Not until he was awarded the Pulitzer Prize for his Third Symphony, in 1947, did Charles Ives receive any degree of recognition for his work.

26. Charles Ives' success in music could be called unusual because he ______.

(A) had a physical handicap

(B) was trained to be a philosopher

(C) did not devote his entire career to music

(D) did not have much financial backing

27. According to the passage, how did Ives feel about the business and musical sides of his life?

(A) They lent support to each other.

(B) They each satisfied his need for recognition.

(C) They represented a conflict in his nature.

(D) They took too much of his time.

28. It can be inferred that all of the following were sources of inspiration for Ives in his early career EXCEPT ______.

(A) church music

(B) folk tunes

(C) Gershwin's compositions

(D) patriotic songs

29. Ives' Third Symphony was first performed in the ______.

(A) late nineteenth century

(B) first decade of the twentieth century

(C) mid-nineteen forties

(D) mid-nineteen sixties

30. It can be inferred from the passage that Ives' symphonies were Not popular with the general public for many years because they were ______.
   (A) heard by very few people
   (B) based on nonclassical themes
   (C) inferior to Gershwin's music
   (D) composed in his spare time

生词及短语

in the glare of		引人注目,显眼
obscurity [əb'skjuəriti]	n.	阴暗,含糊,身份低微
bulk [bʌlk]	n.	大批,大量
composing [kəm'pəuziŋ]	n.	著作,作品
handicap ['hændikæp]	n.	障碍,妨碍
complementary [kɔmplə'mentəri]	a.	补充的,补足的
individualistic [individjuə'listik]	a.	个人主义的
hymn [him]	n.	赞美诗,圣歌
patriotic [pætri'ɔtik]	a.	爱国的,有爱国心的
anthem ['ænθəm]	a.	圣歌,赞美诗
brass band		铜管乐队
march [mɑːtʃ]	n.	进行曲
all but		几乎,差一点
symphony ['simfəni]	n.	交响乐,交响曲
philharmonic [filhɑː'mɔnik]	a.	爱好音乐的
orchestra ['ɔːkistrə]	n.	管弦乐队,交响乐团
premiere ['premiər]	n.	首次公演
under the direction of		由……指挥
Pulitzer Prize		普利策奖

答案与解析

26. [答案] (C)

[解析] 从全文来看,本文从头至尾均未涉及到伊夫斯的身体状况、所受训练或经济条

件,故(A)、(B)、(D) 可基本排除。由第一段第三句可知,他成年后大部分岁月是在保险业工作,其主要音乐作品是在业余时间创作的,因而正确答案为(C)。

27. [答案] (A)

[解析] 从第一段最后一句 "... he regarded his music and ... as complementary activities." 可知音乐家认为保险业与音乐是"互补"的活动,故答案应为(A)。

28. [答案] (C)

[解析] 从第二段第二句中的 "hymns"(圣歌)、"patriotic anthems"(爱国赞美诗) 和 "country dances, and songs"(乡村舞蹈和歌曲) 可排除(A)、(B)、(D),句中未提及格什温及其作品,故正确答案为(C)。

29. [答案] (C)

[解析] 从第三段第四句 "His Third Symphony, completed in 1911, was first performed in 1945."可知首演是在 1945 年,即二十世纪四十年代中期,故答案应为(C)。

30. [答案] (B)

[解析] 从第二段第一句和第三段第一句可知, 伊夫斯的作品都取材于一个小镇的普通音乐生活, 这些作品在完成时一直未得到公众的认可。根据逻辑可以排除(D)、(A);(C) 在文中未被提及,也可排除,正确答案为(B)。

译文

乔治·格什温无论在评论界还是在商业界,都获得了令人注目的成绩,而查尔斯·伊夫斯却在默默无闻地工作着。虽然他于格什温在乐坛崭露头角之前就已经创作出了大量作品,但他的音乐作品直到二十世纪四十年代和五十年代他被"重新发现"之前几乎完全被人忽视。他成年中的大部分时光,是在保险业谋生,而在业余时间中他却创作出美国音乐中一些最为震撼人心的作品。伊夫斯的创作时间仅限于周末、节日、假日和深夜。他本人对此相当理性,从不认为他的业务生涯会妨碍艺术创作。相反,他把音乐和赖以谋生的职业看成是互补的活动。

他全部作品的素材都来自于新英格兰一个小镇的普普通通的音乐生活。在逐步形成他那个性化的音乐语言的过程中,他采用了通俗舞曲、圣歌和爱国主义赞美诗的片断、铜管乐队进行曲、乡村舞曲,并把这些综合成异常复杂的音乐作品。

但伊夫斯的作品在创作的当时在公众中并不流行。他发现几乎不可能使自己的作品上演。例如,伊夫斯于 1897 年至 1902 年间创作的第二交响乐,到 1951 年才由纽约交响乐团在列奥诺德·伯恩斯坦指挥下举行首次演出。他于 1911 年完成的第三交响乐首演于 1945 年。1910 至 1916 年间写成的第四交响乐, 到 1965 年才由利奥波尔德·斯托科夫斯基指挥了首场演出。在他的第三交响乐于 1947 年被授予普利策奖之前,查尔斯·伊夫斯从未因其作品而获得任何程度的承认。

Passage 3

Here in the United States, before agricultural activities destroyed the natural balance, there were great migrations of Rocky Mountain locusts (named Melanoplus spretus). Great migrating hordes of these insects once darkened the skies on the plains east of the Rockies where crops were often destroyed; the worst years were those from 1874 to 1877. One of these migration swarms was estimated to contain 124 billion locusts. During another migration, in Nebraska it was estimated that the swarm of locusts averaged half a mile high and was 100 miles wide and 300 miles long. Usually, these swarms take off from the ground against the wind, but, once airborne, they turn and fly with it. Warm convection currents help to lift them, often to great heights. During the great locust plagues the situation in Nebraska became so serious that the original state constitution had to be rewritten to take care of the economic problems. The new document was known as "The Grasshopper Constitution." It is now believed that these locusts were a migratory form or phase of the lesser migratory locust, which is still common there. In this respect, the North American migratory locusts resemble their African relatives. In both regions the migratory forms arise as a result of crowding and climatic factors. Migratory forms are apparently natural adaptations which bring about dispersal when locust populations become too crowded.

Fortunately for our farmers, the migratory form—the so-called spretus species—no longer seems to occur regularly, although there was a serious outbreak as late as 1938 in midwestern United States and Canada. Actually, there is no reason why the destructive migratory form might not again appear if circumstances should become favorable.

31. Which of the following is the best title for the passage?
   (A) The Life Cycle of Locusts
   (B) Migratory Locusts in the United States
   (C) Locusts Plagues Nebraska
   (D) The Reproductive Capability of the Locust

32. According to the passage, the worst destruction by locusts in the plains area east of the Rockies occurred during the ______.
   (A) eighteenth century
   (B) early nineteenth century
   (C) late nineteenth century
   (D) twentieth century

33. One of the migrating swarms mentioned in the passage averaged how many miles in length?

(A) 100.

(B) 124.

(C) 187.

(D) 300.

34. According to the passage, North American and African migratory locusts are similar in that ______.

(A) they always travel toward mountainous regions

(B) their destructive activities occur only in plains areas

(C) climates affect their development

(D) they are both mentioned in state constitutions

35. The passage supports which of the following conclusions?

(A) The outbreak of locusts in 1938 was more serious than any other in history.

(B) Nebraska farmers had no locust problems in the years 1874—1877.

(C) There is a possibility that crops in the United States might be destroyed by locusts in the future.

(D) There is a chance that African migratory locusts may make their way to the United States.

生词及短语

migration [mai'greiʃən]	*n.*	迁移
locust ['ləukəst]	*n.*	蝗虫，蚱蜢
horde [hɔːd]	*n.*	游牧部落
swarm [swɔːm]	*v.*	涌往，挤满，密集
airborne ['ɛəbɔːn]	*a.*	空运的，空降的，空气支撑的
convection [kən'vekʃən]	*n.*	传送，对流
plague [pleig]	*n.*	瘟疫，灾祸
grasshopper ['grɑːshɔpə]	*n.*	蚱蜢，蝗虫
phase [feiz]	*n.*	阶段，状态，相位
in this respect		在……这一方面
adaptation [ædæp'teiʃən]	*n.*	适应，改编
dispersal [dis'pəːsəl]	*n.*	散布，分散，疏散
spretus	*n.*	（一种蝗虫品种）

答案与解析

31. [答案] (B)

[解析] 本题为主旨题,用排除法可得出答案。文中并未提到蝗虫的生命周期和繁殖力问题,故可将(A) 和(D) 排除。文中不仅叙述了内布拉斯加州(Nebraska)的蝗虫灾害,也叙述了落基山脉以及北美地区的蝗灾情况,所以(C) 也应排除,正确答案为(B)。

32. [答案] (A)

[解析] 从第二句中"... these insects once darkened ... from 1874 to 1877."可知最严重的蝗灾发生在 late nineteenth century,故(A) 应为正确答案。

33. [答案] (D)

[解析] 第三句提到"... the swarm of locusts ... 300 miles long."因此正确答案应为(D)。

34. [答案] (C)

[解析] 第一段倒数二、三句指出北美和非洲蝗虫大迁移是"crowding and climatic factors"所导致的结果,故(C) 应为正确答案。

35. [答案] (C)

[解析] 本文最后一句指出"如果环境条件适合,没有理由认为破坏性的蝗虫迁移不会发生",就是说美国的庄稼有可能在将来被蝗虫所侵害,故(C) 应为正确答案。

译文

在美国的农业生产活动还没有破坏自然平衡之前，就发生了多次落基山脉蝗虫（名为 Melanoplus spretus）大迁移。这些昆虫的大规模迁移曾经遮蔽了落基山脉以东平原的天空，当地的庄稼经常被破坏;最严重的时候是在 1874 至 1877 年间,其中一次大迁移中的蝗虫估计多达 1,240 亿只。另一次在内布拉斯加州发生的蝗虫迁移中,蝗虫群估计平均厚度达半英里,宽 100 英里,长 300 英里。这些蝗虫通常从地面迎风而起,一旦遇上气流,它们就转向顺风而行,热气对流又帮助它们升高,常常到达很高的天空。蝗灾期间内布拉斯加州的形势非常严峻,原州宪法不得不因考虑经济问题而修改。新宪法就是人们熟知的"蝗虫宪法"。现在人们认为,那时的蝗虫是一种该地区现在还常见的、会迁移的较小的蝗虫。从这方面来说,北美的迁移蝗虫和它们的非洲亲戚有些类似，这两个地区的蝗虫迁移是由虫群过于密集和气候的原因而引起。迁移显然是蝗虫的自然适应特性,当蝗虫群太拥挤时,就会发生分散活动。

对农民来说幸运的是,这种迁移类型的迁移——称之为 spretus 的种类——并不是经常发生,尽管后来在 1938 年美国中西部和加拿大又爆发了一次严重的蝗虫迁移。事实上,在环境条件合适的情况下,没有理由认为这种破坏性的蝗虫迁移不会再发生。

Passage 4

An important new industry, oil refining, grew after the Civil War. Crude oil, or petroleum—a dark, thick ooze from the earth—had been known for hundreds of years. But little use had ever been made of it. In the 1850s Samuel M. Kier, a manufacturer in western Pennsylvania, began collecting the oil from local seepages and refining it into kerosene. Refining, like smelting, is a process of removing impurities from a raw material.

Kerosene was used to light lamps. It was a cheap substitute for whale oil, which was becoming harder to get. Soon there was a large demand for kerosene. People began to search for new supplies of petroleum.

The first oil well was drilled by E. L. Drake, a retired railroad conductor. In 1859 he began drilling in Titusville, Pennsylvania. The whole venture seemed so impractical and foolish that onlookers called it "Drake's Folly." But when he had drilled down about 70 feet (21 meters), Drake struck oil. His well began to yield 20 barrels of crude oil a day.

News of Drake's success brought oil prospectors to the scene. By the early 1860s these wildcatters were drilling for "black gold" all over western Pennsylvania. The boom rivaled the California gold rush of 1848 in its excitement and Wild West atmosphere. And it brought far more wealth to the prospectors than any gold rush.

Crude oil could be refined into many products. For some years kerosene continued to be the principal one. It was sold in grocery stores and door-to-door. In the 1880s and 1890s refiners learned how to make other products such as waxes and lubricating oils. Petroleum was not then used to make gasoline or heating oil.

36. What is the best title for the passage?
    (A) Oil Refining: A Historical Perspective
    (B) The California Gold Rush: Get Rich Quickly
    (C) Private Property: Trespassers Will Be Prosecuted
    (D) Kerosene Lamps: A Light in the Tunnel

37. It can be inferred from the passage that kerosene was preferable to whale oil because whale oil was too ______.
    (A) expensive
    (B) thick
    (C) hot
    (D) polluted

38. According to the passage, what is "black gold"?
   (A) Whale oil.
   (B) Gold ore.
   (C) Stolen money.
   (D) Crude oil.

39. Why does the author mention the California gold rush?
   (A) To explain the need for an increased supply of gold.
   (B) To indicate the extent of United States mineral wealth.
   (C) To describe the mood when oil was first discovered.
   (D) To argue that gold was more valuable than oil.

40. The word "one" (Para. 5 Line 2) could best be replaced by which of the following words?
   (A) Oil.
   (B) Door.
   (C) Store.
   (D) Product.

生词及短语

crude oil		原油
ooze [uːz]	*n.*	软泥,渗出
seepage ['siːpidʒ]	*n.*	渗流
refine [ri'fain]	*vt.*	精炼,精制
kerosene ['kerəsiːn]	*n.*	煤油
smelt [smelt]	*vt.*	精炼,冶炼
impurity [im'pjuəriti]	*n.*	杂质,不纯
drill [dril]	*v.*	钻孔
venture ['ventʃə]	*n.*	冒险,投机
impractical [im'præktikəl]	*a.*	不切实际的
folly ['fɔli]	*n.*	愚蠢,荒唐事
prospector [prɔ'spektə(r)]	*n.*	勘探者
scene [siːn]	*n.*	现场,情景,场面
wildcatter ['waildkætə]	*n.*	投机分子
rival ['raivəl]	*v.*	竞争,对抗
grocery ['grəusəri]	*n.*	杂货(店)

wax [wæks]	*n.*	蜡
lubricating [ˈluːbrikeitiŋ]	*a.*	润滑的
gasoline [ˈgæsəliːn]	*n.*	汽油
heating oil		民用燃料油

答案与解析

36. [答案] (A)

[解析] 本题为主旨题。文章在第一句便点明了主题 "An important industry, oil refining, grew after the Civil War",后面段落围绕该主题按历史时间顺序展开叙述。(A)应为正确答案。

37. [答案] (A)

[解析] 从第二段第二句"It was a cheap substitute for whale oil, which was becoming harder to get."可推测出当时鲸油已经难以获得,因此价格昂贵,故答案应为(A)。

38. [答案] (D)

[解析] 第四段指出,德雷克采油成功鼓舞了石油勘探者们,他们在整个宾夕法尼亚西部寻找"black gold"(黑金),即原油。故答案应为(D)。

39. [答案] (C)

[解析] 作者在第四段为了描写人们当时寻找石油的迫切心情,以 1848 年人们淘金热时的情形作比喻,(C) 应为正确答案。

40. [答案] (D)

[解析] 本题应从上下文来分析,与"one"相邻的句子指出"原油可以提炼成许多产品。多年来煤油一直是其中主要的一种。"可以看出,"one"指的是原油所提炼的一种产品,指代前面的"product",(D) 应为正确答案。

译文

一种重要的新兴工业——炼油业,在内战后发展起来。原油或称石油——一种黑色、黏稠的地球渗透物,人们知道它已数百年,但几乎没有怎么利用。在 19 世纪 50 年代,塞缪尔·M.科尔,一位宾夕法尼亚的制造商,开始从当地渗油中收集石油并提炼成煤油。提炼过程与熔炼一样是将原材料中的杂质除去。

煤油用来点灯,是鲸油的廉价替代品,那时鲸油已经越来越难得到。不久,对煤油的需求急剧增加,人们开始寻找新的石油资源。

第一口油井是由一位退休的铁路列车长 E·L·德雷克勘探出来的。1859 年他开始在宾夕法尼亚的泰特斯维尔钻探。这个冒险行动在当时看来既不切实际又愚蠢,以致旁观者称之为

“德雷克的愚蠢”。但当他钻到70英尺(21米)深时,打出了石油。他的油井每天会出产20桶原油。

德雷克成功的消息吸引了石油勘探者们来参观。到19世纪60年代初期,这些盲目的石油勘探者们在整个宾夕法尼亚西部到处钻孔寻找“黑金”。当时的寻油激情和西大荒(Wild West)气氛完全可以和1898年加州的淘金热相提并论。而它为勘探者带来的财富远远超过任何一次淘金热带来的财富。

原油可以提炼成多种产品。多少年来,煤油一直是其中主要的一种。它在杂货店出售或走村串户地出售。到19世纪八九十年代,炼油者已经知道如何炼制诸如蜡和润滑油等其他产品。石油那时还没有被用来提炼汽油或民用燃料油。

阅读B篇

Directions:

In the following article, some sentences have been removed. For Questions 41—45, choose the most suitable one from the list A—G to fit into each of the numbered blanks. There are two extra choices, which do not fit in any of the blanks. Mark your answers on ANSWER SHEET 1. (10 points)

The great American melting *pot* (熔炉) is beautifully simple in theory: colors, creeds and cultures stirred together in the land of the free. But the daily details are more difficult. 41. ________.

There are 43.6 million children attending public schools in America, and 2.6 million of them don't speak English, an increase of 76% in the past decade. 42. ________. Citing the close Quebec secession vote in Canada as a warning signal, U.S. House Speaker Newt Gingrich said last week, “We should insist on English as a common language. That's what binds us together.” Senate majority leader and Republican presidential candidate Robert Dole recently made it an element of his campaign, declaring, “We must stop the practice of multilingual education as a means of *instilling* (渗透) ethnic pride or as a therapy for low self-esteems.” Dole last week endorsed legislation to make English the“official language” of the U.S.. 43. ________.

44. ________. But many critics of *polyglot* (多语言的) America are more direct than Dole: two pending proposals would virtually dismantle the Federal Government's 27-year support for bilingual schooling, congressional budget cuts under consideration would slash present funding as much as two-thirds. Behind these moves lies a backlash against immigration and affirmative action programs to help minorities as well as an impatience with the failures and ideological strictures of some bilingual programs.

45. ______________. New York City classes, for example, are now taught in Spanish, Chinese, Haitian Creole, Russian, Korean, Arabic, Vietnamese, Polish, Bengali and French. In California the *demographic* (人口统计学的) change has been the most breathtaking. Thirty years ago, the state's schools were more than three-quarters filled with white, non-Latino children. Today that proportion has dropped to 44%. A quarter of California's 5 million public school students "do not speak English well enough to understand what is going on in a classroom," according to a 1993 report of a state watchdog agency. The agency charged that California's bilingual bureaucracy had "calcified into a self-serving machine ... an ideologically based program more concerned with the intrinsic values of bilingualism and biculturalism than with teaching English."

(A) Whether these students should be taught in their parental language, in the English of their new home or in bilingual classes has suddenly become a national issue.

(B) Bilingual education refers to using two languages in some proportion in order to facilitate learning by students who have a native proficiency in one language and are acquiring proficiency in the other.

(C) For a start, in explaining this concept to a child growing up in the U.S. racial mix, what language should be used?

(D) A "timely fashion" is a difficult expression for someone wrestling with English.

(E) He says he would not seek to ban the country's many bilingual education programs, provided they "ensure people learn English in a timely fashion."

(F) A polyglot is a person having a speaking, reading, or writing knowledge of several languages.

(G) The biggest test of the language melting pot is in the five states where three-quarters of the young newcomers live: California, New York, Florida, Texas and Illinois.

内容提要

本文对在美国这个多种族国家中选择什么语言对孩子进行教育的问题进行讨论。第一段提到,美国这个大熔炉从理论上说很简单:各种肤色、信仰和文化都融合在这块自由的土地上。但是要说清楚每天的详细生活却很困难。首先,要向一个在美国生活的孩子解释种族混合,应该用什么语言呢?接着叙述了各种民族孩子的语言教育过程。

答案与解析

41. [答案](C)

[解析]第一段提到,美国这个大熔炉从理论上说很简单:各种肤色、信仰和文化都融合在这块自由的土地上。但是要说清楚每天的详细生活却很困难。(C)继续叙述:第一点,要向一个在美国生活的孩子解释种族混合,应该用什么语言呢?

42. [答案](A)

[解析]空白前提到在美国公立学校上学的4,360万孩子,260万不会说英语,(A)提出存在的问题:这些学生是否应该用他们的母语,或是英语,或是双语进行教学呢,这突然间成为一个全国性的问题。

43. [答案](E)

[解析]空白前提到共和党总统候选人多尔签署立法使英语成为美国官方语言。(E)继续提到多尔的言论:他说他不会寻求取缔许多双语教育计划,但要确保人们及时地学习英语。

44. [答案](D)

[解析]前段最后一句提到"timely fashion"即"及时的方式",(D)对此短语进行讨论:对于一个赞同英语教学的人很难以"及时的方式"表达清楚。

45. [答案](G)

[解析]空白后面提到纽约市现在使用西班牙语、中文等语言教学。而(G)提到包括纽约在内的五个州的情况。纽约是举例说明。

阅读C篇

Directions:

Read the following text carefully and then translate the underlined segments into Chinese. Your translation should be written neatly on ANSWER SHEET 2. (10 points)

When I was a psychiatric resident, we had a faculty member who was famous for his messy office: stacks of papers and old journals covered every chair and table as well as much of the floor. Eventually, the faculty member had to be given another office in which to see patients.

Not surprisingly, the psychiatric diagnostic manual does riot list "messy room" in the index. But it does mention a tantalizing symptom: inability "to discard worn-out or worthless objects even when they have no sentimental value". It comes under the diagnosis obsessive-compulsive personality disorder, an obscure cousin of the more famous obsessive-compulsive *disorder* (强迫

性神经官能症).

I was barely aware of the diagnosis. Every era has mental disorders that for cultural or scientific reasons become popular. In Freud's day it was hysteria. Currently, depression has moved to center stage. But other ailments go relatively ignored, and this disorder was one.

(46) It came with a list of additional symptoms: anxiety about spending money, excessive devotion to work to the exclusion of leisure activities, rigidity about following rules, perfectionism in doing tasks—at times to the point of interfering with finishing them.

(47) In moderation, the symptoms seemed to fit right in with our workaholic culture—perhaps explaining the low profile of the diagnosis. Relentless work orientation and perfectionism may even be assets in rule-and-detail-oriented professions like accounting or law.

But when the symptoms are too intense or pervasive, they become crippling. Beneath the seemingly adaptive behaviors lies a central disability. People with this diagnosis have enormous difficulty making decisions. (48) They lack the internal sense of completion that most of us experience at the end of a choice or a task, even one as simple as throwing something out or making a purchase. In obsessive-compulsive personality disorder, this feeling occurs only after endless deliberation and revision, if at all.

(49) The need to come up with the "correct" answer, the best purchase or the perfect proposal leads to excess rumination over each decision. It can even lead to complete paralysis. For such people, rules of all kinds are a godsend—they represent pre-made decisions. Open-ended assignments, like writing papers, are nightmares.

For such a patient or for a psychiatrist, understanding a cluster of diagnostic symptoms can be a revelation. The picture leaps out from the previously disorganized background. (50) But undoubtedly, at times we can become too reductionistic, seeing patterns where none exist: sometimes a messy room is just a messy room.

生词及短语

psychiatric [saiki'ætrik]	*a.*	精神病学的
resident ['rezidənt]	*a.*	居住的,常驻的 *n.* 居民
stack [stæk]	*n.*	堆,堆栈
faculty ['fækəlti]	*n.*	全体教员,院,系
diagnostic manual		诊断手册
riot ['raiət]	*n.*	骚乱,放纵
tantalizing ['tæntəlaiziŋ]	*a.*	非常着急的
symptom ['simptəm]	*n.*	症状
inability [inə'biliti]	*n.*	无能,无力

discard [dis'kɑːd]	*v.*	丢弃,抛弃
sentimental [senti'mentl]	*a.*	感伤的,感情的
obsessive [əb'sesiv]	*a.*	强迫性的,分神的
obsessive-compulsive disorder		强迫性神经官能症
hysteria [his'tiəriə]	*n.*	歇斯底里,癔病
ailment ['eilmənt]	*n.*	疾病,不宁,不安
perfectionism [pə'fekʃənizəm]	*n.*	完美主义,至善论
workaholic [wəːkə'hɔlik]	*n.*	专心工作的人
relentless [ri'lentlis]	*a.*	无情的
orientation [ɔ(ː)rien'teiʃən]	*n.*	方向,倾向,东方的
pervasive [pəː'veisiv]	*a.*	普遍深入的,渗透的
crippling ['kripliŋ]	*a.*	临界的
deliberation [dilib'reiʃən]	*n.*	熟思,考虑
rumination	*n.*	沉思
paralysis [pə'rælisis]	*n.*	瘫痪,麻痹
godsend ['gɔdsend]	*n.*	天赐之物
nightmare ['naitmɛə(r)]	*n.*	恶梦,噩梦
revelation [revi'leʃən]	*n.*	显示,揭露
reductionistic	*a.*	归纳的,还原的

全文译文与答案

在我成为一位精神病科医生时,我们有一个同事,他以杂乱的办公室出名:堆叠的纸张和旧杂志覆盖在每一张椅子、桌子和大部分地板上。最终,这位同事只能被分配另外一间办公室接待病人。

不足为奇,精神病诊断手册上并没有无原则地将"杂乱房间"列入索引。但它确实提到令人担忧的症状:无能力"抛弃废旧或无价值的物品,即便它们已经没有情感价值"。它诊断为强迫性个人病态,属于人们更了解的强迫性神经官能症的一种不出名的同类。

我几乎没有注意到这种诊断。精神失常在每一个时代无论从文化或是科学角度来说都很普遍。在弗洛伊德年代被称为"歇斯底里"。而现在,消沉占据了中心舞台。而其他精神不适相对被忽视,这种精神失常便是其中一种。

(46) 强迫性神经官能症有一系列附加的症状:花钱时感到担心,对工作过于投入以至于没有业余文化生活,僵硬地遵循规定,做事时追求完美,有时到了妨碍任务完成的地步。

(47) 如果不严重的话,这些症状和我们的工作狂文化恰好吻合,这也许解释了为什么这种病症不太为人所知。无休止的工作倾向和完美主义甚至成为像会计或法律这一类追求规矩和细节的职业中的资本。

但当症状加重或深入时，后果便会很严重。在看起来适合的行为之下隐藏了一种重要能力的丧失。表现出这种症状的人在做出决定时都感到巨大的困难。(48) 我们大多数人做出选择或完成一项工作时会体验到一种成就感，而他们内心缺少这种成就感，即使是在扔掉或购买东西这样简单的事情上也是如此。在强迫人群中，这种感觉仅仅发生在不断的深思和纠正之后，并且始终如此。

(49) 要想出"正确的"答案，要买到最合适的东西，要提出完美的提议，这种需要导致患者在做每一个决定时都考虑很多。它甚至可以导致完全的麻痹。对于这些人来说，所有的规则都是天赐之物，它们代表事先做好的决定。开放的作业，像写作文，都是噩梦。

对于这样一个病人或对于一个精神科医生来说，了解这一连串的症状会得到一种启示。从前面杂乱无章的背景中会得出一幅图画。(50) 但是毫无疑问，有时候我们也可能太过简单，无中生有地说看到了这种病症的模式，其实有时候杂乱的房间只是杂乱的房间而已。

阅读强化练习四

阅读A篇

Directions:

Read the following four texts. Answer the questions below each text by choosing A, B, C or D. Mark your answers on ANSWER SHEET 1. (40 points)

Passage 1

With the show *Rodeo*, Agnes de Mille had been an innovator in the world of ballet. But with the show *Oklahoma!* , she revolutionized the Broadway stage—brought to an end the dance routine of high kicks and mechanized movement, and gave in its place dance and plot smoothly integrated, choreography reinforcing the action. Twenty-five years later, in March, 1958, a *New York Times* article by theater critic Walter Kerr, headed "In the Beginning Was *Oklahoma!* ", stated, "*Oklahoma!* had a plot. It had to do with whether a boy would succeed in taking a girl to a picnic lunch. At the end of the first half this great issue was still unresolved, so unresolved that its emotional implications had to be danced out at great length in what remains the most exhilarating dancing ever devised for the United States musical comedy stage."

The impact of *Oklahoma!* was instantaneous. The song "Beautiful Morning" sounded out via radios, in restaurants, from cars passing on the highways, in shoeshine parlors. Full skirts of gingham patterns, street shoes made to look like ballet slippers, the ponytail hairdo, were the rage. The play ran for five years and nine weeks in New York City. A traveling road company played it for nine and a half years. It also toured abroad for several years. In 1955 it became a movie. A newly assembled all-star company was sent abroad by the State Department as representative of a part of the United States culture.

As for Agnes de Mille, her days of giving recitals and losing 300 to 1,000 each time were over. She became the most sought-after choreographer on Broadway.

21. What is the author's main purpose in the passage?

(A) To explain the background of the song "Beautiful Morning".

(B) To compare *Rodeo* and *Oklahoma*.

(C) To describe Agnes de Mille's success with *Oklahoma*.

(D) To discuss the fashions made popular by *Oklahoma*.

22. The author cites Walter Kerr because he was ______.

(A) the composer of the music for *Oklahoma*

(B) a dancer who performed with Agnes de Mille

(C) a critic who praised Agnes de Mille's choreography

(D) the owner of *The New York Times*

23. In Para. 2 Line 3—4, the expression "were the rage" could best be replaced by ______.

(A) created chaos

(B) made people crazed

(C) made people angry

(D) were very popular

24. According to the passage, *Oklahoma*! was selected by the State Department to be performed abroad because it was ______.

(A) considered rather revolutionary

(B) representative of an aspect of American life

(C) poorly received in New York City

(D) an inspiring love story

25. The passage implies that prior to *Oklahoma*! Agnes de Mille had given recitals that were ____.

(A) popular comedy routines

(B) financially unsuccessful

(C) performed at picnics

(D) broadcast over the radio

生词及短语

Rodeo [rəu'deiəu]	*n.*	驱赶牧牛(以盖烙印),牛仔竞技表演
innovator ['inəuveitə]	*n.*	改革者,革新者
high kick		高踢

plot [plɔt]	*n.*	情节,结构
choreography [kɔ(ː) ri'ɔgrəfi]	*n.*	舞台舞蹈
critic ['kritik]	*n.*	批评家,评论家
exhilarating [ig'ziləreitiŋ]	*a.*	令人喜欢的,使人愉快的
instantaneous [instən'teinjəs]	*a.*	瞬间的,即刻的
shoeshine ['ʃuːʃain]	*n.*	鞋油,擦皮鞋
parlor ['pɑːlə]	*n.*	营业室,客厅,会客室
gingham ['giŋəm]	*n.*	有条纹或方格纹的棉布,阳伞
slipper ['slipə]	*n.*	拖鞋
ponytail ['pəuniteil]	*n.*	马尾辫(一种发型)
hairdo ['hɛəduː]	*n.*	发型,发式
be the rage		流行,风靡一时
all-star	*a.*	全明星的
recital [ri'saitl]	*n.*	演出,演唱会
sought-after	*a.*	很吃香的,广受欢迎的

答案与解析

21. [答案] (**D**)

[解析] 从全文内容来看,文章在第一句提了一下《赶牛》(*Rodeo*),之后便全文论述阿格尼丝·戴·米勒的《俄克拉何马》(*Oklahoma!*)。认为它使舞蹈界发生了革命性的变化,得到戏剧评论家的赞扬,并被拍成了电影,多年在国内外巡回演出等等,最后提到阿格尼斯戴·米勒因此成了百老汇最走红的舞蹈家。所以作者的主要意图是要谈论《俄克拉何马》在当时的盛行,故(D) 应为正确答案。

22. [答案] (**C**)

[解析] 从第一段第三句中"..., a *New York Times* article by theater critic Walter Kerr, ..."可知沃尔特·克尔是一位戏剧评论家,对《俄克拉何马》进行了赞扬,故答案应为(C)。

23. [答案] (**D**)

[解析] be the (all) rage 为习惯用语,意为"流行,风靡一时",与(D) 相符。考生也可用排除法将明显与上下文内容逻辑不符的(A)、(B) 和(C) 排除,答案应为(D)。

24. [答案] (**B**)

[解析] 从第二段最后一句中"... sent abroad by the State Department as representative of a part of the United States culture."可知该剧"作为美国文化的一个代表"由全名星

组成的演出公司赴国外演出。故(B)应为正确答案。

25. [答案](B)

[解析]第三段第一句指出"对于阿格尼丝·戴·米勒来说,每举办一次表演就损失300到1,000美元的时代已经结束了",这说明了在此之前她举行的表演在经济上亏损,故答案为(B)。

译文

随着舞剧《赶牛》的上演,阿格尼丝·戴·米勒成为芭蕾舞界的领军人物。而随着《俄克拉何马》的上演,她实现了百老汇舞台的革命——结束了高踢腿常规步法和机械化的动作,将舞蹈和情节有机地结合起来,以舞蹈设计来加强表演效果。25年后,1958年3月,戏剧评论家沃尔特·克尔在《纽约时报》上发表了一篇题为"《俄克拉何马》有开创之功"的文章,文章写道,"《俄克拉何马》有一个剧情,叙述一个男孩能否成功地带一位女孩去野餐。在前半部分的结尾处,这个主要问题还没有结果,所以剧中含蓄的感情需要由一段很长的舞蹈来表现,其中有特别令人愉快的舞蹈动作,在美国音乐喜剧舞台上还没有过这种舞蹈设计。"

《俄克拉何马》的影响显而易见。它的歌曲"美丽的早晨"通过无线电广播回荡在餐厅里、高速公路奔跑的汽车里和擦皮鞋的营业室中。宽大的方格纹棉布裙子、做得像芭蕾舞舞鞋一样的布鞋和女孩的马尾发型都风靡一时。这部舞剧在纽约上演了5年零9周。一支巡回演出团上演了9年半之久,还在国外巡回演出了好几年。1955年,它被拍成了电影。一个由全名星组成的演出队被美国国务院派往国外作为美国文化的一个代表作品演出。

对于阿格尼·戴·米勒来说,每举办一次舞蹈表演会就损失300到1,000美元的时代已经结束,她成了百老汇最红的舞蹈家。

Passage 2

The railroad industry could not have grown as large as it did without steel. The first rails were made of iron. But iron rails were not strong enough to support heavy trains running at high speeds. Railroad executives wanted to replace them with steel rails because steel was ten or fifteen times stronger and lasted twenty times longer. Before the 1870s, however, steel was too expensive to be widely used. It was made by a slow and expensive process of heating, stirring, and reheating iron ore.

Then the inventor Henry Bessemer discovered that directing a blast of air at melted iron in a furnace would burn out the impurities that made the iron brittle. As the air shot through the furnace, the bubbling metal would erupt in showers of sparks. When the fire cooled, the metal had been changed, or converted, to steel. The Bessemer converter made possible the mass production of steel. Now three to five tons of iron could be changed into steel in a matter of minutes.

Just when the demand for more and more steel developed, prospectors discovered huge new deposits of iron ore in the Mesabi Range, a 120-mile-long region in Minnesota near Lake Superior. The Mesabi deposits were so near the surface that they could be mined with steam shovels.

Barges and steamers carried the iron ore through Lake Superior to depots on the southern shores of Lake Michigan and Lake Erie. With dizzying speed Gary, Indiana and Toledo, Youngstown, and Cleveland, Ohio, became major steel-manufacturing centers. Pittsburgh was the greatest steel city of all.

Steel was the basic building material of the industrial age. Production skyrocketed from seventy-seven thousand tons in 1870 to over eleven million tons in 1900.

26. Which of the following is the best title for the passage?

(A) The Railroad Industry

(B) Famous Inventors

(C) Changing Iron into Steel

(D) Steel Manufacturing Centers

27. According to the passage, the railroad industry preferred steel to iron because steel was ____.

(A) cheaper and more plentiful

(B) lighter, and easier to mold

(C) cleaner, and easier to mine

(D) stronger and more durable

28. According to the passage, how did the Bessemer method make the mass production of steel possible?

(A) It director air at melted iron in a furnace, removing all impurities.

(B) It slowly heated iron ore, then stirred it and heated it again.

(C) It changed iron ore into iron, which was a substitute for steel.

(D) It could quickly find deposits of iron ore under the ground.

29. The furnace that Bessemer used to process iron into steel was called a ____.

(A) heater

(B) steamer

(C) converter

(D) shower

30. According to the passage, where were large deposits of iron ore uncovered?

(A) In Pittsburgh.

(B) In the Mesabi Range.

(C) Near Lake Michigan.

(D) Near Lake Erie.

生词及短语

executive [ig'zekjutiv]	n.	主管人员
stir [stəː]	vt.	搅和,摇动
Henry Bessemer		亨利·贝西默(1813—1898,首创转炉钢英国工程师)
blast [blɑːst]	n.	一阵(风),一股(气流)
melt [melt]	v.	(使)融化,(使)熔化
furnace ['fəːnis]	n.	熔炉
brittle ['britl]	a.	易碎的,脆弱的
bubble ['bʌbl]	vi.	起泡
erupt [i'rʌpt]	vi.	喷发,爆发
spark [spɑːk]	n.	火花,火星
a matter of		大约,大概
deposit [di'pɔzit]	n.	矿藏,堆积物
ore [ɔː(r)]	n.	矿石
shovel ['ʃʌvl]	n.	铲,铁铲
barge [bɑːdʒ]	n.	驳船,游艇
depot ['depəu]	n.	库房,仓库
dizzy ['dizi]	a.	眩晕的,昏乱的
skyrocket ['skairɔkit]	v.	飞涨

答案与解析

26. [答案](C)

[解析]本题为主旨题。本文从铁路需要钢、炼钢的方法、钢铁的冶炼、钢产量的增长几个方面谈及了由铁到钢的应用过程,而(A)、(B)、(D)均不为文章主要内容,故答案应为(C)。

27. [答案] (D)

[解析] 第一段第四句指出“Railroad executives wanted ... twenty times longer.”与(D) “更坚硬和耐久”相符,(D) 应为正确答案。

28. [答案] (A)

[解析] 第二段第一句指出“贝西默发现,直接对熔炉中熔化的铁鼓风,会把铁中的杂质除掉”,故(A) 应为正确答案。

29. [答案] (C)

[解析] 第二段第四句明确将贝西默发明的熔炉称之为 converter: “The Bessemer converter made possible the mass production of steel.”故答案应为(C)。

30. [答案] (B)

[解析] 第三段第一句提到“当钢的需求量越来越多时,勘探人员在梅萨比山脉发现了巨大的新铁矿”,(B) 应为正确答案。

译文

没有钢,铁路就不会发展到如此规模。第一条铁轨是用铁制造的。但这种铁轨硬度不够,难以承受高速行驶的沉重的火车。于是铁路主管部门打算把铁轨换成钢轨,因为钢的硬度是铁的 10—15 倍,寿命是铁的 20 倍以上。然而,在 19 世纪 70 年代以前,钢材太贵,无法广泛应用。钢的制造过程既漫长又昂贵,需要对铁矿石进行加温、搅拌和重新加温。

当时的发明家亨利·贝西默发现,直接对熔炉中熔化的铁吹风,就能把铁中使铁脆弱的杂质除掉。当气流穿过熔炉时,冒泡的金属会喷发出火花。当火熄灭后,金属就转变成钢。这种贝西默炼钢术使得钢的大规模生产成为可能。现在,只要几分钟时间,三五吨铁就可以变成钢。

正当钢材的需求日益增加的时候,勘探人员在梅萨比山脉地区发现了丰富的铁矿,位于明尼苏达州,苏必利尔湖附近,一个长 120 英里长的区域。梅萨比的矿床非常浅,用蒸汽挖掘机就可以开采。

船舶和汽艇通过苏必利尔湖把铁矿石运到密执安湖和伊利湖南岸的仓库。印第安纳州的加里、俄亥俄州的托莱多、扬斯敦和克利夫兰迅速成为主要钢铁工业中心。匹兹堡是其中最大的钢城。钢是工业革命时期的基本建筑材料。钢产量由 1870 年的 7.7 万吨直升到 1900 年的 1,100 多万吨。

Passage 3

Certainly one of the most intelligent and best educated women of her day, Mercy Otis Warren produced a variety of poetry and prose. Her farce *The Group* (1776) was the hit of revolutionary Boston; a collection of two plays and poems appeared in 1790; and her three-volume *History of the Rise, Progress, and Termination of the American Revolution, Interspersed with Biographical and Moral Observations* appeared in 1805. She wrote other farces, as well as an anti-Federalist pamphlet, *Observations on the New constitution, and on the Federal and State Conventions*(1788). There is no modern edition of her works, but there are two twentieth-century biographies, one facsimile edition of *The Group*, and a generous discussion of her farces and plays in Arthur Hobson Quinn's *A History of the American Drama*: *From the Beginning to the Civil War*. Of the nondramatic poetry, critics rarely speak.

Mercy Otis was born into a prominent family in Barnstable, Massachusetts. In 1754, she married James Warren, a Harvard friend of James Otis and John Adams. James Warren was to become a member of the Massachusetts legislature just before the war and a financial aide to Washington during the war (with the rank of major general) . The friendship of the Warrens and Adamses was lifelong and close; Abigail Adams was one of Mercy Warren's few close friends. Following the war, James Warren reentered politics to oppose the Constitution because he feared that it did not adequately provide for protection of individual rights. Mercy Warren joined her husband in political battle, but the passage of the Bill of Rights marked the end of their long period of political agitation.

In whatever literary form Warren wrote, she had but one theme—liberty. In her farces and history, it was national and political freedom. In her poems, it was intellectual freedom. In her anti-Federalist pamphlet, it was individual freedom. Throughout all of these words, moreover, runs the thread of freedom (equal treatment) for women. Not militant, she nevertheless urged men to educate their daughters and to treat wives as equals.

31. Which of the following is the main topic of the passage?
   (A) Mercy Otis Warren and other poets of the Revolutionary War period.
   (B) The development of Mercy Otis Warren's writing style.
   (C) Mercy Otis Warren's contributions to American literature and society.
   (D) The friends and acquaintances of Mercy Otis Warren.

32. In what year was Warren's pamphlet about the Constitution written?
   (A) 1776.
   (B) 1788.
   (C) 1790.
   (D) 1805.

33. Which of the following is NOT mentioned as a kind of writing done by Warren?
   (A) Farces.
   (B) Poetry.

(C) Plays.

(D) Advertisements.

34. According to the passage, the kind of liberty emphasized in Warren's poems was ______.

(A) national

(B) intellectual

(C) political

(D) religious

35. In lines 23, the author refers to Warren as "not militant" to indicate that she ______

(A) remained politically aloof

(B) did not continue agitating for a Bill of Rights

(C) did not campaign aggressively for women's rights

(D) did not support military conscription

生词及短语

farce [fɑːs]	n.	笑剧,滑稽剧
termination [təːmiˈneiʃən]	n.	终止
intersperse [intə(ː) ˈspəːs]	vt.	散布,点缀
pamphlet [ˈpæmflit]	n.	小册子
facsimile [fækˈsimili]	n.	摹写,传真
nondramatic [nɔndrəˈmætik]	a.	非戏剧性的
agitation [ædʒiˈteiʃən]	n.	激动,兴奋,煽动
militant [ˈmilitənt]	a.	好战的,过激的

答案与解析

31. [答案] (C)

[解析] 本题为主旨题。本文三段内容分别讨论了莫西·沃伦的作品、生平和政治活动及她的写作主题——自由。(B)、(A) 和 (D) 选项均仅为各段中提到的内容,而只有(C) 概括了全文。故(C) 应为正确答案。

32. [答案] (B)

[解析] 从第三句可知,她的关于"宪法"的小册子是在 1788 年写的,故(B) 为正确答案。

33. [答案](D)

[解析] 文中第一、二句提到她的作品，包括 farces、poems 和 plays，只有(D) 在文中未被提到，故(D) 为正确答案。

34. [答案](B)

[解析] 从第三段第三句"In her poems, it was intellectual freedom."可得出答案应为(B)。

35. [答案](C)

[解析] Not militant 是一个省略的让步状语从句，完整的形式应为"Although she was not militant...",militant 意为"过激的，好战的"，在这里指沃伦在女权问题上并不提倡过激行为，但她还是力劝男人们让他们的女儿受到教育，并平等对待他们的妻子。(A)、(B)、(D) 均与此意无关，只有(C) 贴近题意，为正确答案。

译文

莫西·奥蒂斯·沃伦无疑是她那个时代最有才智和最有教养的女性之一，她写出了各种诗歌和散文。她的闹剧《集团》(*The Group*1776) 轰动了革命时期的波士顿;1790 年出版了两个剧本和诗歌集;1805 年她的三卷本《美国革命的兴起、发展和终结，及其传记性和道德评论》(*History of the Rise, Progress, and Termination of the American Revolution, Interspersed with Biographical and Moral Observations*)问世。她还写了其他闹剧，以及一本反联邦主义者的小册子《对新宪法及联邦、州制宪会议的评论》(*Observation On The New Constitution, and On the Federal and State Conventions*)(1788)。她的作品还没有当代版，但有两部 20 世纪出版的她的传记，一部《集团》(*The Group*)的摹写本，由阿瑟·霍布森·奎恩撰写的《美国戏剧史从早期到内战时期》(*A History of the American Drama: From the Beginning to the Civil War*)一书广泛地评论了她的闹剧和戏剧作品。至于她的非戏剧性诗歌，评论家们很少谈及。

莫西出生在马塞诸塞州巴恩斯泰堡镇的一个很知名的家庭。1754 年她与詹姆斯·沃伦结了婚。詹姆斯·沃伦是詹姆斯·奥蒂斯和约翰·亚当斯哈佛大学时的朋友。詹姆斯·沃伦在独立战争爆发前当上了马塞诸塞州的立法委员，并在战争期间成为华盛顿的财政副官(相当于上将军衔)。沃伦和亚当斯两家人的友谊保持到终生并且一直很亲密。阿比盖尔·亚当斯是莫西·沃伦少数几个亲密朋友之一。随着战争的爆发，詹姆斯·沃伦重入政界反对宪法，因为他担心宪法不能为个人权利提供充分的保护。莫西·沃伦加入了丈夫的政治斗争，但《人权法案》的通过标志着他们长期的政治热情的结束。

无论沃伦用什么样的文学形式写作，她只有一个主题——自由，在她的闹剧和历史作品中，主题是民族和政治自由;在她的诗歌中，是思想自由;在反联邦主义者的小册子中，是个人自由。而且，在她的所有句子中贯穿着妇女自由(平等待遇) 的思想。她并不过激，然而她力劝男人们让他们的女儿受到教育，并平等地对待自己的妻子。

Passage 4

In the past oysters were raised in much the same way as dirt farmers raised tomatoes—by transplanting them. First, farmers selected the oyster bed, cleared the bottom of old shells and other debris, then scattered clean shells about. Next, they "planted" fertilized oyster eggs, which within two or three weeks hatched into larvae. The larvae drifted until they attached themselves to the clean cells on the bottom. There they remained and in time grew into baby oysters called seed or spat. The spat grew larger by drawing in seawater from which they derived microscopic particles of food. Before long, farmers gathered the baby oysters into another body of water to fatten them up.

Until recently the supply of wild oysters and those crudely farmed were more than enough to satisfy people's needs. But today the delectable seafood is no longer available in abundance. The problem has become so serious that some oyster beds have vanished entirely.

Fortunately, as far back as the early 1900s marine biologists realized that if new measures were not taken, oysters would become extinct or at best a luxury food. So they set up well-equipped hatcheries and went to work. But they did not have the proper equipment or the skill to handle the eggs. They did not know when, what, and how to feed the larvae.

And they knew little about the predators that attack and eat baby oysters by the millions. They failed, but they doggedly kept at it. Finally, in the 1940s a significant breakthrough was made.

The marine biologists discovered that by raising the temperature of the water, they could induce oysters to spawn not only in the summer but also in the fall, winter, and spring. Later they developed a technique for feeding the larvae and rearing them to spat. Going still further, they succeeded in breeding new strains that were resistant to diseases, grew faster and larger, and flourished in water of different salinities and temperatures. In addition the cultivated oysters tasted better!

36. Which of the following would be the best title for the passage?
    (A) The Threatened Extinction of Marine Life
    (B) The Cultivation of Oysters
    (C) The Discoveries Made by Marine Biologists
    (D) The Varieties of Wild Oysters

37. In the First paragraph, the production of oysters is compared to what other industry?
    (A) Mining.
    (B) Fishing.

(C) Banking.
(D) Farming.

38. When did scientists discover that oysters were in danger?
(A) In the early part of the nineteenth century.
(B) At the beginning of this century.
(C) In the 1940s.
(D) Just recently.

39. In what paragraph does the author describe successful methods for increasing the oyster population?
(A) First.
(B) Second.
(C) Third.
(D) Fourth.

40. Which of the following best describes the organization of the passage?
(A) Step by step description of the evolution of marine biology.
(B) Discussion of chronological events concerning oyster production.
(C) Random presentation of facts about oysters.
(D) Description of oyster production at different geographic locations.

生词及短语

oyster ['ɔistə]	*n.*	牡蛎
dirt [dəːt]	*n.*	泥土
transplant [træns'plɑːnt]	*v.*	移植,种植
debris ['debriː]	*n.*	碎片,残骸
fertilize ['fəːtilaiz]	*vt.*	施肥,使受精,使多产
hatch [hætʃ]	*vt.*	孵化,孵出
larvae ['lɑːvə]	*n.*	幼虫
spat [spæt]	*n.*	蚝卵
microscopic [maikrə'skɔpik]	*a.*	精微的,用显微镜可见的
fatten ['fætən]	*vt.*	养肥
delectable [di'lektəbl]	*a.*	令人愉快的
marine [mə'riːn]	*a.*	海的,海产的
extinct [iks'tiŋkt]	*a.*	灭绝的,耗尽的

luxury [ˈlʌkʃəri]	*n.*	奢侈
hatchery [ˈhætʃəri]	*n.*	孵卵所
predator [ˈpredətə]	*n.*	食肉动物
doggedly [ˈdɔgidli]	*ad.*	固执地,顽强地
induce [inˈdjuːs]	*vt.*	促使,导致
spawn [spɔːn]	*v.*	产卵
rear [riə]	*vt.*	培养,饲养
breed [briːd]	*v.*	繁殖,抚养
strain [strein]	*n.*	品系,种类,张力,应变
salinity [səˈliniti]	*n.*	盐分,盐度

答案与解析

36. [答案] (B)

[解析] 本题为主旨题。本文从一开始便谈到了过去牡蛎是如何养殖的, 接着描述了20世纪初养殖牡蛎的情况以及20世纪40年代养殖方法有了新突破, 文章自始至终都在谈论牡蛎的养殖,故(B) 应为正确答案。

37. [答案] (D)

[解析] 第一段第一句指出"过去人们就像农民种西红柿一样养殖牡蛎",故(D) 应为正确答案。

38. [答案] (B)

[解析] 第三段第一句指出"... as far back as the early 1900s marine biologists realized that if new measures were not taken, oysters would become extinct ...",科学家在本世纪初发现如果不采取新措施,牡蛎就有灭绝的危险。故(B) 应为正确答案。

39. [答案] (D)

[解析] 第四段提到通过提高水温的方法能够提高牡蛎的产量。显然(D) 为正确答案。

40. [答案] (B)

[解析] 本题考文章的组织结构。第一段谈论牡蛎养殖过去的情况, 第二段说最近的情况,第三段叙述从1900s到1940s的情况,所以文章是按时间顺序来写的。答案也应为(B)。

译文

过去,渔民像农民种植西红柿那样用移植方法养殖牡蛎。首先,渔民们选择牡蛎苗床,清除底部的旧贝壳及其他残骸,然后再将清洁好的贝壳撒下。接着"种植"受精的牡蛎卵,这些卵在两三个星期内就孵成幼虫。幼虫随水游荡,然后就贴在床底干净的贝壳上直到长成称为“种子”和“蚝卵”的幼牡蛎。幼牡蛎靠从海水中吸取微小食物渐渐长大。不久,渔民将这些幼牡蛎采集到别的水域,将它们养肥。

直到不久前,野生和使用这种落后方式养殖的牡蛎一直是供大于求。但今天,这种可口海味的供应已经不再丰富了。问题如此严重,有些地方连牡蛎苗床也完全消失了。

幸运的是,早在二十世纪初海洋生物学家就意识到,如果不采取新措施,牡蛎就会灭绝,或者只能成为奢侈品。于是他们建立起设备先进的孵卵场来养殖牡蛎。但他们没有合适的设备和技术来管理牡蛎卵。

他们不知道什么时候、用什么和怎么样喂养幼牡蛎。他们对那些侵害和吞食上百万幼牡蛎的“食肉动物”也知之甚少。他们失败过,但还是顽强地坚持了下来。终于,在40年代取得了重大的突破。

海洋生物学家发现提高水温可使牡蛎不但在夏天,而且在秋天、冬天和春天都能产卵。后来他们摸索出一种能喂养幼虫并将它们养成幼牡蛎的技术。进一步,他们成功地培养出了抗疾病、生长更快更大的新品种,而且能在不同温度和盐度的水域中繁荣生长。这种培植的牡蛎味道更加鲜美!

阅读B篇

Directions:

In the following article, some sentences have been removed. For Questions 41—45, choose the most suitable one from the list A—G to fit into each of the numbered blanks. There are two extra choices, which do not fit in any of the blanks. Mark your answers on ANSWER SHEET 1. (10 points)

Magazines provide a wide variety of information, opinion, and entertainment. For example, they may cover current events and fashions, discuss foreign affairs, or describe how to repair appliances or prepare food. Subjects addressed in magazines include business, culture, hobbies, medicine, religion, science, and sports. 41. ________________.

42. ________________. For this reason, most magazines have a smaller page size and are printed on better paper. Many have a binding of staples or stitching. In content, magazines often have less concern with daily, rapidly changing events than do newspapers. Most magazines have a cover featuring a photograph or a drawing rather than news stories like the first page of a newspaper.

43. ________________. On the other hand, some weekly newspapers feature long, detailed articles like those found in many magazines. Writing of different types—ranging from factual or practical reporting to a more personal or emotional style—regularly appears in magazines. Some

of the best writers and thinkers in the nation write either occasionally or regularly for magazines. Many well-known authors published their early works in magazines.

44. ______________. Consumer magazines appeal to the broad interests of the general public and are the ones usually seen on newsstands and in stores. Consumer magazines include children's magazines, hobby magazines, intellectual magazines, men's magazines, women's magazines, and news magazines. Service magazines include advice, how-to, medical, self-help, and religious publications. Digests reprint material, in a shorter form, that has appeared in other magazines or in books.

45. ______________. For example, Aviation Week and Space Technology focuses on the informational and product needs of people in the aerospace industry. Many highly specialized trade magazines control their circulation by mailing free copies to people whose jobs make them potential readers. By controlling their circulation, trade magazines limit their costs and attract particular advertisers. As a result, they can succeed with circulations that are much smaller than those of consumer magazines.

(A) Some magazines are designed for young people, some for women, and some for elders, but not so many for children for reason of reading difficulties.

(B) Magazines, like newspapers, represent the work of many writers. But magazines differ from newspapers in form and content. Magazines are designed to be kept much longer than newspapers.

(C) Some periodicals that appear in newspaper form are really magazines.

(D) Magazines are usually divided into several large categories, including consumer magazines and specialized business magazines.

(E) There is a special kind of magazine called campus magazine which is produced by university students and given to anyone who is interested in their college life.

(F) Specialized business magazines, also called trade magazines, appeal to the special interests of business, industrial, and professional groups.

(G) Some magazines seek simply to entertain their readers with fiction, poetry, photography, cartoons, or articles about television shows or motion-picture stars. Thousands of magazines are published in the United States and Canada.

内 容 提 要

本文是一篇关于杂志的叙述文章。本文第一段指出,杂志提供广泛多样的信息、观点和娱乐。接着对这些内容加以举例说明,提到最新事件和时尚、讨论外交事务、讨论家电修理和烹调食物。杂志还谈论生意、文化、爱好、医疗、宗教、科学和运动。在美国和加拿大,有数千杂志出版发行。

答案与解析

41. [答案] (G)

[解析] 本段第一句指出,杂志提供广泛多样的信息、观点和娱乐。接着对这些内容加以举例说明,提到最新事件和时尚、讨论外交事务、讨论家电修理和烹调食物。杂志还谈论生意、文化、爱好、医疗、宗教、科学和运动。由于还没有提到娱乐,所以空白处应该对娱乐加以描述,故应填入(G) 的内容。

42. [答案] (B)

[解析] 本段空白处后面第一句提到,“由于这个原因, 大多数杂志页面尺寸较小但印刷纸的质量较好。”可见空白处叙述的是“这个原因”。而(B) 将杂志与报纸做了比较,指出杂志的设计要比报纸保存更长的时间。这正是杂志页面尺寸较小和纸张质量较好的原因。

43. [答案] (C)

[解析] 本段空白处后面第一句以介词短语“On the other hand”开头,这说明前面空白处表达的是“一方面”的内容,与此句并列。本句难度在于选项中没有出现由“On the one hand”引导的句子,故只能从逻辑和内容上判断。(C) 意为“一些以报纸形式出现的期刊是真实的杂志。”与“另一方面,一些周报像许多杂志那样特别登载了较长和详细的文章。”两句从逻辑和形式两方面相符。

44. [答案] (D)

[解析] 本段空白处后面内容谈到消费者杂志、服务性杂志摘要性杂志,可见本段讨论的是特定的分类,而(D) 正好表达此意:杂志一般分为几大类,包括消费者杂志和专门的商业杂志。

45. [答案] (F)

[解析] 本段空白处后面第一句是举例,可见是为了进一步说明前面提到的内容,所举的例子是关于前段提到的“特定的商业杂志的内容”,明显是继续讨论上一段没有讨论的内容,(F) 讨论的也正是“特定的商业杂志”,从逻辑上相符。

阅读 C 篇

Directions:

Read the following text carefully and then translate the underlined segments into Chinese. Your translation should be written neatly on ANSWER SHEET 2. (10 points)

The time has come for humanity to journey to Mars. We're ready. (46) Though Mars is distant, we are far better prepared today to send humans to Mars than we were to travel to the Moon at the commencement of the space age. Given the will, we could have our first teams on Mars within a decade. The reasons for going to Mars are powerful.

We must go for the knowledge of Mars. Our robotic probes have revealed that Mars was once a warm and wet planet, suitable for hosting life's origin. But did it? A search for fossils on the Martian surface or microbes in groundwater below could provide the answer. If found, they would show that the origin of life is not unique to the Earth, and, by implication, reveal a universe that is filled with life and probably intelligence as well. (47) From the view point of learning our true place in the universe, this would be the most important scientific enlightenment since Copernicus.

We must go for knowledge of Earth. As we begin the twenty-first century, we have evidence that we are changing the Earth's atmosphere and environment in significant ways. It has become a critical matter for us to better understand all aspects of our environment. (48) In this project, comparative planetology is a very powerful tool, a fact already shown by the role that Venusian atmospheric studies played in our discovery of the potential threat of global warming by greenhouse gases. Mars, the planet most like Earth, will have even more to teach us about our home world. The knowledge we gain could be key to our survival.

We must go for the future. (49) Mars is not just a scientific curiosity; it is a world with a surface area equal to all the continents of Earth combined, possessing all the elements that are needed to support not only life, but technological society. (50) It is a New World, filled with history waiting to be made by a new and youthful branch of human civilization that is waiting to be born. We must go to Mars to make that potential a reality. We must go, not for us, but for a people who are yet to be. We must do it for the Martians.

生词及短语

commencement [kə'mensmənt]	n.	开始
go for		寻找,努力获取
host [həust]	v.	做主人招待,寄主,宿主
fossil ['fɔsl]	n.	化石
microbe ['maikrəub]	n.	微生物,细菌
Copernicus [kəu'pəːnikəs]	n.	哥白尼
comparative planetology		比较行星学
Venusian [viːn'juːsiən]	a.	金星的
greenhouse gases		温室气体

全文译文与答案

人类到火星去旅行的时代已经到来。我们已经准备就绪。(46) 尽管火星距离我们很遥远,但与在太空时代之初我们去月球旅行的情形相比,我们今天把人类送上火星的准备就充分多了。如果说愿望,我们可以在十年中将我们的第一个团队送上火星。到火星的理由是很充分的。

我们必须了解火星的知识。我们的火星探测器显示火星曾经是一个温暖潮湿的星球,适合于寄住生命之源。但是不是如此呢?通过对火星表面化石的研究或对地下水微生物的研究可以得到答案。如果能够找到证据,将表明地球不是惟一的生命之源,而这也表示,它将揭示出宇宙充满生命,或许还是智能生命的事实。(47) 从了解我们在宇宙中的真实地位来看,这恐怕是自哥白尼以来最重要的科学启蒙。

我们必须获得地球的知识。当我们开启二十一世纪的时候,我们有证据表明我们正在改变着地球的气候和环境。对于我们来说非常紧要的问题是要了解我们环境的所有方面。(48) 在研究地球环境这一课题中,比较行星学是一个有力的工具。有关金星的大气研究在帮我们发现温室气体所产生的全球气温上升这一潜在威胁方面所起的作用已经说明这一事实。火星是最像地球的星球,它将告诉我们更多有关我们家乡的知识。我们所获得的知识将是我们生存的关键。

我们必须寻找未来。(49) 火星不仅仅是一个科学之谜,它还是一个表面面积等于地球所有大陆面积总和的一个世界,拥有不仅用来维持生命,而且用来支持技术社会的所有要素。(50) 这是一个新的世界,正等待即将诞生的新的年轻人类文明之士去书写它的历史。我们必须到火星上去以使这一潜在的可能性成为现实。我们必须去,不仅仅是为了我们,还为了一个仍然存在的民族。我们必须这样做是为了火星人。

阅读强化练习五

阅读A篇

Directions:

Read the following four texts. Answer the questions below each text by choosing A, B, C or D. Mark your answers on ANSWER SHEET 1. (40 points)

Passage 1

Political controversy about the public-land policy of the United States began with the American Revolution. In fact, even before independence from Britain was won, it became clear that resolving the dilemmas surrounding the public domain might prove necessary to preserve the Union itself.

At the peace negotiations with Britain, Americans demanded, and got, a western boundary at the Mississippi River. Thus the new nation secured for its birthright a vast internal empire rich in agricultural and mineral resources. But under their colonial charters, seven states—Massachusetts, Connecticut, New York, Virginia, North Carolina, South Carolina, and Georgia—claimed portions of the western wilderness. Virginia's claim was the largest, stretching north and west to encompass the later states of Kentucky, Ohio, Indiana, Illinois, Michigan, and Wisconsin. The language of the charters was vague and their validity questionable, but during the war Virginia reinforced its title by sponsoring Colonel George Rogers Clark's 1778 expedition to Vicennes and Raskaskia, which strengthened America's trans-Appalachian pretensions at the peace table.

The six states holding no claim to the trans-mountain region doubted whether a confederacy in which territory was so unevenly apportioned would truly prove what it claimed to be, a union of equals. Already New Jersey, Delaware, Rhode Island , and Maryland were among the smallest and least populous of the States. While they levied heavy taxes to repay state war debts, their larger neighbors might retire debts out of land-sale proceeds. Drawn by fresh lands and low taxes, people would desert the small states for the large, leaving the former to fall into bankruptcy and eventually into political subjugation. All the states shared in the war effort, said the New Jersey legislature, how then could half of them "be left to sink under an enormous debt, while others are enabled, in a short period, to replace all their expenditures from the hard earnings of the whole confederacy?" As the Revolution was a common endeavor, so ought its fruits, including the western lands, to be a common property.

21. With which of the following topics is the passage primarily concerned?
   (A) A controversial public-land policy.
   (B) How independence from Britain was won.
   (C) The land holdings of Massachusetts.
   (D) How New Jersey developed its western land.

22. According to the passage, the British granted the new American nation a western boundary at ______.
   (A) Ohio
   (B) Illinois
   (C) the Mississippi River
   (D) the Appalachian Mountains

23. Which state laid claim to the largest land-holdings?
   (A) North Carolina
   (B) South Carolina
   (C) Virginia
   (D) Georgia

24. Why does the author mention Colonel Clark's expedition?
   (A) To explain how one state strengthened its land claims.
   (B) To criticize an effort to acquire additional agricultural resources.
   (C) To show that many explorers searched for new lands.
   (D) To question the validity of Virginia's claims.

25. According to the passage, the smaller states tried to raise money to pay their war debts by ______.
   (A) collecting taxes
   (B) exporting crops

(C) selling land

(D) raising cattle

生词及短语

dilemma [di'lemə]	*n.*	进退两难的局面，难题
secure [si'kjuə]	*v.*	得到，获得
birthright ['bəːθrait]	*n.*	生来就有的权利
empire ['empaiə]	*n.*	帝国
charter ['tʃɑːtə]	*n.*	宪章
wilderness ['wildənis]	*n.*	荒野，荒地
encompass [in'kʌmpəs]	*v.*	包围，环绕
vague [veig]	*a.*	含糊的，不清楚的
validity [və'liditi]	*n.*	有效性，正确性
sponsor ['spɔnsə]	*vt.*	发起，主办
expedition [ekspi'diʃən]	*n.*	远征，探险队
pretension [priː'tenʃən]	*n.*	借口，要求
confederacy [kən'fedərəsi]	*n.*	联盟，邦联
levy ['levi]	*v.*	征收，征集
proceed [prə'siːd]	*n.*	收入
subjugation [sʌbdʒu'geiʃən]	*n.*	镇压，平息，征服
expenditure [iks'penditʃə]	*n.*	支出，花费
endeavor [in'devə]	*n.*	努力，尽力

答案与解析

21. [答案] (A)

[解析] 本题为主旨题。文章第一句便点明了主题“Political controversy about the public-land policy of the United States began with the American Revolution.” 后面内容谈论了六个州对阿巴拉契山脉以西公共领域所有权问题的争论。故(A) 应为正确答案。

22. [答案] (C)

[解析] 第二段第一句指出 “At the peace negotiations with Britain, Americans demanded, and got, a western boundary at the Mississippi River.” 故(C) 应为正确答案。

23. ［答案］(C)

［解析］第二段第四句指出“Virginia's claim was the largest, ...”,(C) 应为正确答案。

24. ［答案］(A)

［解析］第二段最后一句指出，为了加强自己对西部土地拥有权的理由，弗吉尼亚州于1778 年派出由克拉克上校带领的探险队对温森斯地区和卡斯卡基亚河进行了考察,以加强自己在谈判桌上的理由。故(A) 是正确答案。

25. ［答案］(A)

［解析］第三段第二、三句指出,新泽西、特拉华、罗得岛和马里兰四个州是最小的州,它们靠征税来偿还战争债务 “... they levied heavy taxes to repay state war debts, ...” (A) 应为正确答案。

译文

美国独立革命一开始对公有土地政策就存在政治争议。事实上，在从英国取得独立之前,很清楚,这个联邦要生存下去,就得把困扰公有土地的难题彻底解决。

在与英国进行和平谈判时,美国人要求并实现了以密西西比河为西边地界的要求。这样这个新生国家一诞生就获得了一大块农业、矿产资源都丰富的领土。但根据殖民时期的宪章,马塞诸塞州、康涅狄格州、纽约州、弗吉尼亚州、北卡罗来纳州、南卡罗来纳州和佐治亚州这七个州对西部荒野领域均有部分所有权。其中,弗吉尼亚州的土地拥有权最大——向北以及向西延伸到包括后来的肯塔基州、俄亥俄州、印第安纳州、伊利诺斯州、密歇根州和威斯康星州在内的领土。宪章的言语很含糊,其有效性也令人怀疑。但在战争期间,弗吉尼亚州为加强自己的地位于 1778 年派出乔治·罗杰·克拉克上校为首的探险队到温森斯和卡斯卡基亚河进行考察,这加强了美国在谈判桌上对跨阿巴拉契亚山脉领土所有权的要求。

对跨阿巴拉契亚山脉地区没有领土权的六个州均有疑问，领土分配如此不均的联邦是否能真正证明它所宣称的平等。新泽西州、特拉华州、罗得岛州和马里兰州成了各州中领土最小、人口最少的州。它们的邻州可以用土地出售来偿还战争债务,而它们自己却只能靠增加税收来偿付。受到新土地和低税收吸引,人们将从小州迁移到大州,使小州更无支付能力,最终在政治上受到大州控制。新泽西州议会提出,“既然各州都对战争做出了贡献,为什么要让半数的州因巨额债务而倒下，而其他州却能在短期内靠整个联邦来之不易的收入来填补他们的支出？”既然美国独立革命是大家共同努力的结果,那它的胜利成果,包括西部领土,就应该是大家的共同财产。

Passage 2

Without regular supplies of some hormones our capacity to behave would be seriously impaired; without others we would soon die. Tiny amounts of some hormones can modify our moods and our actions, our inclination to eat or drink, our aggressiveness or submissiveness, and our reproductive and parental behavior. And hormones do more than influence adult behavior; early in life they help to determine the development of bodily form and may even determine an individual's behavioral capacities. Later in life the changing outputs of some endocrine glands and the body's changing sensitivity to some hormones are essential aspects of the phenomena of aging.

Communication within the body and the consequent integration of behavior were considered the exclusive province of the nervous system up to the beginning of the present century. The emergence of endocrinology as a separate discipline can probably be traced to the experiments of Bayliss and Starling on the hormones secretion. This substance is secreted from cells in the intestinal walls when food enters the stomach; it travels through the bloodstream and stimulates the pancreas to *liberate* pancreatic juice, which aids in digestion. By showing that special cells secrete chemical agents that are conveyed by the bloodstream and regulate distant target organs or tissues, Bayliss and Starling demonstrated that chemical integration can occur without participation of the nervous system.

The term "hormone" was first used with reference to secretion. Starling derived the term from the Greek hormon, meaning "to excite or set in motion." The term "endocrine" was introduced shortly thereafter. "Endocrine" is used to refer to glands that secrete products into the bloodstream. The term "endocrine" contrasts with "exocrine," which is applied to glands that secrete their products through ducts to the site of action. Examples of exocrine glands are the tear glands, the sweat glands, and the pancreas, which secretes pancreatic juice through a duct into the intestine. Exocrine glands are also called duct glands, while endocrine glands are called ductless.

26. What is the author's main purpose in the passage?
    (A) To explain the specific functions.
    (B) To provide general information about hormones.
    (C) To explain how the term "hormone" evolved.
    (D) To report on experiments in endocrinology.

27. Which of the following is NOT mentioned as an effect of hormones?
    (A) Modification of behavior.
    (B) Sensitivity to hunger and thirst.
    (C) Aggressive feelings.
    (D) Maintenance of blood pressure.

28. The passage supports which of the following conclusions?
    (A) The human body requires large amounts of most hormones.
    (B) Synthetic hormones can replace a person's natural supply of hormones if necessary.

(C) The quantity of hormones produced and their effects on the body are related to a person's age.

(D) The short child of tall parents very likely had a hormone deficiency early in life.

29. It can be inferred from the passage that, before the Bayliss and Starling experiments, most people believed that chemical integration occurred only ______.

(A) during sleep

(B) in the endocrine glands

(C) under control of the nervous system

(D) during strenuous exercise

30. In Line 14, the word "liberate" could best be replaced by which of the following?

(A) Emancipate.

(B) Discharge.

(C) Surrender.

(D) Save.

生词及短语

hormone ['hɔːməun]	*n.*	激素,荷尔蒙
impair [im'pɛə]	*v.*	削弱
inclination [inkli'neiʃən]	*n.*	倾向,爱好
aggressiveness [ə'gresivnis]	*n.*	积极性,好斗,闯劲
submissiveness [səb'misivnis]	*n.*	柔顺,服从
reproductive [riːprə'dʌktiv]	*a.*	生殖的,再生的
parental [pə'rentl]	*a.*	父母亲的
endocrine ['endəukrain]	*n.*	内分泌
gland [glænd]	*n.*	腺
integration [inti'greiʃən]	*n.*	综合
endocrinology [endəukrai'nɔlədʒi]	*n.*	内分泌学
secretion [si'kriʃən]	*n.*	分泌,分泌物
secrete ['siːkrit]	*vt.*	分泌
intestinal [in'testinl]	*a.*	肠的,肠内的
pancreas ['pænkriəs]	*n.*	胰腺
liberate ['libəreit]	*v.*	释放,解放
digestion [dai'dʒestʃən]	*n.*	消化力

exocrine [ˈeksəkrain]	*a.*	外分泌的
duct [dʌkt]	*n.*	管,输送管,排泄管
intestine [inˈtestin]	*n.*	肠

答案与解析

26. [答案] (B)

[解析] 本题为主旨题。第一段第一句指出了激素的重要性,后面内容详细介绍了有关激素的情况。在选项中,(A) 为第一段的内容,(C) 在第三段提到,(D) 为第二段的内容,都不能概括全文。而(B) 能概括全文,故(B) 为正确答案。

27. [答案] (D)

[解析] 文章提到了激素对人体的各种影响,包括对人的行为、情绪、体格、信息传递、内分泌等,但自始至终未提到过对人的血压的影响,故(D) 应为正确答案。

28. [答案] (C)

[解析] 第一段最后一句指出, 人体激素分泌的多少和人体对某些激素敏感的改变是年龄老化的根本方面。(C) 的内容最贴近题意,故(C) 为正确答案。

29. [答案] (C)

[解析] 第二段第一句指出"直到本世纪初,人体内信息传递和随之产生的举止行为都被认为是只能在神经系统内进行。"故(C) 为正确答案。

30. [答案] (B)

[解析] 第二段三句中 liberate 意为 "分泌, 释放", 指 "刺激胰腺分泌出胰腺液",(B) discharge 意为"释放",与之同义,故应为正确答案。

译文

如果某些激素不能正常提供,我们的活动能力就会受到严重影响;如果缺少另外一些激素,我们不久就会有生命危险。某些少量激素可以改变我们的情绪和行为、饮食喜好,还决定我们是好斗还是顺从,影响我们的生殖和其他行为。激素不仅对成年人的行为有影响,在人的幼年时期,就可以促进人体格的发展,甚至还可能决定个人的行为能力。在后来的生长过程中, 一些内分泌腺分泌量的大小变化和人体对某些激素的敏感程度改变都是年龄老化现象的基本表象。

到本世纪初,人体内的信息传递和随之产生的综合行为被认为只能在神经系统内进行。内分泌学作为一种独立学科的出现,可以追溯到贝利斯和施塔林对激素分泌物的试验。在食物进入胃时肠壁细胞便分泌出这种物质, 它通过血液流动, 刺激胰腺分泌帮助消化的胰腺液。通过向人们展示这些特殊细胞能分泌化学物质,这些物质并由血液传送以控制远处目标器官或组织，贝利斯和施塔林证明，在没有神经系统参与的情况下，这种化合作用照样发生。

"Hormone"一词刚开始是用来指分泌素。由施塔林取自希腊词 hormon，原意为"使激动或使行动"。不久，"endocrine"（内分泌）一词也被引入。"Endocrine"是指那些向血液分泌物质的腺体。与内分泌相对的词是外分泌，它是指那些通过输送管向活动部位排放分泌物的腺体，如泪腺、汗腺和胰腺，胰腺分泌的胰液通过输送管进入肠内。外分泌腺又称为管腺，内分泌腺称为无管腺。

Passage 3

Scattered through the seas of the world are billions of tons of small plants and animals called plankton. Most of these plants and animals are too small for the human eye to see. They drift about lazily with the currents, providing a basic food for many larger animals.

Plankton has been described as the equivalent of grasses that grow on the dry land continents, and the comparison is an appropriate one. In potential food value, however, plankton far outweighs that of the land grasses. One scientist has estimated that while grasses of the world produce about 49 billion tons of valuable carbohydrates each year, the sea's plankton generates more than twice as much.

Despite its enormous food potential, little effort was made until recently to farm plankton as we farm grasses on land. Now, marine scientists have at last begun to study this possibility, especially as the sea's resources loom even more important as a means of feeding an expanding world population.

No one yet has seriously suggested that "plankton burgers" may soon become popular around the world. As a possible farmed supplementary food source, however, plankton is gaining considerable interest among marine scientists.

One type of plankton that seems to have great harvest possibilities is a tiny shrimplike creature called krill. Growing to two or three inches long, krill provide the major food for the giant blue whale, the largest animal ever to inhabit the Earth. Realizing that this whale may grow to 100 feet and weigh 150 tons at maturity, it is not surprising that each one devours more than one ton of krill daily.

Krill swim about just below the surface in huge schools sometimes miles wide, mainly in the cold Antarctic. Because of their pink color, they often appear as a solid reddish mass when viewed from a ship or from the air. Krill are very high in food value. A pound of these crustaceans contains about 460 calories—about the same as shrimp or lobster, to which they are related.

If the krill can feed such huge creatures as whales, many scientists reason, they must certainly be contenders as a new food source for humans.

31. Which of the following statements best describes the organization of the passage?

(A) The author presents the advantages and disadvantages of plankton as a food source.

(B) The author quotes public opinion to support the argument for farming plankton.

(C) The author classifies the different food sources according to amount of carbohydrate.

(D) The author makes a general statement about plankton as a food source and then moves to a specific example.

32. According to the passage, why is plankton considered to be more valuable than land grasses?

(A) It is easier to cultivate.

(B) It produces more carbohydrates.

(C) It does not require soil.

(D) It is more palatable.

33. Blue whales have been known to weigh how much at maturity?

(A) One ton.

(B) Forty tons.

(C) One hundred and fifty tons.

(D) Four hundred and sixty tons.

34. The author mentions all of the following as reasons why plankton could be considered a human food source EXCEPT that it is ______.

(A) high in food value

(B) in abundant supply in the oceans

(C) an appropriate food for other animals

(D) free of chemicals and pollutants

35. Where in the passage does the author first compare plankton to land grasses?

(A) Lines 2—3.

(B) Lines 5—6.

(C) Lines 10—12.

(D) Lines 17—18.

生词及短语

plankton ['plæŋkt(ə)n]	*n.*	浮游生物
equivalent [i'kwivələnt]	*a.*	相当的,相等的
outweigh [aut'wei]	*v.*	在总量(或价值等)上超过

carbohydrate [kɑːbəu'haidreit]	*n.*	碳水化合物
loom [luːm]	*v.*	隐现,迫近
burger ['bəːgə]	*n.*	碎肉夹饼,各种夹饼
supplementary [sʌpli'mentəri]	*a.*	附加的,增补的
shrimp [ʃrimp]	*n.*	小虾
krill [kril]	*n.*	磷虾
devour [di'vauə]	*vt.*	吞吃
reddish ['rediʃ]	*a.*	微红的,略带红色的
crustacean [krʌs'teiʃjən]	*n.*	甲壳类
calories ['kæləri]	*n.*	卡路里
lobster ['lɔbstə]	*n.*	龙虾
contender [kən'tendə(r)]	*n.*	竞争者

答案与解析

31. [答案] (D)

[解析] 从各选项来看,(A) 与(B) 文中均未提及,而(B) 中 carbohydrate 虽在文中出现过,但与文章结构无关。从文章结构来看,第一段首先指出"浮游生物为海洋中众多较大的鱼类提供食物",接着以具体的例子分析浮游生物成为人类食物的可能性。从这两点,可确定(D) 应为正确答案。

32. [答案] (B)

[解析] 第二段最后一句指出,科学家估计,每年世界上的草大约能提供 490 亿吨的碳水化合物,而海水中浮游生物可提供的碳水化合物超过两倍,故(B) 明显应为答案。

33. [答案] (C)

[解析] 第四段第三句指出"Realizing that this whale may grow to 100 feet and weigh 150 tons at maturity ...",故(C) 应为答案。

34. [答案] (D)

[解析] 本题用排除法。(A) 在第二段最后一句提到;(B) 在第一段的第一句谈及;第五段提到了(C);唯有(D) 文中未提及,所以(D) 应为答案。

35. [答案] (B)

[解析] 在第二段 "Plankton has been described as the equivalent of grasses that ... is an appropriate one."作者首次将浮游生物与草相比。故答案应为(B)。

译文

全世界的海洋中散居着数十亿吨我们称之为“浮游生物”的小植物和小动物。它们大多数都很小,不能用肉眼观察到。它们自在地随水流而动,为许多较大的海洋动物提供食物。

人们一直把浮游生物与陆地上生长的草相提并论,这种比较是很合适的。然而从潜在的食物价值角度来讲,浮游生物远远超过草类。一位科学家曾估计,全世界的草每年可产生约490亿吨有价值的碳水化合物,而海洋中的浮游生物产生的数量比这要多两倍多。

虽然浮游生物具有巨大的食物潜力,但直到最近,人们才试图像在陆地上种草一样养殖浮游生物。现在,海洋学家终于开始对这种可能性进行研究,特别是因海洋资源可作为日益增长的世界人口的一种食物来源而显得更为重要。

至今尚未有人认真提出“浮游生物夹饼”不久会风靡全球。然而,作为一种可养殖的食物资源,浮游生物已经引起了海洋学家们的很大兴趣。

有一类浮游生物看来产量可能极大,这是一种称为磷虾的微小生物。它们能长到2—3英寸长,是地球上至今最庞大的动物——蓝鲸的主食。想到这种蓝鲸成熟时能长到100英尺长,150吨重,那么它一天能吞食一吨多磷虾就不会令人惊奇了。

磷虾成群地游于海面下,有时达数英里宽,主要生活在寒冷的南极洲。由于它们是粉红色的,所以当从船上或空中观看时,它们就像一块巨大的红色固体,磷虾的食用价值很高,一磅这类壳类动物含有大约460卡路里,和与它们相关的小虾和龙虾相同。

许多科学家认为,既然磷虾能成为像鲸这样庞大的动物的食物,它也一定会成为人类新食物资源的竞争者。

Passage 4

The years between 1870 and 1895 brought enormous changes to the theater in the United States as the resident company was undermined by touring groups, as New York became the only major center of production, and as the long run superseded the repertory system. By 1870, the resident stock company was at the peak of its development in the United States. The 50 permanent companies of 1870, however, had dwindled to 20 by 1878, to 8 by 1880, to 4 by 1887, and had almost disappeared by 1900.

While the causes of this change are numerous, probably the most important was the rise of the “combination” company (that is, one that travels with star and full company) . Sending out a complete production was merely a logical extension of touring by stars. By the 1840s, many major actors were already taking along a small group of lesser players, for they could not be sure that local companies could supply adequate support in secondary roles.

There is much disagreement about the origin of the combination company. Boucicault claims to have initiated it around 1860 when he sent out a troupe with *Colleen Bawn*, but a book published in 1859 speaks of combination companies as already established. Joseph Jefferson III also declared that he was a pioneer in the movement. In actuality, the practice probably began tentatively during the 1850s, only to be interrupted by the Civil War. *It* mushroomed in the 1870s, as the rapid expansion of the railway system made it increasingly feasible to transport full productions. In 1872, Lawrence Barrett took his company, but no scenery, on tour; in 1876, *Rose Michel* was sent out with full company, scenery, and properties. By the season of 1876—1877 there were nearly 100 combination companies on the road, and by 1886 there were 282.

36. What is the best title for the passage?
   (A) The Development of the Combination Company
   (B) Boucicault's Contribution to the Theater
   (C) How the Repertory System Affected Dramatic Productions
   (D) The Importance of the Theater in the United States

37. Which of the following events is NOT listed as a reason for the decline of the resident stock company?
   (A) The rise of touring companies.
   (B) The outbreak of the Civil War.
   (C) The growing importance of New York as a production center.
   (D) The replacement of the repertory theater by the long run.

38. In what year did the largest number of resident stock companies exist?
   (A) 1840.
   (B) 1860.
   (C) 1870.
   (D) 1895.

39. "It" in Line 5 in the last paragraph refers to the ______.
   (A) the Civil War
   (B) use of combination companies
   (C) westward movement of pioneers
   (D) rapid expansion of the railroad

40. Lawrence Barrett is mentioned in the passage because he ______.
   (A) was the founder of the combination company
   (B) produced the play Rose Michel
   (C) was a well-known actor who traveled with many touring companies
   (D) took one of the early combination companies on tour

生词及短语

resident [ˈrezidənt]	*a.*	常驻的,居住的
supersede [suːpəˈsiːd]	*vt.*	代替,取代
repertory [reˈpətəri]	*n.*	常备,仓库
combination [kɔmbiˈneiʃ(ə) n]	*n.*	联合,混合,结合
troupe [truːp]	*n.*	剧团
tentatively [ˈtentətivli]	*ad.*	试验性地,暂时地

答案与解析

36. [答案] (A)

[解析] 本题为主旨题。本文讲述美国戏剧发生的变化，其中除第一段叙述了驻地剧团(resident company)的衰落,其余内容完全讲述混合剧团(combination company)的兴起与发展的情况,故答案为(A)。其他选项明显与主题无关。

37. [答案] (B)

[解析] 从本文第一句中三个由 as 引导的状语从句“... as the resident company was undermined by touring groups, as New York became the only major center of production, and as the long run superseded the repertory system.”准确地说明了驻地剧团衰落的原因,分别与(A)、(C)、(D) 的内容相符。文中未涉及到内战的爆发,故答案应为(B)。

38. [答案] (C)

[解析] 本文第一段第二句开头“By 1870 ...”给出了正确答案为(C)。

39. [答案] (B)

[解析] 本题为代词的指代问题。一般根据上下文，特别是根据前面所提到的内容来判断。从前句内容来看,主语是 the practice,而 the practice 和前面所说的建立混合剧团的行动是一回事,因而可推断出正确答案为(B)。从内容来看 it 指代(A) 不可能;(C) 的内容本文没有涉及,而(D) 在内容上重复,因而均可排除。

40. [答案] (D)

[解析] 由第三段倒数第二句前半句 “In 1872, Lawrence Barrett took his company, ... on tour;”可知答案为(D)。

译文

在1870至1895年间,美国的戏剧发生了巨大的变化,其原因是因为驻地剧团被巡回剧团所削弱,而纽约成了惟一一个主要的演出中心,同时连台演出取代了常备剧目制度。到1870年,驻地股份剧团公司在美国已经发展到了顶峰。1870年永久性剧团有50个,然而到了1878年已经减少到20个,1880年仅剩下8个,1887年剩下4个,而到了1900年,几乎已经完全消失。

引起这一变化的原因虽然很多,但最重要的也许是"混合"剧团的兴起(混合剧团即明星与整个剧团一起旅行的剧团)。派出一个完整的演出团体不过是明星们巡回演出的必然发展。到了19世纪40年代,许多主要的演员已经带领着演员不多的小戏班子了,因为他们不能确定地方剧团是否能为他们提供足够的次要角色。

关于混合剧团的起源,说法很不相同。布歇柯尔特声称自己是创始人,他在1860年前后就曾派出一个出演《科连·鲍恩》的剧团,但一本1859年出版的著作却说混合剧团已经成立。约瑟夫·杰斐逊三世也宣称他是该运动的先驱。实际上,这种实践在19世纪50年代可能已开始尝试,只不过因内战而中断。到19世纪70年代它又迅速发展,因为铁道系统的迅速扩张使运送整个剧团的可能性增大。1872年劳伦斯·巴雷特带着剧团巡回演出,却没有带布景。到1876年巡回上演《罗丝·米切尔》时,却带着整个剧团、全套布景和财产。到了1876—1877年的演出季节,已有将近一百个混合剧团在巡回演出,而到了1886年,则已达到280个了。

阅读 B 篇

Directions:

In the following article, some sentences have been removed. For Questions 41—45, choose the most suitable one from the list A—G to fit into each of the numbered blanks. There are two extra choices, which do not fit in any of the blanks. Mark your answers on ANSWER SHEET 1. (10 points)

Civil law determines a person's legal rights and obligations in many kinds of activities that involve other people. Such activities include everything from borrowing or lending money to buying a home or signing a job contract.

The great majority of lawyers and judges spend most of their time dealing with private-law matters. Lawyers handle most of these matters out of court. But numerous situations arise in which a judge or jury must decide if a person's private-law rights have been violated. 41.__________.

Private law can be divided into six major branches according to the kinds of legal rights and obligations involved. These branches are contract and commercial law, tort law, property law, inheritance law, family law, and corporation law. 42. ________.

Contract and commercial law deals with the rights and obligations of people who make contracts. A contract is an agreement between two or more persons that can be enforced by law. A wide variety of business activities depend on the use of contracts. A business firm makes contracts both with other firms, such as suppliers and transporters, and with private persons, such as customers and employees.

43. ________. The victim may sue the person or persons responsible. Tort law deals with the rights and obligations of the persons involved in such cases. Many torts are unintentional, such as damages in traffic accidents. But if a tort is deliberate and involves serious harm, it may be treated as a crime.

Property law governs the ownership and use of property. Property may be real, such as land and buildings, or personal, such as an automobile and clothing. The law ensures a person's right to own property. However, the owner must use the property lawfully. 44. ________.

Inheritance law concerns the transfer of property upon the death of the owner. Nearly every country has basic inheritance laws, which list the relatives or other persons who have first rights of inheritance. But in most Western nations, people may will their property to persons other than those specified by law. In such cases, inheritance law also sets the rules for the making of wills.

Family law determines the legal rights and obligations of husbands and wives and of parents and children. It covers such matters as marriage, divorce, adoption, and child support.

Corporation law governs the formation and operation of business corporations. 45. ________.

(A) The dividing line between the various branches is not always clear, however. For example, many cases of property law also involve contract law.

(B) Responsibility is a social, legal, or moral requirement, such as a duty, contract, or promise that compels one to follow or avoid a particular course of action.

(C) A tort is a wrong or injury that a person suffers because of someone else's action. The action may cause bodily harm, damage a person's property, business, or reputation, or make unauthorized use of a person's property.

(D) More than 10 million such cases are filed in United States courts each year. These cases are called lawsuits or civil suits.

(E) People also have the right to sell or lease their property and to buy or rent the property of others. Property law determines a person's rights and obligations involved in such dealings.

(F) Civil law refers to the body of laws of a state or nation dealing with the rights of private citizens.

(G) It deals mainly with the powers and obligations of management and the rights of stockholders. Corporation law is often classed together with contract and commercial law as business law.

内容提要

文章主要谈论民法。第一段指出,民法决定一个人在涉及其他人的多种活动中的法律权利和义务,这些活动包括从借款或贷款买房到签署一份工作合同。

第二段指出,大多数律师和法官花费大部分时间处理个人法律事务。律师在法庭外解决大多数案子。但各种情况均会出现,法官和陪审团必须决定个人的人权是否遭受侵犯。

答案与解析

41. [答案] (D)

[解析] 文章主要谈论民法。本段指出,大多数律师和法官花费大部分时间处理个人法律事务。律师在法庭外解决大多数案子。但各种情况均会出现,法官和陪审团必须决定个人的人权是否遭受侵犯。从上下文来看,空白处应该继续谈论民事案子。而(D) 意为"美国每年有超过 1,000 万的这类案子在法院备案。这些案子称为诉讼或民事诉讼。"其中"such cases"与前面提到的案子相吻合。

42. [答案] (A)

[解析] 本段主要讨论私有法划分的种类包括的有:合同和商业法、民事侵权行为法、财产法、遗产法、家庭法和公司法。空白处内容应与这些种类相关。(A) 指出:然而,这些分类并不是总是很清楚,例如,财产法的许多案例涉及合同法。

43. [答案] (C)

[解析] 空白处后面第一句提到受害者可以起诉当事人或有责任的人。接着谈到民事侵权行为法处理卷入这些案子的当事人的权利和义务。可见本段是在谈论民事侵权行为,而(C) 第一句便解释什么是民事侵权行为,从逻辑上相符。

44. [答案] (E)

[解析] 本段主要叙述财产法,它涉及所有权和财产的使用,这个法律保障个人拥有财产的权利。从上下文看,空白处应该涉及财产和财产法。(E) 的内容与财产和财产法相关,故应为正确答案。

45. [答案] (G)

[解析] 本段叙述公司法,它涉及商业股份公司的组成和经营。空白处应该填入与公司法相关的内容,(G) 的内容涉及公司法,应为正确答案。

阅读 C 篇

Directions:

Read the following text carefully and then translate the underlined segments into Chinese. Your translation should be written neatly on ANSWER SHEET 2.(10 points)

My eldest daughter, an Internet consultant, is only 30, but she has already lived in five different houses in five different places and has had about six different jobs. Every time I visit her, I notice how many new things there are in her house, and how many things lie unused, out of date. What is even more striking is how many things there are which are not expected to last—disposable things. Disposable plates and glasses, disposable towels and babies' nappies. It sometimes seems that we live in an age of the disposable.

(46) This phenomenon of constant change runs through everything in life nowadays, from fashion to music, from medicine to motor cars, from education to employment. Two important factories seem to be driving these changes. The first is the rapid growth in knowledge and the consequent rapid development of technology. The second is the revolution in communications, which means that knowledge is spread faster and more widely than ever. Our times are often called "the information age" and the effect is to bring about "the knowledge economy." New technologies and new knowledge bring about the need for new skills. (47) The speed with which these technologies are being created is such that all of us are faced with the challenge of learning new skills, not just once, but several times. What we knew yesterday is often obsolete today.

I remember my daughter saying to me that she was at "the cutting edge" of her particular field. But within five years, she said, she would have to do something new and different to keep up. There is a greater need for flexibility and problem-solving than before. Tasks require a greater integration of skills. (48) The rewards of life go to the multi-skilled, to flexible teams of workers each capable of contributing in a range of ways. (49) To succeed in this new world of work, individuals will have to regard their careers not just as a process of gathering experience, but as a process of learning new things on an almost continuous basis. All this suggests to me that the relationship between education and employment has changed radically over the last few years.

(50) One could summarize the change by saying that when I grew up. I learned things in order to achieve life-long employment, while my children need to pursue life-long learning in order to stay employed.

生词及短语

consultant [kən'sʌltənt]	*n.*	顾问,咨询师
disposable [dis'pəuzəbl]	*a.*	一次性的,可随意使用的
obsolete ['ɔbsəliːt]	*a.*	陈旧的,荒废的
cutting edge		刀刃,刃口
integration [inti'greiʃən]	*n.*	综合,集成

全文译文与答案

我的大女儿是一位互联网咨询师,30岁,但她已经在5个不同的地方居住过5个不同的房子,有过大概6种不同的工作。每一次我去看她,我都会注意在她房子里有很多新东西,有很多东西堆在那里没有使用过或者已经过期。更令人惊奇的是有很多东西是不打算继续使用的一次性的东西。一次性的盘子和玻璃杯、一次性的毛巾和婴儿尿布。有时候我们像是生活在一个一次性的时代。

(46) 现在,生活都在不断变化中。从时尚到音乐,从医药到汽车,从教育到工作,一切如此。有两项因素似乎在推动这些变化。第一项是知识的快速发展和随之而来的快速技术发展。第二项是通信革命,这意味着知识比任何时候都传播得更快、更广泛。我们的时代通常称为"信息时代",其影响是要产生"知识经济"。新技术和新知识导致新技能的产生。(47) 这些新技术产生的速度是如此之快,以至于我们所有的人都面临学习新技能的挑战,而且不仅仅是学一次,而是要学好几次。昨天我们知道的东西,常常今天就变得陈旧了。

我记得我女儿对我说过,她处于一个自己特殊领域的"刀刃"上。但在五年之内,她说,她会干一些不同的事情以跟上时代。需要比从前有更多的灵活性和解决问题的能力。工作任务需要更多的技能综合来完成。(48) 那些掌握多种技能、灵活多变的人士将得到生活的回报,他们个个都能以多种方式为社会做出贡献。(49) 要想在这片新的工作天地中立于不败之地,人人都必须把自己的事业不仅仅看做是积累经验的过程,而且看做是不断学习新事物的过程。所有这些都在暗示我,在教育和就业之间的关系在最近几年已经发生了根本的变化。

(50) 一个人可能这样总结这种变化:当我成长的时候,我学东西是为了找到终身职业;而我的孩子们都必须一生学习以免失业。

阅读强化练习六

阅读 A 篇

Directions:

Read the following four texts. Answer the questions below each text by choosing A, B, C or D. Mark your answers on ANSWER SHEET 1. (40 points)

Passage 1

The most interesting architectural phenomenon of the 1970s was the enthusiasm for refurbishing older buildings. Obviously, this was not an entirely new phenomenon. What is new is the wholesale in reusing the past, in recycling, in adaptive rehabilitation. A few trial efforts, such as Ghirardelli Square in San Francisco, proved their financial viability in the 1960s, but it was in the 1970s, with strong government support through tax incentives and rapid depreciation, as well as growing interest in ecology issues, that recycling became a major factor on the urban scene.

One of the most comprehensive ventures was the restoration and transformation of Boston's eighteenth century Fancuil Hall and the Quincy Market, designed in 1824. This section had fallen on hard times, but beginning with the construction of a new city hall immediately adjacent, it has returned to life with the intelligent reuse of these fine old buildings under the design leadership of Benjamin Thompson. He has provided a marvelous setting for dining, shopping, professional office, and simply walking.

Butler Square, in Minneapolis, exemplifies major changes in its complex of offices, commercial space, and public amenities carved out of a massive pile designed in 1906 as a hardware warehouse. The exciting interior timber structure of the building was highlighted by cutting light courts through the interior and adding large skylights.

San Antonio, Texas, offers an object lesson for numerous other cities combating urban decay. Rather than bringing in the bulldozers, San Antonio's leaders rehabilitated existing structures, while simultaneously cleaning up the San Antonio River, which meanders through the business district.

21. What is the main idea of the passage?
(A) During the 1970s, old buildings in many cities were recycled for modern use.
(B) Recent interest in ecology issues has led to the cleaning up of many rivers.
(C) The San Antonio example shows that bulldozers are not the way to fight urban decay.
(D) Strong government support has made adaptive rehabilitation a reality in Boston.

22. According to the passage, Benjamin Thompson was the designer for a project in ______.
(A) San Francisco
(B) Boston
(C) Minneapolis
(D) San Antonio

23. When was the Butler Square building originally built?
(A) In the eighteenth century.
(B) In the early nineteenth century.
(C) In the late nineteenth century.
(D) In the early twentieth century.

24. What is the author's opinion of the San Antonio's project?
(A) It is clearly the best of the projects discussed.
(B) It is a good project that could be copied in other cities.
(C) The extensive use of bulldozers made the project unnecessarily costly.
(D) The work done on the river was more important than the work done on the buildings.

25. The passage states that the San Antonio project differed from those in Boston and Minneapolis in which of the following ways?
(A) It consisted primarily of new construction.
(B) It occurred in the business district.
(C) It involved the environment as well as buildings.
(D) It was designed to combat urban decay.

生词及短语

refurbish [riːˈfəːbiʃ] *vt.* 刷新，整修

wholesale ['həulseil]	*a.*	批发的,大规模的
adaptive [ə'dæptiv]	*a.*	适应的
rehabilitation [riː(h) əbili'teiʃən]	*n.*	复原
viability [vaiə'biliti]	*n.*	生存能力
incentive [in'sentiv]	*n.*	动机,激励
depreciation [dipriːʃi'eiʃən]	*n.*	贬值,减价,折旧
restoration [restə'reiʃən]	*n.*	恢复,修复
transformation [trænsfə'meiʃən]	*n.*	变化,转化
adjacent [ə'dʒeisənt]	*a.*	邻近的,接近的
exemplify [ig'zemplifai]	*vt.*	例证,例示
amenity [ə'miːniti]	*n.*	宜人,礼仪
warehouse ['wɛəhaus]	*n.*	仓库,货栈
timber ['timbə]	*n.*	木材,木料
highlight ['hailait]	*vt.*	使显著,突出
skylight ['skailait]	*n.*	天窗
an object lesson		一堂实物教学课
bulldozer ['buldəuzə]	*n.*	推土机
meander [mi'ændə]	*v.*	蜿蜒而流

答案与解析

21. [答案] (**A**)

[解析] 本题为主旨题。文章第一句便点明了主题"20 世纪 70 年代建筑业最有趣的现象便是整修老建筑",而(A) 与此意相符,故(A) 应为正确答案。

22. [答案] (**B**)

[解析] 第二段第一、二句提到,波士顿的一些 18 世纪的老建筑都被翻修,翻修工作是"under the design leadership of Benjamin Thompson",故(B) 应为正确答案。

23. [答案] (**D**)

[解析] 第三段第一句指出巴特勒广场是在 1906 年设计的,即 20 世纪早期,故答案应为(D)。

24. [答案] (**B**)

[解析] 第四段第一句指出, 得克萨斯州的圣安东尼奥市为其他许多城市在与城市环境衰退作斗争方面提供了范例(an object lesson 意为"一堂实物教学课"),这与(B) 的内容相符,故(B) 应为正确答案。

25. [答案] (C)

[解析] 第四段第二句话指出“圣安东尼奥市的领导没有使用推土机推倒现存建筑，而是使其复原，同时也净化了从商业区蜿蜒而过的圣安东尼奥河”，故(C) 应为正确答案。

译文

20 世纪 70 年代建筑界最有趣的现象是对老建筑的修复。显然这并非什么全新现象。新鲜的是人们大规模地重新利用过去的建筑，对其再生利用，适应性地复原。在 60 年代，有几次尝试(例如旧金山的克拉德里广场) 证明了翻修的经济可行性。但直到 70 年代，翻修成为改变都市风景的主要手段，这是因为政府通过税收激励和加快折旧来支持这项行动，同时也由于人们对生态问题越来越关注。

最为复杂的一项工程要算是对波士顿 18 世纪的芬纽尔大厅和 1840 年设计的昆西商场的修复和转变。该街区是在艰难时期败落的，但随着一座紧邻的新市政大厅的开建，在设计师本杰明·汤普森的领导设计下，对这些漂亮的古老建筑巧妙地进行了利用，使它们重获新生。设计师为人们提供了一个就餐、购物、办公或散步的场所。

明尼阿波利斯的巴特勒广场原是 1906 年设计的做五金仓库用的一座高大建筑物，现在展现了重大的变化，它已经被精心改造成为一座集综合性办公室、商业区和公众康乐场所为一体的大厦。最令人惊喜的是这座建筑的内部木质结构是通过内部庭院采光，顶部加开了很大的天窗。

得克萨斯州的圣安东尼奥市在与城市环境退化作斗争方面为其他城市提供了范例。城市领导不是用推土机推倒现有建筑，而是进行修缮，同时也清洁了从商业区蜿蜒而过的圣安东尼奥河。

Passage 2

The classic Neanderthals who lived between about 70,000 and 30,000 years ago, shared a number of special characteristics. Like any biological population, Neanderthals also showed variation in the degree to which those characteristics were expressed. Generally, they were powerfully built, short and stocky, with the lower parts of their arms and legs short in relation to the upper parts, as in modern peoples who live in cold environments. Neanderthal skulls were distinctive, housing brains even larger on average than those of modern humans, a feature that may have had more to do with their large, heavy bodies than with superior intelligence. Seen from behind, Neanderthal skulls look almost spherical, but from the side they are long and flattened, often with a bulging back.

The Neanderthal face, dominated by a projecting and full nose, differed clearly from the faces of other hominids; the middle parts appear to be pulled forward (or the side pulled back), resulting in a rather streamlined face shape. This peculiarity may have been related to the greater importance (in cultural activities as well as food processing) of the front teeth, which are large and part of a row of teeth that lies well forward in the head; it may reflect a reduction in importance of certain jaw muscles operating at the sides of the face; or it may reflect an adaptation to cold. Whether it results from any or all of these three factors or from other, undiscovered causes, this midfacial projection is so characteristic that it unfailingly identifies a Neanderthal to the trained eye. Neanderthal teeth are much more difficult to characterize; the front teeth are large, with strong roots, but the back teeth may be relatively small. This feature may have been an adaptation to cope with heavy tooth wear.

26. What does the passage mainly discuss?
   (A) The eating habits of the Neanderthals.
   (B) A comparison of various prehistoric populations.
   (C) The physical characteristics of the Neanderthals.
   (D) The effect of climate on human development.

27. The author describes the Neanderthals as being all of the following EXCEPT ______.
   (A) short
   (B) swift
   (C) strong
   (D) stocky

28. Which of the following most likely accounts for the fact that the Neanderthal brain was larger than that of the modern human?
   (A) The relatively large size of the Neanderthal.
   (B) The superior intelligence of the Neanderthal.
   (C) The swelling behind the Neanderthal's head.
   (D) The Neanderthal's midfacial projection.

29. In the last line, the author uses the expression "heavy tooth wear" to imply that the Neanderthals ______.
   (A) had unusually heavy teeth
   (B) used their teeth extensively
   (C) regularly pulled out their teeth
   (D) used teeth for ornamentation

30. The paragraph following this passage most probably discusses ______.
   (A) other features of the Neanderthal anatomy
   (B) cave paintings of prehistoric time
   (C) flora and fauna of 70,000 years ago
   (D) difficulties in preserving fossils

生词及短语

Neanderthal [ni'ændətɑːl]	*n.*	尼安德特人
biological [baiə'lɔdʒikəl]	*a.*	生物学的
stocky ['stɔki]	*a.*	矮壮的,健壮结实的
skull [skʌl]	*n.*	头骨,头脑
spherical ['sferikəl]	*a.*	球的,球形的
flatten ['flætn]	*v.*	扁平
bulging ['bʌldʒiŋ]	*n.*	膨胀,凸出(部)
projecting [prəu'dʒektiŋ]	*a.*	突出的,伸出的
hominid ['hɔminid]	*n.*	原始人类
jaw [dʒɔː]	*n.*	颚,下巴
midfacial [mid'feiʃəl]	*a.*	半边脸的
unfailingly [ʌn'feiliŋli]	*ad.*	可靠地

答案与解析

26. [答案] (C)

[解析] 本题为主旨题。本篇文章描述了尼安德特人的身体特征,包括身高、体型、四肢、头盖骨、鼻子、脸和牙齿等的特征,与(C) 相符,故(C) 应为答案。

27. [答案] (B)

[解析] 第一段第三句提到尼安德特人的特点时指出"they were powerfully built, short and stocky ...",故可以排除 (A)、(C) 和(D),只有 (B) swift 文中没有提到,(B) 应为正确答案。

28. [答案] (A)

[解析] 第一段第四句指出,尼安德特人的大脑比现代人大,这一特征不是与智力有关,而是跟他们体型大和重量有关,故(A) 应为正确答案。

29. [答案] (B)

[解析] 文章最后两句指出,尼安德特人的门牙大,牙根牢固,但臼齿相对小。这个特征是

因为牙齿过多磨损所致，故(B) 明显应为正确答案。

30. [答案] (A)

[解析] 在文章的第一段，作者从解剖学角度描述了尼安德特人身体突出的特征，第二段描述头部特点，而其他部分则还没有详细讨论，故可推测作者会继续讨论其他特征，(A) 应为正确答案。

译文

生活在70,000至30,000年以前的典型尼安德特人具有一些特别的特征。和其他生物群体一样，这些特征同样显示出他们变化的程度。一般说来，他们身体强壮、个子矮小，四肢的下半部比上半部短，这与现在生活在寒冷环境的现代人相似。尼安德特人的头盖骨与众不同，头内的脑髓平均比现代人大，这种特征更多的与其粗壮的身体有关而与智力无关。从背后看，尼安德特人的头盖骨几乎是球形的，但从侧面看则是长而扁平的，后部常常突出。

尼安德特人的脸部明显与其他原始人类不同，宽大的鼻子向前突出，面部中间部分往前凸(或说两边部分向后凹)，成为非常流线型的脸形。这一特点或许与前牙(在文化活动和饮食中)起特别重要的作用有关。尼安德特人的门牙很大，整排牙齿在头部很明显地突出在外；这也许是面部两侧一些颚肌退化的结果，或许是为了适应寒冷气候的缘故。不管这是其中一种因素或是以上三种因素，还是其他未发现因素作用的结果，这种脸中部向前突出的特点非常特别，使有经验的人能可靠地确认出尼安德特人。尼安德特人牙的特点很难描述，他们的门牙很大，牙根牢固，但臼齿相对较小。这一特征可能是为了适应繁重的咀嚼。

Passage 3

In the late 1960's, many people in North America turned their attention to environmental problems, and new steel-and-glass skyscrapers were widely criticized. Ecologists pointed out that a cluster of tall buildings in a city often overburdens public transportation and parking lot capacities.

Skyscrapers are also lavish consumers, and wasters of electric power. In one recent year, the addition of 17 million square feet of skyscraper office space in New York City raised the peak daily demand for electricity by 120,000 kilowatts—enough to supply the entire city of Albany, New York, for a day.

Glass walled skyscrapers can be especially wasteful. The heat loss (or gain) through a wall of half-inch plate glass is more than ten times that through a typical masonry wall filled with insulation board. To lessen the strain on heating and air-conditioning equipment, builders of skyscrapers have begun to use double-glazed panels of glass, and reflective glasses coated with silver or gold mirror films that reduce glare as well as heat gain. However, mirror-walled skyscrapers raise the temperature of the surrounding air and affect neighboring buildings.

Skyscrapers put a severe strain on a city's sanitation facilities, too. If fully occupied, the two World Trade Center towers in New York City would alone generate 2.25 million gallons of raw sewage each year—as much as a city the size of Stamford, Connecticut, which has a population of more than 109,000.

Skyscrapers also interfere with television reception, block bird flyways, and obstruct air traffic. In Boston in the late 1960s, some people even feared that shadows from skyscrapers would kill the grass on Boston Common.

Still, people continue to build skyscrapers for all the reasons that they have always built them—personal ambition, civic pride, and the desire of owners to have the largest possible amount of rentable space.

31. The main purpose of the passage is to ______.

(A) compare skyscrapers with other modern structures

(B) describe skyscrapers and their effect on the environment

(C) advocate the use of masonry in the construction of skyscrapers

(D) illustrate some architectural designs of skyscrapers

32. According to the passage, what is one disadvantage of skyscrapers that have mirrored walls?

(A) The exterior surrounding air is heated.

(B) The windows must be cleaned daily.

(C) Construction time is increased.

(D) Extra air-conditioning equipment is needed.

33. According to the passage, in the late 1960s some residents of Boston were concerned with which aspect of skyscrapers?

(A) The noise from their construction.

(B) The removal of trees from building sites.

(C) The harmful effects on the city's grass.

(D) The high cost of rentable office space.

34. The author raises issues that would most concern which of the following groups?

(A) Electricians.

(B) Environmentalists.

(C) Aviators.

(D) Teachers.

35. Where in the passage does the author compare the energy consumption of skyscrapers with that of a city?

(A) Lines 5—8.

(B) Lines 14—15.

(C) Lines 21—22.

(D) Lines 23—25.

生词及短语

ecologist [i'kɔlədʒist]	*n.*	生态学家
cluster ['klʌstə]	*n.*	成群,成串
overburden [əuvə'bəːdn]	*vt.*	负担过重
parking lot		停车场
lavish ['læviʃ]	*vt.*	浪费,滥用
masonry ['meisnri]	*a.*	石工的
insulation [insju'leiʃən]	*n.*	绝缘
double-glazed		双层玻璃的
panel ['pænl]	*n.*	面板
sanitation [sæni'teiʃən]	*n.*	卫生
gallon ['gælən]	*n.*	加仑
sewage ['sju(ː) idʒ]	*n.*	污水,下水道
obstruct [əb'strʌkt]	*v.*	阻碍,妨碍
civic ['sivik]	*a.*	城市的,市民的,公民的
rentable ['rəntəbl]	*a.*	可出租的

答案与解析

31. [答案](B)

[解析]本题为主旨题。文章在开头第一句点明了主题,60年代后期,北美很多人开始关注环境问题,新建摩天大楼遭到了众人的指责。后面段落就摩天大楼对环境的影响进行了详尽的叙述,故答案应为(B)。

32. [答案](A)

[解析]第三段最后一句指出, 以镜子作为墙壁的摩天大楼会使周围空气温度升高并影响邻近的建筑。(A) 应为正确答案。

33. [答案] (C)

[解析] 第五段最后一句指出，在 60 年代末的波士顿，有些人甚至害怕摩天大楼的阴影会伤害波士顿公地的草坪，故(C) 应为正确答案。

34. [答案] (B)

[解析] 文中所列举的由摩天大楼造成的环境问题，环境学家自然会最关心，而不会是一般教师、飞行员和电工所关心的主要问题，故答案应为(B)。

35. [答案] (A)

[解析] 第二段第二句指出，纽约市面积达 1,700 万平方英尺的摩天大楼办公室日需电量达 1.2 万千瓦，足够纽约州整个奥尔巴尼市用一整天的。故(A) 是正确答案。

译文

在 20 世纪 60 年代末，许多北美人开始关注环境问题。新钢铁玻璃结构的摩天大楼受到了大众的批评。生态学家指出，在城市中建造成群的高大建筑会加重城市公共交通和停车场的负担。

摩天大楼也是电力的滥用者和浪费者。在最近一年中，纽约市增加的 1,700 万平方英尺的办公面积使得日用电量高达 1.2 万千瓦，足够纽约州整个奥尔巴尼市一天的用电。

玻璃墙摩天大楼的浪费更是惊人。通过半英寸厚的玻璃板散发(或吸收) 热量的速度要比装有绝缘板的一般砖石墙的速度快 10 多倍。为了减小加热和空调设备的压力，摩天大楼的建筑师们开始使用双层玻璃板，以及镀上银或金镜膜的反光玻璃来降低反光和吸热。然而，以镜子作为墙壁的大楼会使周围空气温度升高而影响相邻建筑。

摩天大楼也给城市卫生设施增加了极大压力。如果纽约市两座世贸大厦都住满人，每年就会排出 225 万加仑的污水——与拥有 10.9 万多人口的康涅狄格州的斯坦福市的排污量一样。摩天大楼还会干扰电视接收，阻挡鸟的飞行并阻碍航空交通。在 60 年代末的波士顿，有些人甚至担心摩天大楼的阴影会伤害波士顿的公用草坪。

但是，人们仍然会有各种理由继续建造摩天大楼——个人雄心、城市的骄傲以及主人对最大出租面积的欲望。

Passage 4

What does a scientist do when he or she "explains" something? Scientific explanation comes in two forms: generalization and reduction. Most psychologists deal with generalization. They explain particular instances of behavior as examples of general laws. For instance most psychologists would explain a pathologically strong fear of dogs as an example of classical conditioning. Presumably, the person was frightened earlier in life by a dog. An unpleasant stimulus was paired with the sight of the animal (perhaps the person was knocked down by an exuberant dog) and the subsequent sight of dogs evokes the earlier response—fear.

Most physiologists deal with reduction. Phenomena are explained in terms of simpler phenomena. For example, the movement of a muscle is explained in terms of changes in the membrane of muscle cells, entry of particular chemicals, and interactions between protein molecules within these cells. A molecular biologist would "explain" these events in terms of forces that bind various molecules together and cause various parts of these molecules to be attracted to one another.

The task of physiological psychology is to "explain" behavior in physiological terms. Like other scientists, physiological psychologists believe that all natural phenomena—including human behavior—are subject to the laws of physics. Thus, the laws of behavior can be reduced to descriptions of physiological processes.

How does one study the physiology of behavior? Physiological psychologists cannot simply be reductionists. It is not enough to observe behaviors and correlate them with physiological events that occur at the same time. Identical behaviors, under different conditions, may occur for different reasons, and thus be initiated by different physiological mechanisms: This means that we must understand "psychologically" why a particular behavior occurs before we can understand what physiological events made it occur.

36. What does the passage mainly discuss?
   (A) The difference between "scientific" and "unscientific" explanations.
   (B) The difference between human and animal behavior.
   (C) How fear would be explained by the psychologist, physiologist, and molecular biologist.
   (D) How scientists differ in their approaches to explaining natural phenomena.

37. In the first paragraph the word "deal" could best be replaced by which of the following?
   (A) Barter.
   (B) Bargain.
   (C) Are playing.
   (D) Are concerned.

38. Which of the following is most clearly analogous to the example in the passage of the person who fears dogs?
   (A) A child chokes on a fishbone and as an adolescent is reluctant to eat fish.
   (B) A person feels lonely and after a while buys a dog for companionship.
   (C) A child studies science in school and later grows up to become a teacher.
   (D) A person hears that a snowstorm is predicted and that evening is afraid to drive home.

39. According to the passage, which of the following is important in explaining a muscle movement?

(A) The flow of blood to the muscles.

(B) Classical conditioning.

(C) Protein interactions.

(D) The entry of unpleasant stimuli through the cell membrane.

40. The author implies that which of the following is the type of scientific explanation most likely used by a molecular biologist?

(A) Experimentation.

(B) Reduction.

(C) Interaction.

(D) Generalization.

生词及短语

generalization [dʒenərəlai'zeiʃ(ə)n]	*n.*	概括
reduction [ri'dʌkʃ(ə)n]	*n.*	归纳，归类
pathological [pæθə'lɔdʒik(ə)l]	*a.*	病理的，病态的
stimulus ['stimjuləs]	*n.*	刺激，刺激物
paired [peə(r)d]	*a.*	成对
exuberant [ig'zjuːbərənt]	*a.*	非凡的
evoke [i'vəuk]	*vt.*	唤起，引起
membrane ['membrein]	*n.*	膜，隔膜
interaction [intər'ækʃ(ə)n]	*n.*	交互作用，交感
protein ['prəutiːn]	*n.*	蛋白质
molecule ['mɔlikjuːl]	*n.*	分子
physiological [fiziə'lɔdʒikəl]	*a.*	生理学的，生理学上的
correlate ['kɔrəleit]	*vt.*	使相互关联

答案与解析

36. [答案] (D)

[解析] 本题为主旨题。本文第一句便提出了全文主题“What does a scientist do when he or she ‘explains’ something?”接着各段分别围绕主题进行了陈述：第一段叙述的

是心理学家解释自然现象的方法,第二段为生理学家使用的方法,第三、四段则为生理心理学家使用的方法。这些方法各不相同,故正确答案应为(D)。

37. [答案] (D)

[解析] 本题采用排除法。barter 意为“交换”;bargain 意为“议价”;playing 意为“玩耍”;concerned 意为“关心,关注”。而原句中 deal with 有“涉及、论及、处理”之意,从上下文来看,只有(D) 在意义和语法上与原句接近。

38. [答案] (A)

[解析] 从第一段中有关对狗怀有恐惧心理的解释, 可知一个人在曾经被狗惊吓过之后一见到狗就会感到恐惧。只有(A) 的内容与这一例子相似,其他几个答案的内容,均不为从前的经验对目前造成的结果。故正确答案为(A)。

39. [答案] (C)

[解析] 从第二段第三句中, 可知生理学家解释肌肉运动的原因是: interaction between protein molecules within these cells。这与(C) “蛋白质的相互作用”同义,故答案应为(C)。

40. [答案] (C)

[解析] 第二段最后一句指出“A molecular biologist would ‘explain’ these events in terms of forces that bind various molecules together and cause various parts of these molecules to be attracted to one another.”其中“将不同的分子聚集在一起,并使这些分子的各个部分相互吸引的力量”与 “相互作用”应为一个意思,故正确答案应为(C)。

译文

科学家在“解释”某件事物时会怎样做呢?科学的解释有两种形式:概括和归纳。大多数心理学家涉足概括法。他们把个别的行为作为一般规律的例证来解释。例如,他们把对狗所产生的强烈病态恐惧作为经典的条件反射的例子来解释。他们推测,这种人从前曾经被狗惊吓过。在看到狗的同时(也许此人曾被一条狗扑倒过),一种不愉快的刺激随之而生,以后只要一看见狗,就会唤起从前的反应——恐惧感。

大多数生理学家常论及归纳法。他们用比较简单的现象来解释现象。例如,肌肉的运动是用肌肉细胞膜的变化、某些化学药品的进入和这些细胞内蛋白质分子之间的相互作用来加以解释。分子生物学家会用将各个分子聚集在一起、并使这些分子的各个部分相互的吸引力来解释这些现象。

生理心理学的任务是用生理方法来“解释”行为。像其他科学家一样,生理心理学家认为,所有自然现象,包括人的行为在内,均受到物理规律的支配。因此,行为的规律可以归纳到对生理过程的描述。

人们如何研究行为生理学呢? 生理心理学家不可能只是归纳主义者。仅仅观察行为,并把它们与同时发生的生理现象关联起来是不够的。在不同条件下发生的同样的行为,可因不同原因而发生，从而很可能是由不同的生理机理所引起的。这意味着，我们必须了解导致某一特定行为产生的心理原因，然后才能明白使之发生的生理现象。

阅读 B 篇

Directions:

In the following article, some sentences have been removed. For Questions 41—45, choose the most suitable one from the list A—G to fit into each of the numbered blanks. There are two extra choices, which do not fit in any of the blanks. Mark your answers on ANSWER SHEET 1. (10 points)

The year 1997 was one in which the computer industry's financial troubles, government investigations, prominent lawsuits, and business consolidations captured as much attention as advancing technology and the continuing growth of the Internet and on-line services.

It also was the year in which the U.S. Supreme Court struck down the Communications Decency Act, an attempt to regulate the content of the Internet. The act had been signed by President Bill Clinton in early 1996 in an attempt to protect children from pornography on the Internet, but opponents had claimed the law was so general it could be used to regulate other, more legitimate types of expression. 41. ____________.

It was a troubled year for Apple Computer, Inc. Already weakened by declining computer sales, Apple was in turmoil in July when Chairman and CEO Gilbert F. Amelio resigned from the company after some 18 months on the job, during which Apple lost nearly $1.5 billion. Apple's board of directors reportedly was displeased by falling sales of Apple's Macintosh computers. Though Amelio, who had been welcomed as a corporate turnaround specialist, was unsuccessful, the roots of Apple's troubles ran deep. 42. ____________.

43. ____________. In October it was accused by the U.S. Justice Department of violating the 1995 court order barring it from anti-competitive licensing activities. The Justice Department asked a federal court to impose a $1 million-a-day fine on the software industry leader for requiring PC manufacturers to use Microsoft's World Wide Web browser, Internet Explorer, on their machines when they installed Microsoft's Windows 95 OS.

The Microsoft-Justice Department battle had the potential to have a major impact on the marketing contest between Microsoft and Netscape Communications Corp, both of which were trying to make their own browser the most widely used on the Internet. Justice Department attorneys said they were trying to prevent Microsoft, which had a virtual monopoly in personal computer operating systems, from using that power to take control of the Internet browser market. At issue was the Justice Department's interpretation of a 1995 consent decree with Microsoft that had settled another antitrust dispute. 44. ______________.

45. ______________. Intel, the world's leading manufacturer of microprocessor chips for PCs, learned in September that it was being investigated by the Federal Trade Commission(FTC) in connection with its business practices in the PC market. The FTC said it wanted to determine if Intel had tried to monopolize or otherwise restrict price competition in its role as supplier of about 85% of the microprocessors used in PCs. Intel also was the subject of an antitrust investigation by the FTC from 1991 to 1993 that did not result in any action against the company.

(A) Microsoft said that far from violating the agreement, it was merely making technological improvements to its existing Windows 95 product by adding browser software to it.

(B) The challenge today is not merely to speed up the development of both advancing technology and Internet.

(C) The legislation made it a crime to publish indecent material on the Internet in a way that would make it available to those under 18; violators could receive up to two years in prison and a $250,000 fine.

(D) Another industry leader, Intel Corp. under Chairman and CEO Andrew Grove, also drew the interest of federal government regulators.

(E) It was obvious that Justice Department had prejudice against Microsoft, which put Microsoft at a disadvantage in the competition with Netscape.

(F) Microsoft had no financial problems but ran into difficulty with the federal government.

(G) They were said to include lack of technical innovation, product-handling mistakes, and management upheaval, plus thousands of layoffs.

内容提要

本文主要叙述1997年所发生的事情。第一段指出,1997年是这样一年:计算机工业财政问题、政府调查、著名的诉讼事件、商业合并等,都像先进技术、持续发展的互联网和在线业务一样引起了广泛注意。

它还是这样一年:美国最高法院否定了通信行为法,该法企图管理互联网内容。它于1996年上半年由克林顿总统签字,目的是保护儿童不受互联网色情内容影响,但反对者声称该法律太过普通,可以被利用来管制其他的和更合法的表达形式。

答案与解析

41. [答案](C)

[解析]从上下文分析,第二段第一、二句提到美国最高法院否决了通信行为法令,它由克林顿于1996年签字生效,目的在于保护儿童免受因特网上的色情危害。反对者认为它的内容过于一般。可见,所填入的内容应与司法和因特网有关,故(C)应为正确选项。

42. [答案](G)

[解析]本段叙述了苹果计算机公司在阿梅利奥任职期间销售滑坡,损失巨大。空白处前一句指出阿梅利奥曾被公认为是可以扭转企业业绩的专家,但没有成功,苹果公司的问题根源很深。后面一句应该继续叙述问题的根源所在,而(G)谈到这些问题,包括缺乏技术革新、产品处理失误、管理大变动及数千职工遭解雇。

43. [答案](F)

[解析]空白处后面几句提到美国司法部谴责它违背了1995年法院禁止它从事反竞争经营活动的命令,法院要求对这个软件工业的领头人处以每天100万美元的罚款。可见文中的it是指微软公司,而在本段最后一句也提到,(F)应为正确答案。

44. [答案](A)

[解析]本段指出美国司法部和微软公司之间争论不休,司法部的目的是要阻止微软在因特网浏览器操作系统上的垄断,微软为此提出了申诉。申诉的内容在(A)中可以找到。

45. [答案](D)

[解析]本题较为简单,空白后面提到英特尔公司于9月也得知受到联邦商业委员会的调查,认为它企图在芯片产品和价格方面形成垄断。故空白处应该填入与英特尔公司有关的信息,答案应为(D)。

阅读C篇

Directions:

Read the following text carefully and then translate the underlined segments into Chinese. Your translation should be written neatly on ANSWER SHEET 2.(10 points)

Historians are understandably reluctant about predicting the future because of all the unknown variables involved. For example, a third world war-employing thermonuclear weapons could conceivably destroy life on this planet. (46) Assuming, however, that mankind can avoid this kind of disaster, it is possible, on the basis of available data, to make meaningful guesses about feasible developments in man's physical, political and societal environments for the year 2,000, and even beyond.

(47) Faced with these prospects, the U.S. government undertook to persuade the Canadian government to join in a continental program to exploit and sell market energy and mineral resources, particularly oil and water, of which Canada is one of the world's major suppliers. For the industrialized countries, a continental strategy of access to energy and fuel resources appeared to be imperative.

We have singled out the North American resource situation because it illustrates a contemporary phenomenon. Peoples everywhere are caught up in the "revolution of rising expectation" so that in underdeveloped countries men look forward to owning at least a few modern western appliances. But this psychological phenomenon of our times poses the question: will the earth's resources last long enough to enable the entire world to approach the living standards in the industrialized countries of today?

It is the application of technology to physical resources that sustains human life and ultimately sets the limits on the number of people who can be fed. But technology also provides the tools and techniques for lengthening life spans and reducing death rates. As a result, high birth rates are no longer closely matched by high death rates as they were until modern times; infectious diseases are much less frequent in most parts of the world, due largely to public health measures; and physical vitality has been increased by improved nutrition. (48) These changes have brought about what is today familiarly called the "population explosion"—which, unless checked, could conceivably become the most serious problem of the next century.

In 1,000 A. D. the estimated population of the world was 275 million, a figure which had approximately doubled by 1650. But whereas it too some years for this increase to occur, the following 300 years brought a sixfold increase to over three billion people in 1962. In those three centuries some 23 billion people had been born, and the factor of acceleration continues.

Asia, Africa and Latin America have been growing more rapidly than Europe, Russia and North America. (49) In other words, the regions possessing the most advanced technology and highest living standards are likely to be a progressively diminishing portion of the global population. Since economic production is growing faster than biological reproduction in the advanced countries of the West while the reverse situation threatens to occur in the rest of the world during the decades ahead, the resulting imbalance between population growth and economic growth is almost certain to generate massive political and social tensions.

(50) The scope and urgency of the questions raised by the population explosion are unprecedented. On the other hand, it is heartening to note that the interaction relationship between population growth, technological change, and the use of resources has at last been

recognized as an international challenge by the member states of the United Nations. It remains to be seen what effective combined efforts can—or will—be made.

生词及短语

variable [ˈvɛəriəbl]	*n.*	变数,变量
conceivably [kənˈsiːvəbli]	*ad.*	令人信服地
imperative [imˈperətiv]	*a.*	紧急的,必要的,命令的
single out		挑选
appliances [ˌæplikəˈbiləti]	*n.*	用具,器具,家用电器
infectious diseases		传染病
vitality [vaiˈtætiti]	*n.*	活力,生命力
nutrition [njuːˈtriʃən]	*n.*	营养,营养学
reproduction [riːprəˈdʌkʃən]	*n.*	繁殖,复制品
interaction [intərˈækʃən]	*n.*	交互作用
it remains to be seen		尚待分晓,还要看情况发展

全文译文与答案

可以理解,历史学家们都很难预测未来,因为存在众多相关和未知的不确定因素。例如,一次使用热核武器的第三次世界大战毫无疑问会摧毁这个星球上的生命。(46) 可是,假定人类能防止这种灾难的话,我们就有可能根据现有的资料对人类在 2,000 年,甚至以后,所处的物质、政治和社会环境等方面所可能取得的进展做出种种有意义的推测。

(47) 面对以上这些前景,美国政府曾一度想说服加拿大政府参与一项开发与出售能源和矿产资源的大陆性计划,尤其是石油和水资源,在这些资源领域,加拿大是世界上主要的供应国之一。对于工业国家来说,使用能源和燃料的大陆战略看起来是必要的。

我们拿北美资源环境为例,因为它说明了当前的现象。各地的人们都被"期望上升的革命"所吸引,以至不发达国家的人们也盼望着拥有几件现代西方家用电器。但我们时代的这种心理现象提出了这样的问题: 地球的资源能够长期维持使整个世界走进像今天工业化国家那样的生活标准吗?

正是技术对物质资源的应用维持着人类的生活, 并最大程度地限制着能够生存的人们的数量。但技术同样为长寿和减少死亡率提供工具和技术。结果,高出生率不再像旧时代那样和高死亡率匹配; 主要因为公共卫生条件的提高, 传染病在世界大多数地方不再频繁出现;人的生命力也由于营养的提高大大增强。(48) 这些变化已经带来了今天人们都熟悉的所谓"人口爆炸",对此如果不加以控制,可以想象得到它可能会成为下半个世纪的一个最严重的问题。

在公元1,000年,世界人口估计为2.75亿,这个数字到1650年几乎翻倍。然而这种增长的发生是在一些年代之后,到1962年,随后的300年人口增长了6倍,超过了30亿。在这3个世纪中大约有23亿人口出生,成为人口加速增长的因素。

亚洲、非洲和拉丁美洲人口增长一直大大高于欧洲、俄国和北美。(49)换句话说,技术最先进,生活水平最高的地区,其人口在世界总人口中所占的比例,很可能会越来越小。在西方发达国家,由于经济产品的增长速度高于生物繁殖,而与此相反的形势在下一个十年中却威胁着其余世界,所产生的人口增长和经济发展之间的不平衡毫无疑问会带来大量的政治和社会问题。

(50)人口爆炸所引起的问题,就其涉及面和迫切性来说,都是前所未有的。另一方面,令人欣慰的是,在人口增长、技术改变和资源利用之间的相互关系终于被联合国成员国认同为是一种国际挑战。能够或将要采取什么有效而联合性的努力,这还尚待分晓。

阅读强化练习七

阅读 A 篇

Directions:

Read the following four texts. Answer the questions below each text by choosing A, B, C or D. Mark your answers on ANSWER SHEET 1. (*40 points*)

Passage 1

George Washington Carver showed that plant life was more than just food for animals and humans. Carver's first *step* was to analyze plant parts to find out what they were made of. He then combined these simpler isolated substances with other substances to create new products.

The branch of chemistry that studies and finds ways to use raw materials from farm products to made industrial products is called chemurgy. Carver was one of the first and greatest chemurgists of all time. Today the science of chemurgy is better known as the science of synthetics. Each day people depend on the use synthetic materials made from raw materials. All his life Carver battled against the disposal of waste materials, and warned of the growing need to develop substitutes for the natural substances being used up by humans.

Carver never cared about getting credit for the new product he created. He never tried to patent his discoveries or get wealthy from them. He turned down many offers to leave Tusgegee Institute to become a rich scientist in private industry. Thomas Edison, inventor of the electric light, offered him a laboratory in Detroit to carry out food research. When the United States government made him a collaborator in the Mycology and Plant Disease Survey of the Department of Agriculture, he accepted the position with the understanding that he wouldn't have to leave Tusgegee. An authority on plant diseases—especially of the fungus variety—Carver sent hundreds of specimens to the United States Department of Agriculture. At the peak of his career, Carver's fame and influence were known on every continent.

21. With what topic is the passage mainly concerned?
(A) The work and career of George Washington Carver.
(B) The research conducted at Tusgegee Institute.
(C) The progress of the science of synthetics.
(D) The use of plants as a source of nutrition.

22. In Line 2, the word "step" could best be replaced by ______.
(A) footprint
(B) action
(C) scale
(D) stair

23. According to passage chemurgy can be defined as the ______.
(A) combination of chemistry and metallurgy
(B) research on chemistry of the soil
(C) study of the relationship between sunlight and energy
(D) development of industrial products from farm products

24. Why does the author mention Thomas Edison's offer to Carver?
(A) To illustrate one of Carver's many opportunities.
(B) To portray the wealth of one of Carver's competitors.
(C) To contrast Edison's contribution with that of Carver.
(D) To describe Carver's dependence on industrial support.

25. Which of the following is NOT discussed in the passage as work done by Carver?
(A) Research on electricity.
(B) Analysis of plant parts.
(C) Invention of new products.
(D) Research on plant diseases.

生词及短语

isolated ['aisəleitid]	*a.*	孤立的,单独的
chemurgy ['keməːdʒi]	*n.*	农业化工
chemurgist ['keməːdʒist]	*n.*	农业化学家
synthetics [sin'θetiks]	*n.*	人工合成材料

substitute [ˈsʌbstitjuːt]	*n.*	代用品,替代者
patent [ˈpeitənt]	*n.*	专利
turn down		拒绝
collaborator [kəˈlæbəreitə(r)]	*n.*	合作者
mycology [maiˈkɔlədʒi]	*n.*	真菌学
fungus [ˈfʌngəs]	*n.*	菌类,蘑菇
specimen [ˈspesimin]	*n.*	标本,样本

答案与解析

21. [答案] (A)

[解析] 本题为主旨题。文章第一句点明了主题"乔治·华盛顿·卡弗指出,植物对于人类和动物并不仅仅只是食物",接着描述了卡弗如何分析植物,合成新产品,成为最伟大的农业化学家之一,最后一句总结出"他的影响遍布全球",故(A) 应为正确答案。

22. [答案] (B)

[解析] 从上下文分析,第二行中的 step 不可能是脚印、刻度、阶梯,而是指卡弗所采取的第一步行动,故(B) 应为正确答案。

23. [答案] (D)

[解析] 第二段第一句指出,农业化学属于化学的一个分支,是研究并探索如何用农产品原料制造工业产品的学科,故(D) 应为正确答案。

24. [答案] (A)

[解析] 第三段第二句指出,卡弗拒绝了很多聘请。接着第三句提到爱迪生的邀请,说明卡弗受聘机会很多,故(A) 应为正确答案。

25. [答案] (A)

[解析] 很明显,卡弗没有从事过电的研究,故(A) 为正确答案。

译文

乔治·华盛顿·卡弗指出,植物对于人类和动物并不仅仅只是食物。他第一步是分析植物的组成成分,弄清楚它们是由什么构成的。然后,他将这些较简单和分离的物质与其他物质结合起来制造出新的产品。

作为化学的一个分支,农业化工是研究和探索利用农产品原材料制造工业产品的方法的科学。卡弗是最早也始终是最伟大的农业化学家之一。今天农业化工被称为大家所知的人工合成材料科学。人们每天都离不开用原料制成的合成产品。卡弗毕生都在与随意处理废弃物质的行为作斗争,并告诫我们需要尽快开发将被人类耗尽的天然物质的替代品。

卡弗从来不想用自己开发的新产品获取荣誉。他从来没有打算为自己的发明申请专利或靠它们发财。他拒绝了许多邀请他离开塔斯基吉研究所到私营企业工作,从而成为一个富有科学家的机会。电灯的发明者托马斯·爱迪生给他提供了一个在底特律的实验室,以从事食物研究。当美国政府让他到农业部"真菌和植物病害研究"部门作合作人时,在取得不会离开塔斯基吉的谅解的前提下,他接受了这一职位。作为植物疾病的权威——特别是在真菌种类方面,卡弗为美国农业部提供了几百种标本。在他事业的顶峰期,他的名气和影响遍及每一个大洲。

Passage 2

Icebergs are among nature's most spectacular creations, and yet most people have never seen one. A vague air of mystery envelops them. They come into being—somewhere—in faraway, line frigid waters, amid thunderous noise and splashing turbulence, which in most cases no one hears or sees, they exist only a short time and then slowly waste away just as unnoticed.

Objects of sheerest beauty, they have been called. Appearing in an endless variety of shapes, they may be dazzlingly white, or they may be glassy blue, green, or purple, tinted faintly or in darker hues. The are graceful, stately, inspiring—in calm, sunlit seas.

But they are also called frightening and dangerous, and that they are—in the night, in the fog, and in storms. Even in clear weather one is wise to stay a safe distance away from them. Most of their bulk is hidden below the water, so their underwater parts may extend out far beyond the visible top. Also, they may roll over unexpectedly, churning the waters around them.

Icebergs are parts of glaciers that break off, drift into the water, float about a while, and finally melt. Icebergs afloat today are made of snowflakes that have fallen over long ages of time. They embody snows that drifted down hundreds, or many thousands, or in some cases maybe a million years ago. The snows fell in polar regions and on cold mountains, where they melted only a little or not at all, and so collected to great depths over the years and centuries.

As each year's snow accumulation lay on the surface, evaporation and melting caused the snowflakes slowly to lose their feathery points and become tiny grains of ice. When new snow fell on top of the old, it too turned to icy grains. So blankets of snow and ice grains mounted layer upon layer and were of such great thickness that the weight of the upper layers compressed the lower ones. With time and pressure from above, the many small ice grains joined and changed to larger crystals, and eventually the deeper crystals merged into a solid mass of ice.

26. Which of the following is the best title for the passage?

(A) The Melting of Icebergs

(B) The Nature and Origin of Icebergs

(C) The Size and Shape of Icebergs

(D) The Dangers of Icebergs

27. The passage mentions all of the following colors for icebergs EXCEPT ______.

(A) yellow

(B) blue

(C) green

(D) purple

28. According to the passage, icebergs are dangerous because they ______.

(A) usually melt quickly

(B) can turn over very suddenly

(C) may create immense snowdrifts

(D) can cause unexpected avalanches

29. The formation of an iceberg is most clearly analogous to which of the following activities?

(A) Walking on fluffy new snow, causing it to become more compact and icy.

(B) Plowing larger areas of earth, leaving the land flat and barren.

(C) Skating across a frozen lake and leaving a trail behind.

(D) Blowing snow into one large pile to clear an area.

30. The attitude of the author toward icebergs is one of ______.

(A) disappointment

(B) humor

(C) disinterest

(D) wonder

生词及短语

spectacular [spek'tækjulə]	*a.*	壮观的，引人入胜的
vague [veig]	*a.*	含糊的，不清楚的，茫然的
frigid ['fridʒid]	*a.*	寒冷的，冷淡的
thunderous ['θʌndərəs]	*a.*	打雷的
turbulence ['təːbjuləns]	*n.*	骚乱，动荡
sheer [ʃiə]	*a.*	纯粹的，绝对的
dazzlingly ['dæzliŋli]	*ad.*	灿烂地，耀眼地

tinted [tintid]	*a.*	带色彩的
faintly ['feintli]	*ad.*	微弱地
hue [hjuː]	*n.*	色调,颜色
sunlit ['sʌnlit]	*a.*	阳光照射的
bulk [bʌlk]	*n.*	体积,大小
roll over		翻身
churn [tʃəːn]	*v.*	搅拌,搅动
glacier ['glæsjə]	*n.*	冰河
afloat [ə'fləut]	*a.*	飘浮的
snowflake ['snəufleik]	*n.*	雪花
embody [im'bɔdi]	*vt.*	具体表达,包含
evaporation [ivæpə'reiʃən]	*n.*	蒸发
feathery ['feðəri]	*a.*	生有羽毛的
blanket ['blæŋkit]	*n.*	毯子
compress [kəm'pres]	*vt.*	压缩

答案与解析

26. [答案] (**B**)

[解析] 本题为主旨题,可以从全文内容来判断。第一段对冰山进行了概述,第二段和第三段具体地描写了冰山的特征,第四、五段描述冰山的形成过程。很明显(B) 最贴近题意,应为正确答案。

27. [答案] (**A**)

[解析] 第二段第二句作者在描写冰山的颜色时提到 blue,green 和 purple, 没有提到 yellow,故答案应为(A)。

28. [答案] (**B**)

[解析] 第三段最后一句谈到冰山的危险性时指出 "... they may roll over unexpectedly, churning the waters around them."它们可能出人意料地突然坍塌,搅动周围的海水。比较各项,(B) 应为正确答案。

29. [答案] (**A**)

[解析] 本文最后一段对雪山的形成进行了描写,每年的雪落在表面,蒸发和融化使雪片慢慢地失去了羽毛状花边而成为小冰粒,当新的雪花落到冰粒上时,它也会变成冰粒。大量的雪花和冰粒一层一层地堆积起来,到了一定的厚度,上层冰层的重量就挤压下层冰雪,随着时间的长久和上层的挤压,很多小冰粒被压成更大的晶

体。最终,深处的晶体融合为巨大坚固的冰团。比较各选项,只有(A) 的过程与此相近,故应为正确答案。

30. [答案] (D)

[解析] 作者在描述冰山时,使用了一些表示惊叹和折服的词汇,例如 spectacular 意为“壮观”,vague 意为“茫然”,mystery 意为“神秘”,sheerest beauty 意为“绝美”,graceful 意为“高雅”,stately 意为“雄伟”,inspiring 意为“令人鼓舞”,同时还有 frightening and dangerous 意为“可怕和危险”,可以看出,作者对冰山的看法是 wonder“惊叹”,故(D) 应为正确答案。

译文

冰山是大自然最壮观的产物之一,但大多数人从未见过。它们有一种神秘的感觉。它们形成于很远的某个地方,在寒冷的水域中,在轰隆的雷声中,在澎湃的急流中。在大多数情况下,没有人可以听见或者看见,它们存在的时间很短,然后悄然融化消失。

它们被称做是最美丽的景观,形态多种多样,颜色可以是耀眼的白色,也可以是蔚蓝、碧绿、紫红,或深或浅。它们在平静的、阳光灿烂的大海中显得优雅、雄伟和令人兴奋。

但是,它们也很吓人很危险,特别是在夜间、雾里和暴风雨中。即使是在晴天,聪明人还是离它们远点。冰山的大部分藏于水下,水下部分可能延伸到距冰尖很远的地方。而且,它可能会出人意料地坍塌,使周围的海水翻腾。

冰山是从冰川上断裂下来并漂浮到海上的一部分,它们漂浮一段时间最终融化。如今海上漂浮的冰山由多年来所下的雪花形成。积在它体内的雪是几百或几千年,有的可能是一百万年前飘落下来的。雪花降落到极地或寒冷的山上,它们只能融化一点儿,或根本不融化,所以经过多年甚至几个世纪之后就堆积得很厚。

每年的雪积聚在表面,蒸发和融化使雪片慢慢地失去了羽毛状花边而成为小冰粒。当新的雪花落到冰粒上时,它也会变成冰粒。大量的雪花和冰粒一层一层地堆积起来,到了一定的厚度,上层冰屑的重量就挤压下层冰雪。随着时间的推移和来自上层压力的挤压,很多小冰粒结合到一起形成了更大的晶体,最终,深处的晶体融合为坚固的冰团。

Passage 3

Native Americans from the southeastern part of what is now the United States believed that the universe in which they lived was made up of three separate, but related, worlds: the Upper World, the Lower World, and This World. In the last there lived humans, most animals, and all plants.

This World, a round island resting on the surface or waters, was suspended from the sky by four cords attached to the island at the four cardinal points of the compass. Lines drawn to connect the opposite points of the compass, from north to south and from east to west, intersected

This World to divide it into four wedge-shaped segments. Thus a symbolic representation of the human world was a cross within a circle, the cross representing the intersecting lines and the circle the shape of This World.

Each segment of This World was identified by its own color. According to Cherokee doctrine, east was associated with the color red because it was the direction of the Sun, the greatest deity of all. Red was also the color of fire, believed to be directly connected with the Sun, with blood, and therefore with life. Finally, red was the color of success. The west was the Moon segment; it provided no warmth and was not life-giving as the Sun was. So its color was black. North was the direction of cold, and so its color was blue (sometimes purple), and it represented trouble and defeat. South was the direction of warmth; its color, white, was associated with peace and happiness.

The southeastern Native Americans' universe was one in which opposites were constantly at war with each other, red against black, blue against white. This World hovered somewhere between the perfect order and predictability of the Upper World and the total disorder and instability of the Lower World. The goal was to find some kind of halfway path, or balance, between those other worlds.

31. Which of the following is the best title for the passage?
   (A) One Civilization's View of the Universe
   (B) The Changing of the Seasons in the Southeast
   (C) The Painting of Territorial Maps by Southeastern Native Americans
   (D) The War Between Two Native American Civilizations

32. The author implies that This World was located ______.
   (A) inside the Upper World
   (B) inside the Lower World
   (C) above the Upper World
   (D) between the Upper World and Lower World

33. According to the passage, southeastern Native Americans compared This World to ______.
   (A) waters
   (B) the sky
   (C) an animal
   (D) an island

34. According to the passage, lines divided This World into how many segments?
   (A) Two.

(B) Three.

(C) Four.

(D) Five.

35. According to the passage, which of the following colors represented the west for southeastern Native Americans?

(A) Blue.

(B) White.

(C) Black.

(D) Purple.

生词及短语

rest on		被搁在,停留在
suspend [səs'pend]	*vt.*	吊,悬挂
cord [kɔːd]	*n.*	绳索
cardinal ['kɑːdinəl]	*a.*	主要的,最重要的
compass ['kʌmpəs]	*n.*	罗盘,指南针
intersect [intə'sekt]	*vi.*	(直线)相交,交叉
wedge-shaped		楔形
deity ['diːiti]	*n.*	神,神性
hover ['hɔvə]	*v.*	盘旋
instability [instə'biliti]	*n.*	不稳定(性)
halfway ['hɑːf'wei]	*a.*	中途的,折中的

答案与解析

31. [答案] (A)

[解析] 本题为主旨题。文章第一句便点明了主题,指出以前居住在美国东南部的美洲土著人对宇宙的认识,认为自己居住的宇宙是由三个独立而又关联的世界组成,接着围绕这个主题进行阐述。比较各选项,答案应为(A)。

32. [答案] (D)

[解析] 第一段第一句提到,宇宙由上界、下界和本界组成。倒数第二句提到,本界盘旋在不稳定的下界上方的某个地方。故可知本界应在上界和下界之间,故答案应为(D)。

33. [答案](D)

[解析]第二段第一句提到,This World 是一个漂浮在表面或水上的圆形岛屿，故答案应为(D)。

34. [答案](C)

[解析]第二段第二句指出,从北到南和从东到西划出的线条把本界(This World)分割成四个楔形部分,故答案应为(C)。

35. [答案](C)

[解析]第三段第四、五句指出:西方是月亮的部分,不给予温暖,也不像太阳那样给予生命,所以它的颜色是黑色。故(C) 应为正确答案。

译文

居住在现在美国东南部的土著美洲人认为他们所生活的宇宙是由三个独立但又相关的世界组成的:上界、下界和本界。在本界生活着人类、动物和植物。

本界是一块漂浮在表面或水面上的圆形岛屿，由四根连接在岛屿四个主要罗盘方位的绳索悬挂在天上。连接罗盘上两个对应点的画线,从北到南和从东到西将本界划分为四个楔形部分。这样,一个内有十字交叉的圆圈就象征人类世界,十字代表交叉线,圆圈代表本界的形状。

本界的每一部分都有自己的颜色加以识别。按照切罗基印第安人的信条,东方跟红色有关,因为它是太阳——万物伟大的神,升起的方向。红色也是火的颜色,被认为直接与太阳、血有联系,因此与生命也有联系。此外,红色还是成功的颜色。西方是月亮的组成部分;它不提供温暖,不像太阳那样能给予生命,所以它是黑色的。北方是寒冷的方向,所以它的颜色是蓝色的(有时为紫色),它代表麻烦和失败。南方是温暖的方向,它的颜色是白色,与和平及幸福相关。

东南美洲土著人的世界是一个对立双方经常处于交战状态的世界,红方与黑方对立,蓝色与白色对立。本界盘旋于具有完美秩序和极有预言性的上界与完全处于混乱和不稳定状态的下界之间。人的目标就是要在其他两个世界之间找到某种折中的途径或平衡。

Passage 4

Grandma Moses is among the most celebrated twentieth-century painters of the United States, yet she had barely started painting before she was in her late seventies. As she once said of herself: "I would never sit back in a rocking chair, waiting for someone to help me." No one could have had a more productive old age.

She was born Anna Mary Robertson on a farm in New York State, one of five boys and five girls ("We came in bunches, like radishes.") At twelve she left home and was in domestic service until, at twenty-seven, she married Thomas Moses, the hired hand of one of her employers. They farmed most of their lives, first in Virginia and then in New York State, at Eagle Bridge. She had ten children, of whom five survived; her husband died in 1927.

Grandma Moses painted a little as a child and made embroidery pictures as a hobby, but only switched to oils in old age because her hands had become too stiff to sew and she wanted to keep busy and pass the time. Her pictures were first sold at the local drugstore and at a fair, and were soon *spotted* by a dealer who bought everything she painted. Three of the pictures were exhibited in the Museum of Modern Art, and in 1940 she had her first exhibition in New York. Between the 1930s and her death she produced some 2,000 pictures: detailed and lively portrayals of the rural life she had known for so long, with a marvelous sense of color and form. "I think real hard till I think of something real pretty, and then I paint it," she said.

36. Which of the following would be the best title for the passage?

(A) Grandma Moses: A Biographical Sketch

(B) The Children of Grandma Moses

(C) Grandma Moses: Her Best Exhibition

(D) Grandma Moses and Other Older Artists

37. According to the passage, Grandma Moses began to paint because she wanted to ______.

(A) decorate her home

(B) keep active

(C) improve her salary

(D) gain an international reputation

38. From Grandma Moses' description of herself in the first paragraph, it can be inferred that she was ______.

(A) independent

(B) pretty

(C) wealthy

(D) timid

39. Grandma Moses spent most of her life ______.

(A) nursing

(B) painting

(C) embroidering

(D) farming

40. In Para. 3 Line 4, the word "spotted" could best be replaced by ______.

(A) speckled

(B) featured

(C) noticed

(D) damaged

生词及短语

Moses		摩西,安娜·玛丽·罗伯特森(1860—1961),美国画家,因其简单而又多彩的乡村风景画而著名
rocking chair		摇椅
productive [prə'dʌktiv]	a.	多产的
bunch [bʌntʃ]	n.	串,束
radish ['rædiʃ]	n.	萝卜
embroidery [im'brɔidəri]	n.	刺绣,装饰
stiff [stif]	a.	僵硬的
portrayal [pɔː'treiəl]	n.	描写,描画

答案与解析

36. [答案] (A)

[解析] 本题为主旨题,第一句点明了主题"Grandma Moses is among the most celebrated twentieth-century painters of the United States, ..." 后面两段按时间顺序叙述了她的生平,故(A) 应为正确答案。

37. [答案] (B)

[解析] 从第三段第一句可知,她画油画是"... she wanted to keep busy and pass the time." 很明显(B) 应为正确答案。

38. [答案] (A)

[解析] 在第一段中,她描绘自己说:"我从不愿意坐在摇椅中,等待别人来帮我"。这说明她具有独立性,故(A) 应为正确答案。

39. [答案] (D)

[解析] 第二段第四句指出"They farmed most of their lives",这说明她和丈夫一生大部分时间在务农,故(D) 应为正确答案。

40. [答案] (C)

[解析] 第三段第四行中的 spotted 意为“发现、认出”，与 notice“注意”近义，故(C) 应为正确答案。

译文

摩西奶奶是 20 世纪美国最负盛名的画家之一，然而她是在 70 多岁之后才开始画画的。她在谈到自己时曾说：“我从不会坐在摇椅中，等待别人来帮助我。”没有哪个人像她那样拥有一个多产的晚年。

她出生在纽约州一个农民家庭，原名叫安娜·玛丽·罗伯特森，有 5 个兄弟和 4 个姐妹（“我们像萝卜似的一连串来到世上。”）12 岁时她离开了家，开始当家仆，一直到 27 岁时才与她雇主的一个名叫托马斯·摩西的帮工结婚。他们一生大部分时间在务农，先在弗吉尼亚州，后定居在纽约州的鹰桥。她生了 10 个孩子，有 5 个活了下来，她丈夫于 1927 年离开人世。

摩西奶奶年幼时画过一点东西，对刺绣很感兴趣，但只是到了晚年才转到油画上，由于手变得僵硬，不适于绣花，而她想让自己忙碌一点以消磨时光。她的画刚开始是在当地的杂货店和集市上出卖，但不久就被一个商人发现，把她的作品全部买了下来。她有 3 幅画在现代艺术博物馆中展出，1940 年她在纽约举办了首次画展。从 30 年代到她去世，她创作了约 2000 幅画，以对色彩和形式绝妙的感觉，细腻而生动地描绘了她长期所熟悉的农村生活。她曾说：“我非常努力地思索，直到想出真正美好的东西，然后才把它画下来。”

阅读 B 篇

Directions:

In the following article, some sentences have been removed. For Questions 41—45, choose the most suitable one from the list A—G to fit into each of the numbered blanks. There are two extra choices, which do not fit in any of the blanks. Mark your answers on ANSWER SHEET 1. (10 points)

Science is committed to the universal. A sign of this is that the more successful a science becomes, the broader the agreement about its basic concepts: there is not a separate Chinese or American or Soviet *thermodynamics* （热力学）, for example; there is simply thermodynamics. 41. ____________.

42. ____________. This is why the spread of technology makes the world look ever more homogeneous. Architectural styles, dress styles, musical styles—even eating styles—tend increasingly to be world styles. The world looks more homogeneous because it is more homogeneous. Children who grow up in this world therefore experience it as a sameness rather than a diversity, and because their identities are shaped by this sameness, their sense of

differences among cultures and individuals diminishes. 43. ______________.

The automobile illustrates the point with great clarity. A technological innovation like streamlining or all-welded body construction may be rejected initially, but if it is important to the efficiency or economics of automobiles, it will reappear in different ways until it is not only accepted but universally regarded as an asset. 44. ______________.

If man creates machines, machines in turn shape their creators. As the automobile is universalized, it universalizes those who use it. Like the World Car he drives, modern man is becoming universal. No longer quite an individual, no longer quite the product of a unique geography and culture, he moves from one climate-controlled shopping mall to another, one airport to the next, from one Holiday Inn to its successor three hundred miles down the road; but somehow his location never changes. He is *cosmopolitan* (四海为家者). The price he pays is that he no longer has a home in the traditional sense of the word. 45. ______________.

The universalizing imperative of technology is irresistible. Barring the catastrophe of nuclear war, it will continue to shape both modern culture and the consciousness of those who inhabit that culture.

(A) Thermodynamics belongs to physics that deals with the relationships between heat and other forms of energy.

(B) As the *corollary* (必然结果) of science, technology also exhibits the universalizing tendency.

(C) Today's automobile is no longer unique to a given company or even to a given national culture, its basic features are found, with variations, in automobiles in general, no matter who makes them.

(D) Genetics is the branch of biology that deals with heredity, especially the mechanisms of hereditary transmission and the variation of inherited characteristics among similar or related organisms.

(E) As buildings become more alike, the people who inhabit the buildings become more alike. The result is described precisely in a phrase that is already familiar: the disappearance of history.

(F) For several decades of the twentieth century there was a Western and a Soviet *genetics* (遗传学), the latter associated with Lysenko's theory that environmental stress can produce genetic *mutations* (变化). Today Lysenko's theory is discredited, and there is now only one genetics.

(G) The benefit is that he begins to suspect home in the traditional sense is another name for limitations, and that home in the modern sense is everywhere and always surrounded by neighbors.

内容提要

本文主要叙述科学技术的发展使世界发生的变化。第一段指出,科学是属于全世界的。其中一个特点是科学越发达,关于它的基础概念便越能达成一致:例如,并没有属于中国、美国或俄国的"热力学",只有热力学。后面继续以遗传学作为例子进行说明。

最后一段指出,技术普遍化的需要是不可抗拒的。在防止核战争带来灾难的同时,科学将继续改变当代文化和生活在这个文化中的人们的意识。

答案与解析

41. [答案] (**F**)

[解析] 第一段提到科学是属于全世界的,例如热力学。(F)继续提到西方和苏联的遗传学,今天都叫遗传学了。

42. [答案] (**B**)

[解析] 第二段空白后面的句子提到为什么技术的发展使世界显得相似,而(B)提到因为科学的必然结果,技术同样表现出这种普遍的趋势。

43. [答案] (**E**)

[解析] 空白前提出由于孩子生长在这个充满相似的世界,他们的身份都被同化,对文化和个人的不同感觉也减弱。(E)继续提到这种同化:由于建筑都类似,居住在这些建筑内的人们也变得相似,结果是"历史的消失"。

44. [答案] (**C**)

[解析] 空白前以汽车为例,(C)继续加以说明:今天的汽车不再属于某个公司特有,或者属于某个民族文化,它的基本特点尽管有所不同,但实质都一样,不管谁制造。

45. [答案] (**G**)

[解析] 空白前提到,今天的现代人也都趋同,以四海为家。(G)提出现代人甚至怀疑传统意义上的家是"限制"的另一种名字,现代意义的家指四海为家,周围都是邻居。

阅读 C 篇

Directions:

Read the following text carefully and then translate the underlined segments into Chinese. Your translation should be written neatly on ANSWER SHEET 2. (10 points)

Old people are always saying that the young are not what they were. The same comment is made from generation to generation and it is always true. It has never been truer than it is today. The young are better educated. They have a lot more money to spend and enjoy more freedom. They grow up more quickly and are not so dependent on their parents. (46) They think more for themselves and do not blindly accept the ideas of their elders. Events which the older generation remembers clearly are nothing more than past history. This is as it should be. Every new generation is different from the one that preceded it. Today the difference is very marked indeed.

The old always assume that they know best for the simple reason that they have been around a bit longer. They don't like to feel that their values are being questioned or threatened. And this is precisely what the young are doing. (47) They are questioning the assumptions of their elders and disturbing their self-satisfaction. They take leave to doubt the older generation has created the best of all possible worlds. What they reject more than anything is conformity.

Who said that human differences can best be solved through conventional politics or by violent means? Why have the older generation so often used violence to solve their problems? (48) Why are they so unhappy and so troubled by a sense of guilt in their personal lives, so occupied with mean ambitions and the desire to accumulate more and more material possessions? Haven't the old lost touch with all that is important in life?

These are not questions the older generation can shrug off lightly. (49) Their record over the past forty years or so hasn't been exactly spotless. Traditionally, the young have turned to their elders for guidance. Today, the situation might be reversed. The old—if they are prepared to admit it—could learn a thing or two from their children. (50) One of the biggest lessons they could learn is that enjoyment is not "sinful". Enjoyment is a principle one could apply to all aspects of life. It is surely not wrong to enjoy your work and enjoy your leisure. It is surely not wrong to live in the present rather than in the past or future.

生词及短语

have been around		见过世面,经验丰富
conformity [kən'fɔːmiti]	n.	一致,符合
spotless ['spɔtlis]	a.	没有污点的

全文译文与答案

老年人总是说,年轻人已经不是他们从前那个样子。同样的评论从一代传到另一代,而这总是事实。但从来没有像今天这样如此真实。年轻人受到良好的教育。他们有更多的钱消费,同时享有更多的自由。他们成长更快,并且不总是依靠自己的父母。(46)他们会更多地独立思考,并且不盲目地接受长辈们的观念。长辈们记得很清楚的一些事情对于年轻人来说只不过是过去的历史。这原本如此。每个新一代都和前一代不同。今天这种差别确实更加明显。

老一辈总是以为他们知道的最多,简单的理由是他们经验丰富。他们不想觉得他们的价值受到置疑或威胁。而这恰恰是年轻人现在正在做的。(47)年轻人怀疑长辈们的观点,这使他们不再自我感觉良好。他们甚至怀疑长辈们创造了最美好的世界。他们最排斥的就是服从。

谁说人类的差异通过传统政治或暴力手段可以解决?为什么年老一代常常使用暴力来解决我们的问题?(48)在他们的个人生活中,他们为什么会不开心?为什么会被负罪感所困扰?为什么会充满野心,渴望积累越来越多的物质财富?老一辈是不是远离了生活中所有重要方面?

这些是老一辈不能轻易回避的问题。(49)他们过去四十来年的历史并不是一点儿问题也没有。传统地,年轻人都向他们的老一辈请教。今天,情况或许已经颠倒。老年人,如果他们准备接受这种事实,可以向他们的孩子学习一件或两件事情。(50)他们能够吸取的一个最大的教训就是:享受不是"罪过"。享受是一种可以应用到生活所有方面的原则。享受你的工作,享受你的闲暇确实不是错。生活在现在而不是过去或将来的确不是错。

阅读强化练习八

阅读 A 篇

Directions:

Read the following four texts. Answer the questions below each text by choosing A, B, C or D. Mark your answers on ANSWER SHEET 1. (40 points)

Passage 1

The total quantity of fresh water on the Earth exceeds all conceivable needs of the human population. Much of the water is inaccessible or otherwise unavailable, however, and the remainder is unevenly distributed from place to place and from season to season. In most parts of the world, therefore, an adequate and reliable supply of water can be had only by active management of water resources, especially under conditions of intrinsic water scarcity. In order to meet the large demands of agriculture and industry and the small but imperative demand of domestic consumption, water must be collected, stored, allocated , and distributed. Water falls freely from the sky but, contrary to popular opinion, water is not free. Human intervention in the natural water cycle always entails some cost, and occasionally the cost is high.

By far the most common method of controlling and augmenting the available water supply is to build dams for impounding the seasonal floods of streams and rivers. Indeed, since the Neolithic period, human settlements have been clustered in the major river basins precisely because water is readily available there. Today, other techniques of water management are also possible, such as tapping underground reservoirs and diverting rivers from one basin into another. The importance of limiting demand and improving the efficiency with which water is delivered to the site of ultimate use has also been recognized since the early twentieth century. A drawback common to almost all these methods of water management is a need for substantial capital investments. Dams, canals, and other devices for regulating the water cycle and compensating for geographical disparities in water resources are among the most elaborate and expensive of all engineering projects.

21. What is the main topic of the passage?
    (A) Water cycles.
    (B) Water shortages.
    (C) Water resource management.
    (D) Water retrieval engineering.

22. According to the passage, the worldwide supply of water suitable for human use is ______.
    (A) now inadequate
    (B) declining rapidly
    (C) not accurately measured
    (D) more than sufficient

23. According to the passage, for how long have people settled in river basins to be near water?
    (A) Since prehistoric times.
    (B) Since the beginning of the twentieth century.
    (C) Since shortages of water were first publicized.
    (D) Since the development of modern engineering techniques.

24. According to the passage, one significant disadvantage of using artificial devices to intervene in the water cycle is that such devices require ______.
    (A) great engineering skill
    (B) cooperation among nations
    (C) large amounts of money
    (D) long periods of time to complete

生词及短语

inaccessible [inæk'sesib(ə) l]	*a.*	难接近的，难得到的
unevenly [ʌn'ivenli]	*ad.*	不规则地，不均匀地
intrinsic [in'trinsik]	*a.*	固有的
scarcity ['skɛəsiti]	*n.*	稀少，缺乏
impounding [im'paundiŋ]	*v.*	储水（于水池等中）
Neolithic [niːəu'liθik]	*a.*	新石器时代的
drawback ['drɔːbæk]	*n.*	缺点，短处

disparity [dis'pæriti] *n.* 不同,不一致

答案与解析

21. [答案](C)

[解析] 本题为主旨题。第一段第三句指出:“因此,全世界大部分地区,只有通过主动管理水源才能保证充足可靠的用水供应。”故答案应为(C),其他三项仅在文中提及。

22. [答案](A)

[解析] 第一段第一、二句指出:“地球上淡水的总量超过全人类所有可能的需求。然而,大量淡水是无法获得的,而剩余部分则因地理和季节不同而分布不均。”答案为(A)。

23. [答案](A)

[解析] 第二段第二句指出:“Indeed, since the Neolithic period, human settlement ...” Neolithic 意为“新石器时代的”,属于史前时期,故答案应为(A)。

24. [答案](C)

[解析] 第二段最后一句指出:“水坝、人工运河以及其他调节水流循环和补偿地理分布不均水源的方法是所有工程项目中最复杂和最昂贵的。”可见答案为应为(C)。

译文

地球上淡水的总量超过全人类所有能想象得到的需求。然而,大量的淡水是无法接近或者说无法获得的,剩余部分则极不均匀地分布于不同地区和不同季节。因此,在全世界大部分地区,只有通过主动管理水源才能保证充足可靠的淡水供应,特别是在本来水资源就稀少的情况下。为了满足工农业的大量需要以及少量但却绝对必不可少的家庭消耗,必须对水进行收集、存贮、分配以及布局。水随意地从天而降,然而与公众的观点相反,水却不是免费得到的。人类对水的自然循环的干预总是要付出一定的代价,而且有时这种代价是很高昂的。

迄今为止,控制及增加可用水供应的最常用的方法就是修筑堤坝以存储季节性的水洪。的确,自新石器时代以来,人类的居住地之所以一直簇集在主要河流盆地,正是因为那些地方的水便于利用。今天其他控制水源的方法也是可能的,例如挖掘地下水库和盆地间引流。自 20 世纪初期以来,人们已经认识到控制水的需求量和提高效益以便将水利用到最大限度的重要性。对所有这些管理水资源的方法存在一个共同的缺点,这就是需要大量的资金投入。水坝、人工运河以及其他调节水流循环和补偿地理分布不均水源的方法是所有工程项目中最复杂和最昂贵的。

Passage 2

When did sport begin? If sport is , in essence, play, the claim might be made that sport is much older than humankind for, as we all have observed, the beasts play. Dogs and cats wrestle and play ball games. Fishes and bird dance. The apes have simple, pleasurable games. Frolicking infants, school children playing tag, and adult arm wrestlers are demonstrating strong, transgenerational and transspecies bonds with the universe of animals—past, present, and future. Young animals, particularly, tumble, chase, run, wrestle, mock, imitate, and laugh (or so it seems) to the point of delighted exhaustion. Their play, and ours, appears to serve no other purpose than to give pleasure to the players, and apparently, to remove temporarily from the anguish of life in earnest.

Some philosophers have claimed that our playfulness is the most noble part of our basic nature. In their generous conceptions, play harmlessly and experimentally permits us to put our creative forces, fantasy, and imagination into action. Play is release from the tedious battles against scarcity and decline which are the incessant, and inevitable, tragedies of life. This is a grand conception that excites and provokes. The holders of this view claim that the origins of our highest accomplishments—liturgy, literature, and law—can be traced to a play impulse which, paradoxically, we see most purely enjoyed by young beasts and children. Our sports, in this rather happy, nonfatalistic view of human nature, are more splendid creations of the nondatable, transspecies play impulse.

25. What is the best title for the passage?

(A) Games for Animals

(B) The Origins and Meaning of Play

(C) A Playful View of Modern Philosophy

(D) The Role of Sport on Child Development

26. It seems to the author that young animals play in order to ______.

(A) gain pleasure

(B) learn specific behavior patterns

(C) delight their owners

(D) exercise their growing muscles

27. The word "noble" in Para. 2 Line 1 could best be replaced by which of the following?

(A) Snobbish.

(B) Wealthy.

(C) Royal.

(D) Admirable.

28. Which of the following conclusions about sports could best be drawn from the passage?

(A) They gradually evolved from play.

(B) They prepare children for conflict in life.

(C) They are becoming more popular among adults.

(D) They developed from conflicting impulses.

生词及短语

wrestle ['res(ə) l]	*v.*	摔跤,角斗
frolic ['frɔlik]	*vi.*	嬉戏,欢闹
play tag		玩鬼抓人游戏
transgenerational [træns'dʒeːnəreiʃənəl]	*a.*	跨代的
transspecies [træns'spiːʃiːz]	*n.*	超类
bond (with)		约定,合同
in earnest		真正地,认真地
anguish ['æŋgwiʃ]	*n.*	苦恼,苦闷
in earnest		认真地,真正地
fantasy ['fæntəsi]	*n.*	空想,幻想,梦想
tedious ['tiːdiəs]	*a.*	乏味的,单调的
liturgy ['litədʒi]	*n.*	礼拜仪式,圣餐仪式
paradoxically [pærə'dɔkskəli]	*ad.*	似是而非地,矛盾地,反论地
nonfatalistic [nɔn'feitə'listik]	*a.*	非宿命论的
nondatable ['nɔndeitəbl]	*a.*	不能测定年代的,不能测定日期的

答案与解析

25. [答案] (B)

[解析] 本题为主旨题。全文阐述了体育运动的起源及其真正含义,答案应为(B)。(A)、(C)只在文中提到,不是主题;(D)未被提到,故可以排除。

26. [答案] (A)

[解析] 第一段最后一句指出 "Their play, and ours, appear to serve no other purpose than to give pleasure to the players",可见答案为(A)。

27. [答案](D)

[解析] notable 意为"值得注意的,显著的",与 admirable"值得称赞的,极好的"在意义上最为接近,故选(D)。

28. [答案](A)

[解析] 本题为推理题,可根据上下文推断或用排除法得出。全文阐述了运动的起源为 play,可见答案明显应为(A)。(B)、(C) 文中未提到,(D) 与文中内容相矛盾,故均可排除。

译文

体育运动始于何时?从本质上讲,如果说体育运动是一种游戏,那么可以说,体育运动要比人类存在的时间长得多。因为正如我们所观察到的,动物也会玩耍。狗和猫会扭打和玩球,鱼和鸟会跳舞,猩猩会做简单有趣的游戏。婴孩嬉闹,小学生捉迷藏,成人掰手腕,都说明了动物世界中存在一种强烈的、超种类和跨代的纽带,无论过去、现在和将来都是如此。特别是小动物兴高采烈地打滚、追逐、奔跑、摔跤、嘲弄、模仿和笑(或看起来像笑)以致到筋疲力尽的地步。他们的玩耍和我们的一样,除了给玩耍者以快乐,而且很明显是要使我们暂时真正摆脱生活中的苦恼。

一些哲学家说过,玩耍是我们基本本质中最高尚的部分。根据他们的大量观点,无害和试验性的玩耍能使我们把创造力、幻想和想象付诸于实施。玩耍就是从同贫穷和衰落——无休止和不可避免的生活悲剧——枯燥乏味的斗争中解脱出来。这是一个令人兴奋和刺激的观念。这种观念的持有者声称,我们的最高成就——礼拜仪式、文学和法律——的源泉可追溯到玩耍冲动,我们发现这个玩耍冲动很矛盾地最受小孩子和年幼动物喜爱。根据这种对人类本性乐观和非宿命论的观点,体育运动是一种不可追溯年代和由超类别玩耍冲动产生的更光辉的产物。

Passage 3

The cost of the First World War to the United States, exclusive of the loss of life and suffering involved and the subsequent payments to veterans, runs into figures almost beyond human comprehension. Including nearly $9,500,000,000 lent to foreign governments, the direct cost for the three years following the declaration of war was around $35,500,000,000. This was three times the total expenditures of the federal government during the first 100 years of its existence, and over $1,000,000 an hour during the 25 months following the declaration of war.

The first problem to be settled in financing the war was, "What proportion of the cost was to be borne by taxes, and what proportion by loans?" In other words, what part of the cost was to be placed on the backs of subsequent generations? As it turned out, about one-third was raised by taxation, and the rest by loans. Beginning with the War Revenue Bill, Congress raised the income, inheritance, and excise taxes, and inaugurated taxes on excess profits and luxuries. Congress, however, stood firm on the principle of low tariffs.

The money that the government borrowed was obtained by means of four "Liberty Loans" and one "Victory Loan." Unlike their practice during former wars, the government made a direct appeal to the people, and by selling the bonds in denominations as low as $50 received aid from millions who until then had never seen a government bond. Over 22,000,000 people subscribed to the "Fourth Liberty Loan." All of the loans were oversubscribed, and about $21,500,000,000 were allotted. Never during the war did the government suffer from inadequate funds or credit.

29. What is the main topic of the passage?
    (A) The patriotism of the United States military.
    (B) One hundred years of United States finance.
    (C) Investment opportunities for the middle class.
    (D) Paying for the First World War.

30. In Line 1, the expression "exclusive of" could best be replaced by ______.
    (A) considering
    (B) restricted to
    (C) not including
    (D) unacceptable to

31. Which of the following is included in the $35,500,000,000 mentioned in the passage?
    (A) Payments to retired soldiers.
    (B) Loans to foreign governments.
    (C) Interest payments on government bonds.
    (D) Salaries paid to members of Congress.

32. Which of the following kinds of taxes was NOT raised to pay for the war?
    (A) Luxury.
    (B) Income.
    (C) Tariff.
    (D) Inheritance.

生词及短语

exclusive of　　除了……之外

veteran ['vetərən]	*n.*	退役军人
expenditure [ek'spenditʃə(r)]	*n.*	支出
inaugurate [i'nɔːgjureit]	*vt.*	开创,开始
denomination [dinɔmi'neiʃ(ə) n]	*n.*	面值,单位
allot [ə'lɔt]	*vt.*	分派,分配

答案与解析

29. [答案] (**D**)

[解析] 本题为主旨题。全文主要叙述了美国为第一次世界大战所付出的巨大代价和获得战争经费的途径,故答案应为(D)。(A)、(B)、(C)均超出文章范围。

30. [答案] (**C**)

[解析] 第一行中的"exclusive of"意为"排除……在外",与(C)同义。

31. [答案] (**B**)

[解析] 从第一段第二句"Including nearly... $35,500,000,000"可见答案为(B)。

32. [答案] (**C**)

[解析] 由第二段第四句"Congress raised ... and luxuries. ..."可排除(A)、(B)和(D),故答案为(C)。

译文

除去人员伤亡的损失和最后对退役军人的赔偿,美国为第一次世界大战所付出的代价数额之高简直令人无法想象。包括给外国政府95亿美元的贷款,宣战之后三年的直接代价大约为355亿美元。这是美国建国100年来联邦政府总支出的三倍,宣战后的25个月之内平均每小时超过100万美元。

为解决战争经费,首先要解决的问题是:多大比例要靠税收获得,多大比例靠贷款获取?换句话说,战争经费的多少要由下一代人承担?结果是,大约1/3的战争费用靠税收收取,其余则靠贷款。从战争税收法开始着手,国会提高了个人所得税、遗产税和消费税,并开创了超利税和奢侈税。然而国会却坚持低关税率的原则。

政府借款的形式包括四种"自由贷款"和一种"胜利贷款"。不同于在以前的战争中的做法,政府直接呼吁民众并通过抛售面额低达50美元的债券,从数以百万计的在那时从未见过政府债券的人手中获得帮助。2,200多万人认购了"第四种自由贷款"。所有债券被超额认购,大约2.15亿美元被分配。战争期间,政府从未感到经费或贷款额不足。

Passage 4

To understand how the elaborate social systems of honeybees or ants may have arisen, let us consider first some members of the order Hymenoptera(bees, wasps, and ants) in which sociality is less highly developed.

A female bee of the subsocial genus Hulictus constructs an underground comb of up to 20 cells, lays an egg in each, provisions the cells with food, and then closes the nest, after which she may remain on guard until her offspring emerge. In some species the young bees have to leave and build their own nests else where, but in some they remain in the parental nest, enlarging it and laying their eggs there. Though there are no castes, and each female is capable of reproduction, there is a breakdown of spatial barriers, and the communal sharing of a resting site can easily be imagined as the evolutionary forerunner of more complex social systems in other bees.

At a more advanced stage of sociality are the bumblebees. Here again the nest is founded in spring by a single female. But unlike the offspring of the Hulictus bee, the young that hatch from the founding bumblebees eggs do not become reproductive in their own right, they serve as workers, enlarging the nest, gathering nectar and pollen, and caring for the young that hatch from later eggs laid by the founder. The founder, who remains in the nest as the queen, now devotes most all her energy to egg laying. Eventually there may be several hundred, or even a thousand, bees in the colony. As the season nears its end, some unfertilized eggs are laid that give rise to males, and some of the fertilized eggs give rise to queens when the young that hatch from them are treated in a special fashion. These new reproductive individuals fly out and mate. The bees in the old hive die with the coming of winter, but the fertilized young queens hibernate and found their own nests the next spring. Because bumblebees have division of labor correlated with sterile castes, they are said to be eusocial (i.e. truly social), but their colonies, which must be founded anew each year because they cannot survive the winter, are by no means as complex as those of honeybees.

33. What is the best title for the passage?
(A) Treatment of the Young by Hulictus Bees and Bumblebees
(B) Division of Labor among Hulictus Bees and Bumblebees
(C) Nest Structures of Hulictus Bees and Bumblebees
(D) Social Systems of Hulictus Bees and Bumblebees

34. According to the passage, what does a female Hulictus Bee generally do after closing a nest?
(A) Migrates to a warmer climate.

(B) Constructs larger underground combs.

(C) Returns to her parental nesting site.

(D) Protects the nest until her offspring hatch.

35. The topic of the passage is developed primarily by means of ______.

(A) comparison and contrast

(B) rhetorical questions and argumentation

(C) describing chronological relationships

(D) drawing a variety of analogies

36. A paragraph following the passage would most probably discuss ______.

(A) the importance of age and social status to queen bees

(B) different types of bee hives

(C) the social structure of honeybees

(D) life patterns of male bumblebees

生词及短语

wasp [wɔsp]	*n.*	胡蜂,黄蜂
genus ['dʒiːnəs]	*n.*	种类,分类
caste [kɑːst]	*n.*	种姓制度
bumblebee ['bʌmblbiː]	*n.*	大黄蜂
nectar ['nektə(r)]	*n.*	(花的)蜜
pollen ['pɔlən]	*n.*	花粉
hibernate ['haibəneit]	*v.*	冬眠
sterile ['sterail]	*a.*	不育的

答案与解析

33. [答案] (**D**)

[解析] 全文详细讲述了有关 Hulictus 蜂和野蜂群居体制以及群居体制的形成。故答案应为(D)。

34. [答案] (**D**)

[解析] 从第二段第一句中 "... after which she may remain on guard until her offspring emerge."可确定答案为(D)。

35. [答案](C)

[解析] 本文以两种特殊的蜂种为例,按照蜂的演化阶段从简单到复杂加以叙述。采用排除法,答案应为(C)。

36. [答案](C)

[解析] 文章最后一句话起着承上启下的作用,Because bumblebees have division of labor ... but their colonies, ... are by no means as complex as those of honeybees.可以推断出下段将叙述 honeybee's colonies,答案应为(C)。

译文

要了解蜜蜂或蚂蚁精密的群居体制是怎样形成的,我们首先来看一下群居程度还不明显但有纪律的膜翅目动物(蜂、黄蜂和蚂蚁)的一些成员。

一个雌性次群居类蜂 Hulictus 会修建一个多达 20 个巢穴的地下蜂房,每个巢穴中产一个卵并供以食物,然后封闭巢穴,之后她会保护巢穴直到其后代破巢而出。在一些种类中,幼蜂要出走,在别处建造自己的蜂房并产卵,而另一些种类的幼蜂则会留住在父母的蜂房,将其扩大并在此产卵,虽然不存在等级之分并且每一个雌蜂都能繁殖,但空间障碍要被打破,如此共同享有一个蜂房使我们不难想像这就是其他更复杂的群居蜂体制的演化前身。

大黄蜂是一种位于较高群居阶段的蜂种。一个雌蜂在春天筑起一个巢房,但不同于 Hulictus 蜂后裔的是,由雌蜂卵所孵出的幼雌蜂天生不会繁殖,它们作为工蜂,担负着扩建巢房、采集花蜜和花粉的任务并看护由母蜂再产卵孵出的小蜂。母蜂留在蜂巢中作为蜂后,专心致志地产卵。最终该群体中可能会有数百或数千只蜂。随着季节结束,一些未受精的卵子产出,孵出雄蜂。而当一些受精卵所孵出的幼蜂受到特殊对待时,则产出蜂王。这些新的会繁殖的蜂飞走并交配。冬天降临时,老巢中的蜂死去,而受精的年轻蜂后则冬眠并在来年春天找到自己的巢房。由于大黄蜂的劳动分工与不生育阶层有关,我们称其为完全群居(即真正的群居)蜂种。由于不能活过冬天,每年必须更新,所以群居体制并不像蜜蜂那样复杂。

阅读 B 篇

Directions:

In the following article, some sentences have been removed. For Questions 37—41, choose the most suitable one from the list A—G to fit into each of the numbered blanks. There are two extra choices, which do not fit in any of the blanks. Mark your answers on ANSWER SHEET 1. (10 points)

Nike is one of the most powerful marketing companies in the business world today, but it had very small beginnings. The global giant company with revenues in 1996 of $6.4 billion and profits of $553 million started in the 1960s with the company's founders selling cheap Japanese sports shoes to American high school athletes at school track meetings, using a supply of shoes they kept in their car.

One of Nike's founders, Phillip Hampson Knight had been a top athlete when he was at the University of Oregon. He moved on to become a student at Stanford Business School, but retained his interest in sport. 37. ______________.

Subsequently, Knight visited Japan and discovered a manufacturer who fitted the model of the ideal firm—Onituska Tiger Company, which made its own inexpensive, high-quality running shoes.

38. ______________. He suggested to his old college track coach. Bill Bowerman, that they could work together using their skills and interests in sport and business, and capitalise on the cheaper cost of sports shoes from Japan. In 1964 they each, contributed $500 to import Tiger shoes, which Knight began selling from his car at high-school track meets.

39. ______________. Knight and Bowerman developed their own brand name, Nike, named after the Greek winged goddess of victory. They paid a local design student at Portland State University $35 to create the famous "Swoosh" logo, and Bowerman created the innovative pattern called the waffle-sole design, by using his wife's waffle iron to impose the pattern on the sole of the shoe. By 1972 Nike began designing its own shoes and was contracting production out to factories in Asia. With excellent timing and a fair share of good luck, the founders of Nike were perfectly placed to cash in on America's sports leisure boom during the 1970s, when millions of Americans began jogging and running as part of their personal campaigns to keep fit and healthy.

40. ______________. But at the heart of its constant campaign is the star athlete, a principle that was put in place early in the huge American company's marketing plans.

41. ______________. Other endorsements came soon after that, such as leading American tennis player Jimmy Connors who won the Wimbledon and the U.S. Open Grand Slam tennis tournaments in 1974 wearing Nike tennis shoes. In 1985, the man who would become one of Nike's biggest successes, Chicago Bulls rookie basketball player Michael Jordan, endorsed his first line of "Air Jordan" shoes. The endorsements by star players, encouraging ordinary consumers to buy the sports gear of the stars and dream of being champions themselves, saw Nike selling close to $1 billion worth of running, basketball, and tennis shoes in 1986, while creating their first sports clothes under the Nike label.

(A) Nowadays, Nike's products include not only basketball and tennis shoes, but also sports clothes, sports bags, sports caps, etc.

(B) Back in the U.S., Knight got to thinking that he could actually put his knowledge into practice, and make money.

(C) In 1973, the newly formed company implemented its first, and most import ant marketing strategy, endorsing its first star athlete, running star Steve Prefontaine who in turn used and praised Nike footwear.

(D) To reinforce its dominant worldwide presence, Nike spent $642 million in 1996 on advertising and promotion.

(E) The name of Nike comes from the goddess of victory in Greek mythology.

(F) At Stanford he brought his enthusiasm for track sports to his studies, writing a paper on how to create a cheaper, better running shoe using Japanese labour, which was cheaper than American.

(G) Worried that the Japanese company might find a more established distributor.

内容提要

本文主要叙述耐克公司的发展过程。第一段指出,耐克是今天商界最强大的销售公司之一,但它在创始的时候规模却很小。这个全球巨人公司 1996 年创下了 64 亿美元的收入,而 60 年代公司开创时利润仅为 5.35 亿美元,它是靠创始人在学校田径比赛时推销日本廉价运动鞋发展起来的。

答案与解析

37. [答案] (F)

[解析] 空白前提到耐克品牌的创始人奈特是一位斯坦福商学院的学生,曾经是优秀的体操运动员,一直对体育情有独钟。(F)继续叙述他在斯坦福商学院提出的对体育服装的观点。

38. [答案] (B)

[解析] 前一段提到奈特访问日本并找到理想的跑鞋制造商,(B)叙述他回到美国考虑将自己的想法付诸实践,并想方设法赚钱。

39. [答案] (G)

[解析] 前一段提到奈特与前教练合作,引进并销售日本老虎牌跑鞋。(G)明显接上段内容:他和教练鲍尔曼担心日本公司会另找代理,因而考虑发展自己的品牌——耐克。

40. [答案] (D)

[解析] 前段提到耐克鞋在亚洲有工场,并且在美国热爱跑步的运动者中得到大发展,(D)进一步指出:为了加强它在世界上的影响,耐克公司在 1996 年投巨资到广告宣传和推广产品中。

41. [答案](C)

[解析] 前段提到最初耐克的战略重点是在美国,(C) 提到这种战略发生改变:1973 年,新组成的公司实施了新的战略,和跑步体育明星签约使用和宣传耐克鞋。后面提到了和其他明星签约,包括篮球明星迈克尔·乔丹。

阅读 C 篇

Directions:

Read the following text carefully and then translate the underlined segments into Chinese. Your translation should be written neatly on ANSWER SHEET 2. (10 points)

(42) Air travel is such an everyday experience these days that we are not surprised when we read about a politician having talks with the Japanese Prime Minister one day, attending a conference in Australia the following morning and having to be off at midday to sign a trade agreement in Hong Kong. But frequent long-distance flying can be so tiring that the traveller begins to feel his brain is in one country, his digestion in another and his powers of concentration nowhere—in short, he hardly knows where he is.

The fatigue we normally experience after a long journey will become even more acute when we fly from east to west or vice versa because we cross time zones. (43) Air travel is so quick nowadays that we can leave London after breakfast and be in New York in eight hours, yet what really disturbs us most is that when we arrive it is only lunch time when we have already had lunch on the plane and are expecting dinner.

(44) Doctors say that since air travellers are in no condition to work after crossing a number of time zones, they should go straight to bed on arrival. Airline pilots, however, often live by their own watches, ignoring local time, and have breakfast at midnight if necessary.

(45) Businessmen who go on long-distance flights, however, are usually proud of having been chosen because it adds to their position in the firm. They are lucky if the boss is clever enough to insist on their taking the doctor's advice and resting for a day before work. Sometimes the managing director is such an energetic person that he expects everyone to be as fit as he is. As he has never felt any ill effects after flying himself, the schedule he lays down is so tight that the employee is too exhausted to carry it out satisfactorily. He must either go straight to an important meeting as soon as his plane touches down or else return as soon as the meeting is over to his boss.

(46) Managers of this type often do not realize how disastrous this policy may be for the man's health and the company's reputation.

生词及短语

powers of concentration		注意力
acute [ə'kjuːt]	*a.*	剧烈的,加剧的
time zones		时区
lay down		制订,规定
touch down		降落

全文译文与答案

(42) 如今空中旅行是一件司空见惯的事,因此当我们在报纸上读到某日某位政治家在和日本首相进行谈判,第二天上午又在澳大利亚参加一个会议,中午还得赶到香港去签署一项贸易协定的报道时,就不会感到奇怪了。但频繁的长途飞行会令人非常疲倦,以至于旅行者开始感觉他的头脑是在一个国家,他的胃口是在另一个国家,而他的注意力却不知道在哪里。一句话,他几乎不知道自己在什么地方。

当我们从东方飞到西方或者反之,我们通常感觉到长途旅行的疲倦会加剧,因为我们跨越了时区。(43) 现在空中旅行的速度是这么快,我们早餐后离开伦敦,八小时后就能到达纽约;但是更使我们感到不适应的是,当我们到达纽约时还只是吃午饭的时候,而我们却已经在飞机上吃过午饭,正等着吃晚饭。

(44) 医生们说,既然空中旅行的人在越过几个时区之后身体状况还不能适应工作,他们到达目的地后应该马上去睡觉。可是飞机驾驶员则是按照自己手表上的时间安排生活,他们不管当地是什么时间,需要时就在半夜里吃早饭。

(45) 可是那些坐长途飞机的商人通常会由于被选中而感到自豪,因为他们在公司里的地位会因此而得到提高。要是那位上司很明智,坚持要他们按照医嘱休息一天再去上班的话,他们就算交上了好运。有时候总经理是精力非常充沛的人,他希望每一个人都像他一样健康。由于他在长途飞行之后从没有什么不适,他所制订的时间表是如此的紧凑以至于他的手下感觉到太疲惫而难以满意完成任务。他必须在飞机刚降落之后就直接奔赴一个重要会议,而在会议刚结束就返回去见自己的老板。

(46) 像这样的经理往往并不了解这样的政策会有损于员工们的健康和公司的声誉。

阅读强化练习九

阅读 A 篇

Directions:

Read the following four texts. Answer the questions below each text by choosing A, B, C or D. Mark your answers on ANSWER SHEET 1. (40 points)

Passage 1

The little art gallery run by Alfred Stieglitz at 291 Fifth Avenue, New York, was never merely a business operation. It was a meeting place, a place to discuss and exchange ideas. It was a place where new art hung on the walls, transferring to the visitor the excitement of discovery. Stieglitz in his little gallery shone like a beacon to those who came to hear him talk , drawn irresistibly as moths. People returned again and again so that the gallery became like the salon of old. One of the new painters shown by Stieglitz was Georgia O'Keeffe, who had been exhibited at "291" a year earlier. Upon her return to New York in 1917, she was given a second exhibition at "291". This time the show was larger and more complete than the original one which had only drawings.

Georgia O'Keeffe's work through there and following years was in the almost purely abstract manner which she had developed while in Texas. She completely *renounced* the styles of her student and commercial art days. To find herself, she had to discover the barest and most basic elements in design. It would never have been her way to paint in abstract style only because other painters were doing so. French art was beginning to cross the Atlantic in waves, turning later to a flood, and the Armory Show of 1913 in New York influenced attitudes in the United States in the direction of abstract art. But Georgia O'Keeffe had already developed her own style using abstract expression as a means of arriving at the basic elements of what she wanted to say. She stripped away everything, and then built again for herself slowly and over a period of time. Although many painters began working in the abstract style, Georgia O'Keeffe followed no one.

21. What is the main subject of the passage?
   (A) New York in the early 1900s.
   (B) Georgia O'Keeffe's work.
   (C) Stieglitz business operation.
   (D) French art in New York.

22. Which of the following can be inferred about Georgia O'Keeffe's second exhibition?
   (A) It was not a success.
   (B) It included more than drawings.
   (C) It was her last one at "291".
   (D) It reflected life in Texas.

23. The word "renounced" in Line 11 is closest in meaning to which of the following?
   (A) Distorted.
   (B) Copied.
   (C) Rejected.
   (D) Repeated.

24. Where in the passage does the author mention an event that influenced people's ideas about the abstract style?
   (A) Lines 6—8.
   (B) Lines 10—11.
   (C) Lines 14—16.
   (D) Lines 19—20.

生词及短语

beacon ['biːkən]	*n.*	灯塔
renounce [ri'nauns]	*vt.*	放弃,抛弃
bare [beə(r)]	*a.*	赤裸的,无修饰的
strip ['strip]	*v.*	剥去,剥下

答案与解析

21. [答案](**B**)

[解析]本题为主旨题。短文主要叙述 Georgia O'Keeffe 的情况和她的抽象艺术风格的形成及其在"291"的展出,故答案应为(B)。

22. [答案](**B**)

[解析]由第一段最后一句 "This time the show was larger and more complete than the original one which had only drawings",可以推断出答案应为(B)。

23. [答案](**C**)

[解析]renounced 意为"抛弃",与 Rejected 同义。答案为(C)。

24. [答案](**C**)

[解析]从 15—16 行中"... and the Armory Show... abstract art",可断定答案为(C)。

译文

由阿尔弗雷德·施蒂格利茨在纽约第五街 291 号经营的小艺术馆决不是纯商业性的。这是一个聚会地,一个讨论和交换思想的场所,一面墙上挂着新的艺术品,为参观者传递创作激情的场所。在她的小艺术馆里,施蒂格利茨像灯塔吸引飞蛾一样吸引前来听他演讲的人们。人们不断地往返于此使得艺术馆变得像古代的沙龙。施蒂格利茨所展出的新画家之一是乔治亚·奥基夫,她在一年前已在 291 号展出过作品。1917 年她返回纽约,在 291 号举行了第二次展览,这次展出比只有绘画的第一次规模更大,内容更丰富。

乔治亚·奥基夫在当地及随后几年在得克萨斯的作品是以几乎纯抽象的艺术形式创作的。她完全抛弃了自己学生和商业艺术时代的艺术风格。为了发现自我,她必须发掘最裸露和最基本的设计素材。她决不会以其他画家也在从事的抽象艺术方式来作画。法国艺术的潮流已经横穿大西洋,随后形成一股洪流,而 1913 年的纽约军械库艺术展(Armory show)影响了美国画家对抽象派艺术的态度。但这时乔治亚·奥基夫已经发展了自己的艺术风格,用抽象艺术来表达她想说明的基本素材。她剥掉了所有一切,经过一段时期又慢慢重建了自己的抽象艺术风格。尽管许多画家以抽象艺术风格进行创作,但乔治亚·奥基夫没有跟随任何人。

Passage 2

Barbara Hasten is an artist who makes photographs of constructions that she creates for the purpose of photographing them. In her studio she arranges objects such as mirrors, solid forms, and flat surfaces into what could be called large still life arrangements, big enough to walk into.

She lights the construction, then rearranges and rephotographs it until she arrives at a final image. She also photographs away from her studio at various architectural sites, bringing camera, lights, mirrors, and a crew of assistants to transform the site into her own abstract image.

Kasten starts a studio construction with a simple problem, such as using several circular and rectangular mirrors. She puts the first objects in place, sets up a camera, then goes back and forth arranging objects and seeing how they appear in the camera. Eventually she makes instant color prints to see what the image looks like. At first she works only with objects, concentrating on their composition, then she lights them and adds color from lights covered with colored filters.

Away from the studio, at architectural sites, the cost of the crew and the equipment rental means she has to know in advance what she wants to do. She visits each location several times to make sketches and tests *shots*. Until she brings in the light, however, she can't predict exactly what they will do to the image, so there is some improvising on the spot.

25. What does the passage mainly discuss?
    (A) The techniques of a photographer.
    (B) The advantages of studio photography.
    (C) Industrial construction sites.
    (D) An architect who appreciates fine art.

26. In Line 2, why does the author mention mirrors?
    (A) They are part of the camera.
    (B) Kasten uses them as subjects.
    (C) The crew needs them.
    (D) Photography mirrors life.

27. The word "*shots*" in Para 3. Line 3 is closest in meaning to which of the following?
    (A) Injections.
    (B) Photographs.
    (C) Loud noises.
    (D) Effective remarks.

28. Why does Kasten visit the location of outdoor work before the day of the actual shooting?
    (A) To plan the photograph.
    (B) To purchase film and equipment.
    (C) To hire a crew.
    (D) To test the lights.

生词及短语

rectangular [rekˈtæŋgjulə(r)]　*a.*　长方形的，成直角的
back and forth　前后地，往复地
rental [ˈrent(ə)l]　*n.*　租金，租赁
improvising [ˈimprəvaiz]　*v.*　即兴，即席创作

答案与解析

25. [答案] (A)
[解析] 本题为主旨题。短文始终围绕卡斯滕如何进行室内外建筑物的摄影而描述，答案明显为(A)。(B)、(C)、(D)文中未提及，故均可排除。

26. [答案] (B)
[解析] 从第一段第二句"In her studio she arranges objects such as mirrors ..."，可知答案应为(B)。

27. [答案] (B)
[解析] shots 意为"照片，快照"，与 photographs"摄影，照片"同义，故答案为(B)。

28. [答案] (A)
[解析] 从第三段 2—3 行 "... she has to know in advance what she wants to do. She visits each location several times to make sketches and test shots." 可推断卡斯滕在实拍之前走访现场的目的是为实拍做安排，答案应为(A)。

译文

芭芭拉·卡斯滕是一位建筑摄影艺术家，她塑造出建筑结构以便对其进行拍照。在摄影棚里，她将诸如镜子、立方体、平面体等物体布置成所谓的大型静物摄影结构，大得足以让人走进去。她照亮这种结构进行拍照，然后重新布置再拍照，直到获得最终的照片。她还走出摄影棚到各种各样的建筑物现场进行拍照，带着相机、灯具、镜子和一组助手将这些建筑物现场变成她自己抽象的照片。

卡斯滕很简单地便开始了摄影棚内建筑造型的布置，诸如使用几个圆形和直角形镜子。她将第一批物体放好，架好相机，然后来回反复地对物体进行摆放，并观察它们在相机中的形象。最终她打印出即时照片看看如何。开始她只对物体进行拍照，注意其组成，随后对物体投以灯光，并通过罩在灯具上的彩色滤光片增加彩光。

走出摄影棚，在建筑物现场时，摄影组成员的花费及设备租金意味着她必须事先知道她

要干什么。她走访每一个场地,多次进行素描和试拍。然而,直到她带着灯具来到现场,她还不能准确预测他们将如何对物体拍照,因而会有一些现场的即兴创作。

Passage 3

To understand the emulsifying process, we must first accept the scientific principle that oil and water do not naturally mix. Quite literally, *they* find each other's presence repulsive. A good illustration of this aversion is homemade oil-and-vinegar salad dressing.

When you shake or beat your salad dressing, you do more than disperse the oil throughout the vinegar: you also break down the oil into droplets minute enough to remain temporarily suspended in the vinegar (which from now on we will call water, because that tart condiment is, in effect, mainly water). The second you stop agitating the dressing, the oil droplets start to combine into units too large to be suspended in the water, and thus slither their way upward, separating from the water in the process. The oil rises to the top and the water sinks because oil has a lower specific density than water.

If you want a stable emulsion, yon need an emulsifying agent, which prevents the oil droplets from combining into larger units. Emulsifying agents occur naturally in many animal substances, including egg yolks and milk.

An emulsifying agent helps to keep the oil particles from combining in three basic ways. First, the agent coats the oil, serving as a physical barrier between the droplets. Second, it reduces the water's surface tension, which, in turn, reduces the water's ability to repulse oil. Third, the agent gives the surfaces of the oil droplets identical electrical charges, since like charges repel each other, the droplets repel each other.

29. What is the author's main purpose in the passage?
    (A) To show how emulsifiers are used to find oil.
    (B) To prove that oil and water do not mix.
    (C) To explain how emulsifiers work.
    (D) To discuss the nature of electrical charges.

30. What does "they" in Para. 1 Line 2 refer to?
    (A) Oil and water.
    (B) Oil droplets.
    (C) Emulsifying agents.
    (D) Animal substances.

31. Which of the following is mentioned as containing an emulsifying agent?

(A) Oil.

(B) Vinegar.

(C) Water.

(D) Milk.

32. If you make a salad dressing, add an emulsifying agent, shake the dressing, and then let it stand for several minutes, where would you expect to find the oil?

(A) At the bottom of the dressing.

(B) At the top of the dressing.

(C) In the middle of the dressing.

(D) Throughout the dressing.

生词及短语

emulsify [iˈmʌlsifai]	*vt.*	使乳化
aversion [əˈvəːʃ(ə) n]	*n.*	讨厌的事情(人或物)
vinegar [ˈvinigə(r)]	*n.*	醋
dressing [ˈdresiŋ]	*n.*	调味汁
droplet [ˈdrɔplit]	*n.*	微滴,小滴
tart [tɑːt]	*a.*	酸的
condiment [ˈkɔndimənt]	*n.*	佐料
agitate [ˈædʒiteit]	*vt.*	搅拌,搅动
slither [ˈsliðə(r)]	*v.*	滑动
yolk [jəuk]	*n.*	蛋黄

答案与解析

29. [答案] (C)

[解析] 本题为主旨题。文章主要说明乳化的基本原理和方法,答案应为(C)。

30. [答案] (A)

[解析] They 应指代前面句子中的成分,明显为 oil and water, 故答案为(A)。

31. [答案] (D)

[解析] 从第三段第二句"Emulsifying agents occur naturally in many animal substances, including egg yolks and milk."可知答案应为(D)。

32. [答案](D)

[解析]从第三、四段中可知,如加上乳化剂,油滴则不会结合,不会上升到表面,而是悬浮在水中。可见答案应为(D)。

译文

要理解乳化过程,我们首先必须接受这样一条科学原则,油和水不能自然混合。不夸张地说,它们相互排斥。自制的油醋色拉调味品就是说明这种讨厌事情的很好例证。

当摇动或搅拌色拉调味品时,要比在醋中扩散油更难:同样还要将油搅碎成微小液滴以暂时悬浮在醋中(从现在起,我们称醋为水,因为这种酸性调味品实质上主要是水)。第二步停止搅拌该调味品,小油滴开始结合成一个个单元体,它们很大以致不能再悬浮于水中,这样便向上滑动,在这个过程中与水分离。因为油的密度比水小,油上升至顶部,而水下沉。

如果希望稳定乳化,需要有乳化剂,它防止小油滴结合成较大的单元体。乳化剂自然产生于许多动物物质中,包括蛋黄和奶。

乳化剂以三种方式帮助防止油滴混合。首先,乳化剂包住油滴,形成油滴间的物理屏障。第二,它减小水表面的张力,反过来减小水排斥油滴的能力。第三,乳化剂给油滴表面以同种电荷,因为同种电荷相斥,油滴就相互排斥。

Passage 4

It is in the joints of the human body that movements of the bones take place. The movement itself is caused by the pull of sheets and cords of very tough tissue called muscle. Muscle tissue has the special ability to shorten itself so that the bone on which it pulls has to move. When muscle tissue shortens, it also bunches up. Muscle tissue covers the body in sheets and bands that lie between the skin and the skeleton. The bones are the framework of the body, but the muscles fill out the body shape. Most muscles extend from one bone to another. When the muscle between the bones shortens, one bone has to move. The point where the muscle is fastened to the unmoving bone is called the origin of the muscle, whereas the point where the muscle is fastened to the bone that is to be moved is called the insertion. Sometimes the muscle is not attached directly to the bone but to a tough, nonstretchable cord, or tendon, that is attached to the bone.

Muscles do not push; they can only pull. To band the arm at the elbow, the muscle at the front of the upper arm has to shorten and bunch up. To unbend the arm, other muscles in the back of the arm have to shorten. These two sets of muscles—the front and the back—are said to act in opposition to each other. When one set is working, the other set is usually relaxed. But there are times when both of them work. Sometimes muscles are called upon to do more than simply pull in one direction. They may have to perform a turning motion. To be able to do this, the muscle must be attached to the bone at an angle. By pulling, the muscle can cause the bone to pivot. A few muscles have special functions. The diaphragm, for example, forces the lungs to take in air. This part of breathing is not primarily a bone-moving operation.

33. What is the main subject of the passage?
   (A) How human muscle develops.
   (B) The differences between major muscle groups in the human body.
   (C) Problems with human muscles.
   (D) The anatomy and operation of human muscles.

34. According to the passage, movement occurs when a muscle ______.
   (A) grows
   (B) shortens
   (C) relaxes
   (D) pushes

35. Why are some muscles attached to bones at an angle?
   (A) To cause the muscles to push.
   (B) To strengthen the muscles.
   (C) To shorten tissues.
   (D) To perform a turning action.

36. Where in the passage does the author mention a bodily organ that is controlled by a particular muscle?
   (A) Lines 2—4.
   (B) Lines 7—9.
   (C) Lines 13—14.
   (D) Lines 19—20.

生词及短语

joint [dʒɔint]	*n.*	关节
cord [kɔːd]	*n.*	韧带,索状组织
bunch [bʌntʃ]	*v.*	形成……一束
tendon [ˈtend(ə) n]	*n.*	腱
pivot [ˈpivət]	*v.*	(以轴为中心的)旋转

diaphragm [ˈdaiəfræm] *n.* 横膈膜

答案与解析

33. [答案] (D)

[解析] 本题为主旨题。全文详细地从解剖学角度描述和说明了人体肌肉的作用和功能，答案明显为(D)。

34. [答案] (B)

[解析] 由文中第一段第2—4行“Muscle tissue has the special ability to shorten itself so that the bone on which it pulls has to move”，可见答案为(B)。

35. [答案] (D)

[解析] 由文中第二段6—7行“They may have to perform a turning motion. To be able to do this, the muscle must be attached to the bone at an angle”，可明确得出答案为(D)。

36. [答案] (D)

[解析] 文中第19行提到“The diaphragm, for example, forces the lungs to take in air”中，横膈膜(diaphragm)为“一块特殊的肌肉”，而肺为一种器官，故答案应为(D)。

译文

骨骼的运动在人体的关节部位发生，其运动自身是由称为肌肉的坚硬带状组织的拉动引起的。肌肉具有特殊的自行收缩能力，以至于它在骨骼上拉动时，骨骼不得不运动。当肌肉组织收缩时，它还形成束状。肌肉组织以位于皮肤和骨骼之间的带状形式覆盖整个身体。骨骼是人体的框架，而肌肉填充起人体的形态。大多数肌肉从一根骨头延伸到另一根骨头。当骨头间的肌肉收缩时，骨头就必须移动。肌肉固定于不移动骨头之点称为肌肉源，而肌肉固定于移动骨头之点称为肌止端。有时肌肉不是直接附着在骨头上，而是附着于骨头上的一种坚硬、不可伸展的韧带或肌腱上。

肌肉不能推动，只能拉动。要将臂在肘处弯曲，上臂前面的组织必须收缩并成束状。要将手臂伸直，手臂后面的其他肌肉必须收缩。这前后两组肌肉在做相反的运动。当一组在工作时，另一组通常处于松弛状态。但有时两者会同时工作。有时肌肉被要求从不止是一个方向拉动。它们还可能要进行转动。要做到这一点，肌肉就必须从一个角度附着于骨头上。通过拉动，肌肉可使骨头做轴性转动。一些肌肉具有特殊功能。例如，膈使肺吸入空气。这部分呼吸运动主要不是一种骨骼运动。

阅读 B 篇

Directions:

In the following article, some sentences have been removed. For Questions 37—41, choose the most suitable one from the list A—G to fit into each of the numbered blanks. There are two extra choices, which do not fit in any of the blanks. Mark your answers on ANSWER SHEET 1. (10 points)

Water is the most common substance on earth. It covers more than 70 percent of the earth's surface. It fills the oceans, rivers, and lakes, and is in the ground and in the air we breathe. Water is everywhere. Without water, there can be no life. In fact, every living thing consists mostly of water. (37) ________.

(38) ________. Rain hammers at the land and washes soil into rivers. The oceans pound against the shores, chiseling cliffs and carrying away land. Rivers knife through rock, carve canyons, and build up land where they empty into the sea. Glaciers plow valleys and cut down mountains.

(39) ________. Land absorbs and releases heat from the sun quickly. But the oceans absorb and release the sun's heat slowly. So breezes from the oceans bring warmth to the land in winter and coolness in summer.

Throughout history, water has been people's slaveand their master. Great civilizations have risen where water supplies were plentiful. They have fallen when these supplies failed. People have killed one another for a muddy water hole. They have worshiped rain gods and prayed for rain. Often when rains have failed to come, crops have withered and starvation has spread across a land. (40) ________.

Today, more than ever, water is both slave and master to people. We use water in our homes for cleaning, cooking, bathing, and carrying away wastes. We use water to irrigate dry farmlands so we can grow more food. Our factories use more water than any other material. We use the water in rushing rivers and thundering waterfalls to produce electricity. Our demand for water is constantly increasing.

Every year, there are more people in the world. Factories turn out more and more products, and need more and more water. We live in a world of water. But almost all of it—about 97 percent—is in the oceans. This water is too salty to be used for drinking, farming, and manufacturing. Only about 3 percent of the world's water is fresh (unsalty). (41) ________.

(A) Ever since the world began, water has been shaping the earth.

(B) When we are running, we feel thirsty and drink a lot of water. In fact, when we eat, the food consists of plenty of water.

(C) Water helps keep the earth's climate from getting too hot or too cold.

(D) Sometimes the rains have fallen too heavily and too suddenly. Then rivers have overflowed their banks, drowning large numbers of people and causing enormous destruction of property.

(E) Your body is about two-thirds water. A chicken is about three-fourths water, and a pineapple is about four-fifths water. Most scientists believe that life itself began in water—in the salty water of the sea.

(F) Nowadays, scientists are considering making use of ocean water. The application of the technology to turn salty water into fresh water will come into being very soon.

(G) Most of this water is not easily available to people because it is locked in icecaps and other glaciers. By the year 2010, the world demand for fresh water may be double what it was in the 1980s. But there will still be enough to meet people's needs.

内容提要

本文主要叙述水的构成和用途。第一段指出,水是地球上最普通的物质。水覆盖了地球表面的70%。它注入海洋、河流和湖泊,藏在地下和我们呼吸的空气中。没有水,就没有生命。实际上,每一个生物的大部分都是由水构成的。

答案与解析

37. [答案] (E)

[解析] 本段提到:水是地球上最普通的物质。什么地方都有水的存在,没有水就没有生命。事实上,每一样有生命的东西大部分都是由水组成的。根据逻辑推理,下文应该是叙述水在一些物质中的构成。故(E) 符合要求。

38. [答案] (A)

[解析] 本段空白处后面的内容提到"雨、海洋、河流和冰川对地球产生的作用",可以推知,本段段首句应该是本段的主题句,概述水对地球产生的作用。而(A) 符合这一要求。

39. [答案] (C)

[解析] 本段叙述了水对气候温度的调节作用:陆地很快地吸收和释放太阳的热量,而海洋缓慢地吸收和释放太阳的热量,这样海洋的微风在冬天将温暖带到陆地,而在

夏天将凉爽送到陆地。可见,空白处内容应该与气候和温度有关,(C) 为正确答案。

40. [答案] (D)

[解析] 本段第一句指出,从历史来看,水既是人们的奴隶又是人们的主人。接着列举了众多例子:人类伟大的文明是由丰富的水源发展起来的。文明随水源的枯竭而衰败,人们为水而互相残杀,他们崇拜水神,祈祷下雨,庄稼因干旱而枯萎,饥荒遍布大地。而空白处应该是继续这种叙述,而(D) 的内容是雨水太多给人们带来的灾难,符合上下文要求。

41. [答案] (G)

[解析] 本段叙述了人口增多与缺水的矛盾:世界人口每年都在增加,工厂在生产更多产品,需要用更多的水。我们生活在水的世界,但大约 97%的水是在海洋中,海水太咸不能饮用、浇灌和生产。世界上只有 3%的水是淡水。从逻辑上分析,空白处应该继续谈论水与人类的关系,而只有(G) 的内容符合。

阅读 C 篇

Directions:

Read the following text carefully and then translate the underlined segments into Chinese. Your translation should be written neatly on ANSWER SHEET 2. (10 points)

(42) Under modern conditions, rail transportation suffers severely from the competition of road transportation. The British railroad system has become relatively uneconomical. In the last decade very few lines have been constructed, except in large towns, and many existing lines have been forced to close. The main lines carry faster traffic and retain much of their earlier importance, but the branch lines have suffered. On those which still operate, many services have been cancelled.

(43) The great advantage of the railroad has always been its superior carrying capacity. It can carry bulky and heavy loads at relatively high speeds for long distances; one engine can pull a load of several hundred tons. Coal, iron ore, and grain are typical commodities for which in many parts of the world rail transportation is employed over long distances, when water transportation is not available. In Britain the main lines are still employed for the long-distance transportation of bulky goods.

(44) Mainline trains are also well suited to passenger and mail traffic. On main lines in Britain modern express trains have been introduced, often driven by powerful diesel engines. For long distances these trains have obvious advantages when compared to buses; they are faster, more comfortable, and probably safer. Seats on these trains are often booked up several days

ahead, and the demand exceeds the supply. (45) Another example of demand exceeding supply is the railroad's contribution to the rush-hour traffic, which is inadequate for present-day requirements. There are serious delays, and the health and leisure of passengers is sacrificed.

But rail transportation suffers from one serious disadvantage. It is inflexible; it is confined to rails, and obviously there cannot be as close a network of rails as of roads. Road transportation goes from door to door. (46) The lower cost per mile of rail transportation is more than balanced by the greater cost of loading and unloading at the beginning and end of many journeys.

生词及短语

bulky [ˈbʌlki]	*a.*	体积大的,笨重的
iron ore		铁矿石
demand exceeding supply		供不应求
confined to		受……限制
from door to door		挨家挨户

全文译文与答案

(42) 在当代的情况下,铁路运输受到了来自公路运输方面的激烈竞争。英国的铁路系统已经变得不够经济。近十年来,除了在大城市以外,极少建造新的线路,而现在的许多线路却被迫关闭。主要的线路运输很快,保持了它们原来的重要地位,但支线却损失惨重。对于这些仍然在经营的,许多业务都被取消。

(43) 长期以来,铁路的主要有利条件就是它那优越的运载能力。它能以较快的速度长途运输笨重而庞大的货物,一台机车就拉得动几千吨重的货物。当不能采用水运时,在世界上大部分国家,这些煤炭、矿产和粮食需要长途运输的货物都会采用铁路运输。在英国,主要铁路线仍然用于庞大货物的长途运输。

(44) 干线火车也很适于载客和运送邮件。在英国的各条铁路干线上,都已经采用了现代化的高速列车,这些火车通常是由大功率的柴油机车来牵引的。对于长途来说,这些火车具有比汽车更明显的优势;它们更快、更舒服,而且更安全。这些火车上的座位通常要提前数天预定,是供不应求的。(45) 供不应求的另一个例子是:铁路对解决高峰出行问题所起的作用仍然无法满足目前的需求的。火车会严重晚点,而且不利于旅客的健康与舒适。

但铁路运输也受到一个严重的不利因素的影响。它不灵活,受铁轨的限制,铁路网明显不能像公路网那样接近。公路运输可以做到送货上门。(46) 铁路运输每英里所收的费用虽然较低,却远远抵不上运程中始发站和终点站所要花的较高装卸费。

阅读强化练习十

阅读 A 篇

Directions:

Read the following four texts. Answer the questions below each text by choosing A, B, C or D. Mark your answers on ANSWER SHEET 1. (40 points)

Passage 1

Gertrude Vanderbilt Whitney announced the founding of the Whitney Museum of American Art in January 1930, but her support of artists from the United States had begun more than twenty years earlier. A sculptor in the academic tradition, she realized that there were few opportunities for independent artists to exhibit or sell their works, and from the early 1900s until her death in 1942, her abiding concern was to aid living artists from the United States. She remains the greatest patron of art of the twentieth century.

As early as 1907, Whitney organized an exhibition of contemporary art in the United States for the Colony Club, a women's club in New York City of which she was a founding member. The following year she purchased four of the seven paintings sold from the landmark exhibition of "The Eight" at the Macbeth Galleries. She contributed funds to the Armory Show of 1913, and for many years paid the deficit of the Society of Independent Artists, founded in 1917 .

In 1914 Whitney converted a townhouse into a small gallery known as the Whitney Studio which featured regular exhibitions of the work of artists from the United States. In 1918 she established the Whitney Studio Club: any artist introduced by a member could join the club, where annual exhibitions gave members a rare opportunity to present their work to the public without first submitting it to a jury.

She aided artists in numerous other ways—sending them abroad to study, paying their hospital bills and studio rents, and, most important, purchasing their works.

By 1929, Whitney owned more than five hundred works by artists from the United States, and she felt the public should have an opportunity to see the collection. That year she offered the collection to the Metropolitan Museum of Modern Art, whose director refused her offer before she even had a chance to express her intention to build and endow a Whitney wing. This abrupt rejection only served to challenge Whitney, who announced in January 1930 that she would establish her own museum with a new and dramatically different mandate to support artists from the United States.

21. What is the main topic of the passage?
   (A) Art movements in the twentieth century.
   (B) The hardships of twentieth-century United States artists.
   (C) The commitment of Whitney to artists from the United States.
   (D) The art collections at two different museums.

22. According to the passage, how was the Whitney Studio Club unusual?
   (A) It featured the works of foreign.
   (B) Membership was exclusive.
   (C) It was easy for artists to display their work.
   (D) The exhibitions were open to the public.

23. Which of the following is NOT mentioned in the passage as a way Whitney financially aided artists during her lifetime?
   (A) Building homes for them in New York.
   (B) Helping With Medical costs.
   (C) Providing Areas where their art could be displayed.
   (D) Paying for their study in foreign countries.

24. According to the passage, the refusal of Whitney's collection by the Metropolitan Museum of Modern Art resulted in her establishment of the ______.
   (A) Colony Club
   (B) Whitney Studio Club
   (C) Society of Independent Artists
   (D) Whitney Museum of American Art

生词及短语

sculptor [ˈskʌlptə(r)] *n.* 雕刻家

abiding [ə'baidiŋ] *a.* 持久的
patron ['peitrən] *n.* (艺术)赞助人,资助人
gallery ['gæləri] *n.* 画廊
deficit ['defisit] *n.* 赤字
endow [in'dau] *v.* 捐赠
mandate ['mændeit] *v.* 委任托管

答案与解析

21. [答案](**C**)

[解析]本题为主旨题。全文叙述了对美国艺术家所提供的各种各样的赞助,故答案应为(C)。commitment 有"aid, support"之意。

22. [答案](**C**)

[解析]根据第三段最后一句"... where annual exhibitions ... submitting it to a jury",可得出答案应为(C),rare=unusual。

23. [答案](**A**)

[解析]从上题和第四段"She aided artists in numerous, ... purchasing their works",可将(B)、(C)、(D)排除,只有(A)在文中没有提到。

24. [答案](**D**)

[解析]从第一段第1—2行"Whitney announced the founding of the Whitney Museum of American Art in January 1930"和最后一句"This abrupt rejection only served to challenge Whitney, ...",可得出答案应为(D)。

译文

格特鲁德·范德比尔特·惠特尼于1930年元月宣布建立惠特尼美国艺术博物馆,然而她对于美国艺术家们的支持早在二十年前就开始了。作为传统学术中的一位雕刻家,她认识到几乎没有任何机会让独立的艺术家们展出和销售他们的作品,自二十世纪初期直到1942年逝世,她一直关心的就是帮助美国还健在的艺术家们。她一直被称为二十世纪最伟大的艺术赞助人。

早在1907年,惠特尼就为侨民俱乐部组织了一次美国现代艺术展,该俱乐部是一个位于纽约的妇女俱乐部,而且她是该俱乐部的奠基人之一。第二年她购买了在麦克贝思美术馆举办的称为"The Eight"划时代画展中展出的七幅画中的四幅。她为1913年举办的军械库艺术展捐款,而且多年来为1917年成立的独立派艺术协会填补财政赤字。

1914年,惠特尼将一座市内住房变成一个小型美术馆,称为惠特尼画室,定期展出美国

艺术家们的作品。1918年,她建立了惠特尼画室俱乐部,任何一位由该俱乐部成员引见的艺术家都可加入该俱乐部,这里一年一度的展览为俱乐部成员把他们的作品展示给公众提供了一个非常宝贵的机会,他们不需要首先将作品交给评奖团。她还以其他各种方式帮助艺术家们:送他们去国外学习,为他们支付医疗费用和画室租金,同时最重要的是购买他们的作品。

到1929年,惠特尼拥有五百多幅美国画家的作品,她认为公众应该有机会来参观这些收藏品。那一年她将这些收藏品赠给大都会现代艺术博物馆,但该馆的馆长在她甚至没有机会说明她想建立并捐赠一个"惠特尼"侧厅的意图之前就拒绝了她。这一突如其来的拒绝只能是对她的一次挑战,她于1930年元月宣布将修建一座她自己的,具有全新的和完全不同托管权的博物馆来帮助美国艺术家。

Passage 2

The Alaska pipeline starts at the frozen edge of the Arctic ocean. It stretches southward across the largest and northern-most state in the United States, ending at a remote ice-free seaport village nearly 800 miles from where it begins. It is massive in size and extremely complicated to operate.

The steel pipe crosses windswept plains and endless miles of delicate tundra that tops the frozen ground. It weaves through crooked canyons, climbs sheer mountains, plunges over rocky crags, makes its way through thick forests, and passes over or under hundreds of rivers and streams. The pipe is 4 feet in diameter, and up to 2 million barrels (or 84 million gallons) of crude oil can be pumped through it daily.

Resting on H-shaped steel racks called "bents", long sections of the pipeline follow a zigzag course high above the frozen earth. Other long sections drop out of sight beneath spongy or rocky ground and return to the surface later on. The pattern of the pipeline's up-and-down route is determined by the often harsh demands of the arctic and subarctic climate. The tortuous lay of the land, and the varied compositions of soil, rock, or permafrost (permanently frozen ground). A little more than half of the pipeline is elevated above the ground. The remainder is buried anywhere from 3 to 12 feet, depending largely upon the type of terrain and the properties of the soil.

One of the largest in the world, the pipeline cost approximately $8 billion and is by far the biggest and most expensive construction project ever undertaken by private industry. In fact, no single business could raise that much money, so 8 major oil companies formed a consortium in order to share the costs. Each company controlled oil rights to particular shares of land in the oil fields and paid into the pipeline-construction fund according to the size of its holdings. Today, despite enormous problems of climate, supply shortages, equipment breakdowns, labor disagreements, treacherous terrain, a certain amount of mismanagement, and even theft, the

Alaska pipeline has been completed and is operating.

25. The passage primarily discusses the pipeline's ______.

(A) operating costs.

(B) employees.

(C) consumers.

(D) construction.

26. The author mentions all of the following as important in determining the pipeline's route EXCEPT the ______.

(A) climate

(B) lay of the land itself

(C) local vegetation

(D) kind of soil and rock

27. How many companies shared the costs of constructing the pipeline?

(A) Three. (B) Four. (C) Eight. (D) Twelve.

28. Which of the following determined what percentage of the construction costs each member of the consortium would pay?

(A) How much oil field land each company owned.

(B) How long each company had owned land in the oil fields.

(C) How many people worked for each company.

(D) How many oil wells were located on the company's land.

生词及短语

delicate [ˈdelikət]	*a.*	棘手的
tundra [ˈtʌndrə]	*n.*	冻土地带
crook [kruk]	*v.*	弯曲
sheer [ʃiə(r)]	*a.*	陡峭的,完全的
crag [kræg]	*n.*	峭壁
rack [ræk]	*n.*	架
bent [bent]	*n.*	弯曲
zigzag [ˈzigzæg]	*a.*	弯曲的
tortuous [ˈtɔːtjuəs]	*a.*	曲折的
spongy [ˈspʌndʒi]	*a.*	柔软的,像海绵的

permafrost [ˈpəːməfrɔst] *n.* 永久冻结带
terrain [teˈrein] *n.* 地形
treacherous [ˈtretʃərəs] *a.* 背叛的

答案与解析

25. [答案] (D)

[解析] 本题为主旨题。文章自始至终介绍了阿拉斯加输油管线的铺设情况,而选项(A)意为"经营成本";(B)意为"雇员";(C)意为"用户";显然不是主题,故答案应为(D)。

26. [答案] (C)

[解析] 从第三段第3—6行 "The pattern of the pipeline's up-and-down route ... or permafrost (permanently frozen ground)."可知(C)未被提及,故答案为(C)。

27. [答案] (C)

[解析] 从第四段第3—4行 "... so 8 major oil companies formed a consortium in order to share the costs."可知答案应为(C)。

28. [答案] (A)

[解析] 从第四段第4—6行"Each company controlled ... the size of its holdings."可得出答案为(A)。

译文

阿拉斯加输油管线起始于冰封的北极洋边缘地带,它向南延伸,横穿美国最大、最北面的州,终止于距起始点近800英里遥远的不冻港村落。该输油管线非常长,铺设工作极为困难。

这条钢制输油管线穿过狂风呼啸的平原以及地表冰冻的冻土地带,迂回过弯曲的峡谷,爬过陡峭的山岭,贯穿峭壁,经过茂密的森林,横跨或穿过数以百计的河流、小溪。这条输油管线直径为4英尺,日原油流量可达两百万桶(即八千四百万加仑)。

置于称为"弯曲"的H型钢制架上,长长的油管管道在冰冻的地面上空形成"之"字形路线,另外一些长管段消失在松软的或充满坚硬岩石的地下,然后钻出地面。油管的上下路线形状取决于北极和亚北极恶劣的气候条件,曲折的地形以及各式各样的土壤、岩石和永久性冻土的构成。只有一半的油管位于地面之上,其余部分则被埋在地下3至12英尺下,这主要是取决于地带类型和土壤的性质。

作为全世界最大的输油管道之一,这条输油管大约耗资80亿美元,并且是迄今为止由私营企业所完成的最大最昂贵的建筑工程。实际上,没有哪一个企业能单独筹集到这么多资金。因此,8个主要的石油公司组成了一个联合财团来分担这项开支,每一个公司都控制了油田地区的一定股份的原油优惠权,并根据自己份额的大小支付输油管道的铺设费用。今天,尽管存在气候恶劣、供应短缺、设备损坏、劳资争议和困难的地理环境,以及一定程度上的管理不善,甚至偷盗等诸多严重问题,但阿拉斯加输油管线已经竣工并且正在运转。

Passage 3

The North American frontier changed some of the characteristics of the pioneers of the 1750s and intensified others. They were, as a group, semiliterate, proud, and stubborn, as dogged in their insistence on their own way of life as pine roots cracking granite to grow. Perhaps their greatest resource was their capacity to endure. They outlasted recurrent plagues of smallpox and malaria and a steady progression of natural accidents. They were incredibly prolific. Squire Boone's family of eight children was small by frontier standards. James Robertson, an eventual neighbor of Boone's and the founder of Nashville, had eleven children. Twice-married John Sevier, the first governor of Tennessee, fathered eighteen; his long-time enemy, John Tipton, also twice married, produced seventeen.

The entire assets of one of these huge families often amounted, in the beginning, to little more than an axe, a hunting knife, an auger, a rifle, a horse or two, some cattle and a few pigs, a sack of seed corn and another of salt, perhaps a crosscut saw, and a loom. Those who moved first into a new region lived for months at a time on wild meat, Indian maize, and native fruits in season. Yet if they were poor at the beginning, they confidently expected that soon they would be rich.

In a way almost impossible to define to urban dwellers, a slice of ground suitable for farming represented not just dollars and cents, but dignity. The obsession brought shiploads of yearners every week to Boston, New York, Philadelphia, Baltimore, Charles Towne, and Savannah. It sent them streaming westward into the wilderness after their predecessors to raise still more children who wanted still more land.

29. In Line 3, the author uses the phrase "as pine roots cracking granite to grow" to suggest that ______.

(A) pioneers could overcome difficult obstacles

(B) pine trees were the most useful trees to grow

(C) pine trees grew best among the rocks

(D) pioneers had to climb nearby mountains

30. How many children did the first governor of Tennessee have?

(A) 8.

(B) 11.

(C) 17.

(D) 18.

31. Upon arrival, the pioneers who settled a new area of the frontier would eat which of the following?

(A) Corn, cattle, and pigs.

(B) Indian maize, native fruits, and wild meat.

(C) Preserved fruits, dried meats, and pine roots.

(D) Fresh fish and native vegetables.

32. It can be inferred from the passage that pioneers differed from city dwellers in that they ____.

(A) thought farming would be easy

(B) were involved in local government

(C) associated land with dignity

(D) wanted to get rich quickly

生词及短语

semiliterate [semi'litərət]	*n.*	半文盲
dogged ['dɔgid]	*a.*	顽固,顽强
granite ['grænit]	*n.*	花岗岩
outlast [aut'lɑːst]	*v.*	比……活得长久
recurrent [ri'kʌrənt]	*a.*	再循环的
plague [pleig]	*n.*	瘟疫,灾祸,麻烦
smallpox ['smɔːlpɔks]	*n.*	天花
malaria [mə'lɛəriə]	*n.*	疟疾
progression [prə'greʃ(ə) n]	*n.*	行进
prolific [prə'lifik]	*a.*	多产的,大量繁殖的
auger ['ɔːgə]	*n.*	螺旋钻
crosscut [krɔs'kʌt]	*n.*	捷径,横切
loom [luːm]	*n.*	织布机
maize [meiz]	*n.*	玉米
obsession [əb'seʃ(ə) n]	*n.*	迷住,困扰
shipload ['ʃipləud]	*n.*	船货
yearner ['jəːnə]	*n.*	渴望者,向往者

答案与解析

29. [答案](A)

[解析]从第二句"They were, as a group, ...cracking granite to grow."可知作者是用这句短语来比喻"拓荒者顽强的精神",故答案应为(A)。

30. [答案](D)

[解析]从第一段最后一句中"Twice-married John Sevier, the first governor of Tennessee, fathered eighteen;"可知答案应为(D)。

31. [答案](B)

[解析]从第二段第二句"Those who moved first ... and native fruits in season."可知答案应为(B)。

32. [答案](C)

[解析]从第三段第一句可得出答案为(C)。

译文

美国北部的边境地区改变了18世纪50年代开拓者们的某些特征，同时加剧了其他一些特征。作为一个群体,他们是半文盲,高傲而固执,就像松树根会使花岗岩裂缝而生长一样固执地坚持着他们自己的生活方式。或许,他们最伟大的就是他们忍耐力,他们挺住了不断复发的天花和疟疾瘟疫以及持续不断的自然灾害。他们不可思议地兴旺起来。斯夸尔·布恩8个孩子的家庭按照边境的标准还是个小家庭。詹姆斯·罗伯逊,布恩家的最后一位邻居和纳什维尔城的奠基人,拥有11个子女。两度结婚的约翰·塞维尔是田纳西州第一任州长,18个孩子的父亲。他长期的政敌约翰·蒂普顿,同样结过两次婚,生育了17个子女。

在创业初期,这样一个巨大家庭的财产总共加起来不过是一把斧头,一把猎刀,一把钻子,一只步枪,一两匹马,一些牛和几头猪,一袋玉米种子和一袋盐,或许还有一把锯子和一台织布机。那些第一次迁移到一个新地区的家庭曾一度要靠野味、印第安玉米及当地的季节性水果生活几个月。诚然,他们在刚开始时很贫穷,但他们坚信不久就会富裕起来。

在一定程度上对城市居民来说几乎无法解释的是，一小块适于种植的土地不只是代表美元与美分,还代表着高贵。这种狂热每周都带着大量的向往者到波士顿、纽约、费城、巴尔的摩、乔治城和萨瓦那。追随着他们的前辈,他们沿河流向西被送到西部荒野地区去生育更多的孩子,而这些孩子们还想要更多的土地。

Passage 4

Over the years, and especially since the Second World War, the realm of landscape architecture has been diversified and its activities classified in response to the needs of a changing world. There now appear to be three clearly definable related stages. First there is landscape planning and assessment. This has a strong ecological and natural science base and is concerned with the systematic evaluation of large areas of land in terms of the land's suitability or capability for any likely future use. The process usually involves a team of specialists. *It* may result in a land use plan or policy, affecting, for example, the distribution and type of development or land use, the alignment of highways, the location of industrial plants, the conservation of water, soil, and amenity values, and the use of countryside for recreation. The study area usually coincides with a natural physiographic region such as the watershed of a major river or some other logical unit of land; unfortunately these seldom coincide with the legal jurisdiction of county and state boundaries. The planning function may at times be less comprehensive and concentrate on the impact of major proposals on the environment or the identification of land suitable for one major use such as recreation.

The second stage is site planning. This represents the more conventional kind of landscape architecture and within this realm lies landscape design. Site planning is the process in which the assessment of the site and the requirements of the program for the use of the site are brought together in creative synthesis. Elements and facilities are located on the land in functional relationships and in a manner fully responsive to the characteristics of the site and its region.

Finally, there is detailed landscape design. This is the selection of components, materials, and plants and their combination as solutions to limited and well-defined problems: paving, steps, fountains, and so forth. This is the process through which specific quality is given to the diagrammatic spaces and areas of the site plan.

33. With what topic is the passage primarily concerned?

(A) The training required for landscape architects.

(B) The history of landscape architecture.

(C) The various aspects of landscape architecture.

(D) The locations of landscape architects' work.

34. According to the passage, the first stage of landscape architecture is firmly grounded in ____.

(A) artistic principles

(B) history

(C) agricultural needs

(D) ecology

35. The word "It" in Para. 1 Line 6 refers to ______.

(A) the future use

(B) the process

(C) a team

(D) a science base

36. Which of the following is NOT mentioned as a possible aspect of detailed landscape design?

(A) Paving.

(B) Soil.

(C) Plants.

(D) Fountains.

生词及短语

landscape architecture		景观建筑学
assessment [ə'sesmənt]	*n.*	估价
ecological [iːkə'lɔdʒikəl]	*a.*	生态学的
alignment [ə'lainmənt]	*n.*	队列
amenity [ə'miːniti]	*n.*	宜人,礼仪
recreation [rekri'eiʃ(ə)n]	*n.*	消遣,娱乐
coincide [kəuin'said]	*v.*	一致,符合
physiographic [fizi'ɔgrəfik]	*a.*	地形学的
watershed ['wɔːtəʃed]	*n.*	分水岭
jurisdiction [dʒuəris'dikʃ(ə)n]	*n.*	权限
synthesis ['sinθisis]	*n.*	综合,合成
diagrammatic [daiəgrə'mætik]	*a.*	图表的,概略的

答案与解析

33. [答案] (C)

[解析] 本题为主旨题。文章分三段分别介绍了景观建筑学的三个不同阶段,答案明显应为(C)。(A)、(B)、(D) 均应排除。

34. [答案] (D)

[解析] 第一段第 4—5 行提到"This has a strong ecological and natural science base...",可见答案应为(D)。

35. [答案] (B)

[解析] 本题要求找出代词指代成分,从第七行 "The process usually involves a team of specialists. It may result in a land use ...",不难确定 It 是指代 the process。

36. [答案] (B)

[解析] 由第三段第二句"This is the selection of components, ... and so forth."可见(B) 未被提到,故答案为(B)。

译文

多年来,尤其是第二次世界大战以来,景观建筑学已经走向多样化,其功能也根据世界变化的需要被加以分类。现在表现出来约有三个可明确定义的相关阶段。首先是环境美化的规划和评估,这要有坚实的生态学和自然科学基础,涉及根据大面积土地的适用性或任何未来可用功能的系统性评估。这个过程通常要有一队专家参与。土地使用计划和政策将由此产生,这将影响到诸如分配和发展类型或土地使用、公路的排列、工厂的位置、水土的保持和舒适宜人的程度,以及乡村娱乐的利用。其研究领域通常与自然地形一致,诸如主要河流分界或某些土地的特点;不幸的是,这却很少与县及州的管辖区界相吻合。所规划的功能常常不够全面,主要侧重于对环境影响提出建议,或对土地是否适宜于娱乐这类主要用途做出鉴别。

第二步是现场规划。这代表更传统的景观建筑学,在此领域涉及环境美化设计。建造地规划是这样的过程,它将把建造地的评估和建造地使用规划的要求创造性地结合在一起。各种设施都按功能关系置于建造地,并且完全能在一定程度上对建造地及其区域的特性做出反应。

最后,还有详细的景观设计。这要选择组成成分、材料和植物,它们的组合能解决有限的和定义明确的问题:铺路、修建楼梯和喷泉等。通过这一过程,所勾画的空间和现场规划的区域获得了特殊的质量效果。

阅读 B 篇

Directions:

In the following article, some sentences have been removed. For Questions 37—41, choose the most suitable one from the list A—G to fit into each of the numbered blanks. There are two extra choices, which do not fit in any of the blanks. Mark your answers on ANSWER SHEET 1. (10 points)

Applicants who have never been issued a passport in their own name must execute an application in person before (1) a passport agent; (2) a clerk of any federal court or state court of record or a judge or clerk of any probate court accepting applications; (3) a postal employee designated by the postmaster at a post office that has been selected to accept passport applications; or (4) a U. S. diplomatic or consular officer abroad.

(37) ______________. If the applicant has no prior passport and was born in the U. S., a certified copy of his/her birth certificate generally must be presented to the agent accepting the passport application. To be acceptable, the certificate must show the given name and surname, the date and place of birth, and that the birth record was filed shortly after birth. A delayed birth certificate (a record filed more than 1 year after the date of birth) is acceptable provided that it shows that acceptable secondary evidence was used for creating this record.

(38) ______________. The notice must be accompanied by the best obtainable secondary evidence, such as a baptismal certificate or a hospital birth record. A naturalized citizen with no previous passport must present a Certificate of Naturalization. A person born abroad claiming U. S. citizenship through either a native-born or naturalized citizen parent must normally submit a Certificate of Citizenship issued by the Immigration and Naturalization Service; or a Consular Report of Birth or Certification of Birth Abroad issued by the Dept. of State. (39) ______________.

Additionally, if citizenship is derived through birth to citizen parent(s), the following documents will be required: parents' marriage certificate showing periods and places of residence or physical presence in the U. S. and abroad, specifying periods spent abroad in the employment of the U. S. government, including the armed forces, or with certain international organizations. (40) ______________.

It is important to apply for a passport as far in advance as possible. Passport offices are busiest between March and September. It can take several weeks to receive your passport. (41) ______________.

(A) If a birth certificate is not obtainable, a notice from a state registrar must be submitted stating that no birth record exists.

(B) Any applicant without prior passport needs a birth certificate provided by a hospital or clinic anywhere in America.

(C) If one of the above documents has not been obtained, evidence of citizenship of the parent(s) through whom citizenship is claimed and evidence that would establish the parent/child relationship must be submitted.

(D) Persons in other circumstances may be eligible to apply for a new passport through interview appointed by email or phone.

(E) If citizenship is derived through naturalization of parents, evidence of admission to the U.S. for permanent residence also will be required.

(F) A full validity passport previously issued to the applicant or one in which he or she was included will be accepted as proof of U. S. citizenship.

(G) Persons who possess the most recent passport issued within the last 12 years and after their 18th birthday may be eligible to apply for a new passport by mail.

内容提要

本文主要叙述如何申请护照。第一段指出,从来没有以自己名字获得护照的申请人必须亲自完成申请过程。最后一段叙述申请护照时需要注意的时间问题,认为最好能提前申请,而三月到九月是护照申请办公部门最忙的时候,可能会等几周才会接受申请。

答案与解析

37. [答案] (F)

[解析] 空白处后面第一句为条件状语从句,意为"如果申请人以前没有护照而又出生在美国,一般要向主管护照申请的部门提交出生证明副件。"可推知前面空白处应该与护照和出生有关,而(F)提到以前颁发护照的问题,与该条件从句有前后逻辑关系。

38. [答案] (A)

[解析] 空白处后面句子指出,"通知必须具有最易取得的次要证据, 诸如洗礼证明或医院出生记录等。"由于"The notice"有定冠词,所以前面句子一定提到过该通知,而(A)符合此要求。

39. [答案] (C)

[解析] 本段提到,移民来的公民如果以前没有护照必须出具国籍证明。在国外出生但父母是本土出生或移民的人申请美国国籍必须正式提交移民局颁发的公民身份证书;或是由国家机关颁发的领事出生报告或国外出生证明。所填内容应该是与这些证明和文件相关的内容,而(C)明显与此内容相关。

40. [答案] (E)

[解析] 本段第一句是一个用if引导的条件句,说明如果公民身份是来自具有公民身份的父母需要提交一些文件。而(E)中也是由If引导,说明如果公民身份是来自移民父母,则还需要提交永久性居住证明。两句在结构上对称,内容上相关,故应为正确答案。

41. [答案] (G)

[解析] 本段叙述申请护照需要注意的时间问题,认为最好能提前申请,而三月到九月是

护照申请办公部门最忙的时候,可能要等几周才会接受你的申请。很明显,空白部分也应该与时间有关系。而(G)符合要求。

阅读C篇

Directions:

Read the following text carefully and then translate the underlined segments into Chinese. Your translation should be written neatly on ANSWER SHEET 2. (10 points)

(42) Electricity is such a part of our everyday life and so much taken for granted nowadays that we rarely think twice when we switch on the light or turn on the radio. At night, roads are brightly lit, enabling people and traffic to move freely. Neon lighting used in advertising has become part of the character of every modern city. In the home, many labour-saving devices are powered by electricity. (43) Even when we turn off the bedside lamp and are fast asleep, electricity is working for us, driving our refrigerators, heating our water, or keeping our rooms air-conditioned. Every day, trains, trolleybuses, and trams take us to and from work. We rarely bother to consider why or how they run until something goes wrong.

One summer something did go wrong with the power plant that provides New York with electricity. For a great many hours, life came almost to a standstill. Trains refused to move and the people in them sat in the dark, powerless to do anything; (44) lifts stopped working, so that even if you were lucky enough not to be trapped between two floors, you had the unpleasant task of finding your way down hundreds of flights of stairs. Famous streets like Broadway and Fifth Avenue in an instant became as gloomy and uninviting as the most remote back streets. (45) People were afraid to leave their houses, for although the police had been ordered to stand by in case of emergency, they were just as confused and helpless as anybody else.

Meanwhile, similar disorder prevailed in the home. New York can be stifling in the summer and this year was no exception. Cool, air-conditioned apartments became furnaces. Food went bad in refrigerators. Cakes and joints of meat remained uncooked in cooling ovens. People sat impatient and frightened in the dark as if an unseen enemy had landed from Mars. One of the strange things that occurred during the power-cut was that some fifty blind people led many sighted workers home.

(46) When the lights came on again, hardly a person in the city can have turned on a switch without reflecting how great a servant he had at his fingertips.

生词及短语

take for granted　　认为理所当然

neon lighting		霓虹灯
trolleybus [ˈtrɔlibʌs]	*n.*	无轨电车
tram [træm]	*n.*	有轨电车
standstill [ˈstændstil]	*n.*	停止,停顿
Broadway [ˈbrɔːdwei]	*n.*	百老汇
Fifth Avenue	*n.*	第五大道
gloomy [ˈɡluːmi]	*n.*	阴沉的,阴郁的
uninviting [ʌninˈvaitiŋ]	*a.*	讨厌的,不受欢迎的
emergency [iˈməːdʒnsi]	*n.*	紧急情况
stifling [ˈstaifliŋ]	*a.*	沉闷的
furnace [ˈfəːnis]	*n.*	熔炉
oven [ˈʌvən]	*n.*	烤箱,烤炉
fingertip [ˈfiŋɡətip]	*n.*	手指

全文译文与答案

(42) 电在我们日常生活中所占的地位是非常重要的,而且现在人们还认为有电是完全理所当然的事,所以我们在开灯或开收音机时就很少会去想电是怎么来的。整晚,道路通明,使人们和交通能自由通行,霓虹灯被用来打广告已经成为每一个现代城市特点的一部分。在家中,许多节省体力劳动的设备都是用电来开动的。(43) 即使在我们关掉了床头灯深深地进入梦乡时,电也在为我们工作,它帮我们运行冰箱,帮我们烧水或使我们房间里的空调保持运转。每天,火车、有轨电车和无轨电车载我们上下班。如果不是因为出故障,我们很少费心去考虑它们是为什么或怎么样运转的。

一个夏天,为纽约提供电力的发电厂出了故障。长达数小时,生活近乎停止。火车不能移动,车厢中的人们坐在漆黑中,无力做任何事情。(44) 电梯停了,因此即使你有幸没有被困在两个楼层的中间,你也得去完成一项不愉快的任务:摸黑往下走几百级楼梯。许多像百老汇和第五大道这样的著名大街瞬间变得像僻巷一样令人郁闷和不受欢迎。(45) 尽管警察都已经接到命令,要做好准备以应付紧急情况,但人们还是不敢出门,因为警察也同其他人一样感到不知所措和无能为力。

同时,家中也同样出现了混乱。纽约在夏季变得沉闷,今年也不例外。凉爽和有空调的公寓变成了火炉。食物在冰箱中腐坏。蛋糕和肉在冷却的烤箱中得不到烘烤。人们在黑暗中不耐烦地坐着,受惊的程度好像是来自火星的看不见的敌人已经登陆。在停电的时候有一件奇怪的事情发生,大约有50个盲人将许多有视力的工人带回家去。

(46) 当电灯再亮时,城里的人在打开电灯开关之前,几乎没有一个人不仔细想一想,他掌控的是一个多么能干的仆人啊。

阅读强化练习十一

阅读 A 篇

Directions:

Read the following four texts. Answer the questions below each text by choosing A, B, C or D. Mark your answers on ANSWER SHEET 1. (*40 points*)

Passage 1

The first navigational lights in the New World were probably lanterns hung at harbor entrances. The first lighthouse was put up by the Massachusetts Bay Colony in 1716 on Little Brewster Island at the entrance to Boston Harbor. Paid for the maintenance by "light dues" levied on ships, the original beacon was blown up in 1776. By then there were only a dozen or so true lighthouses in the colonies. Little over a century later, there were 700 lighthouses.

The first eight erected on the West Coast in the 1850s featured the same basic New England design: a Cape Cod dwelling with the tower rising from the center or standing close by. In New England and elsewhere, though, lighthouses reflected a variety of architectural styles. Since most stations in the Northeast were built on rocky eminences, enormous towers were not the rule. Some were made of stone and brick, others of wood of metal. Some stood on pilings or stilts; some were fastened to rock with iron rods. Farther south, from Maryland through the Florida Keys, the coast was low and sandy. It was often necessary to build tall towers there—massive structures like the majestic Cape Hatteras, North Carolina, lighthouse, which was lit in 1870. At 190 feet, it is the tallest brick lighthouse in the country.

Notwithstanding differences in appearance and construction, most American lighthouse shared several features: a light, living quarters, and sometimes, a bell (or, later, a foghorn). They also had something else in common: a keeper and, usually, the keeper's family. The keeper's essential task was trimming the lantern wick in order to maintain a steady, bright flame. The earliest keepers came from every walk of life—they were seamen, farmers, mechanics, rough mill hands—and appointments were often handed out by local customs commissioners as political plums. After the administration of lighthouses was taken over in 1852 by the United States Lighthouse Board, an agency of the Treasury Department, the keeper corps gradually became highly professional.

21. What is the best title for the passage?
    (A) The Lighthouse on Little Brewster Island
    (B) The Life of a Lighthouse Keeper
    (C) Early Lighthouses in the United States
    (D) The Modern Profession of Lighthouse-Keeping

22. It can be inferred from the passage that lighthouses in the Northeast did not need high towers because ______.
    (A) ships there had high masts
    (B) coastal waters were safe
    (C) the coast was straight and unobstructed
    (D) the lighthouses were built on high places

23. According to the passage, where can the tallest brick lighthouse in the United States be found?
    (A) Little Brewster Island.
    (B) The Florida Keys.
    (C) Cape Hatteras.
    (D) Cape Cod.

24. It can be inferred from the passage that the Treasury Department, after assuming control of the lighthouses, improved which of the following?
    (A) The training of the lighthouse keepers.
    (B) The sturdiness of the lighthouses.
    (C) The visibility of the lights.
    (D) The locations of the lighthouses.

生词及短语

lantern ['læntən]	*n.*	灯笼,提灯
levy ['levi]	*vt.*	征税,征收

beacon [ˈbiːkən] *n.* 灯塔
erect [iˈrekt] *vt.* 竖立,建立
eminence [ˈeminəns] *n.* 出众,显赫
piling [ˈpailiŋ] *n.* 打桩
stilt [stilt] *n.* 支柱,脚柱
foghorn [ˈfɔghɔːn] *n.* 雾号,雾笛
trim [trim] *vt.* 整理,修整
wick [wik] *n.* 灯芯,油绳
mill [mil] *n.* 磨坊,工厂
plum [plʌm] *n.* 洋李;待遇好的工作

答案与解析

21. [答案] (**C**)

[解析] 本文主要叙述了美国早期灯塔的情况,故可排除(A)、(B)、(D)。答案应为(C)。

22. [答案] (**D**)

[解析] 文中第9—10行提到"Since most stations ... were not the rule."在东北部的灯塔站多数建造在岩石高地上,故应排除(A)、(B)、(C)。

23. [答案] (**C**)

[解析] 文中第13—14行提到"like the majestic Cape Hatteras, ...in the country."可见美国最高的砖结构灯塔是在北卡罗来纳州哈特拉斯角,故C为正确答案。

24. [答案] (**A**)

[解析] 文中最后一句提到1852年美国灯塔局接管了灯塔管理之后,灯塔管理者队伍逐渐变得高度专业化了。故应排除(B)、(C)、(D)。

译文

在(北美)新大陆,最初的导航灯大多是悬挂在港湾入口处的灯笼。第一座灯塔于1716年在马塞诸塞海湾殖民地的波士顿港入口处的小布鲁斯特岛上建立,由从过往船只上征收的"灯费"维护。这座最早的灯塔在1776年被炸毁。当时的殖民地仅有大约12座真正意义上的灯塔,一个多世纪之后,达到了700座。

19世纪50年代在西海岸建立的首批8座灯塔有着新英格兰建筑的基本特征:一座在中央或旁边建起塔楼的科德角灯塔。新英格兰和其他地区的灯塔表现出多种多样的建筑风格。由于东北部的大多数灯塔建造在多岩石的高地上,灯塔的高度不标准。一些灯塔用砖石砌筑,其他的为木质或金属结构。有一些灯塔建立在桩基或脚柱之上,另一些灯塔则用铁杆固

定在岩石上。从马里兰向南方延伸到佛罗里达岩礁群,海岸是低平和砂质的,在那里常常需要建造高塔,像北卡罗来纳州宏伟的哈特拉斯灯塔,它于 1870 年启用,高达 190 英尺,是这个国家最高的砖结构灯塔。

尽管在外形和结构上不同,美国的大部分灯塔有几个共同特点:一盏灯,住处,有时有一座钟(或是后来的雾笛)。它们还有其他一些相同之处:一名看守人,通常还有他的家庭。看守人的基本职责是修剪灯芯,保证火焰稳定明亮。最早的看守人来自各行各业:海员、农民、技工、工人。这件工作常作为政治性岗位由地方海关专员委派。当灯塔管理于 1852 年被美国财政部的灯塔局接管以后,看守人队伍逐渐变得高度专业化了。

Passage 2

Homing pigeons are placed in a training program from about the time they are twenty-eight days of age. They are taught to enter the loft through a trap and to exercise above and around the loft, and gradually they are taken away for short distances in wicker baskets and released. They are then expected to find their way home in the shortest possible time.

In their training flights or in actual races, the birds are taken to prearranged distant points and released to find their way back to their own lofts. Once the birds are liberated, their owners, who are standing by at the home lofts, anxiously watch the sky for the return of their entries. Since time is of the essence, the speed with which the birds can be induced to enter the loft trap may make the difference between gaining a win or a second place.

The head of homing pigeon is comparatively small, but its brain is one quarter larger than that of the ordinary pigeon. The homing pigeon is very intelligent and will persevere to the point of stubbornness; some have been known to fly a hundred miles off course to avoid a storm.

Some homing pigeon experts claim that this bird is gifted with a form of built-in radar that helps *it* find its own loft after hours of flight, for hidden under the head feathers are two very sensitive ears, while the sharp, prominent eyes can see great distances in daytime.

Why do homing pigeons fly home? They are not unique in this inherent skill; it is found in most migratory birds, in bees, ants, toads, and even turtles, which have been known to travel hundreds of miles to return to their homes. But in the animal world, the homing pigeon alone can be trusted with its freedom and trained to carry out the missions that people demand.

25. What is the purpose of the passage?

(A) To convince the reader to buy a homing pigeon.

(B) To inform the reader about homing pigeons and their training.

(C) To protect homing pigeons against the threat of extinction.

(D) To encourage the owners of homing pigeons to set the birds free.

26. According to the passage, what happens to homing pigeons when they are about a month old?
   (A) They are kept in a trap.
   (B) They enter their first race.
   (C) They begin a training program.
   (D) They get their wings clipped and marked.

27. According to the passage, what is the difference between a homing pigeon and an ordinary one?
   (A) The span of the wings.
   (B) The shape of the eyes.
   (C) The texture of the feathers.
   (D) The size of the brain.

28. In Para. 4 Line 2, the pronoun "it" refers to which of the following?
   (A) Radar.
   (B) Bird.
   (C) Loft.
   (D) Form.

生词及短语

loft [lɔft]	*n.*	鸽房，阁楼
trap [træp]	*n.*	活板门
wicker ['wikə(r)]	*n.*	柳条
induce [in'djuːs]	*vt.*	引诱，促使
persevere [pəːsi'viə(r)]	*v.*	坚持
stubbornness ['stʌbənnis]	*n.*	顽强，倔强
migratory ['maigrətəri]	*a.*	迁移的
toad [təud]	*n.*	蟾蜍

答案与解析

25. [答案] (**B**)

[解析] 本题为主旨题。全文主要叙述信鸽及其训练过程。故应排除(A)、(C)、(D)。

26.［答案］(C)

［解析］文中第一句指出 "Homing pigeons are placed in a training program from about the time they are twenty-eight days of age." 故可知信鸽满月后便开始一个训练过程。(A) 意为"它们被关在笼子里",(B) 意为"它们开始第一次比赛",(D) 意为"主人修剪它们的翅膀并做记号",均不符合题意。

27.［答案］(D)

［解析］文中第三段第一句提到信鸽的脑比普通鸽子大 1/4,没有提及翅膀的跨度,眼睛的形状,或是羽毛的质地。故答案应为(D)。

28.［答案］(B)

［解析］本题为代词指代成分题,应在代词前面根据逻辑关系找出。很明显,文中第 14 行的 it 是指信鸽找到它的鸽房,it 是指代 bird,而不是雷达,鸽房,或是形式。

译文

信鸽在出生 28 天后便会投入训练,它们被要求通过一扇活板门进入鸽房,同时练习在鸽房上方和周围活动。之后它们被放到柳条篮子中带到不太远的地方,然后放飞。主人希望它们能够在尽可能短的时间之内寻找到返回的路线。

在信鸽的训练飞行和实际比赛中,它们被带到预定的地点,然后放飞,以寻找飞回鸽房的路线。一旦信鸽被放飞,它们的主人便站在鸽房一旁,焦急地看着天空,盼望它们的回归。由于时间很重要,所以信鸽被召回鸽房的速度可能与它获得冠军或亚军有关系。

信鸽的头部较小,但它的脑却比普通鸽子大 1/4。信鸽非常聪明,并且具有不屈不挠的顽强精神,据称有的信鸽曾飞离路线一百英里以躲避一场风暴。

有些信鸽专家称,信鸽天生有雷达结构,这可以帮助它们在飞行数小时之后找到自己的家。因为在信鸽头部的羽毛下藏有两只非常灵敏的耳朵,同时其锐利和卓越的双眼在白昼都会有极远的视野。

为什么信鸽能飞回家呢?这种天生技能并不是独有的,大多数候鸟也是这样,在蜜蜂、蚂蚁、蟾蜍甚至海龟身上也能发现,它们可以旅行数百英里然后返回它们的巢穴。但是,在动物世界中,唯有信鸽可信任地,随意地给其自由,同时加以训练以完成人们要求的任务。

Passage 3

Central Park, emerging from a period of abuse and neglect, remains one of the most popular attractions in New York City, with half a million out-of-towners among the more than 3 million people who visit the park yearly. About 15 million individual visits are made each year.

Summer is the season for softball, concerts, and Shakespeare; fall is stunning; winter is wonderful for sledding, skating, and skiing; and spring time is the loveliest of all. It was all planned that way.

About 130 years ago Frederic Law Olmsted and his collaborator Caivert Vaux submitted their landscaping plan for a rectangular parcel two miles north of the town's center. The barren swampy tract, home for squatters and a bone-boiling works that made glue, was reported as "a pestilential spot where miasmic odors taint every breath of air. " It took 16 years for workers with pickaxes and shovels to move 5 million cubic feet of earth and rock, and to plant half a million tress and shrubs, making a tribute to nature — a romantic nineteenth-century perception of nature.

What exists today is essentially Olmsted and Vaux's plan, with more trees, buildings, and asphalt. Landscape architects still speak reverently of Olmsted's genius and foresight, and the sensitive visitor can see the effects he sought.

29. With what subject is the passage mainly concerned?
   (A) The lives of Olmsted and Vaux.
   (B) New York City's tourist industry.
   (C) Examples of nineteenth century art in New York City.
   (D) The development of Central Park.

30. According to the passage, which is the prettiest time of year in Central Park?
   (A) Winter.
   (B) Spring.
   (C) Summer.
   (D) Fall.

31. According to the passage, before Olmsted and Vaux began their work, the area now occupied by Central Park was ______.
   (A) a romantic place
   (B) an infertile, marshy space
   (C) a green and hilly Park
   (D) a baseball field

32. It can be inferred from the passage that today's landscape architects praise Olmsted for his ______.
   (A) enthusiasm for sport
   (B) skill at designing factories
   (C) concern for New York's homeless people
   (D) foresight in anticipating New York's urbanization

生词及短语

softball ['sɔftbɔːl]	*n.*	垒球
stunning ['stʌniŋ]	*a.*	令人晕倒的;极好的
sledding ['slediŋ]	*n.*	滑雪橇
skating ['skeitiŋ]	*n.*	溜冰
skiing ['skiːiŋ]	*n.*	滑雪
rectangular [rek'tæŋgjulə(r)]	*a.*	矩形的,成直角的
swampy ['swɔmpi]	*a.*	沼泽的
squatter ['skwɔtə]	*n.*	擅自居住者,违章建房者
pestilential [pesti'lenʃ(ə)l]	*a.*	引起瘟疫的
miasmic [mai'æzmik]	*a.*	毒气的
odor ['əudə(r)]	*n.*	气味
taint [teint]	*v.*	感染,污点
pickaxe ['pikæks]	*n.*	镐
shrub [ʃrʌb]	*n.*	灌木丛,灌木
tribute ['tribjuːt]	*n.*	礼物,贡品
asphalt ['æsfælt]	*n.*	沥青
reverently [revə'rəntli]	*ad.*	虔诚地

答案与解析

29. [答案] (**D**)

[解析] 本题为主旨题。本文主要叙述了中央公园规划建设的发展情况，故应排除(A)、(B)、(C)。答案应为(D)。

30. [答案] (**B**)

[解析] 文中第 5 行讲到春季是所有季节中最可爱的“...spring time is the loveliest of all.”。故答案应为(B)。

31. [答案] (**B**)

[解析] 文中第 8—10 行提到当时这里是一片长方形的贫瘠沼泽地带，而不是一处罗曼蒂克的地方,一座绿色的有山的公园,或是一个棒球场。

32. [答案] (**D**)

[解析] 文中第 15—16 行提到景观建筑师们仍然在恭敬地讲述奥姆斯台德的天才和先见而不是赞扬他对体育运动的热情,设计工厂的技能,或是关心纽约无家可归的人们。故答案应为(D)。

译文

产生于一个滥用和被忽视的时期，中央公园是纽约保留下来的最受公众喜爱的景观之一。每年有300多万游客到这个公园观光，来自周围城镇的达50万人之多。每年可保持1,500万人次的客流量。

这里，夏天是垒球、音乐会和莎士比亚戏剧的季节，秋天是极美的，冬天则适合于雪橇、滑冰和滑雪，而春季是所有季节中最可爱的。公园完全是按这个方式来规划的。

130年前，弗莱德里克·劳·奥姆斯台德和他的合作者康沃尔特·沃克斯提出了他们的景观规划，它位于离市中心向北两英里的长方形贫瘠沼泽地带，住有一些占用公地的人和一家熬制骨胶的工厂。这块地方被称为"瘟疫的发源地，臭味污染了呼吸的空气"。工人们用16年的时间挖凿和铲走500万立方英尺的泥土和岩石，种植了50万株树和灌木，为大自然创造了一件礼品——一个19世纪罗曼蒂克的自然景观。

现在的公园基本上是奥姆斯台德和沃克斯规划的格局，具有更多的树木、建筑物和沥青道路。景观建筑师们还在崇敬地讲述着奥姆斯台德的天才和远见，而敏锐的游客也能看出他曾经寻求的效果。

Passage 4

The difference between a liquid and a gas is obvious under the conditions of temperature and pressure commonly found at the surface of the Earth. A liquid can be kept in an open container and fills it to the level of a free surface. A gas forms no free surface but tends to diffuse throughout the space available; it must therefore be kept in a closed container or held by a gravitational field, as in the case of a planet's atmosphere. The distinction was a prominent feature of early theories describing the phases of matter. In the nineteenth century, for example, one theory maintained that a liquid could be "dissolved" in a vapor without losing its identity, and another theory held that the two phases are made up of different kinds of molecules: liquidons and gasons. The theories now prevailing take a quite different approach by emphasizing what liquids and gases have in common. They are both forms of matter that have no permanent structure and they both flow readily. They are fluids.

The fundamental similarity of liquids and gases becomes clearly apparent when the temperature and pressure are raised somewhat. Suppose a closed container partially filled with a liquid is heated. The liquid expands, or in other words becomes less dense; some of it evaporates. In contrast, the vapor above the liquid surface becomes denser as the evaporated molecules are added to it. The combination of temperature and pressure at which the densities become equal is called the critical point. Above the critical point the liquid and the gas can no longer be distinguished; there is a single, undifferentiated fluid phase of uniform density.

33. Which of the following would be the most appropriate title for the passage?
(A) The Properties of Gases and Liquids
(B) High temperature Zones on the Earth
(C) The Beginnings of Modern Physics
(D) New Containers for Fluids

34. According to the passage, the difference between a liquid and a gas under normal conditions on Earth is that the liquid ______.
(A) is affected by changes in pressure
(B) has a permanent structure
(C) forms a free surface
(D) is considerably more common

35. It can be inferred from the passage that the gases of the Earth's atmosphere are contained by ______.
(A) a closed surface
(B) the gravity of the planet
(C) the field of space
(D) its critical point

36. According to the passage, which of the following is the best definition of the critical point?
(A) When the temperature and the pressure are raised.
(B) When the densities of the two phases are equal.
(C) When the pressure and temperature are combined.
(D) When the container explodes.

生词及短语

diffuse [di'fjuːs]	*v.*	散播,扩散
gravitational [grævi'teiʃ(ə) nl]	*a.*	重力的
molecule ['mɔlikjuːl]	*n.*	分子
liquidon ['likwid(ə) n]	*n.*	液态分子
gason ['gæs(ə) n]	*n.*	气态分子

答案与解析

33. [答案] (A)

[解析] 本题为主旨题。全文主要叙述液体和气体的特征,答案明显为(A)。(B)意为“地球上的高温区”;(C)意为“现代物理学的开端”;(D)意为“流体的新容器”,均应排除。

34. [答案] (C)

[解析] 本文第二、三句指出液体可以形成随意的水平表面,而气体不能形成随意的表面,故答案应为(C)。(A)意为“受压力变化的影响”;(B)意为“有永久性的结构”;(D)意为“相当程度上的相同”,均可排除。

35. [答案] (B)

[解析] 第4—5行提到行星的大气层是由重力牵制的,而不是一层密封的表面,空余的场地,或是它的临界点。故答案应为(B)行星的引力。

36. [答案] (B)

[解析] 文中倒数第二句提到在临界点时,密度相等。因此临界点的定义应该是“当两种形态的密度相等的时候”。(A) 意为“当温度和压力被增高的时候”,(C) 意为“当压力和温度被结合的时候”,(D) 意为“当容器爆炸的时候”,均应排除。

译文

液体与气体的区别显然是建立在一般地表温度和压力条件上的。液体能够被保存在开口的容器中,可注入容器中的一个任何表层。气体没有固定的形态,趋向于向空间随意扩散;因此它必须保存在一个封闭的容器中,由重力场来保持,正如一颗行星的大气层的情形。这种区别是早期理论描述物质形态的一个显著的特点。例如,在19世纪,一种理论强调液体能够在蒸汽中“溶解”而不会丧失其特性,另一种理论则认为这两种形态是由不同种类的分子构成:液态分子和气态分子。现在流行的理论采用一种完全不同的方式,强调液体和气体的共同之处。它们都是没有永久性结构的物质形态,都容易流动。它们都是流体。

当温度和压力被稍微增高时,液体和气体的基本共性就显得非常明显。设想一个密封的容器注入部分液体后被加热,液体膨胀,换言之,密度更小,它的一部分蒸发了。对比之下,当蒸发的分子增加,液体上方的气体密度变得更大。在温度和压力的结合点密度变得相等时,就称为临界点。在临界点之上,液体和气体便不再能区别开来;只有一种单一的、无差别的、密度一致的流体形态。

阅读B篇

Directions:

In the following article, some sentences have been removed. For Questions 37—41, choose the most suitable one from the list A—G to fit into each of the numbered blanks. There are two extra choices, which do not fit in any of the blanks. Mark your answers on ANSWER SHEET 1. (10 points)

Just as 2001 was coming to an end, the *USA TODAY-CNN-Gallup Poll*(盖洛普民意测验) asked Americans if they were satisfied with the way things are going in the country. Surprisingly, 70 percent said yes. (37) ________.

What makes the number even more remarkable is that the 70 percent satisfaction *index*(指数) is among the highest of the *Gallup Poll* has measured in the nearly 30 years it has been asking the question. Moreover, the satisfaction rate has usually been lowest in times of economic difficulty. For example, in June 1992, with the economy in recession, just 14 percent said they were satisfied with the way things were going in the country. This time around, while most Americans are concerned about the economy and the accompanying threat of job losses, they're not letting the uncertainty get them down. (38) ________.

(39) ________. Some analysts suggest that it is merely whistling past the graveyard. But other analysts say it is more a reflection of the *indomitable* (不屈不挠) and generous American spirit that showed itself so dramatically in the *aftermath*(不幸后果) of Sept. 11 (9·11). Rather than pull down the shades and hide under the bed in the face of further terrorism threats and the grim realization that the United States is not as invulnerable as most once thought, Americans poured into the streets and came together in a unity of purpose and resolve not seen since World War II. They rallied around the president and strongly supported the use of military force to combat terrorism. (40) ________.

Are 70 percent of the American people really satisfied with the way things are going in the country right now?(41) ________. Yet, there is something running through the American psyche that causes it to refuse to give in to despair. Call it naive. Call it foolish. Call it whistling past the graveyard. Whatever it is, it's good to see. With spirit like that, we can be sure that this too will pass.

(A) At the same time, Americans showed their compassion not only in their generous contributions to funds to aid the thousands of families of victims of the attacks, but also in their support for sending humanitarian aid to the people in war-torn Afghanistan and their insistence that women there be given equal rights with men.

(B) Three of four say they expect the economy to be better a year from now.

(C) Americans are not frightened by terrorism, but showed a particular mood or an emotional state characterized by vigor and animation.

(D) So how can we explain this unexpected expression of optimism that appears to be sweeping through the population?

(E) Probably not. Terrorism threats are still with us. Unemployment is up to 5.8 percent.

(F) Terrorism is unlawful use or threatened use of force or violence by a person or an organized group against people or property with the intention of intimidating or coercing societies or governments, often for ideological or political reasons.

(G) Think about it. Less than four months after the most devastating foreign attack in the nation's history, and with an economy still in recession, one might think most Americans would be in a sour mood and unlikely to think positively about much of anything. Yet, 7 of 10 expressed an upbeat outlook.

内容提要

本文主要叙述 2001 年美国盖洛普民意测验的情况。第一段指出，正当 2001 年即将结束,美国盖洛普民意测验询问美国人,他们是否对国家处理事情的方法感到满意。令人惊奇的是,70%的回答是满意。文中叙述了美国人在灾难之后为什么这么乐观。

答案与解析

37. [答案] (**G**)

[解析] 空白处前一句提到,“令人惊奇的是,70%的被调查者回答满意”,根据逻辑,后面的内容应该是对为什么会令人惊奇做出解释,而(G)给出了回答。

38. [答案] (**B**)

[解析] 空白处前一句提到大多数美国人在关心经济和随着而来的失业问题，但他们没有因这些不确定性而沮丧。后面的内容应与此句内容相关,而(B)提到四分之三的人们回答经济会好转。

39. [答案](D)

[解析]前段提到人们的乐观情绪,该段也继续进行阐述,(D)紧接前面内容解释为什么人们会乐观。

40. [答案](A)

[解析]该段提到美国9·11之后人民没有被恐怖分子吓倒，而是表现出前所未有的团结。后面的内容应该与前部分相关,而(A)提到人们纷纷捐款援助受害家庭。

41. [答案](E)

[解析]空白前面是一个疑问句,后面应该做出回答,(E)明确地做出了回答。

阅读 C 篇

Directions:

Read the following text carefully and then translate the underlined segments into Chinese. Your translation should be written neatly on ANSWER SHEET 2. (10 points)

I am delighted to be guest at this festive occasion celebrating the 50th anniversary of diplomatic relations between Finland and the People's Republic of China. I have been asked to give a comment on the outlook for the common European currency, the Euro. During the past year or so, a lot of different views have been presented about the Euro's performance. (42) Considering the fact that the Euro is a new currency with a major international role in the foreign exchange markets, it is only natural that it has drawn much attention. However, I would like to point out that attempts to measure the success of the Economic and Monetary Union by the Euro's external value are misplaced. The benefits of the Euro stem from elsewhere. Indeed, the benefits that the Euro can and will offer are distinctly of a long-term and structural nature. In the end, a short term misalignment of the Euro has very little to do with these structural developments.

One can come up with number of explanations for the depreciation of the Euro or the strength of the US dollar, which is the other side of the coin. (43) The growth gap, and associated interest rate difference between the Euro area and United States, have been no doubt among the most popular explanations, and there is some truth to this. Most importantly, the dynamic growth in the U.S. has been a source of constant surprise to most of us.

(44) However, in the meantime the economic outlook for the Euro area has improved considerably. The European Central Bank has succeeded very well in delivering price stability for the Euro area, which is its primary and the most important objective. Member States of the Euro area have agreed on, and implemented, a number of important initiatives aiming at raising

the growth potential of the Euro area. Indeed, despite of these facts, it seems that the uncertainties associated with the Euro area have received more attention than those affecting the US economy. This asymmetry has affected the Euro negatively. (45) Accordingly, it is widely recognised that the Euro is significantly undervalued, and the present level does not reflect the strong fundamentals of the Euro area economy.

Most of these challenges reflect the fact that the Euro is still a young currency. (46) In fact, for the citizens of the Euro area, the single currency will not become more tangible until 2002, when the actual notes and coins will be introduced, This is just to say that at this point only tentative conclusions of the functioning of the Euro can be made.

生词及短语

festive occasion		庆祝典礼
misplace [mis'pleis]	*v.*	放错地方
misalignment ['misəlainmənt]	*n.*	未对准,失调
come up with		提出,赶上
initiative [i'niʃiətiv]	*n.*	动议
asymmetry [æ'simətri]	*n.*	不对称
undervalue [ʌndə'væljuː]	*v.*	低估
tangible ['tændʒəbl]	*a.*	可触摸的,切实的

全文译文与答案

我很高兴在庆祝芬兰和中国建交50周年的庆祝典礼上作客。我一直被要求对欧洲货币,即欧元的前景进行评估。在过去的一年来,对欧元的表现曾有过众多不同的观点。(42) 考虑到欧元在外汇交易市场上是一种全新的国际性货币,那么,它所引起的广泛关注就不足为奇了。然而,我想指出的是,任何企图以欧元外部价值来衡量经济或货币同盟的成功与否都是一种误导。欧元的利益来源于其他地方。确实,欧元可以产生也将产生的利益明显具有长期和结构性的性质。最终,欧元短期的失调与这些结构性发展关系不大。

对于欧元的贬值或者美元的升值人们会提出一些解释,这是事情的另一面。(43) 欧元区与美国之间的经济发展差距和相关的利率差异,无疑是得到最广泛认同的一种解释,确实也有点儿道理。最重要的是,美国经济强有力的增长一直是使我们大多数人惊奇的根源。

(44) 但是,与此同时,欧元区的经济发展前景极大地好转。欧洲中央银行已经成功地实现其首要也最重要的目标:保持欧元区的稳定。欧元区成员国已经达成一致并加以实施了一系列旨在提高欧元区经济潜力的重要措施。确实,尽管这些事实,看起来与欧元区相关的不确定因素引起了比影响美国经济因素的更多的注意。这种不对称已经对欧元产生了负面影响。(45) 因此,人们广泛承认欧元的价值被极大地低估了,其当前水平没有反映欧元区经济的坚实基础。

这些挑战大多数反映了这样的事实,即欧元仍然是一种新货币。(46) 事实上,对欧元区的居民而言,要到 2002 年真正的纸币、硬币投入使用时,这种单一货币才会变得更加切实。这就是说,现在关于欧元的结论都只能是试探性的。

阅读强化练习十二

阅读 A 篇

Directions:

Read the following four texts. Answer the questions below each text by choosing A, B, C or D. Mark your answers on ANSWER SHEET 1. (40 points)

Passage 1

Lucinda Childs' spare and orderly dances have both mystified and mesmerized audiences for more than a decade. Like other so-called "postmodern" choreographers. Childs sees dance as pure form. Her dances are mathematical explorations of geometric shapes, and her dancers are expressionless, genderless instruments who etch intricate patterns on the floor in precisely timed, repetitive sequences of relatively simple steps.

The development of Childs' career, from *its* beginning in the now legendary Judson Dance Theater, paralleled the development of minimalist art, although the choreographer herself has taken issue with those critics who describe her work as minimalist. In her view, each of her dances is simply "an intense experience of intense looking and listening." In addition to performing with her troupe, the Lucinda Childs Dance Company, Childs has appeared in the avant-garde opera *Einstein on the Beach*, in two off-Brodway plays, and in the films *Jeanne d'lman* by Marie Jimenez and 21:12 Piano Bar.

As a little girl, Childs had dreamed of becoming an actress. She appeared regularly in student productions throughout her school years, and when she was about eleven she began to take drama lessons. It was at the suggestion of her acting coach that the youngster, who was, by her own admission, "clumsy, shapeless, and on the heavy side," enrolled in a dancing class. Among her early teachers were Hanya Holm, the dancer and choreographer who introduced the Wigman system of modem dance instruction to the United States, and Helen Tamiris, the Broadway choreographer. Pleased with her pupil's progress, Ms. Tamiris eventually asked the girl to perform onstage. After that exhilarating experience, Lucinda Childs "wasn't sure (she) even wanted to be an actress anymore."

21. What is the passage mainly about?
    (A) Minimalist art.
    (B) Mathematical forms.
    (C) A choreographer.
    (D) Broad-way plays.

22. The word "its" in Para. 2 Line 1 refers to ______.
    (A) career
    (B) development
    (C) steps
    (D) the Judson Dance Theater

23. The work of Lucinda Childs has been compared to which of the following?
    (A) Avant-garde opera.
    (B) The Wigman system.
    (C) Realistic drama.
    (D) Minimalist art.

24. In which artistic field did Childs first study?
    (A) Painting.
    (B) Dance.
    (C) Drama.
    (D) Film.

生词及短语

spare [spɛə(r)]	*a.*	少量的，节约的
orderly [ˈɔːdəli]	*ad.*	有次序的，整洁的
mystify [ˈmistifai]	*v.*	迷惑
mesmerize [ˈmezməraiz]	*v.*	施催眠术
choreographer [kɔriˈɔgrəfə(r)]	*n.*	舞蹈指导
geometric [dʒiːəˈmetrik]	*a.*	几何的，几何学的
genderless [ˈdʒendə(r) lis]	*a.*	无性的

etch [etʃ]	*v.*	蚀刻
intricate ['intrikət]	*a.*	复杂的,错综的
legendary ['ledʒəndəri]	*a.*	传说中的,传奇的
minimalist ['minimәlist]	*n.*	极简抽象派艺术
take issue with		与(某人)争论,与(某人)唱反调
troupe [truːp]	*n.*	剧团
avant-garde	*n.*	先锋派
Broadway ['brɔːdwei]	*n.*	百老汇
clumsy ['klʌmzi]	*a.*	笨拙的
enroll [in'rəul]	*v.*	登记,参加
exhilarating [ig'ziləreitiŋ]	*a.*	令人喜欢的,爽快的

答案与解析

21. [答案] (C)

[解析] 本文主要叙述舞美编导卢辛达·恰尔兹的一生,而不是讲简约抽象派艺术,数学的形式,或是百老汇的戏剧。

22. [答案] (**B**)

[解析] 本题测试指代成分, 文中第 6 行的 its 很明显是指代前面提到的恰尔兹的发展。故应排除(A)、(C)、(D)。

23. [答案] (**D**)

[解析] 文中第 8 行提到评论家们将恰尔兹的作品描述为极简抽象派艺术, 并没有同先锋派戏剧,韦格曼系统,或现实主义的戏剧相比拟。故答案应为(D)。

24. [答案] (**C**)

[解析] 文中第三段第 2—3 行提到恰尔兹在 11 岁时开始上戏剧课,未提到过首先学习绘画、舞蹈和电影。故答案为(C)。

译文

卢辛达·恰尔兹简捷而有序的舞蹈拥有着迷的观众达十年之久。像其他所谓的"后现代"舞蹈编导一样,恰尔兹视舞蹈为纯粹的形式。她的舞蹈犹如几何图形的精确探索,而她的舞蹈演员们却显得像呆板而毫无主动性的机器,非常合拍地在地板上刻画复杂的程式,重复着相对简单的步伐。

恰尔兹事业的发展,从她进入传奇式的加德森舞剧院开始,便与简约抽象艺术的发展并存,虽然作为舞蹈编导的她与将其作品视为简约抽象艺术的评论家们有争议。在她看来,她的每组舞蹈纯粹是“强烈视听的一次强烈震撼”。此外,除了和自己剧团——卢辛达·恰尔兹舞蹈团一同演出外,她还在先锋派戏剧《爱因斯坦在海滩上》和两个纽约的非商业性戏剧,以及玛丽·吉姆奈茨的电影《吉妮·德伊曼》中参演,还曾在“21:12 钢琴酒吧”中演出。

当恰尔兹还是一个小女孩的时候就梦想成为一名演员。在上学期间,她始终出现在学生表演中,而且她 11 岁左右时就开始上戏剧课了。在她的舞蹈教练的建议下,这个“笨拙的、没有体形,而且身体偏胖”的年轻人,凭借她持有的入学许可,被一个舞蹈班录取。在她早期的老师中,有舞蹈家兼舞美编导汉雅·赫尔姆,是她把现代舞蹈教育的韦格曼系统介绍到美国来的,还有百老汇的舞美编导海伦·泰米瑞斯。泰米瑞斯女士为学生的进步而感到高兴,她终于要求这位姑娘到台上演出。在那次令人振奋的经历之后,卢辛达·恰尔兹不敢肯定自己是否还想成为一名女演员了。

Passage 2

In 1781 twelve families trooped north from Mexico to California. On a stream along the desert's edge, they built a settlement called Los Angeles. For many years it was a market town, where nearby farmers and ranchers met to trade.

Then in 1876 a railroad linked Los Angeles to San Francisco and, through San Francisco, to the rest of the country. The next year farmers sent their first trainload of oranges east. By 1885 a new railroad provided a direct route between Los Angeles and Chicago.

Then in the 1890s oil was discovered in the city. As derricks went up, workers built many highways and pipe lines. Digging began on a harbor that would make Los Angeles not only an ocean port but also a fishing center. The harbor was completed in 1914. That year the Panama Canal opened. Suddenly Los Angeles was the busiest port on the Pacific Coast.

Today the city is the main industrial center in the West. It produces goods not only for other West Coast communities but also for those in other parts of the country. It leads the nation in making airplanes and equipment for exploring outer space. Many motion pictures and television programs are filmed in Los Angeles. The city is also the business center for states in the West. Improvements in transportation are the main reason for Los Angeles' growth.

25. According to the passage, what was the main commercial activity of Los Angeles during the years directly following its settlement?

(A) Fruit growing.

(B) Oil drilling.

(C) Fishing.

(D) Trading.

26. According to the passage, in which year were oranges first shipped from Los Angeles to the East Coast by train?

(A) 1781.

(B) 1876.

(C) 1877.

(D) 1890.

27. San Francisco is mentioned in the passage for which of the following reasons?

(A) The settlers who founded Los Angeles came from San Francisco.

(B) San Francisco linked Los Angeles with the rest of the country.

(C) San Francisco was a market town where farmers came to trade.

(D) Oil was discovered in San Francisco in the 1890s.

28. Where in the passage does the author state the principal cause of the expansion of Los Angeles?

(A) Lines 4—5.

(B) Line 6.

(C) Line 9.

(D) Lines 14—15.

生词及短语

troop [truːp]	*v.*	结队,群集
derrick ['derik]	*n.*	铁架塔

答案与解析

25. [答案] (**D**)

[解析] 从第一段最后一句“For many years it was a market town, where nearby farmers and ranchers met to trade.”可知,多年来洛杉矶是一座集镇,附近的农场主和工人聚集在这里从事贸易,故答案应为(D)。(A) 意为“水果种植”,(B) 意为“石油钻探”,(C) 意为“渔业,都应排除”。

26. [答案] (**C**)

[解析] 第二段提到,在 1876 年建成洛杉矶到旧金山的铁路之后的第二年,农民用火车向东部发出第一批柑橘。故答案应为(C)。

27. [答案] (B)

[解析] 文中提到旧金山是因为旧金山将洛杉矶同这个国家的其他地区连接起来。本文未曾提及(A)、(C)、(D),故应排除。

28. [答案] (D)

[解析] 本文最后一句谈到交通条件改善是洛杉矶发展的主要原因。

译文

1871 年,12 户家庭结伴从墨西哥北上加利福尼亚。在靠近沙漠边缘的一条小溪旁,他们建立了一处称为洛杉矶的定居点。多年来,洛杉矶都是一座集镇,农场主和工人们聚集在这里从事贸易。

后来,到 1876 年,一条铁路将洛杉矶同旧金山连接起来,并经由旧金山通向这个国家的其他地区。第二年,农民们用火车向东部发送出第一批柑橘。1885 年,一条新铁路将洛杉矶和芝加哥直接连通。

19 世纪 90 年代,这座城市发现了石油。石油井架纷纷竖立起来,工人们建设了许多高速公路和管道线。在一处港湾开始的挖掘工程不仅使洛杉矶成为一座海港,而且成为一个渔业中心。海港于 1914 年完工,当年,巴拿马运河也开放了,洛杉矶成为了太平洋沿岸最繁忙的港口。

今天,这座城市是西部的主要工业中心,它生产的产品不仅供应西海岸的居民区,同时销到这个国家的其他地区。它的飞机制造业和太空探测设备在国内领先。许多电影和电视节目也都在洛杉矶拍摄。它还是西部各州的商业中心。交通的改善是洛杉矶快速发展的主要原因。

Passage 3

As many as one thousand years ago in the Southwest, the Hopi and Zuni tribes of North America were building with adobe-sun-baked brick plastered with mud. Their homes looked remarkably like modern apartment houses. Some were four stories high and contained quarters for perhaps a thousand people, along with storerooms for grain and other goods. These buildings were usually put up against cliffs, both to make construction easier and for defense against enemies. They were really villages in themselves, as later Spanish explorers must have realized since they called them "pueblos", which is Spanish for town.

The people of the pueblos raised what are called "the three sisters"—corn, beans, and squash. They made excellent pottery and wove marvelous baskets, some so fine that they could hold water. The Southwest has always been a dry country, with water scarce. The Hopi and Zuni brought water from streams to their fields and gardens through irrigation and developed elaborate ceremonies and religious rituals to bring rain.

The way of life of less-settled groups was simpler and more strongly influenced by nature. Small tribes such as the Shoshone and Ute wandered the dry and mountainous lands between the Rocky Mountains and the Pacific Ocean. They gathered seeds and hunted small animals such as rabbits and snakes. In the Far North the ancestors of today's Inuit hunted seals, walruses, and the great whales. They lived right on the frozen seas in shelters called igloos built of blocks of packed snow. When summer came, they fished for salmon and hunted the lordly reindeer.

The Cheyenne, Pawnee, and Sioux tribes, known as the Plains Indians, lived on the grasslands between the Rocky Mountains and the Mississippi River. They hunted the bison, commonly called the buffalo. Its meat was the chief food of these tribes, and its hide was used to make their clothing and the covering of their tents and tepees.

29. Which of the following is the best title for the passage?
(A) Building with Adobe
(B) One Thousand Years of Hunting
(C) The Hopi and Zuni Tribes
(D) Early North American Societies

30. It can be inferred from the passage that the dwellings of the Hopi and Zuni were ______.
(A) very small
(B) highly advanced
(C) conveniently located
(D) extremely fragile

31. The author uses the phrase "the three sisters" in Line 8 to refer to ______.
(A) Hopi women
(B) family members
(C) important crops
(D) rain ceremonies

32. The author groups North American Indians according to their ______.
(A) tribes and environment
(B) impact on the Europeans
(C) rituals and ceremonies
(D) date of appearance on the continent

生词及短语

adobe [ə'dəubi]	*n.*	砖坯
quarters ['kwɔːtə(r)]	*n.*	住处
cliff [klif]	*n.*	峭壁
pueblo ['pwebləu]	*n.*	印第安人村庄
squash [skwɔʃ]	*n.*	南瓜
ritual ['ritʃuəl]	*n.*	(宗教)仪式
walruses ['wɔːlrəs]	*n.*	海象
igloo ['igluː]	*n.*	圆顶建筑
salmon ['sæmən]	*n.*	鲑鱼
reindeer ['reindiə(r)]	*n.*	驯鹿
bison ['bais(ə)n]	*n.*	野牛
buffalo ['bʌfələu]	*n.*	水牛
hide [haid]	*n.*	兽皮
tepee ['tiːpiː]	*n.*	美国印第安人的圆锥形帐篷

答案与解析

29. [答案](**D**)

[解析]本文叙述了一千年前生活在北美的8个土著部族的生活情况，故答案应为(D)。而(A)意为“有土墙的建筑物”,(B)意为“狩猎的一千年”,(C)意为“霍皮和祖尼部落”,都只是文中提到的相关内容,不能成为本文标题。

30. [答案](**B**)

[解析]第一段第二句指出“霍皮和祖尼人的房屋看上去很像现代的公寓”,可以推断其房屋是相当先进的,故答案应为(B)。

31. [答案](**C**)

[解析]第二段第一句明确提到“三姐妹”是玉米、蚕豆和南瓜三种农作物,故答案只能是(C)。

32. [答案](**A**)

[解析]本文在对列举的8个土著部族分类时,主要提及他们居住地区的环境、生活特点等,很明显应排除(B)、(C)、(D)。答案只能是(A)。

译文

一千年前，北美的霍皮(Hopi)人和祖尼(Zuni)人在西南部用干土坯和泥浆砌筑起自己的部落。他们的房屋看上去非常像现代的公寓建筑，一些房子有四层楼高，可以容纳大约一千人，还有存放谷物和其他物品的储藏室。这些房子通常背靠峭壁建造，既为了容易修建，也为了防御敌人。它们就是真正的村庄，就像后来的西班牙探险者们也意识到的一样，因为他们称这些村庄为"印第安人村庄(pueblos)"，这是西班牙语对城镇的叫法。

村庄中的人们种植被称为"三姐妹"的农作物：玉米、蚕豆和南瓜。村民们会制造优质的陶器，编织手工篮子，有一些篮子精细得能够盛水。西南部一直是干旱地区，水源缺乏，霍皮人和祖尼人通过水利将水从溪流输送到他们的土地和花园里，并发展出复杂的仪式和宗教典礼来祈雨。

不常定居的部落群的生活方式更加简单，同时会受到大自然的强烈影响。例如游走于落基山脉和太平洋海岸之间的绶绶尼(Shoshone)和尤特(Ute)这样的小部族，他们收集种子，猎取兔子和蛇一类的小动物。在遥远的北方地区，今天因纽特(lnuit)人的祖先们猎取海豹、海象和巨大的鲸，他们居住在冰冻的海面上用夯实雪块砌筑的圆顶屋里。当夏季来临时，他们会捕捉鲤鱼和猎取北美驯鹿。

夏延(Cheyenne)、波尼(Pawnee)和苏(Sioux)族部落被认为是平原印第安人，居住在落基山脉和密西西比河之间的草原上，他们猎取被称为水牛的北美野牛。野牛肉是这些部落的主要食物，野牛皮用来缝制他们的衣服和搭建他们的圆锥形帐篷。

Passage 4

If the salinity of ocean waters is analyzed, it is found to vary only slightly from place to place. Nevertheless, some of these small changes are important. There are three basic processes that cause a change in oceanic salinity. One of these is the subtraction of water from the ocean by means of evaporation—conversion of liquid water to water vapor. In this manner, the salinity is increased, since the salts stay behind. If this is carried to the extreme, of course, white crystals of salt would be left behind; this, by way, is how much of the table salt we use is actually obtained.

The opposite of evaporation is precipitation, such as rain, by which water is added to the ocean. Here the ocean is being diluted so that the salinity is decreased. This may occur in areas of high rainfall or in coastal regions where rivers flow into the ocean. Thus salinity may be increased by the subtraction of water by evaporation, or decreased by the addition of fresh water by precipitation of runoff.

Normally, in tropical regions where the Sun is very strong, the ocean salinity is somewhat higher than it is in other parts of the world where there is not as much evaporation. Similarly in coastal regions where rivers dilute the sea, salinity is somewhat lower than in other oceanic areas.

A third process by which salinity may be altered is associated with the formation and melting of sea ice. When seawater is frozen, the dissolved materials are left behind. In this manner, seawater directly beneath freshly formed sea ice has a higher salinity than it did before the ice appeared. Of course, when this ice melts, it will tend to decrease the salinity of the surrounding water.

In the Weddell Sea, off Antarctica, the densest water in the oceans is formed as a result of this freezing process, which increases the salinity of cold water. This heavy water sinks and is found in the deeper portions of the oceans of the world.

33. What does the passage mainly discuss?

(A) The elements of salt.

(B) The bodies of water of the world.

(C) The many forms of ocean.

(D) The salinity of ocean water.

34. According to the passage, the ocean generally has more salt in ______.

(A) coastal areas

(B) tropical areas

(C) rainy areas

(D) turbulent areas

35. All of the following are processes that decrease salinity EXCEPT ______.

(A) evaporation

(B) precipitation

(C) runoff

(D) melting

36. Which of the following statements about the salinity of a body of water can best be inferred from the passage?

(A) The temperature of the water is the most important factor.

(B) How quickly the water moves is directly related to the amount of salt.

(C) Ocean salinity has little effect on sea life.

(D) Various factors combine to cause variations in the salt content of water.

37. What can be inferred about the water near the bottom of oceans?

(A) It is relatively warm.

(B) Its salinity is relatively high.

(C) It does not move.

(D) It is formed by melting.

生词及短语

salinity [sə'linəti]	*n.*	盐分,含盐量,盐度
subtraction [səb'trækʃ(ə)n]	*n.*	减少
evaporation [ivæpə'reiʃ(ə)n]	*n.*	蒸发(作用)
precipitation [prisipi'teiʃ(ə)n]	*n.*	降雨,降雨量
dilute [dai'ljuːt]	*v.*	稀释,冲淡
runoff	*n.*	流动的雨水

答案与解析

33. [答案] (D)

[解析] 本文主要叙述海洋中不同海域的含盐量差异及其形成的过程,故答案应为(D)。应排除(A)、(B)、(C)。

34. [答案] (B)

[解析] 第三段第一句指出,由于热带强烈的阳光导致海水蒸发,使得热带海域的含盐量稍高于其他海域,故答案应为(B)。(A) 意为“沿岸海域”,(C) 意为“多雨海域”,(D) 意为“汹涌的海域”,均排除。

35. [答案] (A)

[解析] 文中第二段提到降雨,第二、三段提到河流入海,第四段提到冰雪融化,都导致海水含盐量降低,而文中多处提到蒸发是增加含盐量的基本过程,故答案为(A)。

36. [答案] (A)

[解析] 文中第三段和第五段提到, 在热带海域和南极洲的威德尔海含盐量高于其他海域,所以水温过高或过低直接导致含盐量的增加。答案应为(A)。其他选项均不是最重要的因素。

37. [解析] (B)

[解析] 文章最后一句指出, 含盐量增高海域海面会下沉, 能在海洋世界较深的部分发现。可以推断,在海底的海水含盐量较高。答案应为(B)。而洋底的海水不大会是比较温暖,不移动的,或是融化的冰雪形成的。

译文

如果分析海水含盐量,我们会发现不同地点的海水含盐量变化甚微。然而这些细微变化却很重要。有三种基本过程会导致海水含盐量发生变化,一是蒸发使海水量减少,液态水转化为水蒸气,通过这种方式,含盐量增加了,因为盐分都留了下来。如这个过程发展到极端,就只会剩下盐的白色晶体。这实际上获得的就是我们饭桌上使用的大部分盐。

与蒸发相反的过程是降水,例如雨水。雨水汇入海洋中,这样海水被冲淡,盐分就会降低。这种情况会发生在降雨量高的海域以及河流入海的沿岸地区。所以,含盐量可以由蒸发减少水量而增高,也可由降雨和河流汇入海里而降低。

通常地,热带地区的阳光非常强烈,海水含盐量会稍高于世界上其他蒸发不太大的海域。与之相反,海岸线周围的河流冲淡海水,含盐量便稍低于其他海域。

在第三种过程,含盐量的改变与海冰的构成及融化有关。当海水结冰,水中的物质留了下来。这样,在新形成的冰下的海水含盐量比冰块出现之前更高。当然,当这样的冰块融化时,它会降低周围海水的含盐量。

在南极洲附近的威德尔海域,是全球海洋中含盐浓度最大的。其海水的形成便是冰冻过程的结果,冻结过程增加了海水的含盐量。这种较重的海水下沉,在世界各处海洋的较深部位都可找到。

阅读 B 篇

Directions:

In the following article, some sentences have been removed. For Questions 38—42, choose the most suitable one from the list A—G to fit into each of the numbered blanks. There are two extra choices, which do not fit in any of the blanks. Mark your answers on ANSWER SHEET 1. (10 points)

Will America's cities ever again be places most people want to live in? It seems unlikely. Whereas in 1970 America's suburbs contained 25% more families than its cities, today they contain 75 % more. Middle-class families—"the bedrock of a stable community", in the words of the Department of Housing and Urban Development—associate cities with poverty and therefore crime. (38) ________________. No wonder so many families equate the American dream with a home in the suburbs.

But the resulting urban sprawl carries a cost. A report this week from the Sierra Club, which has been preaching ecological sensitivity for more than a century, underlines what it calls "the dark side of the American dream": traffic congestion; commuting journeys that "steal time from family and work"; air and water pollution; lost farmland and recreational space; increased flooding; and more taxes to pay for a suburban infrastructure that ranges from policing to sewage systems. (39) ______________.

Putting numbers to its argument, the Sierra Club reckons air pollution "costs U.S. agriculture more than $2.5 billion every year," and it argues that the paving over of natural wetlands helps produce the floods that cost America an average of $4.3 billion a year. In the period from 1970 to 1990, urban sprawl led the twin cities of Minneapolis—St Paul, in Minnesota, to close 162 schools in and around the city centers while building 78 new ones in the outer suburbs. Between 1970 and 1995, Maine spent over $338 million building new schools even as the number of students in its public schools fell by 27,000. (40) ______________.

(41) ______________. Among the country's largest cities, the most threatened, apparently, are the citizens of Atlanta; among medium-sized cities, it is the people of Orlando, Florida, who have most to fear; and among small cities, the inhabitants of McAllen, Texas. As for Los Angles, the "grand-daddy of sprawl", the city deserves a "dishonorable mention", along with San Diego and Phoenix.

(42) ______________. One idea being tried in parts of Michigan and Maryland is for communities to buy farmland or environmentally sensitive land to prevent its development; another idea, practiced in Oregon and Washington state, is to set an "urban growth boundary" to enclose an urban area within an inviolate green belt; a third is to offer tax inducements to communities that forgo development rights. But in the land of the car, perhaps the most unlikely idea is that Americans will follow the example of New Jersey, which recently voted for higher petrol taxes to preserve a million acres of undeveloped land over the next ten years.

(A) Moreover, as the suburb expands so the inner city's tax base shrinks, setting off a vicious cycle of higher taxes, lower corporate profits, higher joblessness and lower property values.

(B) It was obvious that after 1970 people preferred to live in the suburb while work in the city.

(C) Can urban sprawl be repulsed?

(D) They have a point: the poverty rate in America's urban areas rose from 14.2% in 1970 to 21.5% in 1993, with most of the increase in the inner-city areas from which the middle class has fled.

(E) Meanwhile, the exhaustion of commuters is hardly lessened by new and better roads, since each 1% increase in new lane-miles generates within five years a 0.9% increase in traffic.

(F) The house in the suburb may not be full of conveniences of every sort, so cars are the only means for shopping and transportation.

(G) All this, the Sierra Club maintains, illustrates the threat that urban sprawl represents to the quality of life.

内 容 提 要

本文讨论城市向郊区延伸而产生的一系列问题。第一段指出,美国的城市能再次成为大多数人希望居住的地方吗?看起来未必。尽管1970年美国的郊区居住了比城市多25%的人口,而今天已经达到了75%。用住房和城市发展部的话来说中产阶级家庭是"稳定社会的根基",这将把城市和贫困及犯罪联系到一起。第二段提到城市向郊区延展也产生了许多问题。

答案与解析

38. [答案] (D)

[解析] 空白前一句提到"中产阶级家庭将城市与贫困和犯罪联系到一起",(D)继续论述他们的这种看法。

39. [答案] (A)

[解析] 该段提到城市向郊区延展也产生了许多问题,(A)以"Moreover"将更深层的经济问题进一步加以阐述。

40. [答案] (E)

[解析] 空白前一句提到由于城市延伸,城市中心区的学校关闭,而城郊建起了许多学校,花费巨大,但学生大量减少。后面的内容可能是其他问题,而(E)以Meanwhile引导举出了其他问题:从郊区到城市的往返上班者筋疲力尽,即便修更多更好的路也不会因此减轻奔波的辛苦。

41. [答案] (G)

[解析] 由于前两段一直提到谢拉俱乐部的报告,同时没有结论,而(G)作出了总结:所有这些,谢拉俱乐部认为,说明城市延伸对人们的生活质量造成了威胁。

42. [答案] (C)

[解析] 空白后面提到防止城市延伸的观点,可见空白处应该与此有关,而(C)正提出了这个问题:城市延伸能被制止吗?

阅读C篇

Directions:

Read the following text carefully and then translate the underlined segments into Chinese.

Your translation should be written neatly on ANSWER SHEET 2.(10 points)

(43) Maybe they are too young to know better, or more probably they are young enough to know better than most, but two Internet marketing whizzes from San Francisco say both dotcom companies and the Internet arm of conventional companies will continue to be where client growth and profit is most prolific.

But a marketing strategy, including above-line advertising to drive people to your site, will still be important, say 23-year-old Christopher George and 26-year-old Julio Cabanillas, interactive media specialists from the global advertising agency Foote Cone Belding (FCB).

The two travel the world to instruct their counterparts on the rights and wrongs of Internet as marketing strategies and the correct branding of dotcom companies. They should know. (44) Sixty percent of billings issued by the San Francisco office of FCB are now to dotcom companies including the massive on-line book store Amazon. com, which boasts access to more than a million titles.

(45) On a smaller scale, but equally effective, has been the Listen. com advertising banner, placed on a host of carefully selected music related sites and search engines. The banner has a request function where the user can select an artist and be taken directly to that artist's web page and download MP3 audio tracks.

"The fact that you can search within the banner and condition the user to know what you are offering is key. The creative approach is simple but effective, and conveys exactly what the site is about."

(46) Although the Internet strategies follow the standard 1:3 ratio of conventional advertising campaigns (roughly three times more should be spent on placing advertising in the various media such as television or newspapers than on the production of the advertising campaign), the cost to clients comes before—and after—the online campaign.

For example of what not to do, Senior George and Cabanillas point to the giant supermarket chain Wal-Mart in the U.S. as an Internet site that has not taken advantage of the unique properties of interactivity. "What they've done is to take the bricks andmortar layout—store aisles, for example—and simply put it online," Cabanillas says.

(47) "But the online experience is much more fluid than that, and should provide 'smarter' services like recommendations, discounts and other fun things to enhance the user's experience. Not intrusive, just smarter."

生词及短语

whizz [hwiz]	*n.*	精明的人，专家
client ['klaiənt]	*n.*	客户

prolific [prə'lifik]	*a.*	多产的,丰富的
counterpart ['kauntəpɑːt]	*n.*	搭档,对手,配对
rights and wrongs		事实真相
interactivity		交互性
mortar ['mɔːtə]	*v.*	用水泥涂抹
layout ['leiaut]	*n.*	规划,设计
aisle [ail]	*n.*	走廊,过道
intrusive [in'truːsiv]	*a.*	打扰的,插入的
smart [smaːt]	*a.*	聪明的,机敏的

全文译文与答案

(43)也许是因为他们还太年轻,所以知之甚少;或者,正是由于他们年轻,可能比大多数人知道得更多,但两位来自旧金山的互联网营销高手认为,无论是网络公司还是传统公司的互联网业务都将继续是顾客增长最多和利润最丰的地方。

来自全球广告代理FCB的两位交互式媒体专家——23岁的克里斯托·乔治和26岁的胡利奥·卡瓦尼利亚斯指出,一种市场策略,包括在线广告迫使人们点击你的网址,将仍然非常重要。

两位走遍全球,告知他们的同行有关互联网作为营销策略和网络公司矫正品牌的事实真相。他们必须了解。(44)现在,FCB旧金山营业处的收入有60%来自网络公司,规模巨大的网上书店亚马逊也在其中。亚马逊以拥有超过100万种图书而自豪。

(45)被放置在大量精心挑选出来的涉及音乐的网站和搜索引擎上的"Listen.com"标题广告一直规模较小,但发挥了同等的效力。标题有要求的功能,而用户可以选择一个艺术家,同时被直接带到这个艺术家的网页下载MP3音乐。

"事实是,你可以在标题内进行搜索,而用户知道你提供什么的环境是关键。创造性的途径很简单但也很有效,同时要传达该网址确实是有关什么的。"

(46)尽管网络广告策略遵从传统广告运作中1:3的比例标准(即,将广告通过诸如电视或报纸等各种媒体分布,所支出的费用约为广告本身制作费的3倍),但是对客户的支出在上线运作之前和运作之后,都必须进行。

对于不该做的个案,乔治和卡瓦尼利亚斯指出,美国超级市场连锁店的巨头沃尔玛作为互联网网址并没有利用交互式特有的功能。"例如,他们所做的仅仅是将砖用水泥堆砌,成为店铺的过道,只是简单地把它放到网上。"卡瓦尼利亚斯表示。

(47)"但在线经营比那灵活得多,它应该提供'更聪明'的服务,比如推荐、打折和其他一些有意思的事情,从而丰富用户在线体验。这并非打扰顾客,而只是做得更精确些。"

阅读强化练习十三

阅读A篇

Directions:

Read the following four texts. Answer the questions below each text by choosing A, B, C or D. Mark your answers on ANSWER SHEET 1. (40 points)

Passage 1

Martha Graham's territory of innumerable dances and a self-sufficient dance technique is a vast but closed territory, since to create an art out of one's experience alone is ultimately a self-limiting act. If there had been other choreographers with Graham's gifts and her stature, her work might have seemed a more balanced part of the story of American dance. But as she built her repertory, her own language seemed to shut out all other kinds. Even when an audience thinks it discerns traces of influence from other dance styles, the totality of Graham's theatrical idiom, its control of costumes, lights and every impulse of the dance, makes the reference seem a mirage. Dance is not her main subject. It is only her servant.

Graham had achieved her autonomy by 1931. By that time, three giant figures who had invented the new twentieth-century dance were dead, Sergei Diaghilev, Anna Pavlova, and Isadora Duncan. Their era ended with them, and their dance values nearly disappeared. Their colleagues Michel Fokine and Ruth St. Denis lived on in America like whales on the beach. During the twenties, Martha Graham and her colleagues had rescued art-dance from vaudeville and movies and musical comedy and all the resonances of the idyllic mode in the United States, but in so doing they closed the channels through which different kinds of dance could speak to one another and these stayed closed for half a century. Modern dance dedicated itself to deep significance. It gave up lightness, it gave up a wealth of exotic color, it gave up a certain kind of theatrical wit and that age-old mobile exchange between a dancer and the dancer's rhythmical and musical material. No material in modern dance was neutral. The core of the art became an obsession with meaning and allegory as expressed in bodies. Modern dance excluded its own theatrical traditions of casual play, gratuitous liveliness, the spontaneous pretense, and the rainbow of genres that had formed it. But all these things survived in the public domain, where they had always lived, and they have continued to surface in American dance, if only by accident.

21. What is the main purpose of the passage?
   (A) To discuss Martha Graham's influences on modern dance.
   (B) To trace the origins of different dance techniques.
   (C) To argue the role of modern dance as an artistic form of expression.
   (D) To compare several famous women choreographers of the twentieth century.

22. According to the passage, which of the following most influenced Martha Graham's dances and techniques?
   (A) Her own experience.
   (B) Exotic and idyllic themes.
   (C) Familiar classical stories.
   (D) The works of St. Denis and Duncan.

23. It can be inferred from the passage that Martha Graham had become famous by ______.
   (A) the beginning of the nineteenth century
   (B) the end of the nineteenth century
   (C) the early 1920s
   (D) the early 1930s

24. In Para. 2 Line 4, the author uses the phrase "like whales on the beach" to indicate that Fokine and St. Denis were
   (A) good swimmers.
   (B) physically large.
   (C) out of place.
   (D) very sick.

25. In Lines 15—16, what criticism does the author make of Martha Graham and her colleagues?
   (A) They patterned much of their choreographic style after vaudeville.
   (B) They insisted that all dancers learn the same foreign language.
   (C) They adopted the same dance values of the previous era without interjecting any new ideas.
   (D) They prevented modern dance from expanding beyond their personal interpretations.

生词及短语

stature [ˈstætʃə]	*n.*	身高,高度
repertory [ˈrepətəri]	*n.*	常备节目
discern [diˈsəːn]	*n.*	目睹,辨别
mirage [ˈmirɑːʒ]	*n.*	海市蜃楼,幻想
autonomy [ɔːˈtɔnəmi]	*n.*	自治
vaudeville [ˈvɔːdəvil]	*n.*	歌舞杂耍
idyllic [iˈdilik]	*a.*	田园诗的,牧歌的,生动的
exotic [egˈzɔtik]	*n.*	外来的,异国情调的
allegory [ˈæligəri]	*n.*	寓言
gratuitous [grəˈtjuːitəs]	*a.*	免费的,无理由的
pretense [priˈtens]	*n.*	主张,要求,借口,伪装

答案与解析

21. [答案] (**A**)

[解析] 本题为主旨题。从短文的两段内容可以看出,文章的主要目的是讨论玛莎·格蕾汉姆对现代舞蹈的影响。而(B) 意为"追寻不同舞蹈艺术的起源";(C) 意为"争论现代舞作为一种艺术表现形式的作用";和(D) 意为"对 20 世纪几位著名女舞蹈艺术家加以比较";均不是作者的主要目的。

22. [答案] (**A**)

[解析] 从第一段第一句中 "... since to create an art out of one's experience alone is..."可得出答案应为(A)。

23. [答案] (**D**)

[解析] 由第二段第一句"Graham had achieved her autonomy by 1931."可确定(D) 为正确答案。

24. [答案] (**C**)

[解析] 在第 12 行,作者以短语"巨鲸搁浅滩"比喻福克和丹尼丝是英雄无用武之地,故答案应为(C)。

25. [答案] (**D**)

[解析] 从第 15—16 行可知,她们把现代舞蹈从杂耍和电影等中解脱出来,但同时封锁了各种舞蹈之间的相互交流,故答案为(D)。

译文

玛莎·格蕾汉姆数不胜数的舞蹈和过于自信的舞蹈技巧是一个既广阔又封闭的领地。最终来说,单从一个人的个人经历来创造一门艺术最终是一种自我限制的行为。假如过去存在有格蕾汉姆的天赋和才能的其他芭蕾舞编导的话，格蕾汉姆的舞蹈看起来就更像美国舞蹈史话中并存的一部分。但是,当建立了自己的剧团时,她的舞蹈排斥了所有其他舞蹈,即使有时观众认为可以从她的舞蹈中看到其他舞蹈的蛛丝马迹,但格蕾汉姆的戏剧语言,服装选配和舞蹈的每一个动作总体来说使这些痕迹看起来就好像海市蜃楼。舞蹈并不是她的主体而只是她的附庸。

格蕾汉姆在1931年就到达了她的自由王国。当时发明20世纪新舞蹈的三位大师:史可·迪艾哈罗费、安娜·帕瓦洛瓦和依莎多拉·邓肯已经相继去世,他们的时代也随之成为过去,其舞蹈价值也几乎消失。他们的同行米歇尔·福克和如丝·圣·丹尼丝生活在美国就好像是巨鲸搁浅海滩。在20年代里玛莎·格蕾汉姆及其同行将艺术舞蹈从杂耍、电影、音乐喜剧以及所有其他美国田园式的表演中脱离了出来，但同时也将舞蹈家之间的交流渠道关闭了近半个世纪之久。现代舞寓自己以深刻的含意,它放弃了亮光,放弃了大量的奇光异彩,放弃了某些戏剧的妙语诙谐以及当时舞蹈家与其有节奏的,悦耳的素材间古老的相互交流。在现代舞蹈中没有东西是中性的。艺术的核心变为由身体表达的萦绕于心际的喻意。现代舞排除了自己那些既已形成的随意的表演,无缘无故的活力,冲动的虚假做作和模式化的色彩等,但所有这些东西仍然活在公众中,在那里它们曾一直获得生命并继续在美国舞蹈中出现,而且不只是偶然的。

Passage 2

The invention of the incandescent light bulb by Thomas A. Edison in 1879 created a demand for a cheap, readily available fuel with which to generate large amounts of electric power. Coal seemed to fit the bill, and it fueled the earliest power-stations (which were set up at the end of the nineteenth century by Edison himself) . As more power plants were constructed throughout the country, the reliance on coal increased. Since the First World War, coal-fired power plants have accounted for about half of the electricity produced in the United States each year. In 1986 such plants had a combined generating capacity of 289,000 megawatts and consumed 83% of the nearly 900 million tons of coal mined in the country that year. Given the uncertainty in the future growth of nuclear power and in the supply of oil and natural gas, coal-fired power plants could well provide up to 70% of the electric power in the United States by the end of the century.

Yet, in spite of the fact that coal has long been a source of electricity and may remain one for many years (coal represents about 80% of United States fossil-fuel reserves) , it has actually never been the most desirable fossil fuel for power plants. Coal contains less energy per unit of weight than natural gas or oil, it is difficult to transport, and it is associated with a host of environmental issues, among them acid rain. Since the late 1960s problems of emission control and waste disposal have sharply reduced the appeal of coal-fired power plants. The cost of ameliorating these environmental problems, along with the rising cost of building a facility as large and complex as a coal-fired power plant, have also made such plants less attractive from a purely economic perspective.

Changes in the technological base of coal-fired power plants could restore their attractiveness, however. Whereas some of these changes are evolutionary and are intended mainly to increase the productivity of existing plants, completely new technologies for burning coal cleanly are also being developed.

26. What is the main idea of the passage?
   (A) Coal-fired plants are an important source of electricity in the United States and are likely to remain so.
   (B) Generating electricity from coal is comparatively recent in the United States.
   (C) Coal is a more economical fuel than either oil or nuclear power.
   (D) Coal is a safer and more dependable fossil fuel than oil or gas.

27. Edison's electric light bulb is mentioned in the passage because it ______.
   (A) replaced gas as a light source
   (B) increased the need for electrical power
   (C) was safer than any other method of lighting
   (D) could work only with electricity generated from coal

28. In the author's opinion, the importance of coal-generated electricity could increase in the future for which of the following reasons?
   (A) The possible substitutes are too dangerous.
   (B) The cost of changing to other fuel is too great.
   (C) The future availability of other fuels is uncertain.
   (D) Other fuels present too many environmental problems.

29. Acid rain is mentioned in the passage for which of the following reasons?
   (A) It reduces the efficiency of coal-fired plants.
   (B) It increases the difficulty of transporting coal.
   (C) It is an environmental problem associated with coal use.
   (D) It contains less energy per unit of weight than coal does.

30. According to the passage, which of the following is one of the goals of the new technology in coal-fired plants?
   (A) To adapt the plants to other kinds of fuel.
   (B) To reduce the cost of building more plants.
   (C) To lengthen the lives of plants already in use.
   (D) To make the plants already in use more productive.

生词及短语

incandescent [inkæn'des(ə)nt]	*a.*	遇热发光的,白炽的
fit the bill		符合要求
fossil ['fɔs(ə)l]	*a.*	化石的,矿物的
ameliorate [ə'miːliəreit]	*v.*	改善,改进

答案与解析

26. [答案] (A)
   [解析] 本题为主旨题,由第一段第五句"Since the First World War, ... in the United States each year." 和第一段倒数第一句 "... coal fired power plants could well provide ... by the end of the century."可推断出(A) 为正确答案。
27. [答案] (B)
   [解析] 从第一段第二句 "... created a demand for ... available fuel with which to generate large amounts of electric power."可知答案为(B)。
28. [答案] (C)
   [解析] 从第一段倒数第一句就得知作者的观点应为(C)。
29. [答案] (C)
   [解析] 第二段第二句后半部分指出:"... and it is associated with a host of environmental issues, among them acid rain."表明正确答案为(C)。
30. [答案] (D)
   [解析] 最后一句指出:"... some of these changes are evolutionary and are intended mainly to increase the productivity of existing plants."表明答案为(D)。

译文

1879 年托马斯·爱迪生对白炽灯的发明导致了对能够生产出大量电力的便宜燃料的需

求。而煤很符合这一需求,而最早的电厂(由爱迪生自己于19世纪末创建)就是用煤作燃料的。随着全国范围大量电厂的建设,对煤的需求增加了。第一次世界大战以来,燃煤电厂每年生产出美国一半左右的电能。到1986年,这种电厂总发电能力达289,000兆瓦,消耗了当年美国约9亿吨煤产量的83%。由于将来核电力的增长和石油天然气的供应具有不确定性,到本世纪末燃煤电厂将为美国提供达70%的电力。

然而,尽管长期以来煤被作为电力的资源,而且仍将继续保持这个地位很多年(煤占美国矿物燃料储量的80%),但它实际上一直都不是我们最希望的发电矿物燃料,这是由于煤所含的单位重量能量比天然气和石油低,同时运输不便,还存在诸如酸雨之类的大量环境问题。自20世纪60年代后期以来,排放控制和废物处理的问题大大地降低了燃煤电厂的吸引力。从纯经济学角度看,改善环境问题的费用以及建设像燃煤电厂这样既大又复杂的工厂成本的增加同样减弱了这类工厂的吸引力。

然而,基于技术改造的燃煤电厂能恢复它们的吸引力。鉴于一些技术改造是革命性的,同时主要目的是要提高现有电厂的生产能力,全新的清洁燃煤技术也正在发展中。

Passage 3

The military aspect of the United States Civil War has always attracted the most attention from scholars. The roar of gunfire, the massed movements of uniformed men, the shrill of bugles, and the drama of hand-to-hand combat have fascinated students of warfare for a century. Behind the lines, however, life was less spectacular. It was the story of back-breaking labor to provide the fighting men with food and arms, of nerve-tingling uncertainty about the course of national events, of heartbreak over sons or brothers or husbands lost in battle. If the men on the firing line won the victories, the means to those victories were forged on the home front.

Never in the nation's history had Americans worked harder for victory than in the Civil War. Northerners and Southerners alike threw themselves into the task of supplying their respective armies. Both governments made tremendous demands upon civilians and in general, received willing cooperation.

By 1863 the Northern war economy was rumbling along in high gear. Everything from steamboats to shovels was needed and produced. Denied Southern cotton, textile mills turned to wool for blankets and uniforms. Hides by the hundreds of thousands were turned into shoes and harness and saddles; ironworks manufactured locomotive, ordnance, armor plate. Where private enterprise lagged, the government set up its own factories or arsenals. Agriculture boomed, with machinery doing the job of farm workers drawn into the army.

In short, everything that a nation needed to fight a modern war was produced in uncounted numbers. Inevitably there were profiteers with gold-headed canes and flamboyant diamond stickpins, but for every crooked tycoon there were thousands of ordinary citizens living on fixed incomes who did their best to cope with rising prices and still make a contribution to the war effort. Those who could bought war bonds; others knitted, sewed, nursed, or lent any other assistance in their power.

31. With what topic is the passage primarily concerned?
   (A) Why the south lost the Civil War?
   (B) The causes of the Civil War.
   (C) Where the Civil War battles were fought?
   (D) The civilian response to the Civil War.

32. According to the passage, during the Civil War the South no longer provided the North with ______.
   (A) cotton
   (B) wool
   (C) hides
   (D) shoes

33. In Para. 3 Line 3 the word "Hides" is closest in meaning to which of the following?
   (A) Animal skins.
   (B) Tree trunks.
   (C) Disguises.
   (D) Shelters.

34. The author implies that students of the Civil War usually concentrate on the ______.
   (A) home front
   (B) battlefield
   (C) government
   (D) economy

35. Where in the passage does the author mention a contribution made by the government to the war economy?
   (A) Lines 4—5.
   (B) Lines 10—11.
   (C) Lines 16—17.
   (D) Lines 20—21.

生词及短语

roar [rɔː(r)]	*n.*	吼叫,怒号
bugle [ˈbjuːg(ə) l]	*n.*	喇叭,军号
combat [ˈkɔmbæt]	*n.*	战斗,格斗
warfare [ˈwɔːfɛə(r)]	*n.*	战争,作战
spectacular [spekˈtækjulə(r)]	*a.*	引人入胜的,壮观的
back-breaking	*a.*	非常艰苦的,极累人的
nerve-tingling	*a.*	神经紧张的,神经刺痛的
forge [fɔːdʒ]	*v.*	铸造
rumbling [ˈrʌmb(ə)liŋ]	*n.*	隆隆声
in high gear		高速运转
hide [haid]	*n.*	兽皮,皮革
harness [ˈhɑːnis]	*n.*	马具
saddle [ˈsæd(ə)l]	*n.*	马鞍
ironwork [ˈaiənwəːk]	*n.*	钢铁厂,铁制品
ordnance [ˈɔːdnəns]	*n.*	军火
armor [ˈɑːmə(r)]	*n.*	装甲
arsenal [ˈɑːsən(ə)l]	*n.*	兵工厂
profiteer [prɔfiˈtiə(r)]	*n.*	奸商
cane [kein]	*n.*	杖,藤条
flamboyant [flæmˈbɔiənt]	*a.*	华丽,艳丽
stickpins	*n.*	领带夹
crook [kruk]	*vi.*	弯曲
tycoon [taiˈkuːn]	*n.*	商业大亨
bond [bɔnd]	*n.*	债券,公债
knit [nit]	*v.*	编织

答案与解析

31. [答案] (**D**)

[解析] 本文主要叙述美国内战期间民众对战争的反应及所做的努力,(A)、(B)、(C) 选项的内容文中均未提及,故答案为(D)。

32. [答案](A)

[解析]由第三段第三句 “Denied Southern cotton, textile mills turned to wool for blankets and uniforms.”可得出答案为(A)。

33. [答案](A)

[解析]第三段第四句“Hides ... were turned into shoes and harness and saddles;”可推断出 hides 应为皮革,(A) 为正确答案。

34. [答案](B)

[解析]由第一段第二句 “The roar of gunfire, ...have fascinated students of warfare for a century.”可推断出答案应为(B)。

35. [答案](C)

[解析]从第 16—17 行“... the government set up its own factories or arsenals.”可得出答案为(C)。

译文

美国内战的军事内容一直吸引着学者们的注意。大炮的轰隆声,军队的大规模运动,军号声和肉搏战的激烈场面使学生对战争着迷了一个世纪之久。然而,在后方,生活却并不好。正是后方的艰苦劳动给前线将士们提供了食物和武器,人们紧张地关注着国内事件的进程,承受着被战争夺去儿子、兄弟或丈夫的难忍的悲伤。如果前线的将士们取得了胜利,这些取胜的手段却是在后方铸造成的。

历史上美国人从未像在内战期间那样为取得战争胜利而忘我地工作过。北方人和南方人都同样地把他们投身于为自己所支持的军队提供给养的任务中。双方的政府都对市民提出了最大程度的要求,而一般都得到了他们的配合。

到 1863 年,北方战争经济高速发展。从汽船到铁锹,每一件东西都是必需的,都被生产出来了。在南方拒绝供给棉花后,北方的纺织厂转向用羊毛制作制服和毛毯,成千上万张皮革变成了鞋、马具和马鞍。钢铁厂生产出了火车头、军械和装甲钢板。在落后的私营企业,政府建造了自己的工厂或军工厂。由于机械化取代了参战的农场工人的工作,农业也逐渐繁荣。

总之,一个国家参加一场现代化战争所需的每件东西都陆陆续续地生产出来了。虽然不可避免地出现了一些趁机牟取暴利的投机商,他们拄着金手杖,带着光彩夺目的钻石别针,但是有一个狡诈的大亨,就有数千的靠固定收入生活的平民,在尽力承受着物价上涨的压力,同时仍然为战争做出贡献。这些人有的购买战争公债,有的编织、缝补、看护,或在其能力范围内提供其他的帮助。

Passage 4

The surface of the Earth is the shore of the cosmic ocean. From it we have learned most of what we know about space. Recently, we have waded a little out to sea, enough to dampen our toes or, at most, wet our ankles. The water seems inviting. The ocean calls.

The dimensions of the cosmos are so large that using familiar units of distance, such as meters or miles, chosen for their utility on the Earth, would make little sense. Instead we measure distance with the speed of light. In one second a beam of light travels 186,000 miles, nearly 300,000 kilometers, or seven times around the Earth. In eight minutes it will travel from the Sun to the Earth. We can say the Sun is eight light-minutes away. In a year, it crosses nearly ten trillion kilometers, about six trillion miles, of intervening space. That unit of length, the distance light goes in a year, is called a light-year. *It* measures not time but distances—enormous distances.

The Earth is a place. It is by no means the only place. It is not even a typical place. No planet or star or galaxy can be typical because most of the cosmos is empty. The only typical place is within the vast, cold universal vacuum, the everlasting night of intergalactic space, a place so strange and desolate that by comparison, planets and stars and galaxies seem achingly rare and lovely. If we were randomly inserted into the cosmos, the chance that we would find ourselves on or near a planet would be less than one in a billion trillion trillion. Worlds are precious.

36. If the author's analogy in the first paragraph were extended, which of the following means of transportation would be most appropriate for a trip into space?

(A) A bicycle.

(B) A helicopter.

(C) A wagon.

(D) A boat.

37. It can be inferred from the passage that earthly units of measure are not used for intergalactic distances because these units of measure are ______.

(A) unfamiliar to astronomers

(B) too small

(C) inaccurate for measuring distance

(D) underestimated by scientists

38. According to the passage, how long does it take light to travel from the Sun to the Earth?

(A) 186,000 years.

(B) One year.

(C) Eight minutes.

(D) One second.

39. In Para. 2 Line 7, the word "it" refers to which of the following?
   (A) A spaceship.
   (B) A beam of light.
   (C) The Earth.
   (D) The Sun.

40. According to the passage, where would one find the most ordinary place in the cosmos?
   (A) On a star.
   (B) On a planet.
   (C) In the ocean.
   (D) In intergalactic space.

生词及短语

cosmic ['kɔzmik]	*a.*	宇宙的
dampen ['dæmpən]	*v.*	使潮湿
intervene [intə'viːn]	*vi.*	插入,介入,干涉
desolate ['desəleit]	*a.*	荒凉的,无人烟的

答案与解析

36. [答案] (D)
   [解析] 作者在第一段把地球比做宇宙海洋的海岸,而地球的海洋在呼唤人们去探索,故可以推测出答案应为(D)。

37. [答案] (B)
   [解析] 第二段第一、二句指出:"The dimensions of the cosmos are so large that with the speed of light." 作者认为使用我们熟悉的长度单位去测量宇宙根本没有意义,需要使用光速来进行测量。故答案为(B)。

38. [答案] (C)
   [解析] 由第二段第四句"In eight minutes ... to the Earth."可知答案为(C)

39. [答案] (B)
   [解析] 在 it 的前一句中的主语为 a beam of light,可知答案为(B)。

40. [答案] (D)
   [解析] 从第三段第三句 "The only typical place is within the vast, cold universal vacuum, the everlasting night of intergalactic space, ..."可知答案为(D), typical=ordinary。

译文

地球的表面是宇宙海洋之岸,也使我们学到了大部分关于太空的知识。最近我们向大海迈出了脚步,足以湿到我们的脚趾,至多湿到脚跟。这些水显得诱人,大海在召唤。

宇宙范围太大了,以至于选用我们地球上熟悉的长度单位如米或英里便显得几乎没有意义。于是我们用光速来表示距离。光速一秒钟达 186,000 英里,大约 300,000 公里,相当于绕地球七圈。光用 8 分钟时间就能从太阳到达地球,我们可以说太阳有 8 光分钟远。光用一年时间可穿行约十万亿公里,大约六万亿英里的太空距离。这一长度单位,即光穿越一年的距离,称为光年。它不是用来表示时间,而是用来表示距离的——极远的距离。

地球是一个地方,它绝不是惟一的地方,甚至也不是一个典型的地方。没有任何行星、恒星或银河系是典型的,因为宇宙的绝大部分是空的。惟一典型的地方是在无边和寒冷的宇宙真空中,在银河间太空与世永存的漫漫长夜中,这是一个极其陌生和荒凉的地方,相比之下,行星、恒星和银河系显得极其珍贵和可爱。假如我们随意地进入宇宙的话,我们会发现我们登上或靠近某个星球的机遇不到十亿亿亿亿分之一。世界是如此珍贵!

阅读 B 篇

Directions:

In the following article, some sentences have been removed. For Questions 41—45, choose the most suitable one from the list A—G to fit into each of the numbered blanks. There are two extra choices, which do not fit in any of the blanks. Mark your answers on ANSWER SHEET 1. (10 points)

Time spent in a bookshop can be most enjoyable, whether you are a book-lover or merely there to buy a book as a present. You may even have entered the shop to find shelter from a sudden shower. Whatever the reason, you can soon become totally unaware of your surroundings. The desire to pick up a book with an attractive dust-jacket is irresistible, although this method of selection ought not to be followed, as you might end up with a rather dull book. (41) ________.

(42) ________. There are not many places where it is possible to do this. A music shop is very much like a bookshop. You can wander round such places to your heart's content. If it is a good shop, no assistant will approach you with the inevitable greeting: "Can I help you, sir? " You needn't buy anything you don't want. In a bookshop an assistant should remain in the background until you have finished browsing. Then, and only then, are his services necessary. (43) ________.

You have to be careful not to be attracted by the variety of books in a bookshop. It is very easy to enter the shop looking for a book on, say, ancient coins and to come out carrying a copy of the latest best-selling novel and perhaps a book about brass-rubbing-something which had only vaguely interested you up till then. (44) ________________. This sort of thing can be very dangerous. Apart from running up a huge account, you can waste a great deal of time wandering from section to section. Booksellers must be both long-suffering and indulgent.

(45) ________________. A medical student had to read a textbook which was far too expensive for him to buy. He couldn't obtain it from the library and the only copy he could find was in his bookshop. Every afternoon, therefore, he would go along to the shop and read a little of the book at a time. One day, however, he was dismayed to find the book missing from its usual place and was about to leave when he noticed the owner of the shop beckoning to him. Expecting to be told off, he went towards him. To his surprise, the owner pointed to the book, which was tucked away hidden in a corner. "I put it there in case anyone was tempted to buy it." he said, and left the delighted student to continue his reading.

(A) This opportunity to escape the realities of everyday life is, I think, the main attraction of a bookshop.

(B) The owner of the shop didn't care much about the selling of the book, but hoped that the student could finish his reading.

(C) Of course, you may want to find out where a particular section is, but when he has led you there, the assistant should retire discreetly and look as if he is not interested in selling a single book.

(D) There is a story which illustrate this.

(E) You soon become engrossed in some book or other, and usually it is only much later that you realize you have spent far too much time there and must dash off to keep some forgotten appointment—without buying a book, of course.

(F) You may find much difference between a bookshop and a department store. A bookshop is quiet and the assistant never disturb you when you pick up a book and begin to browse it, while in a department store, the assistant never hesitates to come to introduce loudly the products you show interest.

(G) This volume on the subject, however, happened to be so well illustrated and the part of the text you read proved so interesting, that you just had to buy it.

内 容 提 要

本文讨论人们到书店看书时可能会发生的各种情况。第一段指出,在书店度过的时间是最令人愉快的,不管你是爱书者还是仅仅到这里来买一本书作为礼物。你甚至进到书店是为了躲避一场雨。不管什么理由,你不久就变得完全觉察不到你的环境。

答案与解析

41. [答案] (E)

[解析] 空白前提到如果你偶然进入一家书店拿起一本书看的情况，后面内容当然与此有关，(E) 继续叙述当时可能发生的事。

42. [答案] (A)

[解析] 第二段空白处应该与上段内容有关，(A) 表现了这种关联：这种脱离每天现实生活的机会正是书店吸引人的地方。

43. [答案] (C)

[解析] 空白处前面提到，在书店，只有在你浏览完所需之书后，店员才出来为你提供必要的帮助。(C) 接着叙述了该店员不会打搅你的情况。

44. [答案] (G)

[解析] 空白处后面提到，这类事情是非常危险的，可见前面一定是提到什么事情，而(G)明确给予说明：然而，这本关于该内容的书配有优美的插图，你读到的内容非常吸引你，所有你必须买下它。

45. [答案] (D)

[解析] 本段空白后面举出了一个学医的学生的例子，(D) 明显是引出这个例子的开头句：有一个故事可以对此加以说明。

阅读 C 篇

Directions:

Read the following text carefully and then translate the underlined segments into Chinese. Your translation should be written neatly on ANSWER SHEET 2.(10 points)

When the public demands "law and order" and when newspapers editorials talk about the "rising tide of crime," they have in mind mostly street crime committed by the poor. Even the massive report of the President's Crime Commission, the Challenge of Crime in a Free Society, devoted only two pages to the entire subject of white-collar offenders and business crimes. The deep concern with street crimes is understandable. Unlike a swindler, who merely takes the victim's money, an armed mugger threatens physical injury and even death. (46) Yet the fact remains that a great deal of crime in American society—perhaps most crime, and certainly the most costly crime—is committed by respectable middle-class and upper-class citizens. The term "white-collar crime" was first used by Edwin Sutherland in an address to the American

Sociological Association in 1939. (47) "White-collar crime," he declared, "may be defined approximately as a crime committed by a person of respectability and high status in the course of his occupation." Sutherland documented the existence of this form of crime with a study of the careers of 70 large, reputable corporations, which together had committed 980 violations of the criminal law, or an average of 14 convictions apiece. Behind the offenses of false advertising, unfair labor practices, restraint of trade, price-fixing agreements, stock manipulation, copyright infringement, and outright swindles, were perfectly respectable middle-class executives. (48) Sociologists now use the term "white-collar crime" to refer not only to crimes committed in the course of business activities for corporate benefit but also to crimes, such as embezzlement, typically committed by persons of high status for personal benefits.

As Sutherland pointed out, the full extent of white-collar crime is difficult to assess. Many corporate malpractices go undetected, and many wealthy people are able to commit crimes like expense-account fraud for years without being found out. (49) More important, white-collar crimes are usually regarded as somehow less serious than the crimes of the lower class, and they attract less attention from police and prosecutors. Even the victims may be unwilling to prosecute because of the offender's "standing in the community" and would rather out of court. A company that finds its safe has been burgled in the night will immediately summon the police, but it might not do so if it finds that one of its executives has embezzled some of its funds. (50) To avoid unwelcome publicity, the company officials may simply allow the offender to resign after making an arrangement to repay the missing money.

生词及短语

editorial [edi'tɔːriəl]	*n.*	社论,时评
offender [ə'fendə]	*n.*	罪犯
swindler ['swindlə(r)]	*n.*	骗子
mugger ['mʌɡə]	*n.*	行凶抢劫者
conviction [kən'vikʃən]	*n.*	宣告有罪,定罪
apiece [ə'piːs]	*ad.*	每个,每人
manipulation [mənipju'leiʃən]	*n.*	操纵,操作
infringement [in'frindʒmənt]	*n.*	违反,侵犯
outright [aut'rait]	*a.*	彻底的,完全的
embezzlement [im'bezlmənt]	*n.*	挪用,盗用
malpractice [mæl'præktis]	*n.*	玩忽职守
undetected [ʌndi'tektid]	*a.*	未被发现的
fraud [frɔːd]	*n.*	欺骗,欺诈行为

find out		发现
prosecutor [ˈprɔsikjuːtə]	*n.*	检举人
victim [ˈviktim]	*n.*	受害人
out of court		不经法院
safe [seif]	*n.*	保险柜
burgle [ˈbəːgl]	*v.*	偷窃
summon the police		报警
embezzle [imˈbezl]	*v.*	盗用,挪用
resign [riˈzain]	*v.*	辞职

全文译文与答案

当公众要求"法律和秩序",当报纸评论谈论"犯罪呈上升趋势"时,他们主要想象的是由穷人所犯的街道罪行。甚至在对总统的犯罪委员会和自由社会中的犯罪挑战之类的众多报道中,也只有两页篇幅专门谈论白领犯罪和商业犯罪主题。不像一个骗子,仅仅拿走受害人的钱财,一个武装的行凶抢劫犯威胁到人身安全甚至导致死亡。(46) 然而一个依然存在的事实是,美国社会的大部分犯罪,也许绝大部分犯罪,当然也是高代价的犯罪,是受人尊敬的中层和上层市民犯下的。"白领犯罪"这个术语是由埃德温·萨瑟兰于 1939 年在一次对美国社会学协会演讲时第一次提到的。(47) "白领犯罪",他说,"可以大致上这样来定义,即一个受人尊敬的和有崇高社会地位的人在从业过程中所犯下的罪行"。"萨瑟兰提供的文件证明这种形式犯罪的存在,文件研究了 70 个大型的和有声望的企业的事业,共提交了 980 个违法案例,每个企业平均有 14 项罪名。"在虚假广告、不公平用工、贸易管制、定价协议、操控股市、版权侵犯和诈骗的犯罪后面,是颇受尊敬的中产阶级执行经理们。(48) 社会学家现在使用"白领犯罪"这个术语,不仅是指那些在商务活动中为本公司利益而犯的罪行,也指那些通常由高层人士为个人利益所犯的诸如挪用公款公物之类的罪行。

正如萨瑟兰指出,"白领犯罪"的详细范围很难加以界定。许多企业的玩忽职守没有被觉察,许多富人可以多年犯下消费账目欺骗之类的罪行而未被发现。(49) 更要紧的是,这种白领犯罪总被人们认为不如下层阶级的犯罪那么严重,因此也不那么引起警方和检察官的注意。由于犯罪者在"社群中的身份",甚至受害者也不愿意对其起诉,而宁愿不经过法院解决。一家公司发现保险箱在晚上被盗会立即报警,但如果它发现公司的一位经理挪用了公款,可能就不会这样做了。(50) 为了避免惹人注意,公司官员会只让违法者在偿还了亏空的钱款后辞职。

阅读强化练习十四

阅读 A 篇

Directions:

Read the following four texts. Answer the questions below each text by choosing A, B, C or D. Mark your answers on ANSWER SHEET 1. (40 points)

Passage 1

Bacteria are extremely small living things. While we measure our own sizes in inches or centimeters, bacterial size is measured in microns. One microns is a thousandth of a millimeter: a pinhead is about a millimeter across. Rod-shaped bacteria are usually from two to four microns long, while rounded ones are generally one micron in diameter. Thus, if you enlarged a rounded bacterium a thousand times, it would be just about the size of a pinhead. An adult human magnified by the same amount would be over a mile (1.6 kilometers) tall.

Even with an ordinary microscopy, you must look closely to see bacteria. Using a magnification of 100 times, one finds that bacteria are barely visible as tiny rods or dots. One cannot make out anything of their structure. Using special stains, one can see that some bacteria have attached to them wavy-looking "hairs" called flagella. Others have only one flagellum. The flagella rotate, pushing the bacteria through the water. Many bacteria lack flagella and cannot move about by their own power, while others can glide along over surfaces by some little-understood mechanism.

From the bacterial point of view, the world is a very different place from what it is to humans. To a bacterium, water is as thick as molasses is to us. Bacteria are so small that they are influenced by the movements of the chemical molecules around them.

Bacteria under the microscope, even those with no flagella, often bounce about in the water. This is because they collide with the water molecules and are pushed this way and that. Molecules move so rapidly that within a tenth of a second the molecules around a bacterium have all been replaced by new ones; even bacteria without flagella are thus constantly exposed to a changing environment.

21. Which of the following is the main topic of the passage?
(A) The characteristics of bacteria.
(B) How bacteria reproduce.
(C) The various functions of bacteria.
(D) How bacteria contribute to disease.

22. Bacteria are measured in ______.
(A) inches
(B) centimeters
(C) microns
(D) millimeters

23. Which of the following is the smallest?
(A) A pinhead.
(B) A rounded bacterium.
(C) A microscope.
(D) A rod-shaped bacterium.

24. According to the passage, someone who examines bacteria using only a microscope that magnifies 100 times would see ______.
(A) tiny dots
(B) small "hairs"
(C) large rods
(D) detailed structures

25. The relationship between a bacterium and its flagella is most nearly analogous to which of the following?
(A) A rider jumping on a horse's back.
(B) A ball being hit by a bat.
(C) A boat powered by a motor.
(D) A door closed by a gust of wind.

生词及短语

centimeter ['sentimiːtə(r)]	*n.*	厘米
micron ['maikrɔn]	*n.*	微米
millimeter ['milimiːtə(r)]	*n.*	毫米
pinhead ['pinhed]	*n.*	针头
rod-shaped	*a.*	杆状的,棒状的
magnification [mægnifi'keiʃ(ə)n]	*n.*	放大,扩大
stain [stein]	*n.*	污点
wavy-looking ['weivi-luːkiŋ]	*a.*	波状的,摇摆的
flagella [flə'dʒelə]	*n.*	鞭毛
rotate [rəu'teit]	*v.*	旋转
mechanism ['mekəniz(ə)m]	*n.*	机体,机制
molasses [mə'læsiz]	*n.*	糖蜜
molecule ['mɔlikjuːl]	*n.*	分子
bounce [bauns]	*v.*	跳起,弹起
collide [kə'laid]	*vi.*	碰撞

答案与解析

21. [答案](A)

[解析]本题为主旨题。全文主要讲述有关细菌的一些特性,答案应为(A)。

22. [答案](C)

[解析]从第一段第二句"... bacterial size is measured in microns."可得出答案为(C)。

23. [答案](B)

[解析]从第一段第四句 "Rod-shaped bacteria are usually from two to four microns long, while rounded ones are generally one micron in diameter."可知答案为(B)。

24. [答案](A)

[解析]由第二段第二句 "Using a magnification of 100 times, one finds that bacteria are barely visible as tiny rods or dots."可得知答案为(A)。

25. [答案](C)

[解析]第二段倒数第二句 "The flagella rotate, pushing the bacteria through the water."所表达的意义与(C) 相似,故答案应为(C)。

细菌是极小的生物。我们用英寸或厘米测量尺寸，而细菌的大小是用微米来度量的。1微米是千分之一毫米，别针头的直径大约是1毫米。杆状细菌一般为2—4微米长，而圆形细菌的直径一般是1微米。因此，假如我们将圆形细菌放大1千倍，它将与针尖的大小差不多。如果将一个成人也放大同样的倍数，他将比1英里(1.6公里)还高。

即使使用普通显微镜，也必须仔细观察才能看到细菌。使用一个放大100倍的显微镜，可以发现细菌像几乎看不见的极小的条或点，人们不能辨别它们的结构。采用特殊的染色，可以看到有些细菌身上附着称做鞭毛的波浪形的“发”。另一些细菌只有一条鞭毛。鞭毛不停地旋转，推动细菌在水中游动。许多细菌缺乏鞭毛，不能靠自身运动，有些则通过某些尚不明确的机理沿着表面滑动。

从细菌的角度来看，世界是一个与人类世界完全不同的地方。水对于细菌就像糖浆对于我们那样稠密。细菌是如此的小，连周围的化学分子的运动都会影响它。

在显微镜下，即使是没有鞭毛的细菌也常常在水中到处弹跳，这是因为它们与水分子碰撞，不断受到这样和那样的推动。分子运动的速度非常快，在十分之一秒内细菌周围的分子就全部被新的分子所取代，这样即使没有鞭毛的细菌也常常处在一个变化的环境之中。

Passage 2

One of the most popular literary figures in American literature is a woman who spent almost half of her long life in China, a country on a continent thousands of miles from the United States. In her lifetime she earned this country's most highly acclaimed literary award the Pulitzer Prize, and also the most prestigious form of literary recognition in the world, the Nobel Prize for Literature. Pearl S. Buck was almost a household word throughout much of her lifetime because of her prolific literary output which consisted of some eighty-five published works, including several dozen novels, six collections of short stories, fourteen books for children, and more than a dozen works of nonfiction. When she was eighty years old, some twenty-five volumes were awaiting publication. Many of those books were set in China, the land in which she spent so much of her life. Her books and her life served as a bridge between the cultures of the East and the West. As the product of those two cultures she became as she described herself, “mentally bifocal.” Her unique background made her into an unusually interesting and versatile human being. As we examine the life of Pearl Buck, we cannot help but be aware that we are in fact meeting three separate people; a wife and mother, an internationally famous writer, and a humanitarian and philanthropist. One cannot really get to know Pearl Buck without learning about each of the three. Though honored in her lifetime with the William Dean Howell Medal of the American Academy of Arts and Letters in addition to the Nobel and Pulitzer prizes. Pearl Buck as a total human being, not only a famous author, is a captivating subject of study.

26. What is the author's main purpose in the passage?

(A) To offer a criticism of the works of Pearl Buck.

(B) To illustrate Pearl Buck's views on Chinese literature.

(C) To indicate the background and diverse interests of Pearl Buck.

(D) To discuss Pearl Buck's influence on the cultures of the East and the West.

27. According to the passage, Pearl Buck is known as a writer of all of the following EXCEPT ______.

(A) novels

(B) children's books

(C) poetry

(D) short stories

28. Which of the following is NOT mentioned by the author as an award received by Pearl Buck?

(A) The Nobel Prize.

(B) The Newberry Medal.

(C) The William Dezn Howell Medal.

(D) The Pulitzer Prize.

29. According to the passage, Pearl Buck was an unusual figure in American literature in that she ______.

(A) wrote extensively about a very different culture

(B) published half of her books abroad

(C) won more awards than any other woman of her time

(D) achieved her first success very late in life

30. According to the passage, Pearl Buck described herself as "mentally bifocal" to suggest that she was ______.

(A) capable of resolving the differences between two distinct linguistic systems

(B) keenly aware of how the past could influence the future

(C) capable of producing literary works of interest to both adults and children

(D) equally familiar with two different cultural environments

生词及短语

acclaim [ə'kleim]	v.	欢呼,称赞
prestigious [pre'stidʒəs]	a.	享有声望的,声望很高的

prolific [prə'lifik]	*a.*	多产的,丰富的
nonfiction [nɔn'fikʃ(ə)n]	*n.*	非小说的散文文学
bifocal [bai'fəuk(ə)l]	*a.*	双焦点的
versatile ['vəːsətail]	*a.*	多才多艺的,万能的
humanitarian [hju(ː)mæni'tɛriən]	*n.*	人道主义者
philanthropist [fi'lænθrəpist]	*n.*	慈善家
captivating [kæpti'veitiŋ]	*a.*	迷人的,有魅力的

答案与解析

26. [答案] (**C**)

[解析] 本题提问主题。文章主要介绍了皮艾尔·巴克(赛珍珠)的生平、文学作品以及取得的成就,故(C)与主题贴近,应为正确答案。而文中未对皮艾尔提出过任何批评;(B)在文中未被提到;(D)不为文章主要内容。故均可排除。

27. [答案] (**C**)

[解析] 由文中第6—8行"... including several dozen novels, works of nonfiction."可将(A)、(B)、(D) 排除,答案为(C)。

28. [答案] (**B**)

[解析] 根据文中最后一句可将(A)、(C)、(D) 排除,(B)为正确答案。

29. [答案] (**A**)

[解析] 由文中 9—11 行的两句中"Many of those books ... between the cultures of the East and the West."可看出皮艾尔的多数著作是在中国完成的,其著作和其生活为东西方文化架起了桥梁,因此答案应为(A)。(B)、(C)、(D)在文中均未被提到。

30. [答案] (**D**)

[解析] 由文中第 11—12 行 "As the product of those two cultures she became as she described herself, 'mentally bifocal.'"可知(D) 为正确答案。

译文

美国文学中最著名的一位文学家是一个在远离美国数千英里的中国内地度过近半生的妇女。她在一生中赢得了美国颁发的最高文学奖——普利策奖,还有世界上最有声望的诺贝尔文学奖。由于她多产的文学成就,赛珍珠的名字在其有生之年的多半时间家喻户晓,她共出版了八十五部作品,其中包括几十部小说,六部短篇小说集,十四本儿童读物以及十几本散文作品。当她八十岁时,有二十五卷作品等待出版,其中大部分是在她生活了大半生的中国完成的。她的著作和生活架起了东西方文化的桥梁。由于是这两种文化的产品,她描述自己为“智力双焦点”的人。她的独特背景使她成为一个充满内涵和多才多艺的人。当我们察看赛珍珠的生平时,我们不得不承认我们实际上面对着三个独立的人:妻子和母亲,国际著名作家,人道主义者及慈善家。不了解这三者中的任何一个,就不可能真正了解赛珍珠。除诺贝尔奖和普利策奖之外,她还获得了美国文学艺术科学院的威廉·迪恩·哈威尔奖章。赛珍珠是一个完全的人,不仅仅是一位著名作家,还是一个吸引人的研究主题。

Passage 3

If by “suburb” is meant an urban margin that grows more rapidly than its already developed interior, the process of suburbanization began during the emergence of the industrial city, in the second quarter of the nineteenth century. Before that period the city was a small, highly compact cluster in which people moved about on foot and goods were conveyed by horse and cart. But the early factories, built in the 1830s and 1840s, were located along waterways and near railheads at the edges of cities, and housing was needed for the thousands of people drawn by the prospect of employment. In time, the factories were surrounded by proliferating mill towns of apartments and row houses that abutted the older, main cities. As a defense against this *encroachment*, and to enlarge their tax bases, the cities appropriated their industrial neighbors. In 1854, for example, the city of Philadelphia annexed most of Philadelphia County. Similar municipal maneuvers took place in Chicago and in New York. Indeed, most great cities of the United States achieved such status only by incorporating the communities along their borders.

With the acceleration of industrial growth came acute urban crowding and accompanying social stress, conditions that began to approach disastrous proportions when, in 1888, the first commercially successful electric traction line was developed. Within a few years the horse-drawn trolleys were retired and electric streetcar networks, crisscrossed and connected every major urban area fostering a wave of suburbanization that transformed the compact industrial city into dispersed metropolis. This first phase of mass scale suburbanization was reinforced by the simultaneous emergence of the urban middle class, whose desire for homeownership in neighborhoods far from the aging inner city were satisfied by the developers of single-family housing tracts.

31. Which of the following is the best title for the passage?

(A) The Growth of Philadelphia

(B) The Origin of the Suburb

(C) The Development of City Transportation

(D) The Rise of the Urban Middle Class

32. In Para. 1 Line 8, the word “encroachment” refers to which of the following?

(A) The smell of the factories.

(B) The growth of mill towns.

(C) The development of waterways.

(D) The loss of jobs.

33. Which of the following was NOT mentioned in the passage as a factor in nineteenth-century suburbanization?

(A) Cheaper housing.

(B) Urban crowding.

(C) The advent of an urban middle class.

(D) The invention of the electric streetcar.

34. It can be inferred from the passage that after 1890 most people traveled around cities by ____.

(A) automobile

(B) cart

(C) horse-drawn trolley

(D) electric streetcar

35. Where in the passage does the author describe the cities as they were prior to suburbanization?

(A) Lines 3—5.

(B) Lines 8—10.

(C) Line 11.

(D) Lines 15—17.

生词及短语

suburbanization	*n.*	近郊化
railhead ['reilhed]	*n.*	铁路末端,终点
proliferate [prəu'lifəreit]	*v.*	扩展,增生
abut [ə'bʌt]	*v.*	毗邻,邻接
encroachment [in'krəutʃmənt]	*n.*	侵占,侵犯
annex [æ'neks]	*vt.*	并吞
municipal [mjuː'nisip(ə)l]	*a.*	市政的
maneuver [mə'nuːvə(r)]	*n.*	机动
acute [ə'kjuːt]	*a.*	敏锐的,激烈的

traction ['trækʃ(ə)n] *n.* 牵引
trolley ['trɔli] *n.* 推车,电车
crisscross ['kriskrɔs] *v.* 十字形,交叉往来
foster ['fɔstə(r)] *vt.* 养育,抚育
disperse [di'spəːs] *v.* 使分散,散开

答案与解析

31. [答案](B)

[解析]本题为主旨题,文中第一段第一句便明确提出文章会讨论"suburb"和"suburbanization"(近郊化),故答案应为(B)。(A)、(C)、(D) 的内容均不是主要内容。

32. [答案](B)

[解析]encroachment 意为"侵占,侵犯",从第一段第三句中"... the factories were surrounded by proliferating mill towns ..."可知是由于"mill towns"的发展而产生了这种"侵占"行为,故答案为(B)。而(A)、(C)、(D) 的内容文中均未提到。

33. [答案](A)

[解析]文章第二段提到了城市的拥挤、电车网络的发展和城市中产阶级的出现,可排除(B)、(C)、(D),而未提到(A) 更便宜的住房,故答案应为(A)。

34. [答案](D)

[解析]从第二段 2—6 行 "... in 1888, the first commercially successful electric traction line ... into dispersed metropolis."可知"电车网络"已经取代了"马拉车",答案明显为(D)。

35. [答案](A)

[解析]从文中第 3—5 行 "Before that period the city was a small, highly compact cluster ..."可得出答案为(A)。

译文

如果"郊区"是指比发达的市区发展更快的市郊地区的话,那么近郊化过程早在十九世纪的三四十年代,工业城市出现的时候就开始了。在此之前,城市小而密集,市民出门靠步行,货运由马驮或马车来完成。建于十九世纪三四十年代的早期工厂往往坐落在河道边和城市边缘靠近铁路终点的地方,同时成千上万的雇工需要提供住宿。工厂为毗邻旧城和主城所发展起来的工业城镇住宅和房舍所包围。为了抵抗这种侵占并扩大税收,城市就占据工业邻近地区。例如在 1854 年,费城吞并了费县大部分地区。类似的市政吞并在芝加哥和纽约也曾发生过。的确,绝大多数美国大都市都是通过合并其边缘区而达到今天的地位的。

随着工业的加速发展,市区极度拥挤并伴随着社会压力,在1888年第一条商业化电车线成功地铺设以前,环境恶劣到灾难性的地步。在随后的数年中,马车退出历史,电车网络交叉连接并贯穿了都市的每一个主要区域,大大推进了从拥挤的工业城市向分散的大都市转化的近郊化浪潮。这一大规模近郊化的初期过程由于城市中产阶级的同时出现而加强,他们在郊区而不是在古老的市区拥有自己住房的愿望由开发商通过开发单一家庭住房区的途径得以实现。

Passage 4

Contemporary Western American art has been a very popular and lucrative part of the art marketplace. But unlike some artists who have begun to paint Western subjects precisely because there is a ready market for them, the members who make up the Women Artists of the American West(WAOAW) paint the West because it has always been the primary subject matter for them. For the most part, these women have lived in the American West since birth, and their art is a natural outgrowth of the habitat and habits of their daily lives.

The WAOAW was launched in 1971 by artists Gloria Bilotta and Millie Graham. This organization brought western artists together in the hope of making more of an impact on the art community than any of them could individually and to promote Western art by women.

In the more than 10 years of the organization's existence, the work of WAOAW has become recognized as preeminent by collectors and critics of Western American art. Just what type of subject matter does this art genre include? The scenic landscapes and sprawling vistas of the West are of course popular subjects, but the most recognizable are those landscapes and portraits featuring mountain men, cowboys, and various American Indian tribes. However, WAOAW artists believe that the subject matter for Western art should not be confined to these narrow limitations. It should contain all aspects of ranch and pioneer life, including the large role played by women. Western art should also depict Western wildlife and authentic Western artifacts, as portrayed by Lisa Danicile Lorimer, Esther Mane Versch, Mary Thomson, and other members.

The artists who make up WAOAW currently about thirty-five members, have another characteristic in common apart from their painting genre and that is the high quality of their art. When the group was originally formed, requirements for membership were not stringent and involved a willingness to participate and a membership fee. But as the group grew in prestige, it became necessary to tighten membership requirements considerably in order to justify the many hours and thousands of dollars spent by the group to promote the work of its members.

36. Which of the following is the best title for the passage?

(A) Women Artists of the American West

(B) Western Landscape Paintings

(C) Famous Artists in the West

(D) The Popularity of Western Art

37. Which of the following subjects is NOT mentioned by the author as typical of WAOAW portraits?

(A) Powerful American landowners.

(B) Cowboys.

(C) Mountain men.

(D) Authentic Western artifacts.

38. Which of the following would be an example of a typical WAOAW painting?

(A) A woman participating in a Western horse show.

(B) Men attending an Eastern horse race.

(C) A view of a portrait painter at work.

(D) Collectors at an art auction.

39. Which of the following can be concluded about WAOAW?

(A) Men are eligible for membership.

(B) Acceptance for membership is difficult to obtain today.

(C) The dues are reasonable.

(D) It sets the standards for Western art.

40. What is the author's attitude toward members of WAOAW?

(A) Tolerant.

(B) Ambivalent.

(C) Positive.

(D) Critical.

生词及短语

lucrative [ˈluːkrətiv]	a.	有利的
for the most part		大体上,主要,在极大程度上
habitat [ˈhæbitæt]	n.	生活环境
outgrowth [ˈautgrəuθ]	n.	长出,结果,副产品
preeminent [priːˈeminənt]	a.	卓越的
genre [ˈʒɑːŋr]	n.	流派,类型

sprawling ['sprɔːliŋ] v. 蔓生,蔓延
vista ['vistə] n. 狭长的景色,街景,展望
confine ['kɔnfain] vt. 限制
authentic [ɔː'θentik] a. 可信的,真正的
artifact ['ɑːtifækt] n. 人工制品,加工品
prestige [pre'stiːʒ] n. 声望,威望
tighten ['tait(ə)n] v. 变紧,加强

答案与解析

36. [答案] (A)

[解析] 本题为主旨题。文章主要介绍 WAOAW (Women Artists of the American West) 的创建和绘画艺术等,答案为(A)。

37. [答案] (A)

[解析] 从第三段第三句中"... but the most recognizable...American Indian tribes."及第三段最后一句中 "Western art should also depict Western wildlife and authentic Western artifacts ...",可排除(B)、(C)、(D),故(A) 为正确答案。

38. [答案] (A)

[解析] 从第三段倒数第二句 "It should contain all aspects of ranch and pioneer life, including the large role played by women."可知(A) 为正确答案。

39. [答案] (B)

[解析] 由文中最后一句可知,随着 WAOAW 名声扩大,必须提高会员对入会的要求,所以(B) 为正确答案。文中未提到(A),(C)、(D) 亦非正确答案。

40. [答案] (C)

[解析] 从全文字里行间可感知作者对 WAOAW 的报道较客观和赞赏,因此可排除(A)、(B)、(D),(C) 为正确答案。

译文

当代美国西部艺术一直是艺术市场中一个流行且有利可图的部分。但是,和那些只因为有成熟市场能赚钱而开始西部绘画的艺术家不同的是,组成美国西部妇女艺术家协会(WAOAW)的会员以西部作为创作的主题是因为这一直是她们的原始创作源泉。大体上,她们自出生以来就一直生活在美国西部,她们的艺术作品是其日常生活环境和习惯的自然产物。

WAOAW 由艺术家格勒瑞·比勒特和莫里·格雷厄姆于 1971 年创立,这一组织将西部艺术家召集在一起以便取得比她们个人创作对这个领域产生的更强烈的影响,并通过妇女来

推动西部艺术的发展。

在这一组织存在的十几年间,WAOAW 的工作逐渐被西部艺术评论家和收藏家认可。这一艺术流派究竟包括些什么类型呢？当然，西部秀丽的风景和蔓延起伏的远景是流行的主题,但最出色的是那些风景画和具以山地人、牛仔和各种美洲印第安部落为主题的肖像画。然而 WAOAW 的艺术家认为西部艺术的主题不应该局限在如此窄小的领域,它应该包容农牧场和开拓者生活的各个方面,包括妇女所起到的重要作用,正如丽莎·旦来勒·劳莫尔、爱斯·马瑞·韦斯克、玛丽·汤姆逊和其他会员所描绘的那样,西部绘画还应该描绘西部野生动物和真正的西部人工产品。

目前组成 WAOAW 的艺术家成员已经达到 35 人左右，她们除了绘画流派相同外还有另一个共同的特征,那就是艺术品质高。在组织创建初期,对会员资格的审核要求并不严格,自愿参加并交纳会员费即可。但随着该组织名声的扩大,就有必要在相当程度上提高对会员的要求,以便使协会为促进会员工作而花费的大量时间和金钱受到公正的对待。

阅读 B 篇

Directions:

In the following article, some sentences have been removed. For Questions 41—45, choose the most suitable one from the list A—G to fit into each of the numbered blanks. There are two extra choices, which do not fit in any of the blanks. Mark your answers on ANSWER SHEET 1. (10 points)

Forty years ago, a historic document was signed in Rome that was to change the economic outlook and the future of many countries in Europe. That document was the Treaty of Rome, and this year, on March 25, 1997, the European Union celebrated the 40th anniversary of its signing. A revised draft Treaty on European Union (the Maastricht Treaty) was Presented in Rome on that date. (41) ______________.

(42) ______________. The Treaty set out the three pillars of the European Union— Pillar 1: the three European communities which form its basis; Pillar 2 : the development of a common foreign and security policy; and Pillar 3: cooperation in the areas of justice and home affairs, including immigration and *asylum*(收容所), drug *trafficking*(交易) and international crime.

(43) ______________. EMU means a single monetary policy operating within a single economic market and is therefore the logical complement to the Single Market in Europe today. The EMU will be run by a European Central Bank independent of both national governments and European Union institutions.

(44) ______________. The Euro will enter into circulation in January 1999 in those Member States which meet the criteria for entry to the EMU, and by mid 2002 the changeover

from national currencies to the euro in those countries will be complete. The introduction of the euro will be the most visible measure of integration to date in the daily lives of citizens of the European Union.

The rights of European citizens were further extended by the Maastricht Treaty, so that today citizens of the Member States may travel, reside, work and carry out transactions in any country of the EU without *hindrance* （障碍） and with full protection of the law. The European Union's fields of responsibility were extended to include areas such as consumer protection, public health policy, environmental protection, education and culture and the creation of major transport, communications and energy.

(45) ______________. The first union of six Member States has been enlarged to its present number of fifteen. Added to the original six are Denmark, Ireland, the United Kingdom, Greece, Spain, Portugal, Austria, Sweden and Finland, the last three countries being admitted to the European Union in 1995. The next century will see the inclusion in the Union of a number of countries, mostly from Central and Eastern Europe. Today the European Union is one of the world's greatest single trading powers. Its present population of 370 million has many freedoms and choices, both as citizens and as consumers. Its companies have entered new markets and formed new partnerships to exploit economic opportunities at home and abroad. As the century draws to a close, the vision of a united Europe, made manifest by the Treaty of Rome, made manifest by the Treaty of Rome, is closer to realization than ever before.

(A) In November 1993, the Treaty on European Union(also known as the Maastricht Treaty after the Dutch town where EU leaders met) came into force, creating the European Union and paving the way for greater integration between Member States.

(B) A major aspect of EMU is the single currency, to be known as the euro.

(C) Since the signing of the Treaty of Rome in 1957,Europe has been witness to a remarkable growth in its vitality, homogeneity and strength as a democracy.

(D) As the century comes to an end, a united and enlarged Europe, under the guide of Treaty of Rome, is sure to be realized very soon.

(E) The revised Treaty is a continuation of the process towards integration of the countries of Europe that began in 1957.

(F) The revised treaty is a formal agreement between two or more states, as in reference to terms of peace or trade.

(G) The Treaty also set out the economic criteria Member States must meet to complete Europe's economic and monetary union(EMU), the ultimate goal of economic partnership envisaged by the architects of the Treaty of Rome.

内容提要

文章叙述欧洲国家签订欧洲条约40年来的变化。第一段指出,四十年前一份历史性的文件在罗马签署,使欧洲许多国家的经济面貌和未来发生了改变。这就是《罗马条约》,1997年3月25日,欧盟庆祝文件签署40周年纪念日。这天欧盟在罗马呈交了一份修改的条约。

答案与解析

41. [答案](E)

[解析] 空白处前面提到《罗马条约》40年后进行了修改,(E) 继续说明修改后的条约内容:修改后的条约是1957年欧洲国家一体化条约的延续。

42. [答案](A)

[解析] 空白后面提到"The Treaty",指 The Treaty on European Union,而(A) 先叙述了该条约的内容:1993年11月,欧盟条约正式生效,欧盟诞生,为成员国实现一体化铺平道路。

43. [答案](G)

[解析] 空白后提到 EMU,而(G) 也提到 EMU,可见(G) 应位于前面。

44. [答案](B)

[解析] 空白后提到"欧元",而(B) 首先介绍欧元,故应是前面的内容。

45. [答案](C)

[解析] 空白后提到欧盟不断壮大,(C) 总结了这种形势:自从1957年《罗马条约》签订以来,欧洲明显地成长壮大。

阅读C篇

Directions:

Read the following text carefully and then translate the underlined segments into Chinese. Your translation should be written neatly on ANSWER SHEET 2.(10 points)

All education springs from some image of the future. (46) If the image of the future held by a society is grossly inaccurate, its education system will betray its youth.

Imagine an Indian tribe which for centuries has sailed its dugouts on the river at its doorstep. During all this time the economy and culture of the tribe have depended upon fishing, preparing and cooking the products of the river, growing food in soil fertilized by the river, building boats and appropriate tools. (47) So long as the rate of technological change in such a community stays slow, so long as no wars, invasions, epidemics or other natural disasters upset the even rhythm of life, it is simple for the tribe to formulate a workable image of its own future, since tomorrow merely repeats yesterday.

It is from this image that education flows. Schools may not even exist in the tribe; yet there is a curriculum—a cluster of skills, values and rituals to be learned. Boys are taught to scrape bark and hollow out trees, just as their ancestors did before them. The teacher in such a system knows what he is doing, secure in the knowledge that tradition—the past—will work in the future.

(48) What happens to such a tribe, however, when it pursues its traditional methods unaware that five hundred miles upstream men are constructing a gigantic dam that will dry up their branch of the river? Suddenly the tribe's image of the future, the set of assumptions on which its members base their present behavior, becomes dangerously misleading. Tomorrow will not replicate today. The tribal investment in preparing its children to live in a river culture becomes a pointless and potentially tragic waste. A false image of the future destroys the relevance of the education effort.

This is our situation today-only it is we, ironically, not some distant strangerswho are building the dam that will annihilate the culture of the present. (49) Never before has any culture subjected itself to so intense and prolonged a bombardment of technological, social, and info-psychological change. (50) This change is accelerating and we witness everywhere in the high-technology societies evidence that the old industrial-era structures can no longer carry out their functions.

生词及短语

spring from	*v.*	起源于
grossly ['grəusli]	*ad.*	总计,大体
inaccurate [in'ækjurit]	*a.*	不准确的
dugout ['dʌgaut]	*n.*	独木舟
doorstep ['dɔːstep]	*n.*	门阶
so long as	*ad.*	只要
community [kə'mjuːniti]	*n.*	社团、群体
epidemic [epi'demik]	*n.*	流行病,时疫
upset [ʌp'set]	*n.*	翻到,混乱
rhythm ['riθəm]	*n.*	韵律,节奏
formulate ['fɔːmjuleit]	*v.*	制定,规划

curriculum [kə'rikjuləm]	*n.*	课程
ritual ['ritjuəl]	*n.*	典礼,仪式
scrape [skreip]	*v.*	刮,擦,挖
bark [bɑːk]	*n.*	树皮
hollow out	*v.*	挖空
secure [si'kjuə]	*v.*	保护
upstream [ʌp'striːm]	*ad.*	上游的,逆流而上的
misleading [mis'liːdiŋ]	*ad.*	误导的,引入歧途的
replicate ['replikit]	*v.*	复制
annihilate [ə'naiəˌleit]	*vt.*	消灭,歼灭
prolong [prə'lɔŋ]	*vt.*	延长,拖延
bombardment [bɔm'bɑːdmənt]	*n.*	炮击,轰击
info-psychological	*ad.*	信息—心理的

全文译文与答案

所有教育都起源于对未来的想象。(46) 如果一个社会对未来的想象不实际,它的教育制度将把青年人引向歧途。

想象一个印第安部落,几百年来一直在河上驾驶着独木舟在门前台阶之间穿梭。在这段时间,部落的经济和文化一直依靠捕鱼和烹调河中的产品,在河边肥沃的土壤中种植粮食,建造木船和合适的工具。(47) 只要这样一个部落里技术变化的速度始终缓慢,只要没有战事、侵略、流行病或其他自然疾病打乱生活的平稳节奏,要打造一个本部落切合实际的未来形象很简单,因为明天无非是重复昨天而已。

正是来自于这种形象,教育才永不停息。部落中可能没有学校;然而却有课程,一连串的技巧、价值和礼仪需要学习。男孩要被传授剥树皮和挖空树木的技能,就像他们的前辈在他们之前所做的那样。在这种制度下的教师知道自己在干什么,确保传统,即过去的知识在未来能够有用。

(48) 然而,在继续运用它的传统方法时,意识不到上游五百英里外地方的人们在建造一个大坝,它将抽干支流,那么这样一个部落会碰到什么情况呢? 突然,部落的未来想象,部落成员作为当前行为基础的一套设想,将成为危险的误导。明天将不再复制今天。部落对准备让孩子们生活在河流文化的投资将成为一种毫无意义的和潜在的悲剧性的浪费。一个未来的虚假的想象摧毁了教育的努力成果。

这就是我们今天所处的形势,具有讽刺意义的是,只有我们,而不是某些远方的外国人,正在建设即将消灭当前文化的大坝。(49) 任何文化以前都不曾经受如此激烈而持久的技术、社会、信息、心理上变革的冲击。(50) 这种变革正在加速,我们在高科技社会处处目睹旧工业时代结构再也无法行使其功能的情况。

阅读强化练习十五

阅读 A 篇

Directions:

Read the following four texts. Answer the questions below each text by choosing A, B, C or D. Mark your answers on ANSWER SHEET 1. (40 points)

Passage 1

When Christopher Columbus landed in the New World, the North American continent was an area of astonishing ethnic and cultural diversity. North of the Rio Grande, which now marks the border between the United States and Mexico, was a population of over 12 million people representing approximately 400 distinct cultures, 500 languages, and a remarkable variety of political and religious institutions and physical and ethnic types. Compared to the Europeans, the Indian peoples were extraordinarily heterogeneous, and they often viewed the Europeans as just another tribe.

These varied tribal cultures were as diversified as the land the Indians inhabited. In the high plains of the Dakotas, the Mandan developed a peaceful communal society centered around agriculture. Only a few hundred miles away, however, in northwestern Montana, the Blackfeet turned from agriculture and began to use horses, which had been introduced by the Spaniards. As skilled riders they became hunters and fighters and developed a fierce and aggressive culture centered around the buffalo. In the eastern woodlands surrounding the Great Lakes, the Potawatomis were expert fishermen, canoe builders, and hunters. In the Northeast the six Iroquois nations were among the most politically sophisticated people in the world, forming the famed Iroquois Confederation, which included the Senecas and the Mohawks. This confederation, with its system of checks and balances, provided a model for the United States Constitution.

21. About how many different cultures existed among the fifteenth-century North American Indians?
(A) 400. (B) 500. (C) 600. (D) 1,200.

22. The Mandan tribes could best be classified as ______.
(A) hunters (B) warriors (C) farmers (D) fishermen

23. Before the introduction of horses, the Blackfeet tribes were ______.
(A) peaceful farmers (B) aggressive hunters
(C) fierce warriors (D) skillful sailors

24. It can be inferred from the passage that the life-styles of the various American Indian tribes were influenced most by which of the following?
(A) Contact with other tribes.
(B) Environmental resources.
(C) Contact with Europeans.
(D) Governmental organization.

25. According to the passage, how was the organization of the Iroquois Confederation a forerunner of the United States Constitution?
(A) It was a union of smaller units.
(B) It had a representative government.
(C) Its form of government had a sophisticated way of selecting judges.
(D) Its power was regulated by a system of checks and balances.

生词及短语

ethnic ['eθnik]	a.	人种的，种族的
diversity [di'vəːsitiː]	n.	差异，多样性
heterogeneous [ˌhetərə'dʒiːniːəs]	a.	不同种类的，异类的
famed [feimd]	a.	闻名的，著名的
confederation [kənˌfedə'reiʃən]	n.	联邦

答案与解析

21. [答案] (A)

[解析] 首先，我们都知道哥伦布发现新大陆是在15世纪末，文中第一句话即表明本文讲的是哥伦布发现新大陆时的事；同时，根据第一段第二句中的“... a population of over 12 million people representing approximately 400 distinct cultures, ..." 可知正确答案为(A)。

22. [答案] (A)

[解析] 由第二段第二句中的 "... the Mandan developed a peaceful communal society centered around agriculture."可知这个部落社会是"以农业为中心"的,所以它当然应归入 farmers 一类,故答案为(C)。

23. [答案] (A)

[解析] 第二段第三句中的 "... the Blackfeet turned from agriculture and began to use horses,..."表明他们从事农业在前,使用马匹在后,故答案为(A)。

24. [答案] (B)

[解析] 文中第二段叙述了四个不同地区印第安部落的不同生活方式,由此可以推论,不同的生活环境对他们的生活方式起着最为重要的作用,故答案为(B)。

25. [答案] (D)

[解析] 由文中最后一句 "This confederation, with its system of checks and balances, provided a model for the United States Constitution."可知答案为(D)。

译文

在克里斯托弗·哥伦布登上新大陆时,北美大陆各种不同的种族和文化的数量之多令人吃惊。在现在作为美国与墨西哥边界线的格兰德河以北的区域,当时居住着1,200万人口。他们代表着约400种不同文化和500种语言,明显不同的政治和宗教制度以及不同的体型和种族。与欧洲人相比,印第安人的种族具有极大的差异,他们通常把欧洲人看做是另一个部族。

印第安人各个部族的文化因他们居住地的不同而有所差异。在达科他高地平原,曼丹人建立了一种以农业为中心的和平的公社社会。然而,仅仅在几百英里之外,在西北部的蒙大拿地区,黑脚族人却放弃了农业,开始使用由西班牙人带到美洲来的马匹。作为熟练的骑手,他们成了猎手和战士,发展了一种以捕猎野牛为主的凶猛的攻击型文化。在东部大湖周围的森林地带,波塔瓦托米人既是高明的渔夫,又是独木舟的制造者和猎手。在东北部,那六个易洛魁部族属于全世界政治上最老练的人们之列,组成了著名的易洛魁联邦,包括塞尼加族和莫霍克族。易洛魁联邦建立了相互制衡的制度,为后来的美国宪法提供了一种模式。

Passage 2

By about A.D.500 the Mound Builder culture was declining, perhaps because of attacks from other tribes or perhaps because of severe climatic changes that undermined agriculture. To the west another culture, based on intensive agriculture, was beginning to flourish. Its center was beneath present-day St. Louis, and it radiated out to encompass most of the Mississippi watershed, from Wisconsin to Louisiana and from Oklahoma to Tennessee. Thousands of villages were included in its orbit. By about A. D. 700 this Mississippian culture, as it is known to archaeologists, began to send its influence eastward to transform the life of most of the less technologically advanced woodland tribes. Like the Mound Builders of the Ohio region, these tribes, probably influenced by Meso-American cultures through trade and warfare, built gigantic mounds as burial and ceremonial places. The largest of them, rising in four terraces to a height of one hundred feet, has a rectangular base of nearly fifteen acres, larger than that of the Great Pyramid of Egypt. Built between A.D.900 and 1100, this huge earthwork faces the site of a palisaded Indian city which contained more than one hundred small artificial-mounds marking burial sites. Spread among them was a vast settlement containing some 30,000 people by current estimations. The finely crafted ornaments and tools recovered at Cahokia, as this center of Mississippi culture is called, include elaborate ceramics, finely sculpted stonework, carefully embossed and engraved copper and mica sheets, and one funeral blanket fashioned from 12,000 shell beads. They indicate that Cahokia was a true urban center, with clustered housing, markets, and specialists in toolmaking, hide-dressing, potting, jewelry-making, weaving and salt-making.

26. What is the main topic of the passage?
(A) The Mississippian culture.
(B) The decline of Mound Builder culture.
(C) The architecture of Meso-American Indians.
(D) The eastern woodlands tribes.

27. The paragraph preceding this article most probably discussed ______.
(A) the Mound Builder culture
(B) warfare in A.D.500
(C) the geography of the Mississippi area
(D) agriculture near the Mississippi River

28. The Mississippian culture influenced the culture of the ______.
(A) eastern woodland tribes
(B) Mound Builders.
(C) Meso-Americans
(D) Egyptians.

29. According to the passage, the mounds were used as ______.
(A) palaces for the royal families
(B) fortresses for defense
(C) centers for conducting trade
(D) places for burying the dead

30. The mound at Cahokia was made of ______.
(A) stone (B) dirt (C) ceramics (D) metal

生词及短语

undermine [ˌʌndəˈmain]	*v.*	破坏
radiate [ˈreidieit]	*vi.*	辐射
encompass [inˈkʌmpəs]	*v.*	包围,环绕
watershed [ˈwɔːtəʃed]	*n.*	分水岭
woodland [ˈwudlənd]	*n.*	森林地,林地
warfare [ˈwɔːfɛə(r)]	*n.*	战争,冲突
mound [maund]	*n.*	土墩,土垛,堆积
terrace [ˈterəs]	*n.*	露台,阳台
rectangular [rekˈtæŋgjulə(r)]	*a.*	矩形的,成直角的
acre [ˈeikə(r)]	*n.*	英亩
earthwork		土方工程,土木工程
palisade [ˌpæliˈseid]	*vt.*	用栅栏围护　*n.* 木栅
ceramic [siˈræmik]	*n.*	陶瓷制品
sculpt [skʌlpt]	*v.*	雕刻,造型
emboss [emˈbɔːs]	*vt.*	饰以浮饰,使浮雕出来
mica [ˈmaikə]	*n.*	云母
bead [biːd]	*n.*	珠子,水珠
hide-dressing		皮革物衣
potting		烧罐

答案与解析

26. [答案] (A)

[解析] 本文以第一句作为引导，逐步深入地叙述了密西西比文化中心的发展过程和影响。(A)与第一句相符,故为正确答案。其他选项排除的理由为:文章只在第一句中提到 Mound Builder culture 的衰落及其原因,因此(B)项不是本文讲述的主要内容;(C)在文中只有 probably influenced by Meso-American cultures 这几个字与之相关,不可能是主要内容;(D)不能概括全文内容;故均应排除。

27. [答案] (A)

[解析] 本题问本文前面的段落可能讨论什么内容，解题时应根据文章开头的内容找出线索。本文第一句讲述 the Mound Builder culture 在公元 500 年开始衰落,第二句则转折到密西西比文化的兴起，可见第一句是在两个段落之间起着承上启下作用的过渡句,前面段落最可能讨论的应该是 the Mound Builder culture,因此正确答案为(A)。

28. [答案](A)

[解析] 根据文章第五句 "By about A. D. 700 this Mississippian culture, ...the less technologically advanced woodland tribes."可知正确答案应为(A)——题句是对文章第五句的转述。

29. [答案](D)

[解析] 由第六句中的"... these tribes... built gigantic mounds as burial... places,"可知答案为(D)。

30. [答案](B)

[解析] 本文倒数第四句提到"...this huge earthwork ...",由此可知 mound 是由泥土筑造而成。dirt 有"泥土"之意,符合文意,故(B)项正确。(A)stone、(C)ceramics"陶器"和(D)metal 均为 mound 的装饰物,故均应排除。

译文

大约在公元500年,或许是由于其他部落的攻击,也可能是由于恶劣的气候变化破坏了农业,北美密西西比河流域的筑堤人文化开始衰落。在它的西面,另一个以精耕细作农业为基础的文化开始繁荣。这个文化中心位于今天的圣路易斯之下,并由此向四面八方扩展,其范围包括密西西比河流域的大部分地区,从威斯康星到路易斯安那,从俄克拉何马到田纳西,几千个村庄都在其范围之内。到了公元700年左右,被考古学家们称之为密西西比文化的文化,影响开始向东延伸,改变了东部森林地区技术落后的大多数部族的生活。像俄亥俄地区的史前印第安人一样,这些部落可能由于贸易和战争而受到了中美洲文化的影响,修筑了许多巨大的土墩,作为丧葬和举行仪式的地方。最大的土墩有四级台阶,高达100英尺。其基底呈长方形,差不多有十五英亩,比埃及大金字塔还大。这一个巨大的土方建筑物,修筑于公元900—1100年之间,面对一个围着栅栏的印第安城市,城中有一百多个人工修筑的作为墓地标志的小土墩。据今天的估计,在这些土墩之间散居着的人口多达3万。这个密西西比文化中心叫做卡奥基亚,在这儿出土了制作精细的饰物和工具,包括精致的陶器、优美的石雕、精雕细刻的铜器和云母板,还有一块用1,200颗珍珠装缀的用于丧葬的毯子。这些出土文物说明,卡奥基亚是一个真正的城市中心,有着一群群房舍和市场,还有从事制造工具、皮革服装、陶器、珠宝、纺织品和食盐的工匠。

Passage 3

Archaeology is a source of history, not just a humble auxiliary discipline. Archaeological data are historical documents in their own right, not mere illustrations to written texts. Just as much as any other historian, an archaeologist studies and tries to reconstitute the process that has created the human world in which we live and us ourselves in so far as we are each creatures of our age and social environment. Archaeological data are all changes in the material world resulting from human action or, more succinctly, the fossilized results of human behavior. The sum total of these constitute what may be called the archaeological record. This record exhibits certain peculiarities and deficiencies the consequences of which produce a rather superficial contrast between archaeological history and the more familiar kind based upon written records.

Not all human behavior fossilizes. The words I utter and you hear as vibrations in the air are certainly human changes in the material world. any may be of great historical significance. Yet *they* leave no sort of trace in the archaeological records unless they are captured by the dictaphone or written down by a clerk. The movement of troops on the battlefield may "change the course of history", but this is equally ephemeral from the archaeologist's standpoint. What is perhaps worse, most organic materials are perishable. Everything made of wood, hide, wool, linen, grass, hair, and similar materials will decay and vanish in dust in a few years or centuries, save under very exceptional conditions. In a relatively brief period the archaeological record is reduced to mere scraps of stone, bone, glass, metal, and earthenware. Still modern archaeology, by applying appropriate techniques and comparative methods, aided by a few lucky finds from peat bogs, deserts, and frozen soils, is able to fill up a good deal of the gap.

31. What is the author's main purpose in the passage?

(A) To point out the importance of recent advances in archaeology.

(B) To describe an archaeologist's education.

(C) To explain how archaeology is a source of history.

(D) To encourage more people to become archaeologists.

32. According to the passage, the archaeological record consists of ______.

(A) spoken words of great historical significance

(B) the fossilized results of human activity

(C) organic materials

(D) ephemeral ideas

33. The word "they" in Para. 2 Line 3 refers to ______.

(A) scraps　　(B) words　　(C) troops　　(D) humans

34. Which of the following is NOT mentioned as an example of an organic material?

(A) Stone.　　(B) Wool.　　(C) Grass.　　(D) Hair.

35. The author mentions all of the following archaeological discovery sites EXCEPT ______.

(A) urban areas　　(B) peat bogs

(C) very hot and dry lands　　(D) earth that has been

生词及短语

humble [ˈhʌmb(ə)l]	a.	卑贱的,谦虚的
auxiliary [ɔːgˈziliəri]	a.	辅助的,补助的
reconstitute [riːˈkɔnstitjuːt]	vt.	重新组成,重新建立
in so far as		在……范围之内
succinctly [səkˈsiŋktli]	a.	简洁地,简便地
fossilize [ˈfɔsilaiz]	vt.	使成化石
deficiency [diˈfiʃənsi]	n.	缺乏,不足
superficial [suːpəˈfiʃ(ə)l]	a.	表面的,肤浅的,浅薄的
dictaphone [ˈdiktəfəun]	n.	录音机,口授留声机
ephemeral [iˈfemərəl]	a.	短暂的,短命的
perishable [ˈperiʃəb(ə)l]	a.	容易腐烂的
linen [ˈlinin]	n.	亚麻布,亚麻制品
decay [diˈkei]	vi.	腐朽,腐烂
scrap [skræp]	n.	小片,废料,残余物
earthenware [ˈəːθənweə(r)]	n.	土器,陶器
peat [piːt]	n.	泥煤,泥炭块
bog [bɔg]	n.	沼泽

答案与解析

31. [答案](C)

[解析]本题为主旨题,文章首句即点明主题"Archaeology is a source of history, ..."接着围绕主题进行了叙述,故不难得知答案为(C)。

32. [答案](B)

[解析]由文中第一段第5—6行"Archaeological data are all changes in the material world ..., the fossilized results of human behavior."可得出答案为(B)。(A)、(C)、(D)均可排除。

33. [答案](B)

[解析]本题为代词指代题,可在前面的句子中根据上下文寻找,不难看出本句中出现的两个they均指代上句所提到的words,即答案为(B)。

34. [答案](A)

[解析]从第二段第6—9行"What is perhaps worse, ..."可排除(B)、(C)、(D)。

35. [答案](A)

[解析]从文中最后一句"...a few lucky finds from peat bogs, deserts, and frozen soils, ..."

可排除(B)、(C)、(D)。

译文

考古学是历史的源泉,而不是低下的附属学科。考古学资料本身就是历史文献,而不仅仅是文本的说明。考古学家与其他历史学家一样,研究和试图重建曾经创建我们所生存的世界的过程,以及处于这个时代和社会环境中的我们自己。考古学资料说明了来自于人类活动的物质世界的全部变化过程,或者更简单地说,是人类行为的化石化结果。所有这些构成所谓的考古学记录。这一记录表现出一定特性和缺陷性,其结果造成考古学历史和我们所熟悉的文字记载历史之间相当程度的差异。

并非所有的人类活动都会化石化。我所说的和你听到的是在空气中振动的话,在物质世界中代表了一定的人类变化或许多具有重要的历史意义。除非由录音机录下或者由秘书记录下来,否则它们在考古记载上不会留下任何痕迹。战场上军队的战斗可能"改变历史的进程",但从考古学的观点来看,这同样是瞬息之间的事。或许更糟糕的是,绝大多数有机物易分解腐烂。即使保存在很特殊的条件下,任何由木材、毛皮、羊毛、亚麻、草木、毛发及类似材料制成的物品都将会在若干年或若干世纪内腐朽并消失在尘埃中。在一个相当短暂的时期内,考古学的记载仅限于石器、骨头、玻璃、金属和陶器碎片上。现代考古学只有通过利用适当的技术和比较的方法,在从泥炭、沼泽、沙漠和冻土中得到的一些幸运发现物的辅助下,方能填补起大部分的历史空白。

Passage 4

Many artists late in the last century were in search of a means to express their individuality. Modern dance was one of the ways some of these people sought to free their creative spirit. At the beginning there was no exacting technique, no foundation from which to build. In later years trial, error, and genius founded the techniques and the principles of the movement. Eventually, innovators even drew from what they considered the dread ballet, but first they had to discard all that was academic so that the new could be discovered. The beginnings of modern dance were happening before Isadora Duncan, but she was the first person to bring the new dance to general audiences and see it accepted and acclaimed.

Her search for a natural movement form sent her to nature. She believed movement should be as natural as the swaying of the trees and the rolling waves of the sea, and should be in harmony with the movements of the Earth. Her great contributions are in three areas.

First, she began the expansion of the kinds of movements that could be used in dance. Before Duncan danced, ballet was the only type of dance performed in concert. In the ballet the feet and legs were emphasized, with virtuosity shown by complicated, codified positions and movements. Duncan performed dance by using all her body in the freest possibly way. Her dance stemmed from her soul and spirit. She was one of the the pioneers who broke tradition so others might be able to develop the art.

Her second contribution lies in dance costume. She discarded corset, ballet shoes, and stiff costumes. These were replaced with flowing Grecian tunics, bare feet, and unbound hair. She believed in the natural body being allowed to move freely, and her dress displayed this ideal.

Her third contribution was in the use of music. In her performances she used the symphonies of great masters, including Beethoven and Wagner, which was not the usual custom.

She was as exciting and eccentric in her personal life as in her dance.

36. Which of the following would be the best title for the passage?
   (A) The Evolution of Dance in the Twentieth Century
   (B) Artists of the Last Century
   (C) Natural Movement in Dance
   (D) A Pioneer in Modern Dance

37. According to the passage what did nature represent to Isadora Duncan?
   (A) Something to conquer.
   (B) A model for movement.
   (C) A place to find peace.
   (D) A symbol of disorder.

38. Which of the following is NOT mentioned in the passage as an area of dance that Isadora Duncan worked to change?
   (A) The music.
   (B) The stage sets.
   (C) Costumes.
   (D) Movements.

39. Compared to those of the ballet, Isadora Duncan's costumes were less ______.
   (A) costly
   (B) colorful
   (C) graceful
   (D) restrictive

40. What does the paragraph following the passage most probably discuss?
   (A) Isadora Duncan's further contribution to modern dance.
   (B) The music customarily used in ballet.
   Other aspects of Isadora Duncan's life.
   lience acceptance of the new form of dance.

生词及短语

dread [dred]	*n.*	恐惧,恐怖
virtuosity [vəːtju'ɔsəti]	*n.*	艺术鉴别力
codify ['kəudifai]	*vt.*	编成法典,使法律成文化
stem [stem]	*v.*	滋生
costume ['kɔstjuːm]	*n.*	装束,服装
corset ['kɔːsit]	*n.*	束服,胸衣
Grecian ['griːʃ(ə)n]	*a.*	希腊的,希腊式的
tunic ['tjuːnik]	*n.*	束腰外衣

答案与解析

36. [答案] (D)

[解析] 本题为主旨题。文章主要介绍了现代舞创始人邓肯对现代舞所做的创造性贡献和成就,四个选择项中(D) 最能说明主题,故为正确答案。

37. [答案] (B)

[解析] 从第二段第一、二句"Her search for a natural movement form ... the movements of the Earth."表明(B) 为正确选项。(A)、(C)、(D) 文中均未涉及。

38. [答案] (B)

[解析] 从第三、四、五段中对邓肯三大贡献的介绍先后可排除(D)、(C)、(A)。

39. [答案] (D)

[解析] 从第四段第二、三句 "She discarded corset, ballet shoes, and stiff costumes. These were replaced with flowing Grecian tunics, bare feet, and unbound hair." 可知邓肯的服装不像芭蕾舞那样受严格的限制,答案为(D)。

40. [答案] (C)

[解析] 从文中最后一句 "She was as exciting and eccentric in her personal life as in her dance."可推测出下文将会介绍邓肯的生活,故(C) 为正确选择。

译文

上世纪后期,许多艺术家都在寻找表达他们个性的方式。现代舞就是一些人寻求解放自我创新精神的方式之一。最初,没有确切的技巧,也没有建立的基础。随后几年,尝试、错误和天赋创建了动作的技巧和原则。最后创新者甚至吸收了芭蕾舞中的内容,但他们首先必须抛弃其中学究的东西,这样才能发现新的内容。现代舞在伊沙多拉·邓肯之前就开始出现了,但她是第一位将这种舞蹈带给大众以决定它是否会被接受、会受欢迎的人。

邓肯对自然运动形式的探讨将她送到了大自然。她深信动作应该像树的摇摆和大海的波涛一样自然,并应与地球的运动相协调。她的杰出贡献主要表现在三个方面。

首先,她扩展了舞蹈中应用动作的种类。在邓肯从事舞蹈之前,芭蕾舞是在音乐会上表演的惟一舞蹈。芭蕾舞强调脚和腿,用复杂的、标准的姿势和动作来表现其感染力。而邓肯以全身尽可能最自由的方式来表演舞蹈。她的舞蹈源自其灵魂和精神。她是打破传统的先驱之一,为后人能发展这一艺术铺平了道路。

她的第二个贡献在于舞蹈服饰方面。她抛弃了紧身衣、芭蕾舞鞋和僵硬的服装。它们被飘逸的希腊外衣、赤脚和披发所取代。她深信这样可以使身体的运动更加自如,她的服饰表现了这一思想。

她的第三个贡献是对音乐的使用。在她的表演中使用了音乐大师们的交响乐作品,包括贝多芬和瓦格纳的作品,这是非常规之举。

正像在她的舞蹈中一样,她在个人生活中也是一个令人激动和行为古怪的人。

阅读 B 篇

Directions:

In the following article, some sentences have been removed. For Questions 40—44, choose the most suitable one from the list A—G to fit into each of the numbered blanks. There are two extra choices, which do not fit in any of the blanks. Mark your answers on ANSWER SHEET 1. (10 points)

The start of monetary union in Europe is an exciting event. There is little doubt that it can unleash a new dynamic of enterprise and growth benefiting all of us. (41) ________.

Euro-land faces these risks because it is still an incomplete and unfinished project. It is incomplete because, while monetary policies will now be conducted at the European level, the other tools of macroeconomic management remain firmly in the hands of national authorities. It is unfinished because the European Central Bank (ECB) itself has been left handicapped in the event of major financial crises.

(42) ________. These conflicts will be raised when economic conditions diverge within Euro-land. Inevitably, the difficulties in coordinating different national policies with the monetary policy of the ECB will create tensions and disagreement. Of course, the same thing happens within a nation between the national central bank and the government. But the intensity the conflict is likely to be greater in Euro-land because the national governments bear al responsibility for deteriorating economic conditions, whereas the ECB will be some institution without political accountability.

CB itself will be handicapped by the fact that an essential part of monetary policies—

bank supervision and control—has been left to national authorities, including national banks. This will not matter much in times of financial stability. But in periods of financial upheaval, which inevitably will occur, it could have a substantial impact. The ECB will then lack the information and instruments to act quickly. This may very well exacerbate the crisis.

History tells us that monetary unification must be part of a whole. One cannot simply centralize monetary decision—making without at the same time centralizing the other parts of macroeconomic management. And the fact is that crucial parts of the latter have remained in the hands of the nation states in Europe. In a sense one can say that the start of Euro-land is like a move into a new and beautiful house—which, unfortunately, does not yet have a roof.

So, where does that lead us? Two possible scenarios emerge, an optimistic and a pessimistic one. (43) ______________.

The second scenario is less idyllic. European citizens resist further attempts to transfer power to European institutions. Euro-land lingers in its unfinished state. Economic storms stir rancor between the ECB and the national governments, and among the national governments themselves. Instead of an oasis of monetary stability, Euro-land becomes a source of instability. The Euro would not become the strong and stable currency that so many observers expect it to be. (44) ______________.

Which of the two scenarios is the more likely? (45) ______________. These do not exist. One conclusion, however, can be drawn. If Euro-land fails to move forward toward political union, it will not last.

(A) The simple fact that monetary policies will be governed by a European institution while fiscal policies remain in the hands of the national governments creates the risk of serious conflicts between governments and the ECB.

(B) But the introduction of the Euro is also replete with risks. These are worth keeping in mind even as champagne bottles are uncorked in celebration.

(C) The ECB was deeply stirred by economic reasons raised from national governments.

(D) On the contrary, it would be weak and no match for the dollar.

(E) In the optimistic version, European leaders realize the unfinished nature of the EMU project and act quickly to unify the other parts of macroeconomic policies.

(F) Lack of authorities handicapped the ECB in monetary development.

(G) To attach probabilities to these scenarios, one needs past observations of similar events.

内 容 提 要

本文主要讨论欧元存在的风险及原因。第一段指出,欧洲货币联盟的启动是一件激动人心的事情。没有人会怀疑它会为企业创造新的动力,同时使我们大家受益。后面提到欧元的推出不但有优势也同时会存在有风险。

答案与解析

41. [答案] (B)

[解析] 空白前提到欧元的推出是激动人心的事情,使大家受益。(B) 以 But 转折指出欧元的推出同样充满了风险。

42. [答案] (A)

[解析] 第二段提到这种风险的原因在于财政政策是由欧洲联盟制订, 但整体经济管理却是各个国家控制的。而(A) 继续说明这种情况的风险所在,故第三段的空白处明显为(A)。

43. [答案] (E)

[解析] 空白前提到有两种可能的情况出现,乐观的和悲观的。(E) 首先对乐观的情况加以说明。

44. [答案] (D)

[解析] 空白前内容对欧元的前景不太乐观:不会像观察家希望的那样走强和稳定。(D) 进一步对此观点表示肯定:相反,它将走弱并不能与美元相比。

45. [答案] (G)

[解析] 首句对两种情况的可能性进行提问,而(G) 紧接着问题做出了回答:对于这两种情况的可能性,人们需要对过去的相同的事件进行观察。

阅读 C 篇

Directions:

Read the following text carefully and then translate the underlined segments into Chinese. Your translation should be written neatly on ANSWER SHEET 2. (10 points)

The process of entering the confines of political and economic power can be pictured as a stem in which persons are chosen from a political elite pool. (46) In this reservoir of possible rs are the individuals with the skills, education, and other qualifications needed to fill elite s. It is here that competition does exist, that the highest achievers do display their nd that the best qualified do generally succeed. Here, what is more important is reservoir of qualified people.

(47) Many in the masses may have leadership abilities, but unless they can gain entrance into the elite pool, their abilities will go unnoticed. Those of the higher class and status rank enter more easily into this competition since they have been afforded greater opportunities to acquire the needed qualifications.

(48) In addition to formal qualifications, there are less obvious social-psychological factors which tend to narrow the potential elite pool further. (49) "Self-assertion" and "self-elimination" are processes by which those of higher social status assert themselves and those of lower social status eliminate themselves from competition for elite positions. A young man whose family has been active in politics, who has attended Harvard, and who has established a network of connections to the high position in the business or political world. (50) On the other hand, a young man with less prestigious(有声望的) family background, no connections, and only a high school education or even a college degree from a state university would not likely expect a further place for himself at the top. As Prewitt and Stone explain, such an individual "has few models to follow, no contacts to put him into the right channels, and little reason to think of himself as potentially wealthy or powerful." Thus, self-selection aids in filtering out those of lower income and status groups from the pool of potential elites. Most eliminate themselves from the competition early in the fame.

生词及短语

confine [ˈkɔnfain]	*n.*	界限,边界
elite pool		精英库
reservoir [ˈrezəvwɑː]	*n.*	水库,蓄水池
assertion [əˈsəːʃən]	*n.*	断言,主张
elimination [iˌlimːˈneiʃən]	*n.*	排除,消灭
eliminate [iˈlimineit]	*v.*	消灭
prestigious [ˌpresˈtiːdʒəs]	*a.*	有声望的
contact [ˈkɔntækt]	*n.*	联系,接触
filter out		过滤出
fame [feim]	*n.*	名声,名望

全文译文与答案

进入政治和经济权利圈的过程可以用一个制度来加以描绘,在这个制度中,合适的人选从一个政治精英阵容中选出。(46)在人才库中,有望成为未来领导人的人都具有担任显要职位所需要的技能、学历,以及其他资格。在这里,竞争确实存在,最高成就者展示他们的能力,而最具资格的人才能成功。在这里,更重要的是进入了这个合格人选的人才库。

(47)民众中有许多人可能具有领导者的素质,但是除非他们可以进入这个精英人才库,否则他们的能力就会被忽略。由于他们有更多的机会来获得所需的资格,那些处于较高阶层和地位者才能很容易地进入这种竞争。

(48)除了一些正式的资格外,还有一些不太明显的社会心理因素往往会进一步缩小这个潜在的精英人才库的规模。(49)"坚持己见"和"自我淘汰"是指社会地位较高的人显示自己的权威,以及社会地位较低的人自我淘汰而退出获取显要职位的竞争的过程。一个其家庭在政治领域很活跃的年轻人,还上过哈佛大学,就已经建立好了通向商业或政治世界最高地位的关系网络。(50)另一方面,一位年轻人,如果他不是出生于名门望族,没有社会关系,只有高校教育或某州立学院的学位,他不可能指望自己将来能出人头地。正如普里威特和斯通所说,这样的个人"几乎没有榜样去效仿,没有关系将他引导到正确的途径,也没有理由想象他会有潜力变得富有或有势力。"由此,自我选择帮助从有潜力的精英库中过滤掉这些低收入和低地位的群体。大多数人在成名前就已经在竞争中销声匿迹了。